THE BOOK EVERYONE'S TALKING ABOUT

NO. 1 *NEW YORK TIMES* BESTSELLER

NO. 1 AMAZON UK BESTSELLER

NO. 1 ABA INDIE BESTSELLER

A *NEW YORK TIMES* EDITORS' CHOICE

AN *EW* MOST ANTICIPATED BOOK OF THE YEAR

A *TIME* MAGAZINE NEW BOOK TO READ

TRANSLATED INTO MORE THAN 25 LANGUAGES

"A classic in the making."
The Times

"A masterpiece."
Huffington Post

"A story that places a spotlight on #BlackLivesMatter."
Stylist

"Full of evocative detail and wry humour, with
a charismatic narrator."
The Guardian

"Brimming with pop culture references and humour."
The New York Times

THE HATE U GIVE

ANGIE THOMAS

WALKER
BOOKS

*For Grandma, who showed me there can be
light in the darkness.*

First published in Great Britain 2017 by Walker Books Ltd
87 Vauxhall Walk, London SE11 5HJ

This edition published 2018

4 6 8 10 9 7 5

Text © 2017 A. C. Thomas Writes LLC
Cover design by Nathan Burton

The right of Angie Thomas to be identified as author of this
work has been asserted by her in accordance with the
Copyright, Designs and Patents Act 1988

This book has been typeset in Bembo

Printed and bound by CPI Group (UK) Ltd, Croydon CR0 4YY

British Library Cataloguing in Publication Data: a catalogue record for
this book is available from the British Library

ISBN 978-1-4063-8716-2

www.walker.co.uk

FSC
www.fsc.org

MIX
Paper from
responsible sources
FSC® C020471

PART 1

WHEN IT HAPPENS

CHAPTER 1

I shouldn't have come to this party.

I'm not even sure I *belong* at this party. That's not on some bougie shit, either. There are just some places where it's not enough to be me. Either version of me. Big D's spring break party is one of those places.

I squeeze through sweaty bodies and follow Kenya, her curls bouncing past her shoulders. A haze lingers over the room, smelling like weed, and music rattles the floor. Some rapper calls out for everybody to Nae-Nae, followed by a bunch of "Heys" as people launch into their own versions. Kenya holds up her cup and dances her way through the crowd. Between the headache from the loud-ass music and the nausea from the weed odor, I'll be amazed if I cross the room without spilling my drink.

We break out the crowd. Big D's house is packed wall-to-wall. I've always heard that everybody and their momma comes to his spring break parties – well, everybody except me – but damn, I didn't know it would be this many people. Girls wear their hair colored, curled, laid, and slayed. Got me feeling basic as hell with my ponytail. Guys in their freshest kicks and sagging pants grind so close to girls they just about need condoms. My nana likes to say that spring brings love. Spring in Garden Heights doesn't always bring love, but it promises babies in the winter. I wouldn't be surprised if a lot of them are conceived the night of Big D's party. He always has it on the Friday of spring break because you need Saturday to recover and Sunday to repent.

"Stop following me and go dance, Starr," Kenya says. "People already say you think you all that."

"I didn't know so many mind readers lived in Garden Heights." Or that people know me as anything other than "Big Mav's daughter who works in the store." I sip my drink and spit it back out. I knew there would be more than Hawaiian Punch in it, but this is way stronger than I'm used to. They shouldn't even call it punch. Just straight-up liquor. I put it on the coffee table and say, "Folks kill me, thinking they know what I think."

"Hey, I'm just saying. You act like you don't know nobody 'cause you go to that school."

I've been hearing that for six years, ever since my parents put me in Williamson Prep. "Whatever," I mumble.

"And it wouldn't kill you to not dress like…" She turns up her nose as she looks from my sneakers to my oversized hoodie. "*That*. Ain't that my brother's hoodie?"

Our brother's hoodie. Kenya and I share an older brother, Seven. But she and I aren't related. Her momma is Seven's

8

momma, and my dad is Seven's dad. Crazy, I know. "Yeah, it's his."

"Figures. You know what else people saying too. Got folks thinking you're my girlfriend."

"Do I look like I care what people think?"

"No! And that's the problem!"

"Whatever." If I'd known following her to this party meant she'd be on some *Extreme Makeover: Starr Edition* mess, I would've stayed home and watched *Fresh Prince* reruns. My Jordans are comfortable, and damn, they're new. That's more than some people can say. The hoodie's way too big, but I like it that way. Plus, if I pull it over my nose, I can't smell the weed.

"Well, I ain't babysitting you all night, so you better do something," Kenya says, and scopes the room. Kenya could be a model, if I'm completely honest. She's got flawless dark-brown skin – I don't think she ever gets a pimple – slanted brown eyes, and long eyelashes that aren't store-bought. She's the perfect height for modeling too, but a little thicker than those toothpicks on the runway. She never wears the same outfit twice. Her daddy, King, makes sure of that.

Kenya is about the only person I hang out with in Garden Heights – it's hard to make friends when you go to a school that's forty-five minutes away and you're a latchkey kid who's only seen at her family's store. It's easy to hang out with Kenya because of our connection to Seven. She's messy as hell sometimes, though. Always fighting somebody and quick to say her daddy will whoop somebody's ass. Yeah, it's true, but I wish she'd stop picking fights so she can use her trump card. Hell, I could use mine too. Everybody knows you don't mess with my dad, Big Mav, and you definitely don't mess with his kids. Still, you don't see me going around starting shit.

Like at Big D's party, Kenya is giving Denasia Allen some serious stank-eye. I don't remember much about Denasia, but I remember that she and Kenya haven't liked each other since fourth grade. Tonight, Denasia's dancing with some guy halfway across the room and paying no attention to Kenya. But no matter where we move, Kenya spots Denasia and glares at her. And the thing about the stank-eye is at some point you feel it on you, inviting you to kick some ass or have your ass kicked.

"Ooh! I can't stand her," Kenya seethes. "The other day, we were in line in the cafeteria, right? And she behind me, talking out the side of her neck. She didn't use my name, but I know she was talking 'bout me, saying I tried to get with DeVante."

"For real?" I say what I'm supposed to.

"Uh-huh. I don't want him."

"I know." Honestly? I don't know who DeVante is. "So what did you do?"

"What you think I did? I turned around and asked if she had a problem with me. Ol' trick, gon' say, 'I wasn't even talking about you,' knowing she was! You're so lucky you go to that white-people school and don't have to deal with hoes like that."

Ain't this some shit? Not even five minutes ago, I was stuck-up because I go to Williamson. Now I'm lucky? "Trust me, my school has hoes too. Hoedom is universal."

"Watch, we gon' handle her tonight." Kenya's stank-eye reaches its highest level of stank. Denasia feels its sting and looks right at Kenya. "Uh-huh," Kenya confirms, like Denasia hears her. "Watch."

"Hold up. *We?* That's why you begged me to come to this party? So you can have a tag team partner?"

She has the nerve to look offended. "It ain't like you had nothing else to do! Or anybody else to hang out with. I'm doing your ass a favor."

"Really, Kenya? You do know I have friends, right?"

She rolls her eyes. Hard. Only the whites are visible for a few seconds. "Them li'l bougie girls from your school don't count."

"They're not bougie, and they do count." I think. Maya and I are cool. Not sure what's up with me and Hailey lately. "And honestly? If pulling me into a fight is your way of helping my social life, I'm good. Goddamn, it's always some drama with you."

"Please, Starr?" She stretches the *please* extra long. Too long. "This what I'm thinking. We wait until she get away from DeVante, right? And then we…"

My phone vibrates against my thigh, and I glance at the screen. Since I've ignored his calls, Chris texts me instead.

Can we talk?

I didn't mean for it to go like that.

Of course he didn't. He meant for it to go a whole different way yesterday, which is the problem. I slip the phone in my pocket. I'm not sure what I wanna say, but I'd rather deal with him later.

"Kenya!" somebody shouts.

This big, light-skinned girl with bone-straight hair moves through the crowd toward us. A tall boy with a black-and-blond Fro-hawk follows her. They both give Kenya hugs and talk about how cute she looks. I'm not even here.

"Why you ain't tell me you was coming?" the girl says, and sticks her thumb in her mouth. She's got an overbite from doing that too. "You could've rode with us."

"Nah, girl. I had to go get Starr," Kenya says. "We walked here together."

That's when they notice me, standing not even half a foot from Kenya.

The guy squints as he gives me a quick once-over. He frowns for a hot second, but I notice it. "Ain't you Big Mav's daughter who work in the store?"

See? People act like that's the name on my birth certificate. "Yeah, that's me."

"Ohhh!" the girl says. "I knew you looked familiar. We were in third grade together. Ms. Bridges's class. I sat behind you."

"Oh." I know this is the moment I'm supposed to remember her, but I don't. I guess Kenya was right – I really don't know anybody. Their faces are familiar, but you don't get names and life stories when you're bagging folks' groceries.

12

I can lie though. "Yeah, I remember you."

"Girl, quit lying," the guy says. "You know you don't know her ass."

"'Why you always lying?'" Kenya and the girl sing together. The guy joins in, and they all bust out laughing.

"Bianca and Chance, be nice," Kenya says. "This Starr's first party. Her folks don't let her go nowhere."

I cut her a side-eye. "I go to parties, Kenya."

"Have y'all seen her at any parties 'round here?" Kenya asks them.

"Nope!"

"Point made. And before you say it, li'l lame white-kid suburb parties don't count."

Chance and Bianca snicker. Damn, I wish this hoodie could swallow me up somehow.

"I bet they be doing Molly and shit, don't they?" Chance asks me. "White kids love popping pills."

"And listening to Taylor Swift," Bianca adds, talking around her thumb.

Okay, that's somewhat true, but I'm not telling them that. "Nah, actually their parties are pretty dope," I say. "One time, this boy had J. Cole perform at his birthday party."

"Damn. For real?" Chance asks. "Shiiit. Bitch, next time invite me. I'll party with them white kids."

"Anyway," Kenya says loudly. "We were talking 'bout running up on Denasia. Bitch over there dancing with DeVante."

13

"Ol' trick," Bianca says. "You know she been running her mouth 'bout you, right? I was in Mr. Donald's class last week when Aaliyah told me—"

Chance rolls his eyes. "Ugh! Mr. Donald."

"You just mad he threw you out," Kenya says.

"Hell yes!"

"Anyway, Aaliyah told me—" Bianca begins.

I get lost again as classmates and teachers that I don't know are discussed. I can't say anything. Doesn't matter though. I'm invisible.

I feel like that a lot around here.

In the middle of them complaining about Denasia and their teachers, Kenya says something about getting another drink, and the three of them walk off without me.

Suddenly I'm Eve in the Garden after she ate the fruit – it's like I realize I'm naked. I'm by myself at a party I'm not even supposed to be at, where I barely know anybody. And the person I do know just left me hanging.

Kenya begged me to come to this party for weeks. I knew I'd be uncomfortable as hell, but every time I told Kenya no she said I act like I'm "too good for a Garden party." I got tired of hearing that shit and decided to prove her wrong. Problem is it would've taken Black Jesus to convince my parents to let me come. Now Black Jesus will have to save me if they find out I'm here.

People glance over at me with that "who is this chick, standing against the wall by herself like an idiot?" look. I slip my hands into my pockets. As long as I play it cool and

14

keep to myself, I should be fine. The ironic thing is though, at Williamson I don't have to "play it cool" – I'm cool by default because I'm one of the only black kids there. I have to earn coolness in Garden Heights, and that's more difficult than buying retro Jordans on release day.

Funny how it works with white kids though. It's dope to be black until it's hard to be black.

"Starr!" a familiar voice says.

The sea of people parts for him like he's a brown-skinned Moses. Guys give him daps, and girls crane their necks to look at him. He smiles at me, and his dimples ruin any G persona he has.

Khalil is fine, no other way of putting it. And I used to take baths with him. Not like *that,* but way back in the day when we would giggle because he had a wee-wee and I had what his grandma called a wee-ha. I swear it wasn't perverted though.

He hugs me, smelling like soap and baby powder. "What's up, girl? Ain't seen you in a minute." He lets me go. "You don't text nobody, nothing. Where you been?"

"School and the basketball team keep me busy," I say. "But I'm always at the store. You're the one nobody sees anymore."

His dimples disappear. He wipes his nose like he always does before a lie. "I been busy."

Obviously. The brand-new Jordans, the crisp white tee, the diamonds in his ears. When you grow up in Garden Heights, you know what "busy" really means.

Fuck. I wish *he* wasn't that kinda busy though. I don't know if I wanna tear up or smack him.

But the way Khalil looks at me with those hazel eyes makes it hard to be upset. I feel like I'm ten again, standing in the basement of Christ Temple Church, having my first kiss with him at Vacation Bible School. Suddenly I remember I'm in a hoodie, looking a straight-up mess … and that I actually *have* a boyfriend. I might not be answering Chris's calls or texts right now, but he's still mine and I wanna keep it that way.

"How's your grandma?" I ask. "And Cameron?"

"They a'ight. Grandma's sick though." Khalil sips from his cup. "Doctors say she got cancer or whatever."

"Damn. Sorry, K."

"Yeah, she taking chemo. She only worried 'bout getting a wig though." He gives a weak laugh that doesn't show his dimples. "She'll be a'ight."

It's a prayer more than a prophecy. "Is your momma helping with Cameron?"

"Good ol' Starr. Always looking for the best in people. You know she ain't helping."

"Hey, it was just a question. She came in the store the other day. She looks better."

"For now," says Khalil. "She claim she trying to get clean, but it's the usual. She'll go clean a few weeks, decide she wants one more hit, then be back at it. But like I said, I'm good, Cameron's good, Grandma's good." He shrugs. "That's all that matters."

"Yeah," I say, but I remember the nights I spent with Khalil on his porch, waiting for his momma to come home. Whether he likes it or not, she matters to him too.

The music changes, and Drake raps from the speakers. I nod to the beat and rap along under my breath. Everybody on the dance floor yells out the "started from the bottom, now we're here" part. Some days, we *are* at the bottom in Garden Heights, but we still share the feeling that damn, it could be worse.

Khalil is watching me. A smile tries to form on his lips, but he shakes his head. "Can't believe you still love whiny-ass Drake."

I gape at him. "Leave my husband alone!"

"Your *corny* husband. 'Baby, you my everything, you all I ever wanted,'" Khalil sings in a whiny voice. I push him with my shoulder, and he laughs, his drink splashing over the sides of the cup. "You know that's what he sounds like!"

I flip him off. He puckers his lips and makes a kissing sound. All these months apart, and we've fallen back into normal like it's nothing.

Khalil grabs a napkin from the coffee table and wipes drink off his Jordans – the Three Retros. They came out a few years ago, but I swear those things are so fresh. They cost about three hundred dollars, and that's if you find somebody on eBay who goes easy. Chris did. I got mine for a steal at one-fifty, but I wear kid sizes. Thanks to my small feet, Chris and I can match our sneakers. Yes, we're *that* couple. Shit, we're fly though. If he can stop doing stupid stuff, we'll really be good.

"I like the kicks," I tell Khalil.

"Thanks." He scrubs the shoes with his napkin. I cringe. With each hard rub, the shoes cry for my help. No lie, every time a sneaker is cleaned improperly, a kitten dies.

"Khalil," I say, one second away from snatching that napkin. "Either wipe gently back and forth or dab. Don't scrub. For real."

He looks up at me, smirking. "Okay, Ms. Sneakerhead." And thank Black Jesus, he dabs. "Since you made me spill my drink on them, I oughta make you clean them."

"It'll cost you sixty dollars."

"Sixty?" he shouts, straightening up.

"Hell, yeah. And it would be eighty if they had icy soles." Clear bottoms are a bitch to clean. "Cleaning kits aren't cheap. Besides, you're obviously making big money if you can buy those."

Khalil sips his drink like I didn't say anything, mutters, "Damn, this shit strong," and sets the cup on the coffee table. "Ay, tell your pops I need to holla at him soon. Some stuff going down that I need to talk to him 'bout."

"What kinda stuff?"

"Grown folks business."

"Yeah, 'cause you're so grown."

"Five months, two weeks, and three days older than you." He winks. "I ain't forgot."

A commotion stirs in the middle of the dance floor.

Voices argue louder than the music. Cuss words fly left and right.

My first thought? Kenya walked up on Denasia like she promised. But the voices are deeper than theirs.

Pop! A shot rings out. I duck.

Pop! A second shot. The crowd stampedes toward the door, which leads to more cussing and fighting since it's impossible for everybody to get out at once.

Khalil grabs my hand. "C'mon."

There are way too many people and way too much curly hair for me to catch a glimpse of Kenya. "But Kenya—"

"Forget her, let's go!"

He pulls me through the crowd, shoving people out our way and stepping on shoes. That alone could get us some bullets. I look for Kenya among the panicked faces, but still no sign of her. I don't try to see who got shot or who did it. You can't snitch if you don't know anything.

Cars speed away outside, and people run into the night in any direction where shots aren't firing off. Khalil leads me to a Chevy Impala parked under a dim streetlight. He pushes me in through the driver's side, and I climb into the passenger seat. We screech off, leaving chaos in the rearview mirror.

"Always some shit," he mumbles. "Can't have a party without somebody getting shot."

He sounds like my parents. That's exactly why they don't let me "go nowhere," as Kenya puts it. At least not around Garden Heights.

I send Kenya a text, hoping she's all right. Doubt those bullets were meant for her, but bullets go where they wanna go.

Kenya texts back kinda quick.

I'm fine.

I see that bitch tho. Bout to handle her ass.

Where u at?

Is this chick for real? We just ran for our lives, and she's ready to fight? I don't even answer that dumb shit.

Khalil's Impala is nice. Not all flashy like some guys' cars. I didn't see any rims before I got in, and the front seat has cracks in the leather. But the interior is a tacky lime green, so it's been customized at some point.

I pick at a crack in the seat. "Who you think got shot?"

Khalil gets his hairbrush out the compartment on the door. "Probably a King Lord," he says, brushing the sides of his fade. "Some Garden Disciples came in when I got there. Something was bound to pop off."

I nod. Garden Heights has been a battlefield for the past two months over some stupid territory wars. I was born a "queen" 'cause Daddy used to be a King Lord. But when he left the game, my street royalty status ended. But even if I'd grown up in it, I wouldn't understand fighting over streets nobody owns.

Khalil drops the brush in the door and cranks up his stereo, blasting an old rap song Daddy has played a million times. I frown. "Why you always listening to that old stuff?"

"Man, get outta here! Tupac was the truth."

"Yeah, twenty years ago."

"Nah, even now. Like, check this." He points at me, which means he's about to go into one of his Khalil philosophical moments. "'Pac said Thug Life stood for 'The Hate U Give Little Infants Fucks Everybody.'"

I raise my eyebrows. "What?"

"Listen! The Hate U – the letter U – Give Little Infants Fucks Everybody. T-H-U-G L-I-F-E. Meaning what society give us as youth, it bites them in the ass when we wild out. Get it?"

"Damn. Yeah."

"See? Told you he was relevant." He nods to the beat and raps along. But now I'm wondering what he's doing to "fuck everybody." As much as I think I know, I hope I'm wrong. I need to hear it from him.

"So why have you really been busy?" I ask. "A few months ago Daddy said you quit the store. I haven't seen you since."

He scoots closer to the steering wheel. "Where you want me to take you, your house or the store?"

"Khalil—"

"Your house or the store?"

"If you're selling that stuff—"

"Mind your business, Starr! Don't worry 'bout me. I'm doing what I gotta do."

"Bullshit. You know my dad would help you out."

He wipes his nose before his lie. "I don't need help from

21

nobody, okay? And that li'l minimum-wage job your pops gave me didn't make nothing happen. I got tired of choosing between lights and food."

"I thought your grandma was working."

"She was. When she got sick, them clowns at the hospital claimed they'd work with her. Two months later, she wasn't pulling her load on the job, 'cause when you're going through chemo, you can't pull big-ass garbage bins around. They fired her." He shakes his head. "Funny, huh? The *hospital* fired her 'cause she was sick."

It's silent in the Impala except for Tupac asking *who do you believe in?* I don't know.

My phone vibrates again, probably either Chris asking for forgiveness or Kenya asking for backup against Denasia. Instead, my big brother's all-caps texts appear on the screen. I don't know why he does that. He probably thinks it intimidates me. Really, it annoys the hell out of me.

WHERE R U?

U AND KENYA BETTER NOT BE @ THAT PARTY.

I HEARD SOMEBODY GOT SHOT.

The only thing worse than protective parents is protective older brothers. Even Black Jesus can't save me from Seven.

Khalil glances over at me. "Seven, huh?"

"How'd you know?"

"'Cause you always look like you wanna punch something when he talks to you. Remember that time at your birthday party when he kept telling you what to wish for?"

"And I popped him in his mouth."

"Then Natasha got mad at you for telling her 'boyfriend' to shut up," Khalil says, laughing.

I roll my eyes. "She got on my nerves with her crush on Seven. Half the time, I thought she came over just to see him."

"Nah, it was because you had the Harry Potter movies. What we used to call ourselves? The Hood Trio. Tighter than—"

"The inside of Voldemort's nose. We were so silly for that."

"I know, right?" he says.

We laugh, but something's missing from it. *Someone's* missing from it. Natasha.

Khalil looks at the road. "Crazy it's been six years, you know?"

A *whoop-whoop* sound startles us, and blue lights flash in the rearview mirror.

CHAPTER 2

When I was twelve, my parents had two talks with me.

One was the usual birds and bees. Well, I didn't really get the usual version. My mom, Lisa, is a registered nurse, and she told me what went where, and what didn't need to go here, there, or any damn where till I'm grown. Back then, I doubted anything was going anywhere anyway. While all the other girls sprouted breasts between sixth and seventh grade, my chest was as flat as my back.

The other talk was about what to do if a cop stopped me.

Momma fussed and told Daddy I was too young for that. He argued that I wasn't too young to get arrested or shot.

"Starr-Starr, you do whatever they tell you to do," he said. "Keep your hands visible. Don't make any sudden moves. Only speak when they speak to you."

I knew it must've been serious. Daddy has the biggest mouth of anybody I know, and if he said to be quiet, I needed to be quiet.

I hope somebody had the talk with Khalil.

He cusses under his breath, turns Tupac down, and maneuvers the Impala to the side of the street. We're on Carnation where most of the houses are abandoned and half the streetlights are busted. Nobody around but us and the cop.

Khalil turns the ignition off. "Wonder what this fool wants."

The officer parks and puts his brights on. I blink to keep from being blinded.

I remember something else Daddy said. *If you're with somebody, you better hope they don't have nothing on them, or both of y'all going down.*

"K, you don't have anything in the car, do you?" I ask.

He watches the cop in his side mirror. "Nah."

The officer approaches the driver's door and taps the window. Khalil cranks the handle to roll it down. As if we aren't blinded enough, the officer beams his flashlight in our faces.

"License, registration, and proof of insurance."

Khalil breaks a rule – he doesn't do what the cop wants. "What you pull us over for?"

"License, registration, and proof of insurance."

"I said what you pull us over for?"

"Khalil," I plead. "Do what he said."

Khalil groans and takes his wallet out. The officer follows his movements with the flashlight.

My heart pounds loudly, but Daddy's instructions echo in my head: *Get a good look at the cop's face. If you can remember his badge number, that's even better.*

With the flashlight following Khalil's hands, I make out the numbers on the badge – one-fifteen. He's white, midthirties to early forties, has a brown buzz cut and a thin scar over his top lip.

Khalil hands the officer his papers and license.

One-Fifteen looks over them. "Where are you two coming from tonight?"

"Nunya," Khalil says, meaning none of your business. "What you pull me over for?"

"Your taillight's broken."

"So are you gon' give me a ticket or what?" Khalil asks.

"You know what? Get out the car, smart guy."

"Man, just give me my ticket—"

"Get out the car! Hands up, where I can see them."

Khalil gets out with his hands up. One-Fifteen yanks him by his arm and pins him against the back door.

I fight to find my voice. "He didn't mean—"

"Hands on the dashboard!" the officer barks at me. "Don't move!"

I do what he tells me, but my hands are shaking too much to be still.

He pats Khalil down. "Okay, smart mouth, let's see what we find on you today."

"You ain't gon' find nothing," Khalil says.

One-Fifteen pats him down two more times. He turns up empty.

"Stay here," he tells Khalil. "And you." He looks in the window at me. "Don't move."

I can't even nod.

The officer walks back to his patrol car.

My parents haven't raised me to fear the police, just to be smart around them. They told me it's not smart to move while a cop has his back to you.

Khalil does. He comes to his door.

It's not smart to make a sudden move.

Khalil does. He opens the driver's door.

"You okay, Starr—"

Pow!

One. Khalil's body jerks. Blood splatters from his back. He holds on to the door to keep himself upright.

Pow!

Two. Khalil gasps.

Pow!

Three. Khalil looks at me, stunned.

He falls to the ground.

I'm ten again, watching Natasha drop.

An earsplitting scream emerges from my gut, explodes in my throat, and uses every inch of me to be heard.

Instinct says don't move, but everything else says check on Khalil. I jump out the Impala and rush around to the other side. Khalil stares at the sky as if he hopes to see God. His mouth is open like he wants to scream. I scream loud enough for the both of us.

"No, no, no," is all I can say, like I'm a year old and it's the only word I know. I'm not sure how I end up on the ground next to him. My mom once said that if someone gets shot, try to stop the bleeding, but there's so much blood. Too much blood.

"No, no, no."

Khalil doesn't move. He doesn't utter a word. He doesn't even look at me. His body stiffens, and he's gone. I hope he sees God.

Someone else screams.

I blink through my tears. Officer One-Fifteen yells at me, pointing the same gun he killed my friend with.

I put my hands up.

CHAPTER 3

They leave Khalil's body in the street like it's an exhibit. Police cars and ambulances flash all along Carnation Street. People stand off to the side, trying to see what happened.

"Damn, bruh," some guy says. "They killed him!"

The police tell the crowd to leave. Nobody listens.

The paramedics can't do shit for Khalil, so they put me in the back of an ambulance like I need help. The bright lights spotlight me, and people crane their necks to get a peek.

I don't feel special. I feel sick.

The cops rummage through Khalil's car. I try to tell them to stop. *Please, cover his body. Please, close his eyes. Please, close his mouth. Get away from his car. Don't pick up his hairbrush.* But the words never come out.

One-Fifteen sits on the sidewalk with his face buried in his hands. Other officers pat his shoulder and tell him it'll be okay.

They finally put a sheet over Khalil. He can't breathe under it. I can't breathe.

29

I can't.

Breathe.

I gasp.

And gasp.

And gasp.

"Starr?"

Brown eyes with long eyelashes appear in front of me. They're like mine.

I couldn't say much to the cops, but I did manage to give them my parents' names and phone numbers.

"Hey," Daddy says. "C'mon, let's go."

I open my mouth to respond. A sob comes out.

Daddy is moved aside, and Momma wraps her arms around me. She rubs my back and speaks in hushed tones that tell lies. "It's all right, baby. It's all right."

We stay this way for a long time. Eventually, Daddy helps us out the ambulance. He wraps his arm around me like a shield against curious eyes and guides me to his Tahoe down the street.

He drives. A streetlight flashes across his face, revealing how tight his jaw is set. His veins bulge along his bald head.

Momma's wearing her scrubs, the ones with the rubber ducks on them. She did an extra shift at the emergency room tonight. She wipes her eyes a few times, probably thinking about Khalil or how that could've been me lying in the street.

My stomach twists. All of that blood, and it came out of him. Some of it is on my hands, on Seven's hoodie, on my sneakers. An hour ago we were laughing and catching up. Now his blood…

Hot spit pools in my mouth. My stomach twists tighter. I gag.

Momma glances at me in the rearview mirror. "Maverick, pull over!"

I throw myself across the backseat and push the door open before the truck comes to a complete stop. It feels like everything in me is coming out, and all I can do is let it.

Momma hops out and runs around to me. She holds my hair out the way and rubs my back.

"I'm so sorry, baby," she says.

When we get home, she helps me undress. Seven's hoodie and my Jordans disappear into a black trash bag, and I never see them again.

I sit in a tub of steaming water and scrub my hands raw to get Khalil's blood off. Daddy carries me to bed, and Momma brushes her fingers through my hair until I fall asleep.

Nightmares wake me over and over again. Momma reminds me to breathe, the same way she did before I outgrew asthma. I think she stays in my room the whole night, 'cause every time I wake up, she's sitting on my bed.

But this time, she's gone. My eyes strain against the brightness of my neon-blue walls. The clock says it's five in the morning. My body's so used to waking up at five, it doesn't care if it's Saturday morning or not.

I stare at the glow-in-the-dark stars on my ceiling, trying to recap the night before. The party flashes in my mind, the fight, One-Fifteen pulling me and Khalil over. The first shot rings in my ears. The second. The third.

I'm lying in bed. Khalil is lying in the county morgue.

That's where Natasha ended up too. It happened six years ago, but I still remember everything from that day. I was sweeping floors at our grocery store, saving up for my first pair of J's, when Natasha ran in. She was chunky (her momma told her it was baby fat), dark-skinned, and wore her hair in braids that always looked freshly done. I wanted braids like hers so bad.

"Starr, the hydrant on Elm Street busted!" she said.

That was like saying we had a free water park. I remember looking at Daddy and pleading silently. He said I could go, as long as I promised to be back in an hour.

I don't think I ever saw the water shoot as high as it did that day. Almost everybody in the neighborhood was there too. Just having fun. I was the only one who noticed the car at first.

A tattooed arm stretched out the back window, holding a Glock. People ran. Not me though. My feet became part of the sidewalk. Natasha was splashing in the water, all happy and stuff. Then—

Pow! Pow! Pow!

I dove into a rosebush. By the time I got up, somebody was yelling, "Call nine-one-one!" At first I thought it was me, 'cause I had blood on my shirt. The thorns on the rosebush got me, that's all. It was Natasha though. Her blood mixed in with the water, and all you could see was a red river flowing down the street.

She looked scared. We were ten, we didn't know what happened after you died. Hell, I still don't know, and she was forced to find out, even if she didn't wanna find out.

I know she didn't. Just like Khalil didn't.

My door creaks open, and Momma peeks in. She tries to smile. "Look who's up."

She sinks onto her spot on the bed and touches my forehead, even though I don't have a fever. She takes care of sick kids so much that it's her first instinct. "How you feeling, Munch?"

That nickname. My parents claim I was always munching on something from the moment I got off the bottle. I've lost my big appetite, but I can't lose that nickname. "Tired," I say. My voice has extra bass in it. "I wanna stay in bed."

"I know, baby, but I don't want you here by yourself."

That's all I wanna be, by myself. She stares at me, but it feels like she's looking at who I used to be, her little girl with ponytails and a snaggletooth who swore she was a Powerpuff Girl. It's weird but also kinda like a blanket I wanna get wrapped up in.

"I love you," she says.

"I love you too."

She stands and holds her hand out. "C'mon. Let's get you something to eat."

We walk slowly to the kitchen. Black Jesus hangs from

33

the cross in a painting on the hallway wall, and Malcolm X holds a shotgun in a photograph next to him. Nana still complains about those pictures hanging next to each other.

We live in her old house. She gave it to my parents after my uncle, Carlos, moved her into his humongous house in the suburbs. Uncle Carlos was always uneasy about Nana living by herself in Garden Heights, especially since break-ins and robberies seem to happen more to older folks than anybody. Nana doesn't think she's old though. She refused to leave, talking about how it was her home and no thugs were gonna run her out, not even when somebody broke in and stole her television. About a month after that, Uncle Carlos claimed that he and Aunt Pam needed her help with their kids. Since, according to Nana, Aunt Pam "can't cook worth a damn for those poor babies" she finally agreed to move. Our house hasn't lost its Nana-ness though, with its permanent odor of potpourri, flowered wallpaper, and hints of pink in almost every room.

Daddy and Seven are talking before we get to the kitchen. They go silent as soon as we walk in.

"Morning, baby girl." Daddy gets up from the table and kisses my forehead. "You sleep okay?"

"Yeah," I lie as he guides me to a seat. Seven just stares.

Momma opens the fridge, the door crowded with take-out menus and fruit-shaped magnets. "All right, Munch," she says, "you want turkey bacon or regular?"

"Regular." I'm surprised I have an option. We never have pork. We aren't Muslims. More like "Christlims."

Momma became a member of Christ Temple Church when she was in Nana's belly. Daddy believes in Black Jesus but follows the Black Panthers' Ten-Point Program more than the Ten Commandments. He agrees with the Nation of Islam on some stuff, but he can't get over the fact that they may have killed Malcolm X.

"Pig in my house," Daddy grumbles and sits next to me. Seven smirks across from him. Seven and Daddy look like one of those age-progression pictures they show when somebody's been missing a long time. Throw my little brother, Sekani, in there and you have the same person at eight, seventeen, and thirty-six. They're dark brown, slender, and have thick eyebrows and long eyelashes that almost look feminine. Seven's dreads are long enough to give both bald-headed Daddy and short-haired Sekani each a head full of hair.

As for me, it's as if God mixed my parents' skin tones in a paint bucket to get my medium-brown complexion. I did inherit Daddy's eyelashes – and I'm cursed with his eyebrows too. Otherwise I'm mostly my mom, with big brown eyes and a little too much forehead.

Momma passes behind Seven with the bacon and squeezes his shoulder. "Thank you for staying with your brother last night so we could—" Her voice catches, but the reminder of what happened hangs in the air. She clears her throat. "We appreciate it."

"No problem. I needed to get out the house."

"King spent the night?" Daddy asks.

"More like moved in. Iesha talking about they can be a family—"

"Ay," Daddy says. "That's your momma, boy. Don't be calling her by her name like you grown."

"Somebody in that house needs to be grown," Momma says. She takes a skillet out and hollers toward the hall, "Sekani, I'm not telling you again. If you wanna go to Carlos's for the weekend, you better get up! You're not gonna have me late for work." I guess she's gotta work a day shift to make up for last night.

"Pops, you know what's gonna happen," Seven says. "He'll beat her, she'll put him out. Then he'll come back, saying he changed. Only difference is this time, I'm not letting him put his hands on me."

"You can always move in with us," says Daddy.

"I know, but I can't leave Kenya and Lyric. That fool's crazy enough to hit them too. He don't care that they're his daughters."

"A'ight," Daddy says. "Don't say anything to him. If he puts his hands on you, let me handle that."

Seven nods then looks at me. He opens his mouth and keeps it open a while before saying, "I'm sorry about last night, Starr."

Somebody finally acknowledges the cloud hanging over the kitchen, which for some reason is like acknowledging me.

"Thanks," I say, even though it's weird saying that. I don't deserve the sympathy. Khalil's family does.

36

There's just the sound of bacon crackling and popping in the skillet. It's like a "Fragile" sticker's on my forehead, and instead of taking a chance and saying something that might break me, they'd rather say nothing at all.

But the silence is the worst.

"I borrowed your hoodie, Seven," I mumble. It's random, but it's better than nothing. "The blue one. Momma had to throw it away. Khalil's blood…" I swallow. "His blood got on it."

"Oh…"

That's all anybody says for a minute.

Momma turns around to the skillet. "Don't make any sense. That baby—" she says thickly. "He was just a baby."

Daddy shakes his head. "That boy never hurt anybody. He didn't deserve that shit."

"Why did they shoot him?" Seven asks. "Was he a threat or something?"

"No," I say quietly.

I stare at the table. I can feel all of them watching me again.

"He didn't do anything," I say. "*We* didn't do anything. Khalil didn't even have a gun."

Daddy releases a slow breath. "Folks around here gon' lose their minds when they find that out."

"People from the neighborhood are already talking about it on Twitter," Seven says. "I saw it last night."

"Did they mention your sister?" Momma asks.

"No. Just RIP Khalil messages, fuck the police, stuff

like that. I don't think they know details."

"What's gonna happen to me when the details do come out?" I ask.

"What do you mean, baby?" my mom asks.

"Besides the cop, I'm the only person who was there. And you've seen stuff like this. It ends up on national news. People get death threats, cops target them, all kinds of stuff."

"I won't let anything happen to you," Daddy says. "None of us will." He looks at Momma and Seven. "We're not telling anybody that Starr was there."

"Should Sekani know?" Seven asks.

"No," Momma says. "It's best if he didn't. We're just gonna be quiet for now."

I've seen it happen over and over again: a black person gets killed just for being black, and all hell breaks loose. I've tweeted RIP hashtags, reblogged pictures on Tumblr, and signed every petition out there. I always said that if I saw it happen to somebody, I would have the loudest voice, making sure the world knew what went down.

Now I am that person, and I'm too afraid to speak.

I wanna stay home and watch *The Fresh Prince of Bel-Air*, my favorite show ever, hands down. I think I know every episode word for word. Yeah it's hilarious, but it's also like seeing parts of my life on screen. I even relate to the theme song. A couple of gang members who were up to no good made trouble in my neighborhood and killed Natasha. My parents got scared, and although they didn't send me to my aunt and uncle in a rich neighborhood, they sent me to a bougie private school.

I just wish I could be myself at Williamson like Will was himself in Bel-Air.

I kinda wanna stay home so I can return Chris's calls too. After last night, it feels stupid to be mad at him. Or I could call Hailey and Maya, those girls Kenya claims don't count as my friends. I guess I can see why she says that. I never invite them over. Why would I? They live in mini-mansions. My house is just mini.

I made the mistake of inviting them to a sleepover in seventh grade. Momma was gonna let us do our nails, stay up all night, and eat as much pizza as we wanted. It was gonna be as awesome as those weekends we had at Hailey's. The ones we still have sometimes. I invited Kenya too, so I could finally hang out with all three of them at once.

Hailey didn't come. Her dad didn't want her spending the night in "the ghetto." I overheard my parents say that. Maya came but ended up asking her parents to come get her that night. There was a drive-by around the corner, and the gunshots scared her.

That's when I realized Williamson is one world and Garden Heights is another, and I have to keep them separate.

It doesn't matter what I'm thinking about doing today though – my parents have their own plans for me. Momma tells me I'm going to the store with Daddy. Before Seven leaves for work, he comes to my room in his Best Buy polo and khakis and hugs me.

"Love you," he says.

See, that's why I hate it when somebody dies. People do stuff they wouldn't usually do. Even Momma hugs me longer and tighter with more sympathy than "just because" in it. Sekani, on the other hand, steals bacon off my plate, looks at my phone, and purposely steps on my foot on his way out. I love him for it.

I bring a bowl of dog food and leftover bacon outside to our pit bull, Brickz. Daddy gave him his name 'cause he's always been as heavy as some bricks. Soon as he sees me, he jumps and fights to break free from his chain. And when I get close enough, his hyper butt jumps up my legs, nearly taking me down.

"Get!" I say. He crouches onto the grass and stares up at me, whimpering with wide puppy-dog eyes. The Brickz version of an apology.

I know pit bulls can be aggressive, but Brickz is a baby most of the time. A *big* baby. Now, if somebody tries to break in our house or something, they won't meet the baby Brickz.

While I feed Brickz and refill his water bowl, Daddy picks bunches of collard greens from his garden. He cuts roses that have blooms as big as my palms. Daddy spends hours out here every night, planting, tilling, and talking. He claims a good garden needs good conversation.

About thirty minutes later, we're riding in his truck with the windows down. On the radio, Marvin Gaye asks what's going on. It's still dark out, though the sun peeks through the clouds, and hardly anybody is outside. This early in the morning it's easy to hear the rumbling of eighteen-wheelers on the freeway.

Daddy hums to Marvin, but he couldn't carry a tune if it came in a box. He's wearing a Lakers jersey and no shirt underneath, revealing tattoos all over his arms. One of my baby photos smiles back at me, permanently etched on his arm with *Something to live for, something to die for* written beneath it. Seven and Sekani are on his other arm with the same words beneath them. Love letters in the simplest form.

"You wanna talk 'bout last night some more?" he asks.

"Nah."

"A'ight. Whenever you wanna."

Another love letter in the simplest form.

We turn onto Marigold Avenue, where Garden Heights is waking up. Some ladies wearing floral headscarves come out the Laundromat, carrying big baskets of clothes. Mr. Reuben unlocks the chains on his restaurant. His nephew Tim, the cook, leans against the wall and wipes sleep from his eyes. Ms. Yvette yawns as she goes in her beauty shop. The lights are on at Top Shelf Spirits and Wine, but they're always on.

Daddy parks in front of Carter's Grocery, our family's store. Daddy bought it when I was nine after the former owner, Mr. Wyatt, left Garden Heights to go sit on the beach all day, watching pretty women. (Mr. Wyatt's words, not mine.) Mr. Wyatt was the only person who would hire Daddy when he got out of prison, and he later said Daddy was the only person he trusted to run the store.

Compared to the Walmart on the east side of Garden Heights, our grocery is tiny. White-painted metal bars protect the windows and door. They make the store resemble a jail.

Mr. Lewis from the barbershop next door stands out front, his arms folded over his big belly. He sets his narrowed eyes on Daddy.

Daddy sighs. "Here we go."

We hop out. Mr. Lewis gives some of the best haircuts in Garden Heights – Sekani's high-top fade proves it – but Mr. Lewis himself wears an untidy Afro. His stomach blocks his view of his feet, and since his wife passed nobody tells him that his pants are too short and his socks don't always match. Today one is striped and the other is argyle.

"The store used to open at five fifty-five on the dot," he says. "Five fifty-five!"

It's 6:05.

Daddy unlocks the front door. "I know, Mr. Lewis, but I told you, I'm not running the store the same way Wyatt did."

"It sho' is obvious. First you take down his pictures – who the hell replaces a picture of Dr. King with some nobody—"

"Huey Newton ain't a nobody."

"He ain't Dr. King! Then you hire thugs to work up in here. I heard that Khalil boy got himself killed last night. He was probably selling that stuff." Mr. Lewis looks from Daddy's basketball jersey to his tattoos. "Wonder where he get *that* idea from."

Daddy's jaw tightens. "Starr, turn the coffeepot on for Mr. Lewis."

So he can get the hell outta here, I say to myself, finishing Daddy's sentence for him.

I flick the switch on the coffeepot at the self-serve table, which Huey Newton watches over from a photograph, his fist raised for black power.

I'm supposed to replace the filter and put new coffee and water in, but for talking about Khalil Mr. Lewis gets coffee made from day-old grounds.

He limps through the aisles and gets a honey bun, an apple, and a pack of hog head cheese. He gives me the honey bun. "Heat it up, girl. And you bet' not overcook it."

I leave it in the microwave until the plastic wrapper swells and pops open. Mr. Lewis eats it soon as I take it out.

"That thang hot!" He chews and blows at the same time. "You heated it too long, girl. 'Bout to burn my mouth!"

When Mr. Lewis leaves, Daddy winks at me.

The usual customers come in, like Mrs. Jackson, who insists on buying her greens from Daddy and nobody else. Four red-eyed guys in sagging pants buy almost every bag of chips we have. Daddy tells them it's too early to be that blazed, and they laugh way too hard. One of them licks his next blunt as they leave. Around eleven, Mrs. Rooks buys some roses and snacks for her bridge club meeting. She has droopy eyes and gold plating on her front teeth. Her wig is gold-colored too.

"Y'all need to get some Lotto tickets up in here, baby," she says as Daddy rings her up and I bag her stuff. "Tonight it's at three hundred million!"

Daddy smiles. "For real? What would you do with all that money, Mrs. Rooks?"

"Shiiit. Baby, the question is what I *wouldn't* do with all that money. Lord knows, I'd get on the first plane outta here."

Daddy laughs. "Is that right? Then who gon' make red velvet cakes for us?"

"Somebody else, 'cause I'd be gone." She points to the display of cigarettes behind us. "Baby, hand me a pack of them Newports."

Those are Nana's favorites too. They used to be Daddy's favorites before I begged him to quit. I grab a pack and pass it to Mrs. Rooks.

She's staring at me moments after, patting the pack against her palm, and I wait for *it*. The sympathy. "Baby, I heard what happened to Rosalie's grandboy," she says. "I'm so sorry. Y'all used to be friends, didn't you?"

The "used to" stings, but I just say to Mrs. Rooks, "Yes, ma'am."

"Hmm!" She shakes her head. "Lord, have mercy. My heart 'bout broke when I heard. I tried to go over there and see Rosalie last night, but so many people were already at the house. Poor Rosalie. All she going through and now this. Barbara said Rosalie not sure how she gon' pay to bury him. We talking 'bout raising some money. Think you can help us out, Maverick?"

"Oh, yeah. Let me know what y'all need, and it's done."

She flashes those gold teeth in a smile. "Boy, it's good to

see where the Lord done brought you. Your momma would be proud."

Daddy nods heavily. Grandma's been gone ten years — long enough that Daddy doesn't cry every day, but such a short while ago that if someone brings her up, it brings him down.

"And look at this girl," Mrs. Rooks says, eyeing me. "Every bit of Lisa. Maverick, you better watch out. These li'l boys around here gon' be trying it."

"Nah, they better watch out. You know I ain't having that. She can't date till she forty."

My hand drifts to my pocket, thinking of Chris and his texts. Shit, I left my phone at home. Needless to say, Daddy doesn't know a thing about Chris. We've been together over a year now. Seven knows, because he met Chris at school, and Momma figured it out when Chris would always visit me at Uncle Carlos's house, claiming he was my friend. One day she and Uncle Carlos walked in on us kissing and they pointed out that friends don't kiss each other like that. I've never seen Chris get so red in my life.

She and Seven are okay with me dating Chris, although if it was up to Seven I'd become a nun, but whatever. I can't get the guts to tell Daddy though. And it's not just because he doesn't want me dating yet. The bigger issue is that Chris is white.

At first I thought my mom might say something about it, but she was like, "He could be polka dot, as long as he's not a criminal and he's treating you right." Daddy, on the other hand, rants about how Halle Berry "act like she can't get with brothers anymore" and how messed up that is. I mean, anytime he finds out a black person is with a white person, suddenly something's wrong with them. I don't want him looking at me like that.

Luckily, Momma hasn't told him. She refuses to get in the middle of that fight. My boyfriend, my responsibility to tell Daddy.

Mrs. Rooks leaves. Seconds later, the bell clangs. Kenya struts into the store. Her kicks are cute – Bazooka Joe Nike Dunks that I haven't added to my collection. Kenya always wears fly sneakers.

She goes to get her usual from the aisles. "Hey, Starr. Hey, Uncle Maverick."

"Hey, Kenya," Daddy answers, even though he's not her uncle, but her brother's dad. "You good?"

She comes back with a jumbo bag of Hot Cheetos and a Sprite. "Yeah. My momma wanna know if my brother spent the night with y'all."

There she goes calling Seven "my brother" like she's the only one who can claim him. It's annoying as hell.

"Tell your momma I'll call her later," Daddy says.

"Okay." Kenya pays for her stuff and makes eye contact with me. She jerks her head a little to the side.

"I'm gonna sweep the aisles," I tell Daddy.

Kenya follows me. I grab the broom and go to the produce aisle on the other side of the store. Some grapes have spilled out from those red-eyed guys sampling before buying. I barely start sweeping before Kenya starts talking.

"I heard about Khalil," she says. "I'm so sorry, Starr. You okay?"

I make myself nod. "I … just can't believe it, you know? It had been a while since I saw him, but…"

"It hurts." Kenya says what I can't.

"Yeah."

Fuck, I feel the tears coming. I'm not gonna cry, I'm not gonna cry, I'm not gonna cry…

"I kinda hoped he'd be in here when I walked in," she says softly. "Like he used to be. Bagging groceries in that ugly apron."

"The green one," I mutter.

"Yeah. Talking about how women love a man in uniform."

I stare at the floor. If I cry now, I may never stop.

Kenya pops her Hot Cheetos open and holds the bag toward me. Comfort food.

I reach in and get a couple. "Thanks."

"No problem."

We munch on Cheetos. Khalil's supposed to be here with us.

"So, um," I say, and my voice is all rough. "You and Denasia got into it last night?"

"Girl." She sounds like she's been waiting to drop this story for hours. "DeVante came over to me, right before it got crazy. He asked for my number."

"I thought he was Denasia's boyfriend?"

"DeVante not the type to be tied down. Anyway, Denasia

walked over to start something, but the shots went off. We ended up running down the same street, and I clocked her ass. It was so funny! You should've seen it!"

I would've rather seen that instead of Officer One-Fifteen. Or Khalil staring at the sky. Or all that blood. My stomach twists again.

Kenya waves her hand in front of me. "Hey. You okay?"

I blink Khalil and that cop away. "Yeah. I'm good."

"You sure? You real quiet."

"Yeah."

She lets it drop, and I let her tell me about the second round she has planned for Denasia.

Daddy calls me up front. When I get there, he hands me a twenty. "Get me some beef ribs from Reuben's. And I want—"

"Potato salad and fried okra," I say. That's what he always has on Saturdays.

He kisses my cheek. "You know your daddy. Get whatever you want, baby."

Kenya follows me out the store. We wait for a car to pass, the music blasting and the driver reclined so far back that only the tip of his nose seems to nod to the song. We cross the street to Reuben's.

The smoky aroma hits us on the sidewalk, and a blues song pours outside. Inside, the walls are covered with photographs of civil rights leaders, politicians, and celebrities who have eaten here, like James Brown and pre-heart-bypass Bill Clinton. There's a picture of Dr. King and a much younger Mr. Reuben.

A bulletproof partition separates the customers from the cashier. I fan myself after a few minutes in line. The air conditioner in the window stopped working months ago, and the smoker heats up the whole building.

When we get to the front of the line, Mr. Reuben greets us with a gap-toothed smile from behind the partition. "Hey, Starr and Kenya. How y'all doing?"

Mr. Reuben is one of the only people around here who actually calls me by my name. He remembers everybody's names somehow. "Hey, Mr. Reuben," I say. "My daddy wants his usual."

He writes it on a pad. "All right. Beefs, tater salad, okra. Y'all want fried BBQ wings and fries? And extra sauce for you, Starr baby?"

He remembers everybody's usual orders too somehow. "Yes, sir," we say.

"All right. Y'all been staying out of trouble?"

"Yes, sir," Kenya lies with ease.

"How 'bout some pound cake on the house then? Reward for good behavior."

We say yeah and thank him. But see, Mr. Reuben could know about Kenya's fight and would offer her pound cake regardless. He's nice like that. He gives kids free meals if they bring in their report cards. If it's a good one, he'll make a copy and put it on the "All-Star Wall." If it's bad, as long as they own up to it and promise to do better, he'll still give them a meal.

"It's gon' take 'bout fifteen minutes," he says.

That means sit and wait till your number is called. We find a table next to some white guys. You rarely see white people in Garden Heights, but when you do they're usually at Reuben's. The men watch the news on the box TV in a corner of the ceiling.

I munch on some of Kenya's Hot Cheetos. They would taste much better with cheese sauce on them. "Has there been anything on the news about Khalil?"

She pays more attention to her phone. "Yeah, like I watch the news. I think I saw something on Twitter, though."

I wait. Between a story about a bad car accident on the freeway and a garbage bag of live puppies that was found in a park, there's a short story about an officer-involved shooting that is being investigated. They don't even say Khalil's name. Some bullshit.

We get our food and head back to the store. Right as we cross the street, a gray BMW pulls up beside us, bass thumping inside like the car has a heartbeat. The driver's side window rolls down, smoke drifts out, and the male, three-hundred-pound version of Kenya smiles at us. "What up, queens?"

Kenya leans in through the window and kisses his cheek. "Hey, Daddy."

"Hey, Starr-Starr," he says. "Not gon' say hey to your uncle?"

You ain't my uncle, I wanna say. You ain't shit to me. And if you touch my brother again, I'll— "Hey, King," I finally mumble.

His smile fades like he hears my thoughts. He puffs on a cigar and blows smoke from the corner of his mouth. Two tears are tattooed under his left eye. Two lives he's taken. At least.

"I see y'all been to Reuben's. Here." He holds out two fat rolls of money. "Make up for whatever y'all spent."

Kenya takes one easily, but I'm not touching that dirty money. "No thanks."

"Go on, queen." King winks. "Take some money from your godfather."

"Nah, she good," Daddy says.

He walks toward us. Daddy leans against the car window so he's eye level with King and gives him one of those guy handshakes with so many movements you wonder how they remember it.

"Big Mav," Kenya's dad says with a grin. "What up, king?"

"Don't call me that shit." Daddy doesn't say it loudly or angrily, but in the same way I would tell somebody not to put onions or mayo on my burger. Daddy once told me that King's parents named him after the same gang he later joined, and that's why a name is important. It defines you. King became a King Lord when he took his first breath.

"I was just giving my goddaughter some pocket change," King says. "I heard what happened to her li'l homie. That's fucked up."

"Yeah. You know how it is," Daddy says. "Po-po shoot first, ask questions later."

51

"No doubt. They worse than us sometimes." King chuckles. "But ay? On some business shit, I got a package coming, need somewhere to keep it. Got too many eyes on Iesha's house."

"I already told you that shit ain't going down here."

King rubs his beard. "Oh, okay. So folks get out the game, forget where they come from, forget that if it wasn't for my money, they wouldn't have their li'l store—"

"And if it wasn't for me, you'd be locked up. Three years, state pen, remember that shit? I don't owe you nothing." Daddy leans onto the window and says, "But if you touch Seven again, I'll owe you an ass whooping. Remember that, now that you done moved back in with his momma."

King sucks his teeth. "Kenya, get in the car."

"But Daddy—"

"I said get your ass in the car!"

Kenya mumbles "bye" to me. She goes around to the passenger's side and hops in.

"A'ight, Big Mav. So it's like that?" King says.

Daddy straightens up. "It's exactly like that."

"A'ight then. You just make sure your ass don't get outta line. Ain't no telling what I'll do."

The BMW peels out.

CHAPTER 4

That night, Natasha tries to convince me to follow her to the fire hydrant, and Khalil begs me to go for a ride with him.

I force a smile, my lips trembling, and tell them I can't hang out. They keep asking, and I keep saying no.

Darkness crawls toward them. I try to warn them, but my voice doesn't work. The shadow swallows them up in an instant. Now it creeps toward me. I back away, only to find it behind me...

I wake up. My clock glows with the numbers: 11:05.

I suck in deep breaths. Sweat glues my tank top and basketball shorts to my skin. Sirens scream nearby, and Brickz and other dogs bark in response.

Sitting on the side of my bed, I rub my face, as if that'll wipe the nightmare away. No way I can go back to sleep. Not if it means seeing them again.

My throat is lined with sandpaper and aches for water. When my feet touch the cold floor, goose bumps pop up all over me. Daddy always has the air conditioning on high in the spring and summer, turning the house into a meat locker. The rest of us shiver our butts off, but he enjoys it, saying, "A li'l cold never hurt nobody." A lie.

I drag myself down the hall. Halfway to the kitchen I hear Momma say, "Why can't they wait? She just saw one of her best friends die. She doesn't need to relive that right now."

I stop. Light from the kitchen stretches into the hallway.

"We have to investigate, Lisa," says a second voice. Uncle Carlos, Momma's older brother. "We want the truth as much as anyone."

"You mean y'all wanna justify what that pig did," Daddy says. "Investigate my ass."

"Maverick, don't make this something it's not," Uncle Carlos says.

"A sixteen-year-old black boy is dead because a white cop killed him. What else could it be?"

"Shhh!" Momma hisses. "Keep it down. Starr had the hardest time falling asleep."

Uncle Carlos says something, but it's too low for me to hear. I inch closer.

"This isn't about black or white," he says.

"Bullshit," says Daddy. "If this was out in Riverton Hills and his name was Richie, we wouldn't be having this conversation."

"I heard he was a drug dealer," says Uncle Carlos.

"And that makes it okay?" Daddy asks.

"I didn't say it did, but it could explain Brian's decision if he felt threatened."

A "no" lodges in my throat, aching to be yelled out. Khalil wasn't a threat that night.

And what made the cop think he was a drug dealer?

Wait. *Brian*. That's One-Fifteen's name?

"Oh, so you know him," Daddy mocks. "I ain't surprised."

"He's a colleague, yes and a good guy, believe it or not. I'm sure this is hard on him. Who knows what he was thinking at the time?"

"You said it yourself, he thought Khalil was a drug dealer," Daddy says. "A *thug*. Why he assumed that though? What? By looking at Khalil? Explain that, Detective."

Silence.

"Why was she even in the car with a drug dealer?" Uncle Carlos asks. "Lisa, I keep telling you, you need to move her and Sekani out of this neighborhood. It's poisonous."

"I've been thinking about it."

"And we're not going anywhere," Daddy says.

"Maverick, she's seen two of her friends get killed," Momma says. "Two! And she's only sixteen."

"And one was at the hands of a person who was supposed to protect her! What, you think if you live next door to them, they'll treat you different?"

"Why does it always have to be about race with you?" Uncle Carlos asks. "Other races aren't killing us nearly as much as we're killing ourselves."

"Ne-gro, please. If I kill Tyrone, I'm going to prison. If a cop kills me, he's getting put on leave. Maybe."

55

"You know what? There's no point having this conversation with you," Uncle Carlos says. "Will you at least consider letting Starr speak to the detectives handling the case?"

"We should probably get her an attorney first, Carlos," Momma says.

"That's not necessary right now," he says.

"And it wasn't necessary for that cop to pull the trigger," says Daddy. "You really think we gon' let them talk to our daughter and twist her words around because she doesn't have a lawyer?"

"Nobody's going to twist her words around! I told you, we want the truth to come out too."

"Oh, we know the truth, that's not what we want," says Daddy. "*We* want justice."

Uncle Carlos sighs. "Lisa, the sooner she talks to the detectives, the better. It will be a simple process. All she has to do is answer some questions. That's it. No need to spend money to get an attorney just yet."

"Frankly, Carlos, we don't want anyone to know Starr was there," Momma says. "She's scared. I am too. Who knows what's gonna happen?"

"I get that, but I assure you she'll be protected. If you don't trust the system, can you at least trust me?"

"I don't know," says Daddy. "Can we?"

"You know what, Maverick? I've just about had it with you—"

"You can get out my house then."

"It wouldn't even be your house if it wasn't for me and my mom!"

"Y'all stop!" Momma says.

I shift my weight, and goddamn if the floor doesn't creak, which is like sounding an alarm. Momma glances around the kitchen doorway and down the hall, straight at me. "Starr baby, what you doing up?"

Now I have no choice but to go to the kitchen. The three of them are sitting around the table, my parents in their pajamas and Uncle Carlos in some sweats and a hoodie.

"Hey, baby girl," he says. "We didn't wake you up, did we?"

"No," I say, sitting next to Momma. "I was already awake. Nightmares."

All of them look sympathetic even though I didn't say it for sympathy. I kinda hate sympathy.

"What are you doing here?" I ask Uncle Carlos.

"Sekani has a stomach bug and begged me to bring him home."

"And your uncle was just getting ready to leave," Daddy adds.

Uncle Carlos's jaw twitches. His face has gotten rounder since he made detective. He has Momma's "high yella" complexion, as Nana calls it, and when he gets mad, his face turns deep red, like it is now.

"I'm sorry about Khalil, baby girl," he says. "I was just telling your parents how the detectives would like for you to come in and answer a few questions."

"But you don't have to do it if you don't wanna," Daddy says.

"You know what—" Uncle Carlos begins.

"Stop. Please?" says Momma. She looks at me. "Munch, do you wanna talk to the cops?"

I swallow. I wish I could say yes, but I don't know. On one hand, it's the cops. It's not like I'll be telling just anybody.

On the other hand, *it's the cops*. One of them killed Khalil.

But Uncle Carlos is a cop, and he wouldn't ask me to do something that would hurt me.

"Will it help Khalil get justice?" I ask.

Uncle Carlos nods. "It will."

"Will One-Fifteen be there?"

"Who?"

"The officer, that's his badge number," I say. "I remember it."

"Oh. No, he won't be there. I promise. It'll be okay."

Uncle Carlos's promises are guarantees, sometimes even more than my parents'. He never uses that word unless he absolutely means it.

"Okay," I say. "I'll do it."

"Thank you." Uncle Carlos comes over and gives me two kisses to my forehead, the way he's done since he used to tuck me in. "Lisa, just bring her after school on Monday. It shouldn't take too long."

Momma gets up and hugs him. "Thank you." She walks

him down the hall, toward the front door. "Be safe, okay? And text me when you get home."

"Yes, ma'am. Sounding like our momma," he teases.

"Whatever. You just better text me—"

"Okay, okay. Good night."

Momma comes back to the kitchen, pulling her robe together. "Munch, your father and I are visiting Ms. Rosalie in the morning instead of going to church. You're welcome to come if you want."

"Yeah," Daddy says. "And ain't no uncle pressuring you to go."

Momma cuts him a quick glare, then turns to me. "So, you think you're up for it, Starr?"

Talking to Ms. Rosalie may be harder than talking to the cops, honestly. But I owe it to Khalil to pay his grandmother a visit. She may not even know I was a witness to the shooting. If she somehow does and wants to know what happened, more than anybody she has the right to ask.

"Yeah. I'll go."

"We better find her an attorney before she talks to the detectives," Daddy says.

"Maverick." Momma sighs. "If Carlos doesn't think it's necessary just yet, I trust his judgment. Plus I'll be with her the entire time."

"Good thing somebody trusts his judgment," says Daddy. "And you really been thinking again 'bout moving? We discussed this already."

"Maverick, I'm not going there with you tonight."

"How we gon' change anything around here if we—"

"Mav-rick!" she says through gritted teeth. Whenever Momma breaks a name down like that, you better hope it's not yours. "I said I'm not going there tonight." She side-eyes him, waiting for the comeback. There isn't one. "Try and get some sleep, baby," she tells me, and kisses my cheek before going to their room.

Daddy goes to the refrigerator. "You want some grapes?"

"Yeah. How come you and Uncle Carlos always fighting?"

"'Cause he a buster." He joins me at the table with a bowl of white grapes. "But for real, he ain't never liked me. Thought I was a bad influence on your momma. Lisa was wild when I met her though, like all them other Catholic school girls."

"I bet he was more protective of Momma than Seven is with me, huh?"

"Oh, yeah," he says. "Carlos acted like he was Lisa's daddy. When I got locked up, he moved y'all in with him and blocked my calls. Even took her to a divorce attorney." He grins. "Still couldn't get rid of me."

I was three when Daddy went in prison, six when he got out. A lot of my memories include him, but a lot of my firsts don't. First day of school, the first time I lost a tooth, the first time I rode a bike without training wheels. In those memories, Uncle Carlos's face is where Daddy's should've been. I think that's the real reason they're always fighting.

Daddy drums the mahogany surface of the dining table, making a *thump-thump-thump* beat. "The nightmares will go away after a while," he says. "They're always the worst right after."

That's how it was with Natasha. "How many people have you seen die?"

"Enough. Worst one was my cousin Andre." His finger seems to instinctively trace the tattoo on his forearm – an *A* with a crown over it. "A drug deal turned into a robbery, and he got shot in the head twice. Right in front of me. A few months before you were born, in fact. That's why I named you Starr." He gives me a small smile. "My light during all that darkness."

Daddy chomps on some grapes. "Don't be scared 'bout Monday. Tell the cops the truth, and don't let them put words in your mouth. God gave you a brain. You don't need theirs. And remember that you didn't do nothing wrong – the cop did. Don't let them make you think otherwise."

Something's bugging me. I wanted to ask Uncle Carlos, but I couldn't for some reason. Daddy's different though. While Uncle Carlos somehow keeps impossible promises, Daddy keeps it real with me. "You think the cops want Khalil to have justice?" I ask.

Thump-thump-thump. Thump … thump … thump. The truth casts a shadow over the kitchen – people like us in situations like this become hashtags, but they rarely get justice. I think we all wait for that one time though, *that one time* when it ends right.

Maybe this can be it.

"I don't know," Daddy says. "I guess we'll find out."

Sunday morning, we pull up to a small yellow house. Bright flowers bloom below the front porch. I used to sit with Khalil on that porch.

My parents and I hop out the truck. Daddy carries a foil-covered pan of lasagna that Momma made. Sekani claims he's still not feeling good, so he stayed home. Seven's there with him. I don't buy this "sick" act though – Sekani always gets some kinda bug right as spring break ends.

Going up Ms. Rosalie's walkway floods me with memories. I have scars tattooed on my arms and legs from falls on this concrete. One time I was on my scooter, and Khalil pushed me off 'cause I hadn't given him a turn. When I got up, skin was missing from most of my knee. I never screamed so loud in my life.

We played hopscotch and jumped rope on this walkway too. Khalil never wanted to play at first, talking about how those were girls' games. He always gave in when me and Natasha said the winner got a Freeze Cup – frozen Kool-Aid in a Styrofoam cup – or a pack of "Nileators," a.k.a. Now and Laters. Ms. Rosalie was the neighborhood Candy Lady.

I was at her house almost as much as I was at my own. Momma and Ms. Rosalie's youngest daughter, Tammy, were best friends growing up. When Momma got pregnant with me, she was in her senior year of high school and Nana put her out the house. Ms. Rosalie took her in until my parents eventually got an apartment of their own. Momma says Ms. Rosalie was one of her biggest supporters and cried at her high school graduation like it was her own daughter walking across the stage.

Three years later, Ms. Rosalie saw Momma and me at Wyatt's – this was way before it became our store. She asked my mom how college was going. Momma told her that with Daddy in prison, she couldn't afford daycare and that Nana wouldn't take care of me 'cause I wasn't her baby and therefore I wasn't her problem. So Momma was thinking about dropping out. Ms. Rosalie told her to bring me to her house the next day and that she better not say a word about paying her. She babysat me and later Sekani the whole time Momma was in school.

Momma knocks on the door, rattling the screen. Ms. Tammy answers in a head wrap, T-shirt, and sweatpants. She unhooks the locks, hollering back, "Maverick, Lisa, and Starr are here, Ma."

The living room looks just like it did when Khalil and I played hide-and-seek in it. There's still plastic on the sofa and recliner. If you sit on them too long in the summer while wearing shorts, the plastic nearly glues to your legs.

"Hey, Tammy girl," Momma says, and they hug long and hard. "How you doing?"

"I'm hanging in there." Ms. Tammy hugs Daddy, then me. "Just hate that this is the reason I had to come home."

It's so weird looking at Ms. Tammy. She looks the way Khalil's momma, Ms. Brenda, would look if Ms. Brenda wasn't on crack. A lot like Khalil. Same hazel eyes and dimples. One time Khalil said he wished Ms. Tammy was his momma instead so he could live in New York with her. I used to joke and tell him she didn't have time for him. I wish I never said that.

"Where you want me to put this lasagna, Tam?" Daddy asks her.

"In the refrigerator, if you can find room," she says, as he heads toward the kitchen. "Momma said folks brought food all day yesterday. They were still bringing it when I got here last night. Seems like the whole neighborhood has stopped by."

"That's the Garden for you," Momma says. "If folks can't do anything else, they'll cook."

"You ain't ever lied." Ms. Tammy motions to the sofa. "Y'all, have a seat."

Momma and I sit down, and Daddy comes back and joins us. Ms. Tammy takes the recliner that Ms. Rosalie usually sits in. She gives me a sad smile. "Starr, you know, you sure have grown since the last time I saw you. You and Khalil both grew up so—"

Her voice cracks. Momma reaches over and pats her knee. Ms. Tammy takes a deep breath and smiles at me again. "It's good to see you, baby."

"We know Ms. Rosalie gon' tell us she fine, Tam," Daddy says, "but how she really doing?"

"We're taking one day at a time. The chemo's working, thankfully. I hope I can convince her to move in with me.

That way I can make sure she's getting her prescriptions."
She sighs through her nose. "I had no idea Momma was
struggling like she was. I didn't even know she'd lost her
job. You know how she is. Never wanna ask for help."

"What about Ms. Brenda?" I ask. I have to. Khalil
would've.

"I don't know, Starr. Bren … that's complicated. We hav-
en't seen her since we got the news. Don't know where she
is. If we do find her though … I don't know what we'll do."

"I can help you find a rehab facility near you," Momma
says. "She's gotta wanna get clean though."

Ms. Tammy nods. "And that's the problem. But I
think … I think this will either push her to finally get help
or push her over the edge. I hope it's the former."

Cameron holds his grandma's hand as he leads her into
the living room like she's the queen of the world in a house-
coat. She looks thinner, but strong for somebody going
through chemo and all of this. A scarf wrapped around her
head adds to her majesty – an African queen, and we're
blessed to be in her presence.

The rest of us stand.

Momma hugs Cameron and kisses one of his chubby
cheeks. Khalil called him Chipmunk because of them, but
he'd check anybody stupid enough to call his little brother
fat.

Daddy gives Cameron a palm-slap that ends in a hug.
"What's up, man? You okay?"

"Yes, sir."

A big, wide smile spreads across Ms. Rosalie's face. She holds her arms out, and I walk into the most heartfelt hug I've ever gotten from somebody who's not related to me. There's not any sympathy in it either. Just love and strength. I guess she knows I need some of both.

"My baby," she says. She pulls back and looks at me, tears brimming in her eyes. "Went and grew up on me."

She hugs my parents too. Ms. Tammy lets her have the recliner. Ms. Rosalie pats the end of the sofa closest to her, so I sit there. She holds my hand and rubs her thumb along the top of it.

"Mmm," she says. "Mmm!"

It's like my hand is telling her a story, and she's responding. She listens to it for a while, then says, "I'm so glad you came over. I've been wanting to talk to you."

"Yes, ma'am." I say what I'm supposed to.

"You were the very best friend that boy ever had."

This time I can't say what I'm supposed to. "Ms. Rosalie, we weren't as close—"

"I don't care, baby," she says. "Khalil never had another friend like you. I know that for a fact."

I swallow. "Yes, ma'am."

"The police told me you were the one with him when it happened."

So she knows. "Yes, ma'am."

I'm standing on a track, watching the train barrel toward me, and I tense up and wait for the impact, the moment she asks what happened.

But the train shifts to another track. "Maverick, he wanted to talk to you. He wanted your help."

Daddy straightens up. "For real?"

"Uh-huh. He was selling that stuff."

Something leaves me. I mean, I kinda figured it, but to know it's the truth...

This hurts.

But I swear I wanna cuss Khalil out. How he could sell the very stuff that took his momma from him? Did he realize that he was taking somebody else's momma from them?

Did he realize that if he does become a hashtag, some people will only see him as a drug dealer?

He was so much more than that.

"But he wanted to stop," Ms. Rosalie says. "He told me, 'Grandma, I can't stay in this. Mr. Maverick said it only leads to two things, the grave or prison, and I ain't trying to see either.' He respected you, Maverick. A lot. You were the father he never had."

I can't explain it, but something leaves Daddy too. His eyes dim, and he nods. Momma rubs his back.

"I tried to talk some sense into him," Ms. Rosalie says, "but this neighborhood makes young men deaf to their elders. The money part didn't help. He was going around here, paying bills, buying sneakers and mess. But I know he remembered the things you told him over the years, Maverick, and that gave me a lotta faith.

"I keep thinking if only he had another day or—" Ms. Rosalie covers her trembling lips. Ms. Tammy starts for her,

67

but she says, "I'm okay, Tam." She looks at me. "I'm happy he wasn't alone, but I'm even happier you were with him. That's all I need to know. Don't need details, nothing else. Knowing you were with him is good enough."

Like Daddy, all I can do is nod.

But as I hold Khalil's grandma's hand, I see the anguish in her eyes. His little brother can't smile anymore. So what if people end up thinking he was a thug and never care? We care.

Khalil matters to us, not the stuff he did. Forget everybody else.

Momma leans across me and sets an envelope in Ms. Rosalie's lap. "We want you to have that."

Ms. Rosalie opens it, and I catch a glimpse of a whole lot of money inside. "What in the world? Y'all know I can't take this."

"Yes, you can," Daddy says. "We ain't forgot how you kept Starr and Sekani for us. We weren't 'bout to let you be empty-handed."

"And we know y'all are trying to pay for the funeral," Momma says. "Hopefully that'll help. Plus, we're raising money around the neighborhood too. So don't you worry about a thing."

Ms. Rosalie wipes a new set of tears from her eyes. "I'm gonna pay y'all back every penny."

"Did we say you had to pay us back?" Daddy asks. "You focus on getting better, a'ight? And if you give us any money, we giving it right back, God's my witness."

There are a lot more tears and hugs. Ms. Rosalie gives me a Freeze Cup for the road, red syrup glistening on the top. She always makes them extra sweet.

As we leave, I remember how Khalil used to run up to the car when I was about to go, the sun shining on the grease lines that separated his cornrows. The glimmer in his eyes would be just as bright. He'd knock on the window, I'd let it down, and he'd say with a snaggletooth grin, "See you later, alligator."

Back then I'd giggle behind my own snaggleteeth. Now I tear up. Good-byes hurt the most when the other person's already gone. I imagine him standing at my window, and I smile for his sake. "After a while, crocodile."

CHAPTER 5

On Monday, the day I'm supposed to talk to the detectives, I'm crying out of nowhere, hunched over my bed as the iron in my hand spits out steam. Momma takes it before I burn the Williamson crest on my polo.

She rubs my shoulder. "Let it out, Munch."

We have a quiet breakfast at the kitchen table without Seven. He spent the night at his momma's house. I pick at my waffles. Just thinking about going into that station with all those cops makes me wanna puke. Food would make it worse.

After breakfast, we join hands in the living room like we always do, under the framed poster of the Ten-Point Program, and Daddy leads us in prayer.

"Black Jesus, watch over my babies today," he says. "Keep them safe, steer them from wrong, and help them recognize snakes from friends. Give them the wisdom they need to be their own people.

"Help Seven with this situation at his momma's house, and let him know he can always come home. Thank you for Sekani's miraculous, sudden healing that just so happened to come after he found out they're having pizza at school today." I peek out at Sekani, whose eyes and mouth are open wide. I smirk and close my eyes. "Be with Lisa at the clinic as she helps your people. Help my baby girl get through her situation, Lord. Give her peace of mind, and help her speak her truth this afternoon. And lastly, strengthen Ms. Rosalie, Cameron, Tammy, and Brenda as they go through this difficult time. In your precious name I pray, amen."

"Amen," the rest of us say.

"Daddy, why you put me on the spot like that with Black Jesus?" Sekani complains.

"He knows the truth," Daddy says. He wipes crust from the corners of Sekani's eyes and straightens the collar of his polo. "I'm trying to help you out. Get you some mercy or something, man."

Daddy pulls me into a hug. "You gon' be a'ight?"

I nod into his chest. "Yeah."

I could stay like this all day – it's one of the few places where One-Fifteen doesn't exist and where I can forget about talking to detectives – but Momma says we need to leave before rush hour.

Now don't get it wrong, I can drive. I got my license a week after my sixteenth birthday. But I can't get a car unless I pay for it myself. I told my parents I don't have time for a job with school and basketball. They said I don't have time for a car then either. Messed up.

It takes forty-five minutes to get to school on a good day, and an hour on a slow one. Sekani doesn't have to wear

71

his headphones 'cause Momma doesn't cuss anybody out on the freeway. She hums with gospel songs on the radio and says, "Give me strength, Lord. Give me strength."

We get off the freeway into Riverton Hills and pass all these gated neighborhoods. Uncle Carlos lives in one of them. To me, it's so weird to have a gate around a neighborhood. Seriously, are they trying to keep people out or keep people in? If somebody puts a gate around Garden Heights, it'll be a little bit of both.

Our school is gated too, and the campus has new, modern buildings with lots of windows and marigolds blooming along the walkways.

Momma gets in the carpool lane for the lower school. "Sekani, you remembered your iPad?"

"Yes, ma'am."

"Lunch card?"

"Yes, ma'am."

"Gym shorts? And you better have gotten the clean ones too."

"Yes, Momma. I'm almost nine. Can't you give me a little credit?"

She smiles. "All right, big man. Think you can give me some sugar?"

Sekani leans over the front seat and kisses her cheek. "Love you."

"Love you too. And don't forget, Seven's bringing you home today."

He runs over to some of his friends and blends in with

all the other kids in khakis and polos. We get in the carpool lane for my school.

"All right, Munch," Momma says. "Seven's gonna bring you to the clinic after school, then you and I will go to the station. Are you absolutely sure you're up for it?"

No. But Uncle Carlos promised it'll be okay. "I'll do it."

"Okay. Call me if you don't think you can make it the whole day at school."

Hold up. I could've stayed home? "Why are you making me come in the first place?"

"'Cause you need to get out the house. Out that neighborhood. I want you to at least try, Starr. This will sound mean, but just because Khalil's not living doesn't mean you stop living. You understand, baby?"

"Yeah." I know she's right, but it feels wrong.

We get to the front of the carpool line. "Now I don't have to ask if you brought some funky-ass gym shorts, do I?" she says.

I laugh. "No. Bye, Momma."

"Bye, baby."

I get out the car. For at least seven hours I don't have to talk about One-Fifteen. I don't have to think about Khalil. I just have to be normal Starr at normal Williamson and have a normal day. That means flipping the switch in my brain so I'm Williamson Starr. Williamson Starr doesn't use slang – if a rapper would say it, she doesn't say it, even if her white friends do. Slang makes them cool. Slang makes her "hood." Williamson Starr holds her tongue when people piss her off so nobody will think she's the "angry black girl." Williamson Starr is approachable. No stank-eyes, side-eyes, none of that. Williamson Starr is nonconfrontational. Basically, Williamson Starr doesn't give anyone a reason to call her ghetto.

I can't stand myself for doing it, but I do it anyway.

I sling my backpack over my shoulder. As usual it matches my J's, the blue-and-black Elevens like Jordan wore in *Space Jam*. I worked at the store a month to buy them. I hate dressing like everybody else, but *The Fresh Prince* taught me something. See, Will always wore his school uniform jacket inside out so he could be different. I can't wear my uniform inside out, but I can make sure my sneakers are always dope and my backpack always matches them.

I go inside and scan the atrium for Maya, Hailey, or Chris. I don't see them, but I see that half the kids have tans from spring break. Luckily I was born with one. Someone covers my eyes.

"Maya, I know that's you."

She snickers and moves her hands. I'm not tall at all, but Maya has to stand on her tiptoes to cover my eyes. And the chick actually wants to play center on the varsity basketball team. She wears her hair in a high bun because she probably thinks it makes her look taller, but nope.

"What's up, Ms. I Can't Text Anyone Back?" she says, and we do our little handshake. It's not complicated like Daddy and King's, but it works for us. "I was starting to wonder if you were abducted by aliens."

74

"Huh?"

She holds up her phone. The screen has a brand-new crack stretching from corner to corner. Maya's always dropping it. "You haven't texted me in two days, Starr," she says. "Not cool."

"Oh." I've barely looked at my phone since Khalil got ... since the incident. "Sorry. I was working at the store. You know how crazy that can get. How was your spring break?"

"Okay, I guess." She munches on some Sour Patch Kids. "We visited my great-grandparents in Taipei. I ended up taking a bunch of snapbacks and basketball shorts, so all week long I heard, 'Why do you dress like a boy?' 'Why do you play a boy sport?' Blah, blah, blah. And it was awful when they saw a picture of Ryan. They asked if he was a rapper!"

I laugh and steal some of her candy. Maya's boyfriend, Ryan, happens to be the only other black kid in eleventh grade, and everybody expects us to be together. Because apparently when it's two of us, we have to be on some Noah's Ark type shit and pair up to preserve the blackness of our grade. Lately I'm super aware of BS like that.

We head for the cafeteria. Our table near the vending machines is almost full. There's Hailey, sitting on top of it, having a heated discussion with curly-haired, dimpled Luke. I think that's foreplay for them. They've liked each other since sixth grade, and if your feelings can survive the awkwardness of middle school you should stop playing around and go out.

Some of the other girls from the team are there too: Jess the co-captain and Britt the center who makes Maya look like an ant. It's kinda stereotypical that we all sit together, but it worked out that way. I mean, who else will listen to us bitch about swollen knees and understand inside jokes born on the bus after a game?

Chris's boys from the basketball team are at the table next to ours, egging Hailey and Luke on. Chris isn't there yet. Unfortunately and fortunately.

Luke sees me and Maya and reaches his arms toward us. "Thank you! Two sensible people who can end this discussion."

I slide onto the bench beside Jess. She rests her head on my shoulder. "They've been at it for fifteen minutes."

Poor girl. I pat her hair. I have a secret crush on Jess's pixie cut. My neck's not long enough for one, but her hair is perfect. Every strand is where it should be. If I were into girls, I would totally date her for her hair, and she would date me for my shoulder.

"What's it about this time?" I ask.

"Pop Tarts," Britt says.

Hailey turns to us and points at Luke. "This jerk actually said they're better warmed up in the microwave."

"Eww," I say, instead of my usual "Ill," and Maya goes, "Are you serious?"

"I know, right?" says Hailey.

"Jesus Christ!" Luke says. "I only asked for a dollar to buy one from the machine!"

76

"You're not wasting my money to destroy a perfectly good Pop Tart in a microwave."

"They're supposed to be heated up!" he argues.

"I actually agree with Luke," Jess says. "Pop Tarts are ten times better heated up."

I move my shoulder so her head isn't resting on it. "We can't be friends anymore."

Her mouth drops open, and she pouts.

"Fine, fine," I say, and she rests her head on my shoulder with a wide grin. Total weirdo. I don't know how she'll survive without my shoulder when she graduates in a few months.

"Anyone who heats up a Pop Tart should be charged," Hailey says.

"And imprisoned," I say.

"And forced to eat uncooked Pop Tarts until they accept how good they are," Maya adds.

"It is law," Hailey finishes, smacking the table like that settles it.

"You guys have issues," Luke says, hopping off the table. He picks at Hailey's hair. "I think all that dye seeped into your brain."

She swats at him as he leaves. She's added blue streaks to her honey-blond hair and cut it shoulder-length. In fifth grade, she trimmed it with some scissors during a math test because she felt like it. That was the moment I knew she didn't give a shit.

"I like the blue, Hails," I say. "And the cut."

"Yeah." Maya grins. "It's very Joe Jonas of you."

Hailey whips her head around so fast, her eyes flashing. Maya and I snicker.

So there's a video deep in the depths of YouTube of the three of us lip-syncing to the Jonas Brothers and pretending to play guitars and drums in Hailey's bedroom. She decided she was Joe, I was Nick, and Maya was Kevin. I really wanted to be Joe – I secretly loved him the most, but Hailey said she should have him, so I let her.

I let her have her way a lot. Still do. That's part of being Williamson Starr, I guess.

"I so have to find that video," Jess says.

"Nooo," Hailey goes, sliding off the tabletop. "It must never be found." She sits across from us. "Never. Ne-ver. If I remembered that account's password, I'd delete it."

"Ooh, what was the account's name?" Jess asks. "JoBro Lover or something? Wait, no, JoBro *Lova*. Everybody liked to misspell shit in middle school."

I smirk and mumble, "Close."

Hailey looks at me. "Starr!"

Maya and Britt crack up.

It's moments like this that I feel normal at Williamson. Despite the guidelines I put on myself, I've still found my group, my table.

"Okay then," Hailey says. "I see how it is, Maya Jonas and Nick's Starry Girl 2000—"

"So, Hails," I say before she can finish my old screen name. She grins. "How was your spring break?"

Hailey loses her grin and rolls her eyes. "Oh, it was wonderful. Dad and Stepmother Dearest dragged me and Remy to the house in the Bahamas for 'family bonding.'"

And bam. That normal feeling? Gone. I suddenly remember how different I am from most of the kids here. Nobody would have to drag me or my brothers to the Bahamas – we'd swim there if we could. For us, a family vacation is staying at a local hotel with a swimming pool for a weekend.

"Sounds like my parents," says Britt. "Took us to fucking Harry Potter World for the third year in a row. I'm sick of Butter Beer and corny family photos with wands."

Holy shit. Who the fuck complains about going to Harry Potter World? Or Butter Beer? Or wands?

I hope none of them ask about my spring break. They went to Taipei, the Bahamas, Harry Potter World. I stayed in the hood and saw a cop kill my friend.

"I guess the Bahamas wasn't so bad," Hailey says. "They wanted us to do family stuff, but we ended up doing our own thing the entire time."

"You mean you texted me the entire time," Maya says.

"It was still my own thing."

"All day, every day," Maya adds. "Ignoring the time difference."

"Whatever, Shorty. You know you liked talking to me."

"Oh," I say. "That's cool."

Really though, it's not. Hailey never texted me during spring break. She barely texts me at all lately. Maybe once a week now, and it used to be every day. Something's changed between us, and neither one of us acknowledges it. We're normal when we're at Williamson, like now. Beyond here though, we're no longer best friends, just ... I don't know.

Plus she unfollowed my Tumblr.

She has no clue that I know. I once posted a picture of Emmett Till, a fourteen-year-old black boy who was murdered for whistling at a white woman in 1955. His mutilated body didn't look human. Hailey texted me immediately after, freaking out. I thought it was because she couldn't believe someone would do that to a kid. No. She couldn't believe I would reblog such an awful picture.

Not long after that, she stopped liking and reblogging my other posts. I looked through my followers list. Aww, Hails was no longer following me. With me living forty-five minutes away, Tumblr is supposed to be sacred ground where our friendship is cemented. Unfollowing me is the same as saying "I don't like you anymore."

Maybe I'm being sensitive. Or maybe things have changed, maybe *I've* changed. For now I guess we'll keep pretending everything is fine.

The first bell rings. On Mondays AP English is first for me, Hailey, and Maya. On the way they get into this big discussion-turned-argument about NCAA brackets and the Final Four. Hailey was born a Notre Dame fan. Maya hates them almost unhealthily. I stay out that discussion. The NBA is more my thing anyway.

We turn down the hall, and Chris is standing in the

doorway of our class, his hands stuffed in pockets and a pair of headphones draped around his neck. He looks straight at me and stretches his arm across the doorway.

Hailey glances from him to me. Back and forth, back and forth. "Did something happen with you guys?"

My pursed lips probably give me away. "Yeah. Sort of."

"That douche," Hailey says, reminding me why we're friends – she doesn't need details. If someone hurts me in any way, they're automatically on her shit list. It started in fifth grade, two years before Maya came along. We were those "crybaby" kids who bust out crying at the smallest shit. Me because of Natasha, and Hailey because she lost her mom to cancer. We rode the waves of grief together.

That's why this weirdness between us doesn't make sense. "What do you want to do, Starr?" she asks.

I don't know. Before Khalil, I planned to cold-shoulder Chris with a sting more powerful than a nineties R&B breakup song. But after Khalil I'm more like a Taylor Swift song. (No shade, I fucks with Tay-Tay, but she doesn't serve like nineties R&B on the angry-girlfriend scale.) I'm not happy with Chris, yet I miss him. I miss *us*. I need him so much that I'm willing to forget what he did. That's scary as fuck too. Someone I've only been with for a year means *that* much to me? But Chris … he's different.

You know what? I'll Beyoncé him. Not as powerful as a nineties R&B breakup song, but stronger than a Taylor Swift. Yeah. That'll work. I tell Hailey and Maya, "I'll handle him."

They move so I'm between them like they're my body-guards, and we go to the door together.

Chris bows to us. "Ladies."

"Move!" Maya orders. Funny considering how much Chris towers over her.

He looks at me with those baby blues. He got a tan over break. I used to tell him he was so pale he looked like a marshmallow. He hated that I compared him to food. I told him that's what he got for calling me caramel. It shut him up.

Dammit though. He's wearing the *Space Jam* Elevens too. I forgot we decided to wear them the first day back. They look good on him. Jordans are my weakness. Can't help it.

"I just wanna talk to my girl," he claims.

"I don't know who that is," I say, Beyoncé'ing him like a pro.

He sighs through his nose. "Please, Starr? Can we at least talk about it?"

I'm back to Taylor Swift because the *please* does it. I nod at Hailey and Maya.

"You hurt her, and I'll kill you," Hailey warns, and she and Maya go in to class without me.

Chris and I move away from the door. I lean against a locker and fold my arms. "I'm listening," I say.

A bass-heavy instrumental plays in his headphones. Probably one of his beats. "I'm sorry for what happened. I should've talked to you first."

I cock my head. "We did talk about it. A week before. Remember?"

"I know, I know. And I heard you. I just wanted to be prepared in case—"

"You could push the right buttons and convince me to change my mind?"

"No!" His hands go up in surrender. "Starr, you know I wouldn't – that's not – I'm sorry, okay? I took it too far."

Understatement. The day before Big D's party, Chris and I were in Chris's ridiculously large room. The third floor of his parents' mansion is a suite for him, a perk of being the last born to empty-nesters. I try to forget that he has an entire floor as big as my house and hired help that looks like me.

Fooling around isn't new for us, and when Chris slipped his hand in my shorts, I didn't think anything of it. Then he got me going, and I really wasn't thinking. At all. For real, my thought process went out the door. And right as I was at *that* moment, he stopped, reached into his pocket, and pulled out a condom. He raised his eyebrows at me, silently asking for an invitation to go all the way.

All I could think about was those girls I see walking around Garden Heights, babies propped on their hips. Condom or no condom, shit happens.

I went off on Chris. He knew I wasn't ready for that, we already talked about it, and yet he had a condom? He said he wanted to be responsible, but if I said I'm not ready, I'm not ready.

I left his house pissed *and* horny, the absolute worst way to leave.

My mom may have been right though. She once said that after you go there with a guy, it activates all these feelings, and you wanna do it all the time. Chris and I went far enough that I notice every single detail about his body now. His cute nostrils that flare when he sighs. His soft brown hair that my fingers love to explore. His gentle lips, and his tongue that wets them every so often. The five freckles on his neck that are in the perfect spots for kissing.

More than that, I remember the guy who spends almost every night on the phone with me talking about nothing and everything. The one who loves to make me smile. Yeah, he pisses me off sometimes, and I'm sure I piss him off, but we mean something. We actually mean a lot.

Fuckity fuck, fuck, fuck. I'm crumbling. "Chris…"

He goes for a low blow and beatboxes an all-too-familiar, *"Boomp … boomp, boomp, boomp."*

I point at him. "Don't you dare!"

"'Now, this is a story all about how, my life got flipped – turned upside down. And I'd like to take a minute, just sit right there, I'll tell you how I became the prince of a town called Bel-Air.'"

He beat-boxes the instrumental and pops his chest and booty to the rhythm. People pass by us, laughing. A guy whistles suggestively. Someone shouts, "Shake that ass, Bryant!"

My smile grows before I can stop it.

The Fresh Prince isn't just my show, it's *our* show. Sophomore year he followed my Tumblr, and I followed him back. We knew of each other from school, but we didn't *know* each other. One Saturday, I reblogged a bunch of *Fresh Prince* GIFs and clips. He liked and reblogged every single one. That Monday morning in the cafeteria, he paid for my Pop Tarts and grape juice and said, "The first Aunt Viv was the best Aunt Viv."

It was the beginning of us.

Chris gets *The Fresh Prince,* which helps him get me. We once talked about how cool it was that Will remained himself in his new world. I slipped up and said I wish I could be like that at school. Chris said, "Why can't you, Fresh Princess?"

Ever since, I don't have to decide which Starr I have to be with him. He likes both. Well, the parts I've shown him. Some things I can't reveal, like Natasha. Once you've seen how broken someone is it's like seeing them naked – you can't look at them the same anymore.

I like the way he looks at me now, as if I'm one of the best things in his life. He's one of the best things in mine too.

I can't lie, we get the "why is he dating *her*" stare that usually comes from rich white girls. Sometimes I wonder the same thing. Chris acts like those looks don't exist. When he does stuff like this, rapping and beatboxing in the middle of a busy hall just to make me smile, I forget about those looks too.

He starts the second verse, swaying his shoulders and looking at me. The worst part? His silly butt knows it's working. "'In West Philadelphia, born and raised' – c'mon, babe. Join in."

He grabs my hands.

One-Fifteen follows Khalil's hands with the flashlight.

He orders Khalil to get out with his hands up.

He barks at me to put my hands on the dashboard.

I kneel beside my dead friend in the middle of the street with my hands raised. A cop as white as Chris points a gun at me.

As white as Chris.

I flinch and snatch away.

Chris frowns. "Starr, you okay?"

Khalil opens the door. "You okay, Starr—"

Pow!

There's blood. Too much blood.

The second bell rings, jolting me back to normal Williamson, where I'm not normal Starr.

Chris leans down, his face in front of mine. My tears blur him. "Starr?"

It's a few tears, yeah, but I feel exposed. I turn to go to class, and Chris grabs my arm. I yank away and whirl on him.

His hands go up in surrender. "Sorry. I was…"

I wipe my eyes and walk into the classroom. Chris is right behind me. Hailey and Maya shoot him the dirtiest looks. I lower myself into the desk in front of Hailey.

She squeezes my shoulder. "That jackwad."

★ ★ ★

Nobody mentioned Khalil at school today. I hate to admit it, because it's like throwing him the middle finger, but I'm relieved.

Since basketball season is over, I leave when everybody else does. Probably for the first time in my life I wish it wasn't the end of the day. I'm that much closer to talking to the cops.

Hailey and I trek across the parking lot, arm in arm. Maya has a driver to pick her up. Hailey has her own car, and I have a brother with a car; the two of us always end up walking out together.

"Are you absolutely sure you don't want me to kick Chris's ass?" Hailey asks.

I told her and Maya about Condomgate, and as far as they're concerned Chris is eternally banished to Asshole Land.

"Yes," I say, for the hundredth time. "You're violent, Hails."

"When it comes to my friends, possibly. Seriously though, why would he even? God, boys and their fucking sex drive."

I snort. "Is that why you and Luke haven't gotten together?"

She lightly elbows me. "Shut up."

I laugh. "Why won't you admit you like him?"

"What makes you think I like him?"

"Really, Hailey?"

"Whatever, Starr. This isn't about me. This is about you and your sex-driven boyfriend."

"He's not sex-driven," I say.

"Then what do you call it?"

"He was horny at that moment."

"Same thing!"

I try to keep a straight face and she does too, but soon we're cracking up. God, it feels good to be normal Starr and Hailey. Has me wondering if I imagined a change.

We part at the halfway point to Hailey's car and Seven's. "The ass-kicking offer is still on the table," she calls to me.

"Bye, Hailey!"

I walk off, rubbing my arms. Spring has decided to go through an identity crisis and get chilly on me. A few feet away, Seven keeps a hand on his car as he talks to his girl-friend, Layla. Him and that damn Mustang. He touches it more than he touches Layla. She obviously doesn't care. She plays with the dreadlock near his face that isn't pulled into his ponytail. Eye-roll worthy. Some girls do too much. Can't she play with all them curls on her own head?

Honestly though, I don't have a problem with Layla. She's a geek like Seven, smart enough for Harvard but Howard bound, and real sweet. She's one of the four black girls in the senior class, and if Seven just wants to date black girls, he picked a great one.

I walk up to them and go, *"Hem-hem."*

Seven keeps his eyes on Layla. "Go sign Sekani out."

"Can't," I lie. "Momma didn't put me on the list."

"Yeah, she did. Go."

I fold my arms. "I am not walking halfway across campus to get him and halfway back. We can get him when we're leaving."

He side-eyes me, but I'm too tired for all that, and it's cold. Seven kisses Layla and goes around to the driver's side. "Acting like that's a long walk," he mumbles.

"Acting like we can't get him when we're leaving," I say, and hop in.

He starts the car. This nice mix Chris made of Kanye and my other future husband J. Cole plays from Seven's iPod dock. He maneuvers through the parking lot traffic to Sekani's school. Seven signs him out of his after-school program, and we leave.

"I'm hungry," Sekani whines not even five minutes out the parking lot.

"Didn't they give you a snack in after-school?" Seven asks.

"So? I'm still hungry."

"Greedy butt," Seven says, and Sekani kicks the back of his seat. Seven laughs. "Okay, okay! Ma asked me to bring some food to the clinic anyway. I'll get you something too." He looks at Sekani in the rearview mirror. "Is that cool—"

Seven freezes. He turns Chris's mix off and slows down.

"What you turn the music off for?" Sekani asks.

"Shut up," Seven hisses.

We stop at a red light. A Riverton Hills patrol car pulls up beside us.

Seven straightens up and stares ahead, barely blinking and gripping the steering wheel. His eyes move a little like he wants to look at the cop car. He swallows hard.

"C'mon, light," he prays. "C'mon."

I stare ahead and pray for the light to change too.

It finally turns green, and Seven lets the patrol car go first. His shoulders don't relax until we get on the freeway. Mine neither.

We stop at this Chinese restaurant Momma loves and get food for all of us. She wants me to eat before I talk to the detectives. In Garden Heights, kids play in the streets. Sekani presses his face against my window and watches them. He won't play with them though. Last time he played with some neighborhood kids, they called him "white boy" 'cause he goes to Williamson.

Black Jesus greets us from a mural on the side of the clinic. He has locs like Seven. His arms stretch the width of the wall, and there are puffy white clouds behind him. Big letters above him remind us that *Jesus Loves You.*

Seven passes Black Jesus and goes into the parking lot behind the clinic. He punches in a code to open the gate and parks next to Momma's Camry. I get the tray of sodas, Seven gets the food, and Sekani doesn't take anything because he never takes anything.

I hit the buzzer for the back door and wave up at the camera. The door opens into a sterile-smelling hall with bright-white walls and white-tile floors that reflect us. The hall takes us to the waiting room. A handful of people watch the news on the old box TV in the ceiling or read magazines that have been there since I was little. When this shaggy-haired man sees that we have food, he straightens up and sniffs hard as if it's for him.

"What y'all bringing up in here?" Ms. Felicia asks at the front desk, stretching her neck to see.

Momma comes from the other hallway in her plain yellow scrubs, following a teary-eyed boy and his mom. The boy sucks on a lollipop, a reward for surviving a shot.

"There go my babies," Momma says when she sees us. "And they got my food too. C'mon. Let's go in the back."

"Save me some!" Ms. Felicia calls after us. Momma tells her to hush.

We set the food out on the break room table. Momma gets some paper plates and plastic utensils that she keeps in a cabinet for days like this. We say grace and dig in.

Momma sits on the countertop and eats. "Mmm-mm! This is hitting the spot. Thank you, Seven baby. I only had a bag of Cheetos today."

"You didn't have lunch?" Sekani asks, with a mouth full of fried rice.

Momma points her fork at him. "What did I tell you about talking with your mouth full? And for your information, no I did not. I had a meeting on my lunch break. Now, tell me about y'all. How was school?"

Sekani always talks the longest because he gives every single detail. Seven says his day was fine. I'm as short with my "It was all right."

Momma sips her soda. "Anything happen?"

I freaked out when my boyfriend touched me, but –
"Nope. Nothing."

Ms. Felicia comes to the door. "Lisa, sorry to bother you, but we have an *issue* up front."

"I'm on break, Felicia."

"Don't you think I know that? But she asking for you. It's Brenda."

Khalil's momma.

My mom sets her plate down. She looks straight at me when she says, "Stay here."

I'm hardheaded though. I follow her to the waiting room. Ms. Brenda sits with her face in her hands. Her hair is uncombed, and her white shirt is dingy, almost brown. She has sores and scabs on her arms and legs, and since she's real light-skinned they show up even more.

Momma kneels in front of her. "Bren, hey."

Ms. Brenda moves her hands. Her red eyes remind me of what Khalil said when we were little, that his momma had turned into a dragon. He claimed that one day he'd become a knight and turn her back.

It doesn't make sense that he sold drugs. I would've thought his broken heart wouldn't let him.

"My baby," his momma cries. "Lisa, my baby."

Momma sandwiches Ms. Brenda's hands between hers and rubs them, not caring that they're nasty looking. "I know, Bren."

"They killed my baby."

"I know."

"They killed him."

"I know."

"Lord Jesus," Ms. Felicia says from the doorway. Next to her, Seven puts his arm around Sekani. Some patients in the waiting room shake their heads.

"But Bren, you gotta get cleaned up," Momma says. "That's what he wanted."

"I can't. My baby ain't here."

"Yes, you can. You have Cameron, and he needs you. Your momma needs you."

Khalil needed you, I wanna say. He waited for you and cried for you. But where were you? You don't get to cry now. Nuh-uh. It's too late.

But she keeps crying. Rocking and crying.

"Tammy and I can get you some help, Bren," Momma says. "But you gotta really want it this time."

"I don't wanna live like this no more."

"I know." Momma waves Ms. Felicia over and hands Ms. Felicia her phone. "Look through my contacts and find Tammy Harris's number. Call and tell her that her sister is here. Bren, when was the last time you ate?"

"I don't know. I don't – my baby."

Momma straightens up and rubs Ms. Brenda's shoulder. "I'm gonna get you some food."

I follow Momma back. She walks kinda fast but passes the food and goes to the counter. She leans on it with her back to me and bows her head, not saying a word.

Everything I wanted to say in the waiting room comes bubbling out. "How come she gets to be upset? She wasn't there for Khalil. You know how many times he cried about her? Birthdays, Christmas, all that. Why does she get to cry now?"

"Starr, please."

"She hasn't acted like a mom to him! Now all of a sudden, he's her baby? It's bullshit!"

Momma smacks the counter, and I jump. "Shut up!" she screams. She turns around, tears streaking her face. "That wasn't some li'l friend of hers. That was her son, you hear me? Her son!" Her voice cracks. "She carried that boy, birthed that boy. And you have no right to judge her."

I have cotton-mouth. "I—"

Momma closes her eyes. She massages her forehead. "I'm sorry. Fix her a plate, baby, okay? Fix her a plate."

I do and put a little extra of everything on it. I take it to Ms. Brenda. She mumbles what sounds like "thank you" as she takes it.

When she looks at me through the red haze, Khalil's eyes stare back at me, and I realize my mom's right. Ms. Brenda is Khalil's momma. Regardless.

CHAPTER 6

My mom and I arrive at the police station at four thirty on the dot.

A handful of cops talk on phones, type on computers, or stand around. Normal stuff, like on *Law & Order,* but my breath catches. I count: One. Two. Three. Four. I lose count around twelve because the guns in their holsters are all I can see.

All of them. Two of us.

Momma squeezes my hand. "Breathe."

I didn't realize I had grabbed hers.

I take a deep breath and another, and she nods with each one, saying, "That's it. You're okay. We're okay."

Uncle Carlos comes over, and he and Momma lead me to his desk, where I sit down. I feel eyes on me from all around. The grip tightens around my lungs. Uncle Carlos hands me a sweating bottle of water. Momma puts it up to my lips.

I take slow sips and look around Uncle Carlos's desk to avoid the curious eyes of the officers. He has almost as many pictures of me and Sekani on display as he has of his own kids.

"I'm taking her home," Momma tells him. "I'm not putting her through this today. She's not ready."

"I understand, but she has to talk to them at some point, Lisa. She's a vital part of this investigation."

Momma sighs. "Carlos—"

"I get it," he says, in a noticeably lower voice. "Believe me, I do. Unfortunately, if we want this investigation done right, she has to talk to them. If not today, then another day."

Another day of waiting and wondering what's gonna happen.

I can't go through that.

"I wanna do it today," I mumble. "I wanna get it over with."

They look at me, like they just remembered I'm here.

Uncle Carlos kneels in front of me. "Are you sure, baby girl?"

I nod before I lose my nerve.

"All right," Momma says. "But I'm going with her."

"That's totally fine," Uncle Carlos says.

"I don't care if it's not fine." She looks at me. "She's not doing this alone."

Those words feel as good as any hug I've ever gotten.

Uncle Carlos keeps an arm around me and leads us to a small room that has nothing in it but a table and some chairs. An unseen air conditioner hums loudly, blasting freezing air into the room.

"All right," Uncle Carlos says. "I'll be outside, okay?"

"Okay," I say.

He kisses my forehead with his usual two pecks. Momma takes my hand, and her tight squeeze tells me what she doesn't say out loud – *I got your back.*

We sit at the table. She's still holding my hand when the two detectives come in – a young white guy with slick black hair and a Latina with lines around her mouth and a spiky haircut. Both of them wear guns on their waists.

Keep your hands visible.

No sudden moves.

Only speak when spoken to.

"Hi, Starr and Mrs. Carter," the woman says, holding out her hand. "I'm Detective Gomez, and this is my partner, Detective Wilkes."

I let go of my mom's hand to shake the detectives' hands. "Hello." My voice is changing already. It always happens around "other" people, whether I'm at Williamson or not. I don't talk like me or sound like me. I choose every word carefully and make sure I pronounce them well. I can never, ever let anyone think I'm ghetto.

"It's so nice to meet you both," Wilkes says.

"Considering the circumstances, I wouldn't call it nice," says Momma.

Wilkes's face and neck get extremely red.

"What he means is we've heard so much about you both," Gomez says. "Carlos always gushes about his wonderful family. We feel like we know you already."

She's laying it on extra thick.

"Please, have a seat." Gomez points to a chair, and she and Wilkes sit across from us. "Just so you know, you're being recorded, but it's simply so we can have Starr's statement on record."

"Okay," I say. There it is again, all perky and shit. I'm never perky.

Detective Gomez gives the date and time and the names of the people in the room and reminds us that we're being recorded. Wilkes scribbles in his notebook. Momma rubs my back. For a moment there's only the sound of pencil on paper.

"All right then." Gomez adjusts herself in her chair and smiles, the lines around her mouth deepening. "Don't be nervous, Starr. You haven't done anything wrong. We just want to know what happened."

I know I haven't done anything wrong, I think, but it comes out as, "Yes, ma'am."

"You're sixteen, right?"

"Yes, ma'am."

"How long did you know Khalil?"

"Since I was three. His grandmother used to babysit me."

"Wow," she says, all teacher-like, stretching out the word. "That's a long time. Can you tell us what happened the night of the incident?"

"You mean the night he was killed?"

Shit.

Gomez's smile dims, the lines around her mouth aren't

as deep, but she says, "The night of the incident, yes. Start where you feel comfortable."

I look at Momma. She nods.

"My friend Kenya and I went to a house party hosted by a guy named Darius," I say.

Thump-thump-thump. I drum the table.

Stop. No sudden moves.

I lay my hands flat to keep them visible.

"He has one every spring break," I say. "Khalil saw me, came over, and said hello."

"Do you know why he was at the party?" Gomez asks.

Why does anybody go to a party? To party. "I assume it was for recreational purposes," I say. "He and I talked about things going on in our lives."

"What kind of things?" she questions.

"His grandmother has cancer. I didn't know until he told me that evening."

"I see," Gomez says. "What happened after that?"

"A fight occurred at the party, so we left together in his car."

"Khalil didn't have anything to do with the fight?"

I raise an eyebrow. "Nah."

Dammit. Proper English.

I sit up straight. "I mean, no, ma'am. We were talking when the fight occurred."

"Okay, so you two left. Where were you going?"

"He offered to take me home or to my father's grocery store. Before we could decide, One-Fifteen pulled us over."

"Who?" she asks.

"The officer, that's his badge number," I say. "I remember it."

Wilkes scribbles.

"I see," Gomez says. "Can you describe what happened next?"

I don't think I'll ever forget what happened, but saying it out loud, that's different. And hard.

My eyes prickle. I blink, staring at the table.

Momma rubs my back. "Look up, Starr."

My parents have this thing where they never want me or my brothers to talk to somebody without looking them in their eyes. They claim that a person's eyes say more than their mouth, and that it goes both ways – if we look someone in their eyes and mean what we say, they should have little reason to doubt us.

I look at Gomez.

"Khalil pulled over to the side of the road and turned the ignition off," I say. "One-Fifteen put his brights on. He approached the window and asked Khalil for his license and registration."

"Did Khalil comply?" Gomez asks.

"He asked the officer why he pulled us over first. Then he showed his license and registration."

"Did Khalil seem irate during this exchange?"

"Annoyed, not irate," I say. "He felt that the cop was harassing him."

"Did he tell you this?"

"No, but I could tell. I assumed the same thing myself."

Shit.

Gomez scoots closer. Maroon lipstick stains her teeth, and her breath smells like coffee. "And why was that?"

Breathe.

The room isn't hot. You're nervous.

"Because we weren't doing anything wrong," I say. "Khalil wasn't speeding or driving recklessly. It didn't seem like he had a reason to pull us over."

"I see. What happened next?"

"The officer forced Khalil out the car."

"Forced?" she says.

"Yes, ma'am. He pulled him out."

"Because Khalil was hesitant, right?"

Momma makes this throaty sound, like she was about to say something but stopped herself. She purses her lips and rubs my back in circles.

I remember what Daddy said – *"Don't let them put words in your mouth."*

"No, ma'am," I say to Gomez. "He was getting out on his own, and the officer yanked him the rest of the way."

She says "I see" again, but she didn't see it so she probably doesn't believe it. "What happened next?" she asks.

"The officer patted Khalil down three times."

"Three?"

Yeah. I counted. "Yes, ma'am. He didn't find anything. He then told Khalil to stay put while he ran his license and registration."

"But Khalil didn't stay put, did he?" she says.

"He didn't pull the trigger on himself either."

Shit. Your fucking big mouth.

The detectives glance at each other. A moment of silent conversation.

The walls move in closer. The grip around my lungs returns. I pull my shirt away from my neck.

"I think we're done for today," Momma says, taking my hand as she starts to stand up.

"But Mrs. Carter, we're not finished."

"I don't care—"

"Mom," I say, and she looks down at me. "It's okay. I can do this."

She gives them a glare similar to the one she gives me and my brothers when we've pushed her to her limit. She sits down but holds on to my hand.

"Okay," Gomez says. "So he patted Khalil down and told him he would check his license and registration. What next?"

"Khalil opened the driver's side door and—"

Pow!

Pow!

Pow!

Blood.

Tears crawl down my cheeks. I wipe them on my arm. "The officer shot him."

"Do you—" Gomez starts, but Momma holds a finger toward her.

"Could you *please* give her a second," she says. It sounds more like an order than a question.

Gomez doesn't say anything. Wilkes scribbles some more.

My mom wipes some of my tears for me. "Whenever you're ready," she says.

I swallow the lump in my throat and nod.

"Okay," Gomez says, and takes a deep breath. "Do you know why Khalil came to the door, Starr?"

"I think he was coming to ask if I was okay."

"You think?"

I'm not a telepath. "Yes, ma'am. He started asking but didn't finish because the officer shot him in the back."

More salty tears fall on my lips.

Gomez leans across the table. "We all want to get to the bottom of this, Starr. We appreciate your cooperation. I understand this is hard right now."

I wipe my face on my arm again. "Yeah."

"Yeah." She smiles and says in that same sugary, sympathetic tone, "Now, do you know if Khalil sold narcotics?"

Pause.

What the fuck?

My tears stop. For real, my eyes get dry with the quickness. Before I can say anything, my mom goes, "What does that have to do with anything?"

"It's only a question," Gomez says. "Do you, Starr?"

All the sympathy, the smiles, the understanding. This chick was baiting me.

Investigating or justifying?

I know the answer to her question. I knew it when I saw Khalil at the party. He never wore new shoes. And jewelry? Those little ninety-nine-cent chains he bought at the beauty supply store didn't count. Ms. Rosalie just confirmed it.

But what the hell does that have to do with him getting murdered? Is that supposed to make all of this okay?

Gomez tilts her head. "Starr? Can you please answer the question?"

I refuse to make them feel better about killing my friend.

I straighten up, look Gomez dead in her eyes, and say, "I never saw him sell drugs or do drugs."

"But do you know if he sold them?" she asks.

"He never told me he did," I say, which is true. Khalil never flat-out admitted it to me.

"Do you have knowledge of him selling them?"

"I heard things." Also true.

She sighs. "I see. Do you know if he was involved with the King Lords?"

"No."

"The Garden Disciples?"

"No."

"Did you consume any alcohol at the party?" she asks.

I know that move from *Law & Order.* She's trying to discredit me. "No. I don't drink."

"Did Khalil?"

"Whoa, wait one second," Momma says. "Are y'all putting Khalil and Starr on trial or the cop who killed him?"

Wilkes looks up from his notes.

"I – I don't quite understand, Mrs. Carter?" Gomez sputters.

"You haven't asked my child about that cop yet," Momma says. "You keep asking her about Khalil, like he's the reason he's dead. Like she said, he didn't pull the trigger on himself."

"We just want the whole picture, Mrs. Carter. That's all."

"One-Fifteen killed him," I say. "And he wasn't doing anything wrong. How much of a bigger picture do you need?"

Fifteen minutes later, I leave the police station with my mom. Both of us know the same thing:

This is gonna be some bullshit.

CHAPTER 7

Khalil's funeral is Friday. Tomorrow. Exactly one week since he died.

I'm at school, trying not to think about what he'll look like in the coffin, how many people will be there, what he'll look like in the coffin, if other people will know I was with him when he died … what he'll look like in the coffin.

I'm failing at not thinking about it.

On the Monday night news, they finally gave Khalil's name in the story about the shooting, but with a title added to it – Khalil Harris, a Suspected Drug Dealer. They didn't mention that he was unarmed. They said that an "unidentified witness" had been questioned and that the police were still investigating.

After what I told the cops, I'm not sure what's left to "investigate."

In the gym everyone's changed into their blue shorts and gold Williamson T-shirts, but class hasn't started yet. To pass time, some of the girls challenged some of the boys to a basketball game. They're playing on one end of the gym, the floor squeaking as they run around. The girls are all *"Staawp!"* when the guys guard them. Flirting, Williamson style.

Hailey, Maya, and I are in the bleachers on the other end. On the floor, some guys are supposedly dancing, trying to get their moves ready for prom. I say *supposedly* because there's no way that shit can be called dancing. Maya's boyfriend, Ryan, is the only one even close, and he's just doing the dab. It's his go-to move. He's a big, wide-shouldered linebacker, and it looks a little funny, but that's an advantage of being the sole black guy in class. You can look silly and still be cool.

Chris is on the bottom bleacher, playing one of his mixes on his phone for them to dance to. He glances over his shoulder at me.

I have two bodyguards who won't allow him near me – Maya on one side, cheering Ryan on, and Hailey, who's laughing her ass off at Luke and recording him. They're still pissed at Chris.

I'm honestly not. He made a mistake, and I forgive him. *The Fresh Prince* theme and his willingness to embarrass himself helped with that.

But that moment he grabbed my hands and I flashed back to that night, it's like I suddenly really, *really* realized that Chris is white. Just like One-Fifteen. And I know, I'm sitting here next to my white best friend, but it's almost as if I'm giving Khalil, Daddy, Seven, and every other black guy in my life a big, loud "fuck you" by having a white boyfriend.

Chris didn't pull us over, he didn't shoot Khalil, but

am I betraying who I am by dating him?

I need to figure this out.

"Oh my God, that's sickening," says Hailey. She's stopped recording to watch the basketball game. "They're not even trying."

They're really not. The ball sails past the hoop from an attempted shot by Bridgette Holloway. Either homegirl's hand-eye coordination is way off or she missed that on purpose, because now Jackson Reynolds is showing her how to shoot. Basically, he's all up on her. And shirtless.

"I don't know what's worse," Hailey says. "The fact that they're going soft on them because they're girls, or that the girls are letting them go soft on them."

"Equality in basketball. Right, Hails?" Maya says with a wink.

"Yes! Wait." She eyes Maya suspiciously. "Are you making fun of me or are you serious, Shorty?"

"Both," I say, leaning back on my elbows, my belly pooching out my shirt – a food baby. We just left lunch, and the cafeteria had fried chicken, one of the foods Williamson gets right. "It's not even a real game, Hails," I tell her.

"Nope." Maya pats my stomach. "When are you due?"

"Same day as you."

"Aww! We can raise our food offspring as siblings."

"I know, right? I'm naming mine Fernando," I say.

"Why Fernando?" Maya asks.

"Dunno. It sounds like a food baby name. Especially when you roll the *r*."

"I can't roll my *r*'s." She tries, but she makes some weird noise, spit flying, and I'm cracking up.

Hailey points at the game. "Look at that! It's that whole 'play like a girl' mind-set the male gender uses to belittle women, when we have as much athleticism as they do."

Oh my Lord. She's seriously upset over this.

"Take the ball to the hole!" she hollers to the girls.

Maya catches my eye, hers glimmering sneakily, and it's middle school déjà vu.

"And don't be afraid to shoot the outside J!" Maya shouts.

"Just keep ya head in the game," I say. "Just keep ya head in the game."

"And don't be afraid to 'shoot the outside J,'" Maya sings.

"'Just get'cha head in the game,'" I sing.

We bust out with "Get'cha Head in the Game" from *High School Musical*. It'll be stuck in my head for days. We were obsessed with the movies around the same time as our Jonas Brothers obsession. Disney took all our parents' money.

We're loud with it now. Hailey's trying to glare at us. She snorts.

"C'mon." She gets up and pulls me and Maya up too. "Get'cha head in *this* game."

I'm thinking, *Oh, so you can drag me to play basketball during one of your feminist rages, but you can't follow my Tumblr because of Emmett Till?* I don't know why I can't make myself bring it up. It's Tumblr.

But then, it's *Tumblr*.

"Hey!" Hailey says. "We wanna play."

"No we don't," Maya mutters. Hailey nudges her.

I don't wanna play either, but for some reason Hailey makes decisions and Maya and I follow along. It's not like we planned it to be this way. Sometimes the shit just happens, and one day you realize there's a leader among you and your friends and it's not you.

"Come on in, ladies." Jackson beckons us into the game. "There's always room for pretty girls. We'll try not to hurt you."

Hailey looks at me, I look at her, and we have the same deadpan expression that we've had mastered since fifth grade, mouths slightly open, eyes ready to roll at any moment.

"Alrighty then," I say. "Let's play."

"Three on three," Hailey says as we take our positions. "Girls versus boys. Half court. First to twenty. Sorry, ladies, but me and my girls are gonna handle this one, mm-kay?"

Bridgette gives Hailey some serious stank-eye. She and her friends move to the sideline.

The dance party stops and those guys come over, Chris included. He whispers something to Tyler, one of the boys who played in the previous game. Chris takes Tyler's place on the court.

Jackson checks the ball to Hailey. I run around my guard, Garrett, and Hailey passes to me. No matter what's going on, when Hailey, Maya, and I play together, it's rhythm, chemistry, and skill rolled into a ball of amazingness.

Garrett's guarding me, but Chris runs up and elbows him aside. Garrett goes, "The hell, Bryant?"

"I've got her," Chris says.

He gets in his defensive stance. We're eye to eye as I dribble the ball.

"Hey," he says.

"Hey."

I do a chest-pass to Maya, who's wide open for a jump shot.

She makes it.

Two to zero.

"Good job, Yang!" says Coach Meyers. She's come out her office. All it takes is a hint of a real game, and she's in coaching mode. She reminds me of a fitness trainer on a reality TV show. She's petite yet muscular, and God that woman can yell.

Garrett's at the baseline with the ball.

Chris runs to get open. Stomach full, I have to push harder to stay on him. We're hip to hip, watching Garrett try to decide who to pass to. Our arms brush, and something in me is activated; my senses are suddenly consumed by Chris. His legs look so good in his gym shorts. He's wearing Old Spice, and even just from that little brush, his skin feels so soft.

"I miss you," he says.

No point in lying. "I miss you too."

The ball sails his way. Chris catches it. Now I'm in my defensive stance, and we're eye to eye again as he dribbles.

My gaze lowers to his lips; they're a little wet and begging me to kiss them. See, this is why I can never play ball with him. I get too distracted.

"Will you at least talk to me?" Chris asks.

"Defense, Carter!" Coach yells.

I focus on the ball and attempt to steal. Not quick enough. He gets around me and goes straight for the hoop, only to pass it to Jackson, who's open at the three-point line.

"Grant!" Coach shouts for Hailey.

Hailey runs over. Her fingertips graze the ball as it leaves Jackson's hand, changing its course.

The ball goes flying. I go running. I catch it.

Chris is behind me, the only thing between me and the hoop. Let me clarify – my butt is against his crotch, my back against his chest. I'm bumping up against him, trying to figure out how to get the ball in the hole. It sounds way dirtier than it actually is, especially in this position. I understand why Bridgette missed shots though.

"Starr!" Hailey calls.

She's open at the three. I bounce-pass it to her.

She shoots. Nails it.

Five to zero.

"C'mon, boys," Maya taunts. "Is that all you can do?"

Coach claps. "Good job. Good job."

Jackson's at the baseline. He passes to Chris. Chris chest-passes it back to him.

"I don't get it," Chris says. "You practically freaked out the other day in the hall. What's going on?"

Garrett passes to Chris. I get in my defensive stance, eyes on the ball. Not on Chris. Cannot look at Chris. My eyes will give me away.

"Talk to me," he says.

I attempt to steal again. No luck.

"Play the game," I say.

Chris goes left, quickly changes direction, and goes right. I try to stay on him, but my heavy stomach slows me down. He gets to the hoop and makes the layup. It's good.

Five to two.

"Dammit, Starr!" Hailey yells, recovering the ball. She passes it to me. "Hustle! Pretend the ball is some fried chicken. Bet you'll stay on it then."

What.

The.

Actual.

Fuck?

The world surges forward without me. I hold the ball and stare at Hailey as she jogs away, blue-streaked hair bouncing behind her.

I can't believe she said… She couldn't have. No way.

The ball falls out my hands. I walk off the court. I'm breathing hard, and my eyes burn.

The smell of postgame funk lingers in the girls' locker room. It's my place of solace when we lose a game, where I can cry or cuss if I want.

I pace from one side of the lockers to the other.

Hailey and Maya rush in, out of breath. "What's up with you?" Hailey asks.

"Me?" I say, my voice bouncing off the lockers. "What the hell was that comment?"

"Lighten up! It was only game talk."

"A fried chicken joke was only game talk? Really?" I ask.

"It's fried chicken day!" she says. "You and Maya were just joking about it. What are you trying to say?"

I keep pacing.

Her eyes widen. "Oh my God. You think I was being *racist*?"

I look at her. "You made a fried chicken comment to the only black girl in the room. What do you think?"

"Ho-ly shit, Starr! Seriously? After everything we've been through, you think I'm a racist? Really?"

"You can say something racist and not be a racist!"

"Is something else going on, Starr?" Maya says.

"Why does everyone keep asking me that?" I snap.

"Because you're acting so weird lately!" Hailey snaps back. She looks at me and asks, "Does this have something to do with the police shooting that drug dealer in your neighborhood?"

"Wh-what?"

"I heard about it on the news," she says. "And I know you're into that sort of thing now—"

That sort of thing? What the fuck is "that sort of thing"?

"And then they said the drug dealer's name was Khalil," she says, and exchanges a look with Maya.

"We've wanted to ask if it was the Khalil who used to come to your birthday parties," Maya adds. "We didn't know how, though."

The drug dealer. That's how they see him. It doesn't matter that he's suspected of doing it. "Drug dealer" is louder than "suspected" ever will be.

If it's revealed that I was in the car, what will that make me? The thug ghetto girl with the drug dealer? What will my teachers think about me? My friends? The whole fucking world, possibly?

"I—"

I close my eyes. Khalil stares at the sky.

"Mind your business, Starr," he says.

I swallow and whisper, "I don't know that Khalil."

It's a betrayal worse than dating a white boy. I fucking deny him, damn near erasing every laugh we shared, every hug, every tear, every second we spent together. A million "I'm sorry"s sound in my head, and I hope they reach Khalil wherever he is, yet they'll never be enough.

But I had to do it. I had to.

"Then what is it?" Hailey asks. "Is this, like, Natasha's anniversary or something?"

I stare at the ceiling and blink fast to keep from bawling. Besides my brothers and the teachers, Hailey and Maya are the only people at Williamson who know about Natasha. I don't want all the pity.

"Mom's anniversary was a few weeks ago," Hailey says. "I was in a shitty mood for days. I understand if you're upset,

115

but to accuse me of being racist, Starr? How can you *even*?"

I blink faster. God, I'm pushing her away, Chris away. Hell, do I deserve them? I don't talk about Natasha, and I just flat-out denied Khalil. I could've been the one killed instead of them. I don't have the decency to keep their memories alive, yet I'm supposed to be their best friend.

I cover my mouth. It doesn't stop the sob. It's loud and echoes off the walls. One follows it, and another and another. Maya and Hailey rub my back and shoulders.

Coach Meyers rushes in. "Carter—"

Hailey looks at her and says, "Natasha."

Coach nods heavily. "Carter, go see Ms. Lawrence."

What? No. She's sending me to the school shrink? All the teachers know about poor Starr who saw her friend die when she was ten. I used to bust out crying all the time, and that was always their go-to line – see Ms. Lawrence. I wipe my eyes. "Coach, I'm okay—"

"No, you're not." She pulls a hall pass from her pocket and holds it toward me. "Go talk to her. It'll help you feel better."

No it won't, but I know what will.

I take the pass, grab my backpack out my locker, and go back into the gym. My classmates follow me with their eyes as I hurry toward the doors. Chris calls out for me. I speed up.

They probably heard me crying. Great. What's worse than being the Angry Black Girl? The *Weak* Black Girl.

By the time I get to the main office, I've dried my eyes and my face completely.

"Good afternoon, Ms. Carter," Dr. Davis, the headmaster, says. He's leaving as I'm going in and doesn't wait for my response. Does he know all the students by name, or just the ones who are black like him? I hate that I think about stuff like that now.

His secretary, Mrs. Lindsey, greets me with a smile and asks how she can assist me.

"I need to call someone to come get me," I say. "I don't feel good."

I call Uncle Carlos. My parents would ask too many questions. A limb has to be missing for them to take me out of school. I only have to tell Uncle Carlos that I have cramps, and he'll pick me up.

Feminine problems. The key to ending an Uncle Carlos interrogation.

Luckily he's on lunch break. He signs me out, and I hold my stomach for added effect. As we leave he asks if I want some fro-yo. I say yeah, and a short while later we're going into a shop that's walking distance from Williamson. It's in a brand-new mini mall that should be called Hipster Heaven, full of stores you'd never find in Garden Heights. On one side of the fro-yo place, there's Indie Urban Style and on the other side, Dapper Dog, where you can buy outfits for your dog. Clothes. For a dog. What kinda fool would I be, dressing Brickz in a linen shirt and jeans?

On a serious tip – white people are crazy for their dogs.

We fill our cups with yogurt. At the toppings bar, Uncle

Carlos breaks out into his fro-yo rap. "I'm getting fro-yo, yo. Fro-yo, yo, yo."

He loves his fro-yo. It's kinda adorable. We take a booth in a corner that's got a lime-green table and hot-pink seats. You know, typical fro-yo decor.

Uncle Carlos looks over into my cup. "Did you seriously ruin perfectly good fro-yo with Cap'n Crunch?"

"You can't talk," I say. "Oreos, Uncle Carlos? Really? And they're not even the Golden Oreos, which are by far the superior Oreos. You got the regular ones. *Ill*."

He devours a spoonful and says, "You're weird."

"*You're* weird."

"So cramps, huh?" he says.

Shit. I almost forgot about that. I hold my stomach and groan. "Yeah. They're real bad today."

I know who *won't* win an Oscar anytime soon. Uncle Carlos gives me his hard detective stare. I groan again; this one sounds a little more believable. He raises his eyebrows.

His phone rings in his jacket pocket. He sticks another spoonful of fro-yo in his mouth and checks it. "It's your mom calling me back," he says around the spoon. He holds the phone with his cheek and shoulder. "Hey, Lisa. You get my message?"

Shit.

"She's not feeling good," Uncle Carlos says. "She's got, you know, *feminine* problems."

Her response is loud but muffled. Shit, shit.

Uncle Carlos holds the nape of his neck and slowly

118

releases a long, deep breath. He turns into a little boy when Momma raises her voice at him, and he's supposed to be the oldest.

"Okay, okay. I hear you," he says. "Here, you talk to her."

Shit, shit, shit.

He passes me the piece of dynamite formerly known as his phone. There's an explosion of questioning as soon as I say, "Hello?"

"Cramps, Starr? Really?" she says.

"They're bad, Mommy," I whine, lying my butt off.

"Girl, please. I went to class in labor with you," she says. "I pay too much money for you to go to Williamson so you can leave because of cramps."

I almost point out that I get a scholarship too, but nah. She'd become the first person in history to hit someone through a phone.

"Did something happen?" she asks.

"No."

"Is it Khalil?" she asks.

I sigh. This time tomorrow I'll be staring at him in a coffin.

"Starr?" she says.

"Nothing happened."

Ms. Felicia calls for her in the background. "Look, I gotta go," she says. "Carlos will take you home. Lock the door, stay inside, and don't let anybody in, you hear me?"

Those aren't zombie survival tips. Just normal instructions for latchkey kids in Garden Heights. "I can't let

119

Seven and Sekani in? Great."

"Oh, somebody's trying to be funny. Now I know you ain't feeling bad. We'll talk later. I love you. Mwah!"

It takes a lot of nerve to go off on somebody, call them out, and tell them you love them within a span of five minutes. I tell her I love her too and pass Uncle Carlos his phone.

"All right, baby girl," he says. "Spill it."

I stuff some fro-yo in my mouth. It's melting already. "Like I said. Cramps."

"I'm not buying that, and let's be clear about something: you only get one 'Uncle Carlos, get me out of school' card per school year, and you're using it right now."

"You got me in December, remember?" For cramps also. I didn't lie about those. They were a bitch that day.

"All right, one per *calendar* year," he clarifies. I smile. "But you gotta give me a little more to work with. So talk."

I push Cap'n Crunch around my fro-yo. "Khalil's funeral is tomorrow."

"I know."

"I don't know if I should go."

"What? Why?"

"Because," I say. "I hadn't seen him in months before the party."

"You still should go," he says. "You'll regret it if you don't. I thought about going. Not sure if that's a good idea, considering."

Silence.

"Are you really friends with that cop?" I ask.

"I wouldn't say friends, no. Colleagues."

"But you're on a first-name basis, right?"

"Yes," he says.

I stare at my cup. Uncle Carlos was my first dad in some ways. Daddy went to prison around the time I realized that "Mommy" and "Daddy" weren't just names, but they meant something. I talked to Daddy on the phone every week, but he didn't want me and Seven to ever set foot in a prison, so I didn't see him.

I saw Uncle Carlos though. He fulfilled the role and then some. Once I asked if I could call him Daddy. He said no, because I already had one, but being my uncle was the best thing he could ever be. Ever since, "Uncle" has meant almost as much as "Daddy."

My uncle. On a first-name basis with that cop.

"Baby girl, I don't know what to say." His voice is gruff. "I wish I could – I'm sorry this happened. I am."

"Why haven't they arrested him?"

"Cases like this are difficult."

"It's not that difficult," I say. "He killed Khalil."

"I know, I know," he says, and wipes his face. "I know."

"Would you have killed him?"

He looks at me. "Starr – I can't answer that."

"Yeah, you can."

"No, I can't. I'd like to think I wouldn't have, but it's hard to say unless you're in that situation, feeling what that officer is feeling—"

"He pointed his gun at me," I blurt out.

"What?"

My eyes prickle like crazy. "While we were waiting on help to show up," I say, my words wobbling. "He kept it on me until somebody else got there. Like I was a threat. I wasn't the one with the gun."

Uncle Carlos stares at me for the longest time.

"Baby girl." He reaches for my hand. He squeezes it and moves to my side of the table. His arm goes around me, and I bury my face in his rib cage, tears and snot wetting his shirt.

"I'm sorry. I'm sorry. I'm sorry." He kisses my hair with each apology. "But I know that's not enough."

CHAPTER 8

Funerals aren't for dead people. They're for the living.

I doubt Khalil cares what songs are sung or what the preacher says about him. He's in a casket. Nothing can change that.

My family and I leave thirty minutes before the funeral starts, but the parking lot at Christ Temple Church is already full. Some kids from Khalil's school stand around in "RIP Khalil" T-shirts with his face on them. A guy tried to sell some to us yesterday, but Momma said we weren't wearing them today – T-shirts are for the streets, not for church.

So here we are, getting out the car in our dresses and suits. My parents hold hands and walk in front of me and my brothers. We used to go to Christ Temple when I was younger, but Momma got tired of how people here act like their shit don't stank, and now we go to this "diverse" church in Riverton Hills. Way too many people go there, and praise and worship is led by a white guy on guitar. Oh, and service lasts less than an hour.

Going back in Christ Temple is like when you go back

to your old elementary school after you've been to high school. When you were younger it seemed big, but when you go back you realize how small it is. People fill up the tiny foyer. It has cranberry-colored carpet and two burgundy high-back chairs. One time Momma brought me out here because I was acting up. She made me sit in one of those chairs and told me not to move until service was over. I didn't. A painting of the pastor hung above the chairs, and I could've sworn he was watching me. All these years later and they still have that creepy painting up.

There's a line to sign a book for Khalil's family and another line to go into the sanctuary. To see him.

I catch a glimpse of the white casket at the front of the sanctuary, but I can't make myself try to see more than that. I'll see him eventually, but — I don't know. I wanna wait until I don't have any other choice.

Pastor Eldridge greets people in the doorway of the sanctuary. He's wearing a long white robe with gold crosses on it. He smiles at everyone. I don't know why they made him look so creepy in that painting. He's not creepy at all.

Momma glances back at me, Seven, and Sekani, like she's making sure we look nice, then she and Daddy go up to Pastor Eldridge. "Morning, Pastor," she says.

"Lisa! So good to see you." He kisses her cheek and shakes Daddy's hand. "Maverick, good to see you as well. We miss y'all around here."

"I bet y'all do," Daddy mumbles. Another reason we left Christ Temple: Daddy doesn't like that they take up so many offerings. But he doesn't even go to our diverse church.

"And these must be the children," Pastor Eldridge says. He shakes Seven's and Sekani's hands and kisses my cheek. I feel more of his bristly mustache than anything. "Y'all sure have grown since I last saw you. I remember when the little one was an itty-bitty thing wrapped up in a blanket. How's your momma doing, Lisa?"

"She's good. She misses coming here, but the drive is a little long for her."

I side-eye the hell — excuse me, heck; we're in church — out of her. Nana stopped coming to Christ Temple because of some incident between her and Mother Wilson over Deacon Rankin. It ended with Nana storming off from the church picnic, banana pudding in hand. That's all I know though.

"We understand," says Pastor Eldridge. "Let her know we're praying for her." He looks at me with an expression I know too well — pity. "Ms. Rosalie told me you were with Khalil when this happened. I am so sorry you had to witness it."

"Thank you." It's weird saying that, like I'm stealing sympathy from Khalil's family.

Momma grabs my hand. "We're gonna find some seats. Nice talking to you, Pastor."

Daddy wraps his arm around me, and the three of us walk into the sanctuary together.

My legs tremble and a wave of nausea hits me, and we aren't even at the front of the viewing line yet. People go up to the casket in twos, so I can't see Khalil at all.

Soon there are six people in front of us. Four. Two. I keep my eyes closed the whole time with the last two. Then it's our turn.

My parents lead me up. "Baby, open your eyes," Momma says.

I do. It looks more like a mannequin than Khalil in the casket. His skin is darker and his lips are pinker than they should be, because of the makeup. Khalil would've had a fit if he knew they put that on him. He's wearing a white suit and a gold cross pendant.

The real Khalil had dimples. This mannequin version of him doesn't.

Momma brushes tears from her eyes. Daddy shakes his head. Seven and Sekani stare.

That's not Khalil, I tell myself. *Like it wasn't Natasha.*

Natasha's mannequin wore a white dress with pink and yellow flowers all over it. It had on makeup too. Momma had told me, "See, she looks asleep," but when I squeezed her hand, her eyes never opened.

Daddy carried me out the sanctuary as I screamed for her to wake up.

We move so the next set of people can look at Khalil's mannequin. An usher is about to direct us to some seats, but this lady with natural twists gestures toward the front row of the friends' side, right in front of her. No clue who she is, but she must be somebody if she's giving orders like that. And she must know something about me if she thinks my family deserves the front row.

We take our seats, and I focus on the flowers instead. There's a big heart made out of red and white roses, a "K" made out of calla lilies, and an arrangement of flowers in orange and green, his favorite colors.

When I run out of flowers, I look at the funeral program. It's full of pictures of Khalil, from the time he was a curly-haired baby up until a few weeks ago with friends I don't recognize. There are pictures of me and him from years ago and one with us and Natasha. All three of us smile, trying to look gangster with our peace signs. The Hood Trio, tighter than the inside of Voldemort's nose. Now I'm the only one left.

I close the program.

"Let us stand." Pastor Eldridge's voice echoes throughout the sanctuary. The organist starts playing, and everyone stands.

"And Jesus said, 'Do not let your hearts be troubled,'" he says, coming down the aisle. "'You believe in God, believe also in me.'"

Ms. Rosalie marches behind him. Cameron walks alongside her, gripping her hand. Tears stain his chubby cheeks. He's only nine, a year older than Sekani. Had one of those bullets hit me, that could've been my little brother crying like that.

Khalil's aunt Tammy holds Ms. Rosalie's other hand. Ms. Brenda is wailing behind them, wearing a black dress that once belonged to Momma. Her hair has been combed into a ponytail. Two guys, I think they're Khalil's cousins, hold her up. It's easier to look at the casket.

"'My Father's house has many rooms; if that were not so, would I have told you that I am going there to prepare a place for you?'" Pastor Eldridge says. "'And if I go and prepare a place for you, I will come back and take you to be with me that you also may be where I am.'"

At Natasha's funeral, her momma passed out when she saw her in the casket. Somehow Khalil's momma and grandma don't.

"I wanna make one thing clear today," Pastor Eldridge says once everyone is seated. "No matter the circumstances, this is a homegoing celebration. Weeping may endure for a night, but how many of you know that JOY—!" He doesn't even finish and people shout.

The choir sings upbeat songs, and almost everyone claps and praises Jesus. Momma sings along and waves her hands. Khalil's grandma and auntie clap and sing too. A praise break even starts, and people run around the sanctuary and do the "Holy Ghost Two-Step," as Seven and I call it, their feet moving like James Brown and their bent arms flapping like chicken wings.

But if Khalil's not celebrating, how the hell can they? And why praise Jesus, since he let Khalil get shot in the first place?

I put my face in my hands, hoping to drown out the drums, the horns, the shouting. This shit doesn't make any sense.

After all that praising, some of Khalil's classmates – the

ones who were in the parking lot in the T-shirts – make a presentation. They give his family the cap and gown Khalil would've worn in a few months and cry as they tell funny stories I'd never heard. Yet I'm the one in the front row on the friends' side. I'm such a fucking phony.

Next, the lady with the twists goes up to the podium. Her black pencil skirt and blazer are more professional-looking than church-looking, and she's wearing an "RIP Khalil" T-shirt too.

"Good morning," she says, and everyone responds. "My name is April Ofrah, and I'm with Just Us for Justice. We are a small organization here in Garden Heights that advocates for police accountability.

"As we say farewell to Khalil, we find our hearts burdened with the harsh truth of how he lost his life. Just before the start of this service, I was informed that, despite a credible eyewitness account, the police department has no intentions of arresting the officer who murdered this young man."

"What?" I say, as people murmur around the sanctuary. Everything I told them, and they're not arresting him?

"What they don't want you to know," Ms. Ofrah says, "is that Khalil was unarmed at the time of his murder."

People *really* start talking then. A couple of folks yell out, including one person who's bold enough to shout "This is bullshit" in a church.

"We won't give up until Khalil receives justice," Ms. Ofrah says over the talking. "I ask you to join us and Khalil's family after the service for a peaceful march to the cemetery. Our route happens to pass the police station. Khalil was silenced, but let's join together and make our voices heard for him. Thank you."

The congregation gives her a standing ovation. As she returns to her seat, she glances at me. If Ms. Rosalie told the pastor I was with Khalil, she probably told this lady too. I bet she wants to talk.

Pastor Eldridge just about preaches Khalil into heaven. I'm not saying Khalil didn't make it to heaven – I don't know – but Pastor Eldridge tries to make sure he gets there. He sweats and breathes so hard I get tired looking at him.

At the end of the eulogy, he says, "If anybody wishes to view the body, now is the—"

He stares at the back of the church. Murmurs bubble around the sanctuary.

Momma looks back. "What in the world?"

King and a bunch of his boys post up in the back in their gray clothes and bandanas. King has his arm hooked around a lady in a tight black dress that barely covers her thighs. She has way too much weave in her head – for real, it comes to her ass – and way too much makeup on.

Seven turns back around. I wouldn't wanna see my momma looking like that either.

But why are they here? King Lords only show up at King Lord funerals.

Pastor Eldridge clears his throat. "As I was saying, if anyone wishes to view the body, now is the time."

King and his boys swagger down the aisle. Everybody stares. Iesha walks alongside him, all proud and shit, not realizing she looks a hot mess. She glances at my parents and smirks, and I can't stand her ass. I mean, not just because of how she treats Seven, but because every time she shows up, there's suddenly an unspoken tension between my parents. Like now. Momma shifts her shoulder so it's not as close to Daddy, and his jaw is clenched. She's the Achilles' heel of their marriage, and it's only noticeable if you've been watching it for sixteen years like I have.

King, Iesha, and the rest of them go up to the casket. One of King's boys hands him a folded gray bandana, and he lays it across Khalil's chest.

My heart stops.

Khalil was a King Lord too?

Ms. Rosalie jumps up. "Like hell you will!"

She marches to the coffin and snatches the bandana off Khalil. She starts toward King, but Daddy catches her halfway and holds her back. "Get outta here, you demon!" she screams. "And take this mess with you!"

She throws the bandana at the back of King's head.

He stills. Slowly, he turns around.

"Now look, bi—"

"Ay!" Daddy says. "King, man, just go! Leave, a'ight?"

"You ol' hag," Iesha snarls. "Got some nerve treating my man like this after he offered to pay for this funeral."

"He can keep his filthy money!" Ms. Rosalie says. "And you can take your behind right out the door too. Coming in

131

the Lord's house, looking like the prostitute you are!"

Seven shakes his head. It's no secret that my big brother is the result of a "for hire" session Daddy had with Iesha after a fight with Momma. Iesha was King's girl, but he told her to "hook Maverick up," not knowing Seven would come along looking exactly like Daddy. Fucked up, I know.

Momma reaches behind me and rubs Seven's back. There are rare times, when Seven's not around and Momma thinks Sekani and I can't hear her, that she'll tell Daddy, "I still can't believe you slept with that nasty ho." But Seven can't be around. When he's around, none of that matters. She loves him more than she hates Iesha.

The King Lords leave, and conversations break out all around.

Daddy leads Ms. Rosalie to her seat. She's so mad she's shaking.

I look at the mannequin in the coffin. All those horror stories Daddy told us about gangbanging, and Khalil became a King Lord? How could he even *think* about doing that?

It doesn't make sense though. He had green in his car. That's what Garden Disciples do, not King Lords. And he didn't run to help out with the fight at Big D's party.

But the bandana. Daddy once said that's a King Lord tradition – they crown their fallen comrades by putting a folded bandana on the body, as if to say they're going into heaven repping their set. Khalil must've joined to get that honor.

I could've talked him out of it, I know it, but I abandoned

him. Fuck the friends' side. I shouldn't even be at his funeral.

Daddy stays with Ms. Rosalie for the rest of the service and later helps her when the family follows the casket out. Aunt Tammy motions us over to join them.

"Thank you for being here," she tells me. "You meant a lot to Khalil, I hope you know that."

My throat tightens too much for me to tell her he means a lot to me too.

We follow the casket with the family. Just about everyone we pass has tears in their eyes. For Khalil. He really is in that casket, and he's not coming back.

I've never told anyone, but Khalil was my first crush. He unknowingly introduced me to stomach butterflies and later heartbreak when he got his own crush on Imani Anderson, a high schooler who wasn't even thinking about fourth-grade him. I worried about my appearance for the first time around him.

But fuck the crush, he was one of the best friends I ever had, no matter if we saw each other every day or once a year. Time didn't compare to all the shit we went through together. And now he's in a casket, like Natasha.

Big fat tears fall from my eyes, and I sob. A loud, nasty, ugly sob that everybody hears and sees as I come up the aisle.

"They left me," I cry.

Momma wraps her arm around me and presses my head onto her shoulder. "I know, baby, but we're here. We aren't going anywhere."

Warmth brushes my face, and I know we're outside. All

of the voices and noises make me look. There are more people out here than in the church, holding posters with Khalil's face on them and signs that say "Justice for Khalil." His classmates have posters saying "Am I Next?" and "Enough Is Enough!" News vans with tall antennas are parked across the street.

I bury my face in Momma's shoulder again. People – I don't know who – pat my back and tell me it'll be okay.

I can tell when it's Daddy who's rubbing my back without him even saying anything. "We gon' stay and march, baby," he tells Momma. "I want Seven and Sekani to be a part of this."

"Yeah, I'm taking her home. How are y'all getting back?"

"We can walk to the store. I gotta open up anyway." He kisses my hair. "I love you, baby girl. Get some rest, a'ight?"

Heels clack toward us, then someone says, "Hi, Mr. and Mrs. Carter, I'm April Ofrah with Just Us for Justice."

Momma tenses up and pulls me closer. "How may we help you?"

She lowers her voice and says, "Khalil's grandmother told me that Starr is the one who was with Khalil when this happened. I know she gave a statement to the police, and I want to commend her on her bravery. This is a difficult situation, and that must've taken a lot of strength."

"Yeah, it did," Daddy says.

I move my head off Momma's shoulder. Ms. Ofrah shifts her weight from foot to foot and fumbles with her fingers. My parents aren't helping with the hard looks they're giving her.

"We all want the same thing," she says. "Justice for Khalil."

"Excuse me, Ms. Ofrah," Momma says, "but as much as I want that, I want my daughter to have some peace. And privacy."

Momma looks at the news vans across the street. Ms. Ofrah glances back at them.

"Oh!" she says. "Oh no. No, no, no. We weren't – I wasn't – I don't want to put Starr out there like that. Quite the opposite, actually. I want to protect her privacy."

Momma loosens her hold. "I see."

"Starr offers a unique perspective in this, one you don't get a lot with these cases, and I want to make sure her rights are protected and that her voice is heard, but without her being—"

"Exploited?" Daddy asks. "Pimped?"

"Exactly. The case is about to gain national media attention, but I don't want it to be at her expense." She hands each of us a business card. "Besides being an advocate, I'm also an attorney. Just Us for Justice isn't providing the Harris family with legal representation – someone else is doing that. We're simply rallying behind them. However, I'm available and willing to represent Starr on my own. Whenever you're ready, please give me a call. And I am so sorry for your loss."

She disappears into the crowd.

Call her when I'm ready, huh? I'm not sure I'll ever be ready for the shit that's about to happen.

CHAPTER 9

My brothers come home with a message – Daddy's spending the night at the store.

He also leaves instructions for us – stay inside.

A chain-link fence surrounds our house. Seven puts the big lock on the gate, the one we use when we go out of town. I bring Brickz inside. He doesn't know how to act, walking around in circles and jumping on the furniture. Momma doesn't say anything until he gets on her good sofa in the living room.

"Ay!" She snaps her fingers at him. "Get your big behind off my furniture. You crazy?"

He whimpers and scurries over to me.

The sun sets. We're in the middle of saying grace over pot roast and potatoes when the first gunshots ring out.

We open our eyes. Sekani flinches. I'm used to gunshots, but these are louder, faster. One barely sounds off before another's right behind it.

"Machine guns," says Seven. More shots follow.

"Take your dinner to the den," Momma says, getting

up from the table. "And sit on the floor. Bullets don't know where they're supposed to go."

Seven gets up too. "Ma, I can—"

"Seven, den," she says.

"But—"

"Se-ven." She breaks his name down. "I'm turning the lights off, baby, okay? Please, go to the den."

He gives in. "All right." When Daddy isn't home, Seven acts like he's the man of the house by default. Momma always has to break his name down and put him in his place.

I grab my plate and Momma's and head for the den, the one room without exterior walls. Brickz is right behind me, but he always follows food. The hallway darkens as Momma turns off the lights throughout the house.

We have one of those old-school big-screen TVs in the den. It's Daddy's prized possession. We crowd around it, and Seven turns on the news, lighting up the den.

There are at least a hundred people gathered on Magnolia Avenue. They chant for justice and hold signs, fists high in the air for black power.

Momma comes in, talking on the phone. "All right, Mrs. Pearl, as long as you sure. Just remember we got enough room over here for you if you don't feel comfortable being alone. I'll check in later."

Mrs. Pearl is this elderly lady who lives by herself across the street. Momma checks on her all the time. She says Mrs. Pearl needs to know that somebody cares.

Momma sits next to me. Sekani rests his head in her lap.

Brickz mimics him and puts his head in my lap, licking my fingers.

"Are they mad 'cause Khalil died?" Sekani asks.

Momma brushes her fingers through his high-top fade. "Yeah, baby. We all are."

But they're *really* mad that Khalil was unarmed. Can't be a coincidence this is happening after Ms. Ofrah announced that at his funeral.

The cops respond to the chants with tear gas that blankets the crowd in a white cloud. The news cuts to footage inside the crowd of people running and screaming.

"Damn," Seven says.

Sekani buries his face in Momma's thigh. I feed Brickz a piece of my pot roast. The clenching in my stomach won't let me eat.

Sirens wail outside. The news shows three patrol cars that have been set ablaze at the police precinct, about a five-minute drive away from us. A gas station near the freeway gets looted, and the owner, this Indian man, staggers around bloody, saying he didn't have anything to do with Khalil's death. A line of cops guard the Walmart on the east side.

My neighborhood is a war zone.

Chris texts to see if I'm okay, and I immediately feel like shit for avoiding him, Beyoncé'ing him, and everything else. I would apologize, but texting "I'm sorry" combined with every emoji in the world isn't the same as saying it face-to-face. I do let him know I'm okay though.

Maya and Hailey call, asking about the store, the house, my family, me. Neither of them mention the fried chicken drama. It's weird talking to them about Garden Heights. We never do. I'm always afraid one of them will call it "the ghetto."

I get it. Garden Heights is the ghetto, so it wouldn't be a lie, but it's like when I was nine and Seven and I got into one of our fights. He went for a low blow and called me Shorty McShort-Short. A lame insult now when I think about it, but it tore me up back then. I knew there was a possibility I was short — everybody else was taller than I was — and I could call myself short if I wanted. It became an uncomfortable truth when Seven said it.

I can call Garden Heights the ghetto all I want. Nobody else can.

Momma stays on her phone too, checking on some neighbors and getting calls from others who are checking on us. Ms. Jones down the street says that she and her four kids are holed up in their den like we are. Mr. Charles next door says that if the power goes out we can use his generator.

Uncle Carlos checks on us too. Nana takes the phone and tells Momma to bring us out there. Like we're about to go through the shit to get out of it. Daddy calls and says the store is all right. It doesn't stop me from tensing up every time the news mentions a business that's been attacked.

The news does more than give Khalil's name now — they show his picture too. They only call me "the witness." Sometimes "the sixteen-year-old black female witness."

The police chief appears onscreen and says what I was afraid he'd say: "We have taken into consideration the evidence as well as the statement given by the witness, and as of now we see no reason to arrest the officer."

Momma and Seven glance at me. They don't say anything with Sekani right here. They don't have to. All of this is my fault. The riots, gunshots, tear gas, all of it, are ultimately my fault. I forgot to tell the cops that Khalil got out with his hands up. I didn't mention that the officer pointed his gun at me. I didn't say something right, and now that cop's not getting arrested.

But while the riots are my fault, the news basically makes it sound like it's Khalil's fault he died.

"There are multiple reports that a gun was found in the car," the anchor claims. "There is also suspicion that the victim was a drug dealer as well as a gang member. Officials have not confirmed if any of this is true."

The gun stuff can't be true. When I asked Khalil if he had anything in the car, he said no.

He also wouldn't say if he was a drug dealer or not. And he didn't even mention the gangbanging stuff.

Does it matter though? He didn't deserve to die.

Sekani and Brickz start breathing deeply around the same time, fast asleep. That's not an option for me with the helicopters, the gunshots, and the sirens. Momma and Seven stay up too. Around four in the morning, when it's quieted down, Daddy comes in bleary-eyed and yawning.

"They didn't hit Marigold," he says between bites of pot

140

roast at the kitchen table. "Looks like they keeping it mostly on the east side, near where he was killed. For now at least."

"For now," Momma repeats.

Daddy runs his hand over his face. "Yeah. I don't know what's gon' stop them from coming this way. Shit, much as I understand it, I dread it if they do."

"We can't stay here, Maverick," she says, and her voice is shaky, like she's been holding something in this entire time and is just now letting it out. "This won't get better. It'll get worse."

Daddy reaches for her hand. She lets him take it, and he pulls her onto his lap. Daddy wraps his arms around her and kisses the back of her head.

"We'll be a'ight."

He sends me and Seven to bed. Somehow I fall asleep.

Natasha runs into the store again. "Starr, come on!"

Her braids have dirt in them, and her once-fat cheeks are sunken. Blood soaks through her clothes.

I step back. She runs up to me and grabs my hand. Hers feels icy like it did in her coffin.

"Come on." She tugs at me. "Come on!"

She pulls me toward the door, and my feet move against my will.

"Stop," I say. "Natasha, stop!"

A hand extends through the door, holding a Glock.

Bang!

I jolt awake.

Seven bangs his fist against my door. He doesn't text normal, and he doesn't wake people up normal either. "We're leaving in ten."

My heart beats against my chest like it's trying to get out. *You're fine,* I remind myself. *It's Seven's stupid butt.* "Leaving for what?" I ask him.

"Basketball at the park. It's the last Saturday of the month, right? Isn't this what we always do?"

"But – the riots and stuff?"

"Like Pops said, that stuff happened on the east. We're good over here. Plus the news said it's quiet this morning."

What if somebody knows I'm the witness? What if they know that it's my fault that cop hasn't been arrested? What if we come across some cops and they know who I am?

"It'll be all right," Seven says, like he read my mind. "I promise. Now get your lazy butt up so I can kill you on the court."

If it's possible to be a sweet asshole, that's Seven. I get out of bed and put on my basketball shorts, LeBron jersey, and my Thirteens like Jordan wore before he left the Bulls. I comb my hair into a ponytail. Seven waits for me at the front door, spinning the basketball between his hands.

I snatch it from him. "Like you know what to do with it."

"We'll see 'bout that."

I holler to let Momma and Daddy know we'll be back later and leave.

At first Garden Heights looks the same, but a couple of blocks away at least five police cars speed by. Smoke lingers in the air, making everything look hazy. It stinks too.

We make it to Rose Park. Some King Lords sit in a gray Escalade across the street, and a younger one's on the park merry-go-round. Long as we don't bother them, they won't bother us.

Rose Park occupies a whole block, and a tall chain-link fence surrounds it. I'm not sure what it's protecting – the graffiti on the basketball court, the rusting playground equipment, the benches that way too many babies have been made on, or the liquor bottles, cigarette butts, and trash that litter the grass.

We're right near the basketball courts, but the entrance to the park is on the other side of the block. I toss the ball to Seven and climb the fence. I used to jump down from the top, but one fall and a sprained ankle stopped me from doing that again.

When I get over the fence Seven tosses the ball to me and climbs. Khalil, Natasha, and I used to take a shortcut through the park after school. We'd run up the slides, spin on the merry-go-round till we were dizzy, and try to swing higher than one another.

I try to forget all that as I check the ball to Seven. "First to thirty?"

"Forty," he says, knowing damn well he'll be lucky if he gets twenty points. He can't play ball just like Daddy can't play ball.

As if to prove it, Seven dribbles using the palm of his hand. You're supposed to use your fingertips. Then this fool shoots for a three.

The ball bounces off the rim. Of course. I grab it and look at him. "Weak! You knew that shit wasn't going in."

"Whatever. Play the damn game."

Five minutes in, I have ten points to his two, and I basic-ally gave him those. I fake left, make a quick right in a smooth crossover, and go for the three. That baby goes in nicely. This girl's got game.

Seven makes a *T* with his hands. He pants harder than I do, and I'm the one who used to have asthma. "Time out. Water break."

I wipe my forehead with my arm. The sun glares on the court already. "How about we call it?"

"Hell no. I got some game in me. I gotta get my angles right."

"Angles? This is ball, Seven. Not selfies."

"Ay, yo!" some boy calls.

We turn around, and my breath catches. "Shit."

There are two of them. They look thirteen, fourteen years old and are wearing green Celtics jerseys. Garden Disciples, no doubt. They cross the courts, coming straight for us.

The tallest one steps to Seven. "Nigga, you Kinging?"

I can't even take this fool seriously. His voice squeaks. Daddy says there's a trick to telling OGs from Young Gs, besides their age. OGs don't start stuff, they finish it. Young Gs always start stuff.

144

"Nah, I'm neutral," Seven says.

"Ain't King your daddy?" the shorter one asks.

"Hell, no. He just messing with my momma."

"It don't even matter." The tall one flicks out a pocket knife. "Hand your shit over. Sneakers, phones, everything."

Rule of the Garden – if it doesn't involve you, it doesn't have shit to do with you. Period. The King Lords in the Escalade see everything going down. Since we don't claim their set, we don't exist.

But the boy on the merry-go-round runs over and pushes the GDs back. He lifts up his shirt, flashing his piece. "We got a problem?"

They back up. "Yeah, we got a problem," the shorter one says.

"You sure? Last time I checked, Rose Park was King territory." He looks toward the Escalade. The King Lords inside nod at us, a simple way of asking if things are cool. We nod back.

"A'ight," the tall GD says. "We got you."

The GDs leave the same way they came.

The younger King Lord slaps palms with Seven. "You straight, bruh?" he asks.

"Yeah. Good looking out, Vante."

I can't lie, he's kinda cute. Hey, just 'cause I have a boyfriend doesn't mean I can't look, and as much as Chris drools over Nicki Minaj, Beyoncé, and Amber Rose, I dare him to get mad at me for looking.

On a side note – my boyfriend clearly has a type.

This Vante guy's around my age, a little taller, with a big Afro puff and the faint signs of a mustache. He has some nice lips too. Real plump and soft.

I've looked at them too long. He licks them and smiles. "I had to make sure you and li'l momma were okay."

And that ruins it. Don't call me by a nickname if you don't know me. "Yeah, we're fine," I say.

"Them GDs helped you out anyway," he tells Seven. "She was killing you out here."

"Man, shut up," Seven says. "This is my sister, Starr."

"Oh yeah," the guy says. "You the one who work up in Big Mav's store, ain't you?"

Like I said, I get that all. The. Time. "Yep. That's me."

"Starr, this is DeVante," Seven says. "He's one of King's boys."

"DeVante?" So this is the dude Kenya fought over.

"Yeah, that's me." He looks at me from head to toe and licks his lips again. "You heard 'bout me or something?"

All that lip licking. Not cute. "Yeah, I've heard about you. And you may wanna get some Chapstick if your lips that dry, since you're licking them so much."

"Damn, it's like that?"

"What she means is thanks for helping us out," Seven says, even though that's not what I meant. "We appreciate it."

"It's all good. Them fools running around here 'cause the riots happening on their side. It's too hot for them over there."

"What you doing in the park this early anyway?" Seven asks.

He shoves his hands in his pockets and shrugs. "Posted up. You know how it go."

He's a d-boy. Damn, Kenya really knows how to pick them. Anytime drug-dealing gangbangers are your type, you've got some serious issues. Well, King *is* her daddy.

"I heard about your brother," Seven says. "I'm sorry, man. Dalvin was a cool dude."

DeVante kicks at a pebble on the court. "Thanks. Mom's taking it real hard. That's why I'm here. Had to get out the house."

Dalvin? DeVante? I tilt my head. "Your momma named y'all after them dudes from that old group Jodeci?" I only know because my parents love them some Jodeci.

"Yeah, so?"

"It was just a question. You don't have to have an attitude."

A white Tahoe screeches to a stop on the other side of the fence. Daddy's Tahoe.

His window rolls down. He's in a wifebeater and pillow marks zigzag across his face. I pray he doesn't get out because knowing Daddy his legs are ashy and he's wearing Nike flip-flops with socks. "What the hell y'all thinking, leaving the house without telling nobody?" he yells.

The King Lords across the street bust out laughing. DeVante coughs into his fist like he wants to laugh too. Seven and I look at everything but Daddy.

147

"Oh, y'all wanna act like y'all don't hear me? Answer me when I'm talking to you!"

The King Lords howl with laughter.

"Pops, we just came to play ball," Seven says.

"I don't care. All this shit going on, and y'all leave? Get in this truck!"

"Goddamn," I say under my breath. "Always gotta act a fool."

"What you say?" he barks.

The King Lords howl louder. I wanna disappear.

"Nothing," I say.

"Nah, it was something. Tell you what, don't climb the fence. Go round to the entrance. And I bet' not beat y'all there."

He drives off.

Shit.

I grab my ball, and Seven and I haul ass across the park. The last time I ran this fast, Coach was making us do suicides. We get to the entrance as Daddy pulls up. I climb in the back of the truck, and Seven's dumb butt gets in the passenger seat.

Daddy drives off. "Done lost y'all minds," he says. "People rioting, damn near calling the National Guard around here, and y'all wanna play ball."

"Why you have to embarrass us like that?" Seven snaps.

I'm so glad I'm in the backseat. Daddy turns toward Seven, not even looking at the road, and growls, "You ain't too old."

148

Seven stares ahead. Steam is just about coming off him.

Daddy looks at the road again. "Got some goddamn nerve talking to me like that 'cause some King Lords were laughing at you. What, you Kinging now?"

Seven doesn't respond.

"I'm talking to you, boy!"

"No, sir," he bites out.

"So why you care what they think? You wanna be a man so damn bad, but men don't care what nobody thinks."

He pulls into our driveway. Not even halfway up the walkway I see Momma through the screen on the door in her nightgown, her arms folded and her bare foot tapping.

"Get in this house!" she shouts.

She paces the living room as we come in. The question isn't if she'll explode but when.

Seven and I sink onto her good sofa.

"Where were y'all?" she asks. "And you better not lie."

"The basketball court," I mumble, staring at my J's.

Momma leans down close to me and puts her hand to her ear. "What was that? I didn't hear you good."

"Speak up, girl," Daddy says.

"The basketball court," I repeat louder.

"The basketball court." Momma straightens up and laughs. "She said the basketball court." Her laughter stops, and her voice gets louder with each word. "I'm walking around here, worried out my mind, and y'all at the damn basketball court!"

Somebody giggles in the hallway.

"Sekani, go to your room!" Momma says without looking that way. His feet thump hurriedly down the hall.

"I hollered and told y'all we were leaving," I say.

"Oh, she hollered," Daddy mocks. "Did you hear anybody holler, baby? 'Cause I didn't."

Momma sucks her teeth. "Neither did I. She can wake us up to ask for some money, but she can't wake us up to tell us she's going in a war zone."

"It's my fault," Seven says. "I wanted to get her out the house and do something normal."

"Baby, there's no such thing as normal right now!" says Momma. "You see what's been happening. And y'all were crazy enough to go out there like that?"

"Dumb enough is more like it," Daddy adds.

I keep my eyes on my shoes.

"Hand over your phones," Momma says.

"What?" I shriek. "That's not fair! I hollered and told y'all—"

"Starr Amara," she says through her teeth. Since my first name is only one syllable, she has to throw my middle name in there to break it down. "If you don't hand me that phone, I swear to God."

I open my mouth, but she goes, "Say something else! I dare you, say something else! I'll take all them Jordans too!"

This is some bullshit. For real. Daddy watches us; her attack dog, waiting for us to make a wrong move. That's how they work. Momma does the first round, and if it's not

150

successful, Daddy goes for the KO. And you never want Daddy to go for the KO.

Seven and I hand her our phones.

"I thought so," she says, and passes them to Daddy. "Since y'all want 'normal' so much, go get your stuff. We're going to Carlos's for the day."

"Nah, not him." Daddy motions Seven to get up. "He going to the store with me."

Momma looks at me and jerks her head toward the hall. "Go. I oughta make you take a shower, smelling like outside." As I'm leaving, she hollers, "And don't get any skimpy stuff to wear to Carlos's either!"

Ooh, she gets on my nerves. See, Chris lives down the street from Uncle Carlos. I am glad she didn't say any more in front of Daddy though.

Brickz meets me at my bedroom door. He jumps up my legs and tries to lick my face. I had about forty shoe boxes stacked in a corner, and he knocked all of them over.

I scratch behind his ears. "Clumsy dog."

I would take him with us, but they don't allow pits in Uncle Carlos's neighborhood. He settles on my bed and watches me pack. I only really need my swimsuit and some sandals, but Momma could decide to stay out there the whole weekend because of the riots. I pack a couple of outfits and get my school backpack. I throw each backpack over a shoulder. "C'mon, Brickz."

He follows me to his spot in the backyard, and I hook him up to his chain. While I refill Brickz's food and water

151

bowls, Daddy crouches beside his roses and examines the petals. He waters them like he's supposed to, but for some reason they're dry looking.

"C'mon, now," he tells them. "Y'all gotta do better than this."

Momma and Sekani wait for me in her Camry. I end up in the passenger's seat. It's childish, but I don't wanna sit this close to her right now. Unfortunately it's either sit next to her or next to Sir-Farts-a-Lot Sekani. I'm staring straight ahead, and out the corner of my eye I see her looking at me. She makes this sound like she's about to speak, but her words decide to come out as a sigh.

Good. I don't wanna talk to her either. I'm being petty as hell and don't even care.

We head for the freeway, passing the Cedar Grove projects, where we used to live. We get to Magnolia Avenue, the busiest street in Garden Heights, where most of the businesses are located. Usually on Saturday mornings, guys around the neighborhood have their cars on display, cruising up and down the street and racing each other.

Today the street's blocked off. A crowd marches down the middle of it. They're holding signs and posters of Khalil's face and are chanting, "Justice for Khalil!"

I should be out there with them, but I can't join that march, knowing I'm one of the reasons they're protesting.

"You know none of this is your fault, right?" Momma asks.

How in the world did she do that? "I know."

"I mean it, baby. It's not. You did everything right."

"But sometimes right's not good enough, huh?"

She takes my hand, and despite my annoyance I let her. It's the closest thing I get to an answer for a while.

Saturday morning traffic on the freeway moves smoothly compared to weekday traffic. Sekani puts his headphones on and plays with his tablet. Some nineties R&B songs play on the radio, and Momma sings along under her breath. When she really gets into it, she attempts all kinds of runs and goes, "Yes, girl! Yes!"

Out of nowhere she says, "You weren't breathing when you were born."

My first time hearing that. "For real?"

"Uh-huh. I was eighteen when I had you. Still a baby myself, but I thought I was grown. Wouldn't admit to anybody that I was scared to death. Your nana thought there was no way in hell I could be a good parent. Not wild Lisa.

"I was determined to prove her wrong. I stopped drinking and smoking, went to all of my appointments, ate right, took my vitamins, the whole nine. Shoot, I even played Mozart on some headphones and put them on my belly. We see what good that was. You didn't finish a month of piano lessons."

I laugh. "Sorry."

"It's okay. Like I was saying, I did everything right. I remember being in that delivery room, and when they pulled you out, I waited for you to cry. But you didn't. Everybody ran around, and your father and I kept asking what was

153

wrong. Finally the nurse said you weren't breathing.

"I freaked out. Your daddy couldn't calm me down. He was barely calm himself. After the longest minute of my life, you cried. I think I cried harder than you though. I knew I did something wrong. But one of the nurses took my hand" – Momma grabs my hand again – "looked me in the eye, and said, 'Sometimes you can do everything right and things will still go wrong. The key is to never stop doing right.'"

She holds my hand the rest of the drive.

I used to think the sun shone brighter out here in Uncle Carlos's neighborhood, but today it really does – there's no smoke lingering, and the air is fresher. All the houses have two stories. Kids play on the sidewalks and in the big yards. There are lemonade stands, garage sales, and lots of joggers. Even with all that going on, it's real quiet.

We pass Maya's house, a few streets over from Uncle Carlos's. I would text her and see if I could come over, but, you know, I don't have my phone.

"You can't visit your li'l friend today," Momma says, reading my mind once a-freaking-gain. "You're grounded."

My mouth flies wide open.

"But she can come over to Carlos's and see you."

She glances at me out the corner of her eye with a half smile. This is supposed to be the moment I hug her and thank her and tell her she's the best.

Not happening. I say, "Cool. Whatever," and sit back.

She busts out laughing. "You are so stubborn!"

"No, I'm not!"

"Yes, you are," she says. "Just like your father."

Soon as we pull into Uncle Carlos's driveway, Sekani jumps out. Our cousin Daniel waves at him from down the sidewalk with some other boys, and they're all on their bikes.

"Later, Momma," Sekani says. He runs past Uncle Carlos, who's coming out the garage, and grabs his bike. Sekani got it for Christmas, but he keeps it at Uncle Carlos's house because Momma's not about to let him ride around Garden Heights. He pedals down the driveway.

Momma hops out and calls after him, "Don't go too far!"

I get out, and Uncle Carlos meets me with a perfect Uncle Carlos hug – not too tight, but so firm that it tells me how much he loves me in a few seconds.

He kisses the top of my head twice and asks, "How are you doing, baby girl?"

"Okay." I sniff. Smoke's in the air. The good kind though. "You barbecuing?"

"Just heated the grill up. Gonna throw some burgers and chicken on for lunch."

"I hope we don't end up with food poisoning," Momma teases.

"Ah, look who's trying to be a comedian," he says. "You'll be eating your words and everything I cook, baby sis, because I'm about to throw down. Food Network doesn't have anything on me." And he pops his collar.

Lord. He's so corny sometimes.

Aunt Pam tends to the grill on the patio. My little cousin Ava sucks her thumb and hugs Aunt Pam's leg. The second she sees me, she comes running. "Starr-Starr!"

Her ponytails fly as she runs, and she launches herself into my arms. I swing her around, getting a whole lot of giggles out of her. "How's my favorite three-year-old in the whole wide world doing?"

"Good!" She sticks her wrinkly, wet thumb back in her mouth. "Hey, Auntie Leelee."

"Hey, baby. You've been good?"

Ava nods too much. No way she's been *that* good.

Aunt Pam lets Uncle Carlos handle the grill and greets Momma with a hug. She has dark-brown skin and big curly hair. Nana likes her because she comes from a "good family." Her mom is an attorney, and her dad is the first black chief of surgery at the same hospital where Aunt Pam works as a surgeon. Real-life Huxtables, I swear.

I put Ava down, and Aunt Pam hugs me extra tight. "How are you doing, sweetie?"

"Okay."

She says she understands, but nobody really does.

Nana comes busting out the back door with her arms outstretched. "My girls!"

That's the first sign something's up. She hugs me and Momma and kisses our cheeks. Nana never kisses us, and she never lets us kiss her. She says she doesn't know where our mouths have been. She frames my face with her hands, talking about, "Thank the Lord. He spared your life. Hallelujah!"

So many alarms go off in my head. Not that she wouldn't be happy that "the Lord spared my life," but this isn't Nana. At all.

She takes me and Momma by our wrists and pulls us toward the poolside loungers. "Y'all come over here and talk to me."

"But I was gonna talk to Pam—"

Nana looks at Momma and hisses through gritted teeth, "Shut the hell up, sit down, and talk to me, goddammit."

Now *that's* Nana. She sits back in a lounger and fans herself all dramatically. She's a retired theater teacher, so she does everything dramatically. Momma and I share a lounger and sit on the side of it.

"What's wrong?" Momma asks.

"When—" she begins, but plasters on a fake smile when Ava waddles over with her baby doll and a comb. Ava hands both to me and goes to play with some of her other toys.

I comb the doll's hair. That girl has me trained. Doesn't have to say anything, and I do it.

Once Ava's out of earshot, Nana says, "When y'all taking me back to my house?"

"What happened?" Momma asks.

"Keep your damn voice down!" Ironically, she's not keeping hers down. "Yesterday morning, I took some catfish out for dinner. Was gonna fry it up with some hush puppies, fries, the whole nine. I left to run some errands."

"What kinda errands?" I ask for the hell of it.

Nana cuts me "the look" and it's like seeing Momma in thirty years, with a few wrinkles and gray hairs she missed when coloring her hair (she'd whoop my behind for saying that).

"I'm grown, li'l girl," she says. "Don't ask me what I do. Anyway, I come home and that *heffa* done covered my catfish in some damn cornflakes and baked it!"

"Cornflakes?" I say, parting the doll's hair.

"Yes! Talking 'bout, 'It's healthier that way.' If I want healthy, I eat a salad."

Momma covers her mouth, and the edges of her lips are turned up. "I thought you and Pam got along."

"We did. Until she messed with my food. Now, I've dealt with a lotta things since I've been here. But that" – she holds up a finger – "is taking it too damn far. I'd rather live with you and that ex-con than deal with this."

Momma stands and kisses Nana's forehead. "You'll be all right."

Nana waves her off. When Momma leaves, she looks at me. "You okay, li'l girl? Carlos told me you were in the car with that boy when he was killed."

"Yes, ma'am, I'm okay."

"Good. And if you're not, you will be. We're strong like that."

I nod, but I don't believe it. At least not about myself.

The doorbell rings up front. I say, "I'll get it," put Ava's doll down, and go inside.

Crap. Chris is on the other side of the door. I wanna apologize to him, but dammit, I need time to prepare.

Weird though. He's pacing. The same way he does when we study for tests or before a big game. He's afraid to talk to me.

I open the door and lean against the frame. "Hey."

"Hey." He smiles, and despite everything I smile too.

"I was washing one of my dad's cars and saw you guys pull up," he says. That explains his tank top, flip-flops, and shorts. "Are you okay? I know you said you were in your text, but I wanted to be sure."

"I'm okay," I say.

"Your dad's store didn't get hit, did it?" he asks.

"Nope."

"Good."

Staring and silence.

He sighs. "Look, if this is about the condom stuff, I'll never buy one again."

"Never?"

"Well, only when you want me to." He quickly adds, "Which doesn't have to be anytime soon. Matter of fact, you don't have to ever sleep with me. Or kiss me. Hell, if you don't want me to touch you, I—"

"Chris, Chris," I say, my hands up to get him to slow down, and I'm fighting a laugh. "It's okay. I know what you mean."

"Okay."

"Okay."

159

Another round of staring and silence.

"I'm sorry, actually," I tell him, shifting my weight from foot to foot. "For giving you the silent treatment. It wasn't about the condom."

"Oh…" His eyebrows meet. "Then what was it about?"

I sigh. "I don't feel like talking about it."

"So you can be mad at me, but you can't even tell me why?"

"It has nothing to do with you."

"Yeah, it does if you're giving *me* the silent treatment," he says.

"You wouldn't understand."

"Maybe you should let me determine that myself?" he says. "Here I am, calling you, texting you, everything, and you can't tell me why you're ignoring me? That's kinda shitty, Starr."

I give him this look, and I have a strong feeling I look like Momma and Nana right now with their "I know you didn't just say that" glare.

"I told you, you wouldn't understand. So drop it."

"No." He folds his arms. "I came all the way down here—"

"All the way? Bruh, all *what* way? Down the street?"

Garden Heights Starr is all up in my voice right now.

"Yeah, down the street," he says. "And guess what? I didn't have to do that. But I did. And you can't even tell me what's going on!"

"You're white, okay?" I yell. "You're white!"

160

Silence.

"I'm white?" he says, like he's just hearing that for the first time. "What the fuck's that got to do with anything?"

"Everything! You're white, I'm black. You're rich, I'm not."

"That doesn't matter!" he says. "I don't care about that kinda stuff, Starr. I care about you."

"That kinda stuff is part of me!"

"Okay, and...? It's no big deal. God, seriously? This is what you're pissed about? *This* is why you're giving me the silent treatment?"

I stare at him, and I know, I *know*, I'm straight up looking like Lisa Janae Carter. My mouth is slightly open like hers when I or my brothers "get smart," as she calls it, I've pulled my chin back a little, and my eyebrows are raised. Shit, my hand's even on my hip.

Chris takes a small step back, just like my brothers and I do. "It just ... it doesn't make sense to me, okay? That's all."

"So like I said, you don't understand. Do you?"

Bam. If I am acting like my mom, this is one of her "see, I told you" moments.

"No. I guess I don't," he says.

Another round of silence.

Chris puts his hands in his pockets. "Maybe you can help me understand? I don't know. But I do know that not having you in my life is worse than not making beats or playing basketball. And you know how much I love making beats and playing basketball, Starr."

161

I smirk. "You call that a line?"

He bites his bottom lip and shrugs. I laugh. He does too.

"Bad line, huh?" he asks.

"Awful."

We go silent again, but it's the type of silence I don't mind. He puts his hand out for mine.

I still don't know if I'm betraying who I am by dating Chris, but I've missed him so much it hurts. Momma thinks coming to Uncle Carlos's house is normal, but Chris is the kind of normal I really want. The normal where I don't have to choose which Starr to be. The normal where nobody tells you how sorry they are or talks about "Khalil the drug dealer." Just ... normal.

That's why I can't tell Chris I'm the witness.

I take his hand, and everything suddenly feels right. No flinching and no flashbacks.

"C'mon," I say. "Uncle Carlos should have the burgers ready."

We go into the backyard, hand in hand. He's smiling, and surprisingly I am too.

CHAPTER 10

We spend the night at Uncle Carlos's house because the riots started again as soon as the sun went down. Somehow the store got spared. We should go to church and thank God for that, but Momma and I are too tired to sit through less than an hour of anything. Sekani wants to spend another day at Uncle Carlos's, so Sunday morning we return to Garden Heights without him.

Right as we get off the freeway, we're met by a police roadblock. Only one lane of traffic isn't blocked by a patrol car, and officers talk to drivers before letting them pass through.

Suddenly it's as if someone grabbed my heart and twisted it. "Can we—" I swallow. "Can we get around them?"

"Doubt it. They probably got these all around the neighborhood." Momma glances over at me and frowns. "Munch? You okay?"

I grab my door handle. They can easily grab their guns and leave us like Khalil. All the blood in our bodies pooling on the street for everybody to see. Our mouths wide open.

Our eyes staring at the sky, searching for God.

"Hey." Momma cups my cheek. "Hey, look at me."

I try to, but my eyes are filled with tears. I'm so sick of being this damn weak. Khalil may have lost his life, but I lost something too, and it pisses me off.

"It's okay," Momma says. "We got this, all right? Close your eyes if you have to."

I do.

Keep your hands visible.

No sudden moves.

Only speak when spoken to.

The seconds drag by like hours. The officer asks Momma for her ID and proof of insurance, and I beg Black Jesus to get us home, hoping there won't be a gunshot as she searches through her purse.

We finally drive off. "See, baby," she says. "Everything's fine."

Her words used to have power. If she said it was fine, it was fine. But after you've held two people as they took their last breaths, words like that don't mean shit anymore.

I haven't let go of the car door handle when we pull into our driveway.

Daddy comes out and knocks on my window. Momma rolls it down for me. "There go my girls." He smiles, but it fades into a frown. "What's wrong?"

"You about to go somewhere, baby?" Momma asks, meaning they'll talk later.

"Yeah, gotta run to the warehouse and stock up." He taps my shoulder. "Ay, wanna hang out with your daddy? I'll get you some ice cream. One of them big fat tubs that'll last 'bout a month."

I laugh even though I don't feel like it. Daddy's talented like that. "I don't need all that ice cream."

"I ain't say you needed it. When we get back, we can watch that Harry Potter shit you like so much."

"Noooooooo."

"What?" he asks.

"Daddy, you're the worst person to watch Harry Potter with. The whole time you're talking about" – I deepen my voice – "'Why don't they shoot that nigga Voldemort?'"

"Ay, it don't make sense that in all them movies and books, nobody thought to shoot him."

"If it's not that," Momma says, "you're giving your 'Harry Potter is about gangs' theory."

"It is!" he says.

Okay, so it *is* a good theory. Daddy claims the Hogwarts houses are really gangs. They have their own colors, their own hideouts, and they are always riding for each other, like gangs. Harry, Ron, and Hermione never snitch on one another, just like gangbangers. Death Eaters even have matching tattoos. And look at Voldemort. They're scared to say his name. Really, that "He Who Must Not Be Named" stuff is like giving him a street name. That's some gang-banging shit right there.

"Y'all know that make a lot of sense," Daddy says. "Just

'cause they was in England don't mean they wasn't gang-banging." He looks at me. "So you down to hang out with your old man today or what?"

I'm always down to hang out with him.

We roll through the streets, Tupac blasting through the subwoofers. He's rapping about keeping your head up, and Daddy glances at me as he raps along, like he's telling me the same thing Tupac is.

"I know you're fed up, baby" – he nudges my chin – "but keep your head up."

He sings with the chorus about how things will get easier, and I don't know if I wanna cry 'cause that's really speaking to me right now, or crack up 'cause Daddy's singing is so horrible.

Daddy says, "That was a deep dude right there. Real deep. They don't make rappers like that no more."

"You're showing your age, Daddy."

"Whatever. It's the truth. Rappers nowadays only care 'bout money, hoes, and clothes."

"Showing your age," I whisper.

"'Pac rapped 'bout that stuff too, yeah, but he also cared 'bout uplifting black people," says Daddy. "Like he took the word 'nigga' and gave it a whole new meaning – Never Ignorant Getting Goals Accomplished. And he said Thug Life meant—"

"The Hate U Give Little Infants F---s Everybody," I censor myself. This is my daddy I'm talking to, you know?

"You know 'bout that?"

"Yeah. Khalil told me what he thought it means. We were listening to Tupac right before … you know."

"A'ight, so what do you think it means?"

"You don't know?" I ask.

"I know. I wanna hear what *you* think."

Here he goes. Picking my brain. "Khalil said it's about what society feeds us as youth and how it comes back and bites them later," I say. "I think it's about more than youth though. I think it's about us, period."

"Us who?" he asks.

"Black people, minorities, poor people. Everybody at the bottom in society."

"The oppressed," says Daddy.

"Yeah. We're the ones who get the short end of the stick, but we're the ones they fear the most. That's why the government targeted the Black Panthers, right? Because they were scared of the Panthers?"

"Uh-huh," Daddy says. "The Panthers educated and empowered the people. That tactic of empowering the oppressed goes even further back than the Panthers though. Name one."

Is he serious? He always makes me think. This one takes me a second. "The slave rebellion of 1831," I say. "Nat Turner empowered and educated other slaves, and it led to one of the biggest slave revolts in history."

"A'ight, a'ight. You on it." He gives me dap. "So, what's the hate they're giving the 'little infants' in today's society?"

"Racism?"

167

"You gotta get a li'l more detailed than that. Think 'bout Khalil and his whole situation. Before he died."

"He was a drug dealer." It hurts to say that. "And possibly a gang member."

"Why was he a drug dealer? Why are so many people in our neighborhood drug dealers?"

I remember what Khalil said – he got tired of choosing between lights and food. "They need money," I say. "And they don't have a lot of other ways to get it."

"Right. Lack of opportunities," Daddy says. "Corporate America don't bring jobs to our communities, and they damn sure ain't quick to hire us. Then, shit, even if you do have a high school diploma, so many of the schools in our neighborhoods don't prepare us well enough. That's why when your momma talked about sending you and your brothers to Williamson, I agreed. Our schools don't get the resources to equip you like Williamson does. It's easier to find some crack than it is to find a good school around here.

"Now, think 'bout this," he says. "How did the drugs even get in our neighborhood? This is a multibillion-dollar industry we talking 'bout, baby. That shit is flown into our communities, but I don't know anybody with a private jet. Do you?"

"No."

"Exactly. Drugs come from somewhere, and they're destroying our community," he says. "You got folks like Brenda, who think they need them to survive, and then you got the Khalils, who think they need to sell them to survive.

The Brendas can't get jobs unless they're clean, and they can't pay for rehab unless they got jobs. When the Khalils get arrested for selling drugs, they either spend most of their life in prison, another billion-dollar industry, or they have a hard time getting a real job and probably start selling drugs again. That's the hate they're giving us, baby, a system designed against us. That's Thug Life."

"I hear you, but Khalil didn't *have* to sell drugs," I say. "You stopped doing it."

"True, but unless you're in his shoes, don't judge him. It's easier to fall into that life than it is to stay outta it, especially in a situation like his. Now, one more question."

"Really?" Damn, he's messed with my head enough.

"Yeah, really," he mocks in a high voice. I don't even sound like that. "After everything I've said, how does Thug Life apply to the protests and the riots?"

I have to think about that one for a minute. "Everybody's pissed 'cause One-Fifteen hasn't been charged," I say, "but also because he's not the first one to do something like this and get away with it. It's been happening, and people will keep rioting until it changes. So I guess the system's still giving hate, and everybody's still getting fucked?"

Daddy laughs and gives me dap. "My girl. Watch your mouth, but yeah, that's about right. And we won't stop getting fucked till it changes. That's the key. It's gotta change."

A lump forms in my throat as the truth hits me. Hard. "That's why people are speaking out, huh? Because it won't change if we don't say something."

"Exactly. We can't be silent."

"So *I* can't be silent."

Daddy stills. He looks at me.

I see the fight in his eyes. I matter more to him than a movement. I'm his baby, and I'll always be his baby, and if being silent means I'm safe, he's all for it.

This is bigger than me and Khalil though. This is about Us, with a capital U; everybody who looks like us, feels like us, and is experiencing this pain with us despite not knowing me or Khalil. My silence isn't helping Us.

Daddy fixes his gaze on the road again. He nods. "Yeah. Can't be silent."

The trip to the warehouse is hell.

You got all these people pushing big flatbeds around, and them things are hard to push as it is, and you gotta maneuver it while it's stacked with stuff. By the time we leave, I feel like Black Jesus snatched me from the depths of hell. Daddy does get me ice cream though.

Buying the stuff is only the first step. We unload it at the store, put it on the shelves, and we (scratch that, *I*) put price stickers on all those bags of chips, cookies, and candies. I should've thought about that before I agreed to hang out with Daddy. While I do the hard work, he pays bills in his office.

I'm putting stickers on the Hot Fries when somebody knocks on the front door.

"We're closed," I yell without looking. We have a sign, can't they read?

Obviously not. They knock again.

Daddy appears in the doorway of his office. "We closed!"

Another knock.

Daddy disappears into his office and returns with his Glock. He's not supposed to carry it since he's a felon, but he says that technically he doesn't carry it. He keeps it in his office.

He looks out at the person on the other side of the door. "What you want?"

"I'm hungry," a guy says. "Can I buy something?"

Daddy unlocks the door and holds it open. "You got five minutes."

"Thanks," DeVante says as he comes in. His Afro puff has become a full-blown Afro. He has this wild look about him, and I don't mean 'cause of his hair, but like in his eyes. They're puffy and red and darting around. He barely gives me a nod when he passes.

Daddy waits at the cash register with his piece.

DeVante glances outside. He looks at the chips. "Fritos, Cheetos, or Dori—" His voice trails off as he glances again. He notices me watching him and looks at the chips. "Doritos."

"Your five minutes getting shorter," Daddy says.

"Damn, man. A'ight!" DeVante grabs a bag of Fritos. "Can I get something to drink?"

"Hurry up."

DeVante goes to the refrigerators. I join Daddy at the cash register. It's so obvious something is up. DeVante keeps stretching his neck to look outside. His five minutes pass at least three times. It doesn't take anybody that long to choose between Coke, Pepsi, or Faygo. I'm sorry but it doesn't.

"A'ight, Vante." Daddy motions him to the cash register. "You trying to get the nerve to stick me up or you running from somebody?"

"Hell nah, I ain't trying to stick you up." He takes out a wad of money and sets it on the counter. "I'm paid. And I'm a King. I don't run from no-damn-body."

"No, you hide in stores," I say.

He glares at me, but Daddy tells him, "She right. You hiding from somebody. Kings or GDs?"

"It's not those GDs from the park, is it?" I ask.

"Why don't you mind your business?" he snaps.

"You came in my daddy's business, so I am minding my business."

"Ay!" Daddy says. "But for real, who you hiding from?"

DeVante stares at his scuffed-up Chucks that are beyond the help of my cleaning kit. "King," he mumbles.

"Kings or King?" Daddy asks.

"King," DeVante repeats louder. "He wants me to handle the dudes that killed my brother. I'm not trying to have that on me though."

"Yeah, I heard 'bout Dalvin," Daddy says. "I'm sorry. What happened?"

"We were at Big D's party, and some GDs stepped to him. They got into it, and one of them cowards shot him in the back."

Oh, damn. That was the same party Khalil and I were at. Those were the gunshots that made us leave.

"Big Mav, how'd you get out the game?" DeVante asks.

Daddy strokes his goatee, studying DeVante. "The hard way," he eventually says. "My daddy was a King Lord. Adonis Carter. A straight up OG."

"Yo!" DeVante says. "That's your pops? Big Don?"

"Yep. Biggest drug dealer this city ever seen."

"Yo! Man, that's crazy." DeVante's seriously fangirling right now. "I heard he had cops working for him and everything. He pulled in big money."

I heard my granddaddy was so busy pulling in big money that he didn't have time for Daddy. There are lots of pictures of Daddy when he was younger wearing mink coats, playing with expensive toys, flashing jewelry, and Grandpa Don isn't in any of the pictures.

"Probably so," Daddy says. "I wouldn't know too much 'bout that. He went to prison when I was eight. Been there ever since. I'm his only child, his son. Everybody expected me to pick up where he left off.

"I became a King Lord when I was twelve. Shit, that was the only way to survive. Somebody was always coming at me 'cause of my pops, but if I was a King Lord I had folks to watch my back. Kinging became my life. I was down to die for it, say the word."

He glances at me. "Then I became a daddy, and I realized that King Lord shit wasn't worth dying for. I wanted out. But you know how the game work, it ain't as easy as

173

saying you done. King was the crown and he was my boy, but he couldn't let me out like that. I was making good money too, and it was honestly hard to consider walking away from it."

"Yeah, King says you one of the best d-boys he ever knew," DeVante says.

Daddy shrugs. "I got it from my pops. But really I was only good 'cause I never got caught. One day, me and King took a trip to do a pickup, and we got busted. Cops wanted to know who the weapons belonged to. King had two strikes, and that charge would've meant life. I didn't have a record, so I took the charge and got a few years and probation. Loyal like a motha.

"Those were the hardest three years of my life. Growing up I was pissed at my daddy for going to prison and leaving me. And there I was, in the same prison as him, missing out on my babies' lives."

DeVante's eyebrows meet. "You were in prison with your pops?"

Daddy nods. "All my life, people made him sound like a real king, you know what I'm saying? A legend. But he was a weak old man, regretting the time he missed with me. Realest thing he ever told me was, 'Don't repeat my mistakes.'" Daddy looks at me again. "And I was doing that. I missed first days of school, all that. Had my baby wanting to call somebody else daddy 'cause I wasn't there."

I look away. He knows how close Uncle Carlos and I became.

"I was officially done with the King Lord shit, drug shit, all of it," Daddy says. "And since I took that charge, King agreed to let me out. It made those three years worth it."

DeVante's eyes dim like they do when he talks about his brother. "You had to go to prison to get out?"

"I'm the exception, not the rule," Daddy says. "When people say it's for life, it's for life. You gotta be willing to die in it or die for it. You want out?"

"I don't wanna go to prison."

"He didn't ask you that," I say. "He asked if you wanted out."

DeVante is quiet for a long time. He looks up at Daddy and says, "I just wanna be alive, man."

Daddy strokes his goatee. He sighs. "A'ight. I'll help you. But I promise, you go back to slinging or banging, you'll wish King would've got you when I'm done. You go to school?"

"Yeah."

"What your grades look like?" Daddy asks.

He shrugs.

"What the hell is this?" Daddy imitates DeVante's shrug. "You know what grades you get, so what kind?"

"I mean, I get As and Bs and shit," DeVante says. "I ain't dumb."

"A'ight, good. We gon' make sure you stay in school too."

"Man, I can't go back to Garden High," DeVante says. "All them King Lords up in there. You know that's a death wish, right?"

"I ain't say you was going there. We'll figure something out. In the meantime you can work here in the store. You been staying home at night?"

"Nah. King got his boys watching for me over there."

"Of course he do," Daddy mumbles. "We'll figure something out with that too. Starr, show him how to do the price stickers."

"You're really hiring him, just like that?" I ask.

"Whose store is this, Starr?"

"Yours, but—"

"'Nuff said. Show him how to do the price stickers."

DeVante snickers. I wanna punch him in his throat.

"C'mon," I mumble.

We sit crossed-legged in the chip aisle. Daddy locks the front door and goes back in his office. I grab a jumbo bag of Hot Cheetos and slap a ninety-nine-cent sticker on them.

"You supposed to show me how to do it," DeVante says.

"I am showing you. Watch."

I grab another bag. He leans real close over my shoulder. Too close. Breathing in my ear and shit. I move my head and look at him. "Do you mind?"

"What's your problem with me?" he asks. "You caught an attitude yesterday, soon as I walked up. I ain't did nothing to you."

I put a sticker on some Doritos. "No, but you did it to Denasia. And Kenya. And who knows how many other girls in Garden Heights."

"Hold up, I ain't do nothing to Kenya."

"You asked for her number, didn't you? Even though you're with Denasia."

"I'm not with Denasia. I just danced with her at that party," he says. "She the one who wanted to act like she was my girlfriend and got mad 'cause I was talking to Kenya. If I wouldn't have been dealing with them, I could've—" He swallows. "I could've helped Dalvin. By the time I got to him, he was on the floor, bleeding. All I could do was hold him."

I see myself sitting in a pool of blood too. "And try to tell him it would be okay, even though you knew—"

"There was no chance in hell it would be."

We go quiet.

I get one of those weird déjà-vu moments though. I see myself sitting cross-legged like I am now, but I'm showing Khalil how to do the price stickers.

We couldn't help Khalil with his situation before he died. Maybe we can help DeVante.

I hand him a bag of Hot Fries. "I'm only gonna explain how to use this price gun one time, and you better pay attention."

He grins. "My attention's all yours, li'l momma."

Later, when I'm supposed to be asleep, my mom tells my dad in the hallway, "So he's hiding from King, and you think he should hide here?"

DeVante. Apparently, Daddy couldn't "figure it out" and decided that DeVante should stay with us. Daddy dropped the two of us off a couple of hours ago before heading back to the store to protect it from the rioters. He just got back. He said our house is the one place King won't look for DeVante.

"I had to do something," Daddy says.

"I understand that, and I know you think this is your do-over with Khalil—"

"It ain't like that."

"Yeah, it is," she says softly. "I get it, baby. I have a ton of regrets regarding Khalil myself. But this? This is dangerous for our family."

"It's just for now. DeVante can't stay in Garden Heights. This neighborhood ain't good for him."

"Wait. It's not good for him, but it's fine for our kids?"

"C'mon, Lisa. It's late. I'm not trying to hear this right now. I been at that store all night."

"And I've been up all night, worried about you! Worried about my babies being in this neighborhood."

"They fine! They ain't involved in none of that banging shit."

Momma scoffs. "Yeah, so fine that I have to drive almost an hour to get them to a decent school. And God forbid Sekani wants to play outside. I gotta drive to my brother's house, where I don't have to worry about him getting shot like his sister's best friend did."

It's messed up that she could mean either Khalil or Natasha.

"A'ight, let's say we move," Daddy said. "Then what?

We just like all the other sellouts who leave and turn their backs on the neighborhood. We can change stuff around here, but instead we run? That's what you wanna teach our kids?"

"I want my kids to enjoy life! I get it, Maverick, you wanna help your people out. I do too. That's why I bust my butt every day at that clinic. But moving out of the neighborhood won't mean you're not real and it won't mean you can't help this community. You need to figure out what's more important, your family or Garden Heights. I've already made my choice."

"What you saying?"

"I'm saying I'll do what I gotta do for my babies."

There are footsteps, then a door closes.

I stay up most of the night, wondering what that means for them. Us. Okay, yeah, they've talked about moving before, but they weren't arguing about it like this until after Khalil died.

If they break up, it'll be one more thing One-Fifteen takes from me.

CHAPTER 11

Monday morning, I know something is up when I first step into Williamson. Folks are quiet as hell. Well, whispering really, in little huddles in the halls and the atrium like they're discussing plays during a basketball game.

Hailey and Maya find me before I find them. "Did you get the text?" Hailey asks.

That's the first thing she says. No hey or anything. I still don't have my phone, so I'm like, "What text?"

She shows me hers. There's a big group text with about a hundred names on it. Hailey's older brother, Remy, sent out the first message.

Protesting today @ 1st period.

Then curly-haired, dimpled Luke replied:

Hell yeah. Free day. I'm game.

And Remy came back with:

That's the point, dumbass.

It's like somebody hit a pause button on my heart. "They're protesting for Khalil?"

"Yeah," Hailey says, all giddy and shit. "Perfect timing

too. I so did not study for that English exam. This is, like, the first time Remy actually came up with a good idea to get out of class. I mean, it's kinda messed up that we're protesting a *drug dealer's* death, but—"

All my Williamson rules go out the door, and Starr from Garden Heights shows up. "What the fuck that got to do with it?"

Their mouths open into perfectly shaped *O*'s. "Like, I mean … if he was a drug dealer," Hailey says, "that explains why…"

"He got killed even though he wasn't doing shit? So it's cool he got killed? But I thought you were protesting it?"

"We are! God, lighten up, Starr," she says. "I thought you'd be all over this, considering your obsession on Tumblr lately."

"You know what?" I say, one second from *really* going off. "Leave me alone. Have fun in your little protest."

I wanna fight every person I pass, Floyd Mayweather style. They're so damn excited about getting a day off. Khalil's in a grave. He can't get a day off from that shit. I live it every single day too.

In class I toss my backpack on the floor and throw myself into my seat. When Hailey and Maya come in, I give them a stank-eye and silently dare them to say shit to me.

I'm breaking all of my Williamson Starr rules with zero fucks to give.

Chris gets there before the bell rings, headphones draped around his neck. He comes down my aisle and squeezes my nose, going, "Honk, honk," because for some reason it's hilarious to him. Usually I laugh and swat at him, but today… Yeah, I'm not in the mood. I just swat. Kinda hard too.

He goes, "Ow," and gives his hand a quick shake. "What's wrong with you?"

I don't respond. If I open my mouth, I'll explode.

He crouches beside my desk and shakes my thigh. "Starr? You okay?"

Our teacher, balding, stumpy Mr. Warren, clears his throat. "Mr. Bryant, my class is not the *Love Connection*. Please have a seat."

Chris slides into the desk next to mine. "What's wrong with her?" he whispers to Hailey.

She plays dumb and says, "Dunno."

Mr. Warren tells us to take out our MacBooks and begins the lesson on British literature. Not even five minutes in, someone says, "Justice for Khalil."

"Justice for Khalil," the others chant. "Justice for Khalil."

Mr. Warren tells them to stop, but they get louder and pound their fists on the desks.

I wanna puke and scream and cry.

My classmates stampede toward the door. Maya's the last one out. She glances back at me then at Hailey who motions her to come on. Maya follows her out.

I think I'm done following Hailey.

In the hall, chants for Khalil go off like sirens. Unlike Hailey, some of them may not care that he was a drug dealer. They might be almost as upset as I am. But since I know *why*

182

Remy started this protest, I stay in my seat.

Chris does too for some reason. His desk scrapes the floor as it scoots closer to mine until they touch. He brushes my tears with his thumb.

"You knew him, didn't you?" he says.

I nod.

"Oh," says Mr. Warren. "I am so sorry, Starr. You don't have to — you can call your parents, you know?"

I wipe my face. The last thing I want is Momma making a fuss because I can't handle all this. Worse, I don't wanna be unable to handle it. "Can you continue with the lesson, sir?" I ask. "The distraction would be nice."

He smiles sadly and does as I ask.

For the rest of the day, sometimes Chris and I are the only ones in our classes. Sometimes one or two other people join us. People go out of their way to tell me they think Khalil's death is bullshit, but that Remy's reason for protesting is bullshit too. I mean, this sophomore girl comes up to me in the hall and explains that she supports the cause but decided to go back to class after she heard why they were really protesting.

They act like I'm the official representative of the black race and they owe me an explanation. I think I understand though. If I sit out a protest, I'm making a statement, but if they sit out a protest, they look racist.

At lunch, Chris and I head to our table near the vending machines. Jess with her perfect pixie cut is the only one there, eating cheese fries and reading her phone.

"Hey?" I ask more than say. I'm surprised she's here.

"S'up?" She nods. "Have a seat. As you can see, there's plenty of room."

I sit beside her, and Chris sits on the other side of me. Jess and I have played basketball together for three years, and she's put her head on my shoulder for two of them, but I'm ashamed to admit I don't know much about her. I do know she's a senior, her parents are attorneys, and she works at a bookstore. I didn't know that she'd skip the protest.

I guess I'm staring at her hard, because she says, "I don't use dead people to get out of class."

If I wasn't straight I would totally date her for saying that. This time I rest my head on her shoulder.

She pats my hair and says, "White people do stupid shit sometimes."

Jess is white.

Seven and Layla join us with their trays. Seven holds his fist out to me. I bump it.

"Sev-en," Jess says, and they fist-bump too. I had no idea they were cool like that. "I take it we're protesting the 'Get Out of Class' protest?"

"Yep," Seven says. "Protesting the 'Get Out of Class' protest."

Seven and I get Sekani after school, and he won't shut up about the news cameras he saw from his classroom window, because he's Sekani and he came into this world looking for a camera. I have too many selfies of him on my phone

184

giving the "light skin face," his eyes squinted and eyebrows raised.

"Are y'all gonna be on the news?" he asks.

"Nah," says Seven. "Don't need to be."

We could go home, lock the door, and fight over the TV like we always do, or we could help Daddy at the store. We go to the store.

Daddy stands in the doorway, watching a reporter and camera operator set up in front of Mr. Lewis's shop. Of course, when Sekani sees the camera, he says, "Ooh, I wanna be on TV!"

"Shut up," I say. "No you don't."

"Yes, I do. You don't know what I want!"

The car stops, and Sekani pushes my seat forward, sending my chin into the dashboard as he jumps out. "Daddy, I wanna be on TV!"

I rub my chin. His hyper butt is gonna kill me one day.

Daddy holds Sekani by the shoulders. "Calm down, man. You not gon' be on TV."

"What's going on?" Seven asks when we get out.

"Some cops got jumped around the corner," Daddy says, one arm around Sekani's chest to keep him still.

"Jumped?" I say.

"Yeah. They pulled them out their patrol car and stomped them. Gray Boys."

The code name for King Lords. Damn.

"I heard what happened at y'all school," Daddy says. "Everything cool?"

"Yeah." I give the easy answer. "We're good."

Mr. Lewis adjusts his clothes and runs a hand over his Afro. The reporter says something, and he lets out a belly-jiggling laugh.

"What this fool 'bout to say?" Daddy wonders.

"We go live in five," says the camera operator, and all I can think is, *Please don't put Mr. Lewis on live TV.* "Four, three, two, one."

"That's right, Joe," the reporter says. "I'm here with Mr. Cedric Lewis Jr., who witnessed the incident involving the officers today. Can you tell us what you saw, Mr. Lewis?"

"He ain't witness nothing," Daddy tells us. "Was in his shop the whole time. I told him what happened!"

"I sholl can," Mr. Lewis says. "Them boys pulled those officers out their car. They weren't doing nothing either. Just sitting there and got beat like dogs. Ridiculous! You hear me? Re-damn-diculous!"

Somebody's gonna turn Mr. Lewis into a meme. He's making a fool out of himself and doesn't even know it.

"Do you think that it was retaliation for the Khalil Harris case?" the reporter asks.

"I sholl do! Which is stupid. These thugs been terrorizing Garden Heights for years, how they gon' get mad now? What, 'cause they didn't kill him themselves? The president and all'a them searching for terrorists, but I'll name one right now they can come get."

"Don't do it, Mr. Lewis," Daddy prays. "Don't do it."

Of course, he does. "His name King, and he live right

here in Garden Heights. Probably the biggest drug dealer in the city. He over that King Lords gang. Come get him if you wanna get somebody. Wasn't nobody but his boys who did that to them cops anyway. We sick of this! Somebody march 'bout that!"

Daddy covers Sekani's ears. Every cuss word that follows equals a dollar in Sekani's jar if he hears it. "Shit," Daddy hisses. "Shit, shit, shit. This motha—"

"He snitched," says Seven.

"On live TV," I add.

Daddy keeps saying, "Shit, shit, shit."

"Do you think that the curfew the mayor announced today will prevent incidents like this?" the reporter asks Mr. Lewis.

I look at Daddy. "What curfew?"

He takes his hands off Sekani's ears. "Every business in Garden Heights gotta close by nine. And nobody can be in the streets after ten. Lights out, like in prison."

"So you'll be home tonight, Daddy?" Sekani asks.

Daddy smiles and pulls him closer. "Yeah, man. After you do your homework, I can show you a thang or two on Madden."

The reporter wraps up her interview. Daddy waits until she and the camera operator leave and then goes over to Mr. Lewis. "You crazy?" he asks.

"What? 'Cause I told the truth?" Mr. Lewis says.

"Man, you can't be going on live TV, snitching like that. You a dead man walking, you know that, right?"

"I ain't scared of that nigga!" Mr. Lewis says real loud, for everybody to hear. "You scared of him?"

"Nah, but I know how the game work."

"I'm too old for games! You oughta be too!"

"Mr. Lewis, listen—"

"Nah, you listen here, boy. I fought a war, came back, and fought one here. See this?" He lifts up his pants leg, revealing a plaid sock over a prosthetic. "Lost it in the war. This right here." He lifts his shirt to his underarm. There's a thin pink scar stretching from his back to his swollen belly. "Got it after some white boys cut me 'cause I drank from their fountain." He lets his shirt fall down. "I done faced a whole lot worse than some so-called King. Ain't nothing he can do but kill me, and if that's how I gotta go for speaking the truth, that's how I gotta go."

"You don't get it," Daddy says.

"Yeah I do. Hell, I get you. Walking around here, claiming you ain't a gangster no more, claiming you trying to change stuff, but still following all'a that 'don't snitch' mess. And you teaching them kids the same thing, ain't you? King still controlling your dumb ass, and you too stupid to realize it."

"Stupid? How you gon' call me stupid when you the one snitching on live TV!"

A familiar *whoop-whoop* sound alarms us.

Oh God.

The patrol car with flashing lights cruises down the street. It stops next to Daddy and Mr. Lewis.

Two officers get out. One black, one white. Their hands linger too close to the guns at their waists.

No, no, no.

"We got a problem here?" the black one asks, looking squarely at Daddy. He's bald just like Daddy, but older, taller, bigger.

"No, sir, officer," Daddy says. His hands that were once in his jeans pockets are visible at his sides.

"You sure about that?" the younger white one asks. "It didn't seem that way to us."

"We were just talking, officers," Mr. Lewis says, much softer than he was minutes ago. His hands are at his sides too. His parents must've had the talk with him when he was twelve.

"To me it looks like this young man was harassing you, sir," the black one says, still looking at Daddy. He hasn't looked at Mr. Lewis yet. I wonder if it's because Mr. Lewis isn't wearing an NWA T-shirt. Or because there aren't tattoos all on his arms. Or because he's not wearing somewhat baggy jeans and a backwards cap.

"You got some ID on you?" the black cop asks Daddy.

"Sir, I was about to go back to my store—"

"I said do you have some ID on you?"

My hands shake. Breakfast, lunch, and everything else churns in my stomach, ready to come back up my throat. They're gonna take Daddy from me.

"What's going on?"

I turn around. Tim, Mr. Reuben's nephew, walks over

189

to us. People have stopped on the sidewalk across the street.

"I'm gonna reach for my ID," Daddy says. "It's in my back pocket. A'ight?"

"Daddy—" I say.

Daddy keeps his eyes on the officer. "Y'all, go in the store, a'ight? It's okay."

We don't move though.

Daddy's hand slowly goes to his back pocket, and I look from his hands to theirs, watching to see if they're gonna make a move for their guns.

Daddy removes his wallet, the leather one I bought him for Father's Day with his initials embossed on it. He shows it to them.

"See? My ID is in here."

His voice has never sounded so small.

The black officer takes the wallet and opens it. "Oh," he says. *"Maverick Carter."*

He exchanges a look with his partner.

Both of them look at me.

My heart stops.

They've realized I'm the witness.

There must be a file that lists my parents' names on it. Or the detectives blabbed, and now everyone at the station knows our names. Or they could've gotten it from Uncle Carlos somehow. I don't know how it happened, but it happened. And if something happens to Daddy...

The black officer looks at him. "Get on the ground, hands behind your back."

"But—"

"On the ground, face-down!" he yells. "Now!"

Daddy looks at us. His expression apologizes for the fact that we have to see this.

He gets down on one knee and lowers himself to the ground, face-down. His hands go behind his back, and his fingers interlock.

Where's that camera operator now? Why can't this be on the news?

"Now, wait a minute, Officer," Mr. Lewis says. "Me and him were just talking."

"Sir, go inside," the white cop tells him.

"But he didn't do anything!" Seven says.

"Boy, go inside!" the black cop says.

"No! That's my father, and—"

"Seven!" Daddy yells.

Even though he's lying on the concrete, there's enough authority in his voice to make Seven shut up.

The black officer checks Daddy while his partner glances around at all of the onlookers. There's quite a few of us now. Ms. Yvette and a couple of her clients stand in her doorway, towels around the clients' shoulders. A car has stopped in the street.

"Everyone, go about your own business," the white one says.

"No, sir," says Tim. "This is our business."

The black cop keeps his knee on Daddy's back as he searches him. He pats him down once, twice, three times,

191

just like One-Fifteen did Khalil. Nothing.

"Larry," the white cop says.

The black one, who must be Larry, looks up at him, then at all the people who have gathered around.

Larry takes his knee off Daddy's back and stands. "Get up," he says.

Slowly, Daddy gets to his feet.

Larry glances at me. Bile pools in my mouth. He turns to Daddy and says, "I'm keeping an eye on you, boy. Remember that."

Daddy's jaw looks rock hard.

The cops drive off. The car that had stopped in the street leaves, and all of the onlookers go on about their business. One person hollers out, "It's all right, Maverick."

Daddy looks at the sky and blinks the way I do when I don't wanna cry. He clenches and unclenches his hands.

Mr. Lewis touches his back. "C'mon, son."

He guides Daddy our way, but they pass us and go into the store. Tim follows them.

"Why did they do Daddy like that?" Sekani asks softly. He looks at me and Seven with tears in his eyes.

Seven wraps an arm around him. "I don't know, man."

I know.

I go in the store.

DeVante leans against a broom near the cash register, wearing one of those ugly green aprons Daddy tries to make me and Seven wear when we work in the store.

There's a pang in my chest. Khalil wore one too.

DeVante's talking to Kenya as she holds a basket full of groceries. When the bell on the door clangs behind me, both of them look my way.

"Yo, what happened?" DeVante asks.

"Was that the cops outside?" says Kenya.

From here I see Mr. Lewis and Tim standing in the doorway of Daddy's office. He must be in there.

"Yeah," I answer Kenya, heading toward the back. Kenya and DeVante follow me, asking about fifty million questions that I don't have time to answer.

Papers are scattered all on the office floor. Daddy's hunched over his desk, his back moving up and down with each heavy breath.

He pounds the desk. "Fuck!"

Daddy once told me there's a rage passed down to every black man from his ancestors, born the moment they couldn't stop the slave masters from hurting their families. Daddy also said there's nothing more dangerous than when that rage is activated.

"Let it out, son," Mr. Lewis tells him.

"Fuck them pigs, man," Tim says. "They only did that shit 'cause they know 'bout Starr."

Wait. What?

Daddy glances over his shoulder. His eyes are puffy and wet, like he's been crying. "The hell you talking 'bout, Tim?"

"One of the homeboys saw you, Lisa, and your baby girl getting out an ambulance at the crime scene that night,"

Tim says. "Word spread around the neighborhood, and folks think she's the witness they been talking 'bout on the news."

Oh.

Shit.

"Starr, go ring Kenya up," Daddy says. "Vante, finish them floors."

I head for the cash register, passing Seven and Sekani.

The neighborhood knows.

I ring Kenya up, my stomach knotted the whole time. If the neighborhood knows, it won't be long until people outside of Garden Heights know. And then what?

"You rang that up twice," Kenya says.

"Huh?"

"The milk. You rang it up twice, Starr."

"Oh."

I cancel one of the milks and put the carton into a bag. Kenya's probably cooking for herself and Lyric tonight. She does that sometimes. I ring up the rest of her stuff, take her money, and hand her the change.

She stares at me a second, then says, "Were you really the one with him?"

My throat is thick. "Does it matter?"

"Yeah, it matters. Why you keeping quiet 'bout it? Like you hiding or something."

"Don't say it that way."

"But it is that way. Right?"

I sigh. "Kenya, stop. You don't understand, all right?"

Kenya folds her arms. "What's to understand?"

194

"A lot!" I don't mean to yell, but damn. "I can't go around telling people that shit."

"Why not?"

"Because! You ain't see what the cops just did to my dad 'cause they know I'm the witness."

"So you gon' let the police stop you from speaking out for Khalil? I thought you cared about him way more than that."

"I do." I care more than she may ever know. "I already talked to the cops, Kenya. Nothing happened. What else am I supposed to do?"

"Go on TV or something, I don't know," she says. "Tell everybody what really happened that night. They're not even giving his side of the story. You're letting them trash-talk him—"

"Excuse— How the hell am I letting them do anything?"

"You hear all the stuff they're saying 'bout him on the news, calling him a thug and stuff, and you know that ain't Khalil. I bet if he was one of your private school friends, you'd be all on TV, defending him and shit."

"Are you for real?"

"Hell yeah," she says. "You dropped him for them bougie-ass kids, and you know it. You probably would've dropped me if I didn't come around 'cause of my brother."

"That's not true!"

"You sure?"

I'm not.

Kenya shakes her head. "Fucked-up part about this?

195

The Khalil I know would've jumped on TV in a hot second and told everybody what happened that night if it meant defending you. And you can't do the same for him."

It's a verbal slap. The worst kind too, because it's the truth.

Kenya gets her bags. "I'm just saying, Starr. If I could change what happens at my house with my momma and daddy, I would. Here you are, with a chance to help change what happens in our *whole neighborhood*, and you staying quiet. Like a coward."

Kenya leaves. Tim and Mr. Lewis aren't far behind her. Tim gives me the black power fist on his way out. I don't deserve it though.

I head to Daddy's office. Seven's standing in the doorway, and Daddy's sitting on his desk. Sekani's next to him, nodding along to whatever Daddy's saying but looking sad. Reminds me of the time Daddy and Momma had the talk with me. Guess Daddy decided not to wait until Sekani's twelve.

Daddy sees me. "Sev, go cover the cash register. Take Sekani with you. 'Bout time he learned."

"Aww, man," Sekani groans. Don't blame him. The more you learn to do at the store, the more you're expected to do at the store.

Daddy pats the now-empty spot beside him on the desk. I hop up on it. His office has just enough space for the desk and a file cabinet. Framed photographs crowd the walls, like the one of him and Momma at the courthouse the day they got married, her belly (a.k.a. me) big and round; pictures of me and my brothers as babies, and this one picture from about seven years ago when my parents took the three of us to the mall for one of those J. C. Penney family portraits. They dressed alike in baseball jerseys, baggy jeans, and Timberlands. Tacky.

"You a'ight?" Daddy asks.

"Are you?"

"I will be," he says. "Just hate that you and your brothers had to see that shit."

"They only did it 'cause of me."

"Nah, baby. They started that before they knew 'bout you."

"But that didn't help." I stare at my J's as I kick my feet back and forth. "Kenya called me a coward for not speaking out."

"She didn't mean it. She going through a lot, that's all. King throwing Iesha around like a rag doll every single night."

"But she's right." My voice cracks. I'm this close to crying. "I am a coward. After seeing what they did to you, I don't wanna say shit now."

"Hey." Daddy takes my chin so I have no choice but to look at him. "Don't fall for that trap. That's what they want. If you don't wanna speak out, that's up to you, but don't let it be because you're scared of them. Who do I tell you that you have to fear?"

"Nobody but God. And you and Momma. Especially Momma when she's extremely pissed."

He chuckles. "Yeah. The list ends there. You ain't got nothing or nobody else to fear. You see this?" He rolls up his shirt sleeve, revealing the tattoo of my baby picture on his upper arm. "What it say at the bottom?"

"Something to live for, something to die for," I say, without really looking. I've seen it my whole life.

"Exactly. You and your brothers are something to live for, and something to die for, and I'll do whatever I gotta do to protect you." He kisses my forehead. "If you're ready to talk, baby, talk. I got your back."

CHAPTER 12

I'm luring Brickz inside when it passes out front.

I watch it crawl down the street for the longest time till I get the sense to alert somebody. "Daddy!"

He looks up from pulling weeds around his bell peppers. "Are they for real with that?"

The tank resembles the ones they show on the news when talking about war in the Middle East. It's the size of two Hummers. The blue-and-white lights on the front make the street almost as bright as it is in daytime. An officer is positioned on top, wearing a vest and a helmet. He points his rifle ahead.

A voice booms from the armored vehicle, "All persons found violating the curfew will be subject to arrest."

Daddy pulls more weeds. "Some bullshit."

Brickz follows the piece of bologna I dangle in front of him all the way to his spot in the kitchen. He sits there all content, chomping on it and the rest of his food. Brickz won't act crazy as long as Daddy's home.

All of us are kinda like Brickz, really. Daddy being

home means Momma won't sit up all night, Sekani won't flinch all the time, and Seven won't have to be the man of the house. I'll sleep better too.

Daddy comes in, dusting caked dirt off his hands. "Them roses dying. Brickz, you been pissing on my roses?"

Brickz's head perks up. He locks his eyes with Daddy's but eventually lowers his head.

"I bet' not catch you doing it," Daddy says. "Or we gon' have a problem."

Brickz lowers his eyes too.

I grab a paper towel and a slice of pizza from the box on the counter. This is like my fourth slice tonight. Momma bought two huge pies from Sal's on the other side of the freeway. Italians own it, so the pizza is thin, herby (is that a word?), and good.

"You finished your homework?" Daddy asks.

"Yep." A lie.

He washes his hands at the kitchen sink. "Got any tests this week?"

"Trig on Friday."

"You studied for it?"

"Yep." Another lie.

"Good." He gets the grapes out the refrigerator. "You still got that old laptop? The one you had before we bought you that expensive-ass fruit one?"

I laugh. "It's an Apple MacBook, Daddy."

"It damn sure wasn't the price of an apple. Anyway, you got the old one?"

"Yeah."

"Good. Give it to Seven. Tell him to look over it and make sure it's a'ight. I want DeVante to have it."

"Why?"

"You pay bills?"

"No."

"Then I ain't gotta answer that."

That's how he gets out of almost every argument with me. I should buy one of those cheap magazine subscriptions and say, "Yeah, I pay a bill, and what?" It won't matter though.

I head to my room after I finish my pizza. Daddy's already gone to his and Momma's room. Their TV's on, and they're both lying on their stomachs on the bed, one of her legs on his as she types on her laptop. It's oddly adorable. Sometimes I watch them to get an idea of what I want one day.

"You still mad at me 'bout DeVante?" Daddy asks her. She doesn't answer, keeping her eyes on her laptop. He scrunches up his nose and gets all in her face. "You still mad at me? Huh? You still mad at me?"

She laughs and playfully pushes at him. "Move, boy. No, I'm not mad at you. Now give me a grape."

He grins and feeds her a grape, and I just can't. The cuteness is too much. Yeah, they're my parents, but they're my OTP. Seriously.

Daddy watches whatever she's doing on the computer, feeding her a grape every time he eats one. She's probably uploading the latest family snapshots on Facebook for our out-of-town relatives. With everything that's going on, what can she say? "Sekani saw cops harass his daddy, but he's doing so well in school. #ProudMom." Or, "Starr saw her best friend die, keep her in your prayers, but my baby made the honor roll again. #Blessed." Or even, "Tanks are rolling by outside, but Seven's been accepted into six colleges so far. #HeIsGoingPlaces."

I go to my room. Both my old and new laptops are on my desk, which is a mess. There's a huge pair of Daddy's Jordans next to my old laptop. The yellowed bottoms of the sneakers face the lamp, and a layer of Saran Wrap protects my concoction of detergent and toothpaste that'll eventually clean them. Watching yellowed soles turn icy again is as satisfying as squeezing a blackhead and getting all the gunk out. Ah-maz-ing.

According to the lie I told Daddy, my homework is supposed to be done, but I've been on a "Tumblr break," a.k.a. I haven't started my homework and have spent the last two hours on Tumblr. I started a new blog – *The Khalil I Know*. It doesn't have my name on it, just pictures of Khalil. In the first one he's thirteen with an Afro. Uncle Carlos took us to a ranch so we could "get a taste of country life," and Khalil's looking side-eyed at a horse that's beside him. I remember him saying, "If this thing makes a wrong move, I'm running!"

On Tumblr, I captioned the picture: "The Khalil I know was afraid of animals." I tagged it with his name. One person liked it and reblogged it. Then another and another.

That made me post more pictures, like one of us in a bathtub when we were four. You can't see our private parts because of all the suds, and I'm looking away from the camera. Ms. Rosalie's sitting on the side of the tub, beaming at us, and Khalil's beaming right back at her. I wrote, "The Khalil I know loved bubble baths almost as much as he loved his grandma."

In just two hours, hundreds of people have liked and reblogged the pictures. I know it's not the same as getting on the news like Kenya said, but I hope it helps. It's helping me at least.

Other people posted about Khalil, uploaded artwork of him, posted pictures of him that they show on the news. I think I've reblogged every single one.

Funny though: somebody posted a video clip of Tupac from back in the day. Okay, so every video clip of Tupac is from back in the day. He's got a little kid on his lap and is wearing a backwards snapback that would be fly now. He explains Thug Life like Khalil said he did – The Hate U Give Little Infants Fucks Everybody. 'Pac spells out "Fucks" because that kid is looking dead in his face. When Khalil told me what it meant I kinda understood it. I really understand it now.

I grab my old laptop when my phone buzzes on my desk. Momma returned it earlier – hallelujah, thank you, Black Jesus. She said it's only in case there's another situation at school. I got it back though, don't really care why. I'm hoping it's a text from Kenya. I sent her the link to my new Tumblr earlier. Thought she'd like to see it since she kinda pushed me to do it.

But it's Chris. He took note from Seven with his all-caps texts:

OMG!

THIS *FRESH PRINCE* EPISODE

WILL'S DAD DIDN'T TAKE HIM WITH HIM

THE ASSHOLE CAME BACK AND LEFT HIM AGAIN

NOW HE'S HAVING A BREAKDOWN WITH UNCLE PHIL

MY EYES ARE SWEATING

Understandable. That's seriously the saddest episode ever. I text Chris back:

Sorry :(. And your eyes aren't sweating. You're crying, babe.

He replies:

LIES!

I say:

You ain't gotta lie, Craig. You ain't gotta lie.

He responds:

DID YOU REALLY USE A LINE FROM FRIDAY ON ME???

So watching nineties movies is kinda our thing too. I text back:

Yep ;)

He replies:

BYE, FELICIA!

I take the laptop to Seven's room, phone in hand in case

204

Chris has another *Fresh Prince* breakdown. Some reggae chants meet me in the hall, followed by Kendrick Lamar rapping about being a hypocrite. Seven sits on the side of the lower bunk, an open computer tower at his feet. With his head down, his dreads hang loosely and make a curtain in front of his face. DeVante sits cross-legged on the floor. His Afro bobs to the song.

A zombie version of Steve Jobs watches them from a poster on the wall along with all these superheroes and *Star Wars* characters. There's a Slytherin comforter on the bottom bunk that I swear I'll steal one day. Seven and I are reverse HP fans – we liked the movies first, then the books. I got Khalil and Natasha hooked on them too. Momma found the first movie for a dollar at a thrift store back when we lived in the Cedar Grove projects. Seven and I said we were Slytherins since almost all Slytherins were rich. When you're a kid in a one-bedroom in the projects, rich is the best thing anybody can be.

Seven removes a silver box from the computer and examines it. "It's not even that old."

"What are you doing?" I ask.

"Big D asked me to fix his computer. It needs some new DVD drives. He burnt his out making all them bootlegs."

My brother is the unofficial Garden Heights tech guy. Old ladies, hustlers, and everybody in between pay him to fix their computers and phones. He makes good money like that too.

A black garbage bag leans against the foot of the bunk

bed with some clothes sticking out the top of it. Somebody put it over the fence and left it in our front yard. Seven, Sekani, and I found it when we came home from the store. We thought it may have been DeVante's, but Seven looked inside and everything in it belonged to him. The stuff he had at his momma's house.

He called Iesha. She said she was putting him out. King told her to.

"Seven, I'm sorry—"

"It's okay, Starr."

"But she shouldn't have—"

"I said it's okay." He glances up at me. "All right? Don't sweat it."

"All right," I say as my phone vibrates. I hand DeVante the laptop and look. Still no response from Kenya. Instead it's a text from Maya.

Are u mad @ us?

"What's this for?" DeVante asks, staring at the laptop.

"Daddy wants you to have it. But he said let Seven check it out first," I tell him as I reply to Maya.

What do u think?

"What he want me to have it for?" DeVante asks.

"Maybe he wants to see if you actually know how to operate one," I tell DeVante.

"I know how to use a computer," DeVante says. He hits Seven, who's snickering.

My phone buzzes three times. Maya has responded.

Definitely mad.

Can the 3 of us talk?

Things have been awkward lately.

Typical Maya. If Hailey and I have any kind of disagreement, she tries to fix it. She has to know this won't be a "Kumbaya" moment. I reply:

Okay. Will let u know when I'm @ my uncle's.

Gunshots fire at rapid speed in the distance. I flinch.

"Goddamn machine guns," Daddy says. "Folks acting like this Iran or some shit."

"No cussing, Daddy!" Sekani says from the den.

"Sorry, man. I'll add a dollar to the jar."

"Two! You said the 'g-d' word."

"A'ight, two. Starr, come to the kitchen for a second."

In the kitchen, Momma speaks in her "other voice" on the phone. "Yes, ma'am. We want the same thing." She sees me. "And here's my lovely daughter now. Could you hold, please?" She covers the receiver. "It's the DA. She would like to talk to you this week."

Definitely not what I expected. "Oh…"

"Yeah," Momma says. "Look, baby, if you're not comfortable with it—"

"I am." I glance at Daddy. He nods. "I can do it."

"Oh," she says, looking from me to Daddy and back. "Okay. As long as you're sure. I think we should meet with Ms. Ofrah first though. Possibly take her up on her offer to represent you."

"Definitely," Daddy says. "I don't trust them folks at the DA office."

"So how about we see her tomorrow and meet with the DA later on this week?" Momma asks.

I grab another slice of pizza and take a bite. It's cold now, but cold pizza is the best pizza. "So two days of no school?"

"Oh, you're going to school," she says. "And did you eat any salad while you're eating all that pizza?"

"I've had veggies. These little bitty peppers."

"They don't count when they're that little."

"Yeah, they do. If babies can count as humans when they're little, veggies can count as veggies when they're little."

"That logic ain't working with me. So, we'll meet with Ms. Ofrah tomorrow and the DA on Wednesday. Sound like a plan?"

"Yeah, except the school part."

Momma uncovers the phone. "Sorry for the delay. We can come in on Wednesday morning."

"In the meantime tell your boys the mayor and the police chief to get them fucking tanks out my neighborhood," Daddy says loudly. Momma swats at him, but he's going down the hall. "Claim folks need to act peaceful, but rolling through here like we in a goddamn war."

"Two dollars, Daddy," Sekani says.

When Momma hangs up, I say, "It wouldn't kill me to miss one day of school. I don't wanna be there if they try that protest mess again." I wouldn't be surprised if Remy tried to get a whole week off because of Khalil. "I need two days, that's all." Momma raises her brows. "Okay, one and a half. Please?"

208

She takes a deep breath and lets it out slowly. "We'll see. But not a word of this to your brothers, you hear me?"

Basically, she said yes without saying yes outright. I can deal with that.

Pastor Eldridge once preached that "Faith isn't just believing but taking steps toward that belief." So when my alarm goes off Tuesday morning, by faith I don't get up, believing that Momma won't make me go to school.

And to quote Pastor Eldridge, hallelujah, God shows up and shows out. Momma doesn't make me get up. I stay in bed, listening as everybody else gets ready for the day. Sekani makes it his business to tell Momma I'm not up yet.

"Don't worry about her," she says. "Worry about yourself."

The TV in the den blares some morning news show, and Momma hums around the house. When Khalil and One-Fifteen are mentioned, the volume lowers a whole lot and doesn't go back up until a political story comes on.

My phone buzzes under my pillow. I take it out and look. Kenya finally texted me back about my new Tumblr. She would make me wait hours for a response, and her comment is short as hell:

It's aight

I roll my eyes. That's about as close as I'm gonna get to a compliment from her. I text back.

I love you too

Her response?

I know ☺

She's so petty. Part of me wonders though if she didn't respond last night 'cause of drama at her house. Daddy said King's still beating Iesha up. Sometimes he hits Kenya and Lyric too. Kenya's not the type to talk about it like that, so I ask:

Everything okay?

The usual, she writes back.

Short, but it says enough. There isn't much I can do, so I just remind her:

I'm here if you need me

Her response?

You better be

See? Petty.

Here's the messed-up part about missing school: you wonder what you would be doing if you went. At eight, I figure Chris and I would just be getting to history since it's our first class on Tuesdays. I send him a quick text.

Won't be at school today.

Two minutes later, he replies.

Are you sick? Need me to kiss it and make it better? Wink wink

He seriously typed "wink wink" instead of two wink emojis. I'll admit, I smile. I write back:

What if I'm contagious?

He says:

Doesn't matter. I'll kiss you anywhere. Wink wink.

I reply:

Is that another line?

He responds in less than a minute.

It's whatever you want it to be. Love you Fresh Princess.

Pause. That "L" word completely catches me off guard, like a player from the other team stealing the ball right as you're about to make a layup. It takes all of your momentum and you spend a week wondering how that steal slipped up on you.

Yeah. Chris saying "love you" is like that, except I can't waste a week wondering about it. By not answering, I'm answering, if that makes sense. The shot clock is winding down, and I need to say something.

But what?

By not saying "I" before "love you," he's making it more casual. Seriously, "love you" and "I love you" are different. Same team, different players. "Love you" isn't as forward or aggressive as "I love you." "Love you" can slip up on you, sure, but it doesn't make an in-your-face slam dunk. More like a nice jump shot.

Two minutes pass. I need to say something.

Love you too.

It's as foreign as a Spanish word I haven't learned yet, but funny enough it comes pretty easily.

I get a wink emoji in return.

Just Us for Justice occupies the old Taco Bell on Magnolia Avenue, between the car wash and the cash advance place. Daddy used to take me and Seven to that Taco Bell every Friday and get us ninety-nine-cent tacos, cinnamon twists, and a soda to share. This was right after he got out of prison, when he didn't have a lot of money. He usually watched us eat. Sometimes he asked the manager, one of Momma's girlfriends, to keep an eye on us, and he went to the cash advance place next door. When I got older and discovered that presents don't just "show up," I realized Daddy always went over there around our birthdays and Christmas.

Momma rings the doorbell at Just Us, and Ms. Ofrah lets us in.

"Sorry about that," she says, locking the door. "It's just me here today."

"Oh," Momma says. "Where are your colleagues?"

"Some of them are at Garden Heights High doing a roundtable discussion. Others are leading a march on Carnation where Khalil was murdered."

It's weird to hear somebody say "Khalil was murdered" as easily as Ms. Ofrah does. She doesn't bite her tongue or hesitate.

Short-walled cubicles take up most of the restaurant. They have almost as many posters as Seven has, but the kind Daddy would love, like Malcolm X standing next to a window holding a rifle, Huey Newton in prison with his fist up for black power, and photographs of the Black Panthers at rallies and giving breakfast to kids.

Ms. Ofrah leads us to her cubicle next to the drive-through window. It's kinda funny too 'cause she has a Taco Bell cup on her desk. "Thank you so much for coming," she says. "I was so happy when you called, Mrs. Carter."

"Please, call me Lisa. How long have you all been in this space?"

"Almost two years now. And if you're wondering, yes, we do get the occasional prankster who pulls up to the window and tells me they want a chalupa."

We laugh. The doorbell rings up front.

"That's probably my husband," Momma says. "He was on his way."

Ms. Ofrah leaves, and soon Daddy's voice echoes through the office as he follows her back. He grabs a third chair from another cubicle and sets it halfway in Ms. Ofrah's office and halfway in the hall. That's how small her cubicle is.

"Sorry I'm late. Had to get DeVante situated with Mr. Lewis."

"Mr. Lewis?" I ask.

"Yeah. Since I'm here, I asked him to let DeVante help around the shop. Mr. Lewis needs somebody to look out for his dumb behind. Snitching on live TV."

"You're talking about the gentleman who did the interview about the King Lords?" Ms. Ofrah asks.

"Yeah, him," says Daddy. "He owns the barbershop next to my store."

"Oh, wow. That interview definitely has people talking. Last I checked it had almost a million views online."

I knew it. Mr. Lewis has become a meme.

"It takes a lot of guts to be as upfront as he is. I meant what I said at Khalil's funeral, Starr. It was very brave of you to talk to the police."

"I don't feel brave." With Malcolm X watching me on her wall, I can't lie. "I'm not running my mouth on TV like Mr. Lewis."

"And that's okay," Ms. Ofrah says. "It seemed Mr. Lewis impulsively spoke out in anger and frustration. In a case like Khalil's, I would much rather that you spoke out in a more deliberate and planned way." She looks at Momma. "You said the DA called yesterday?"

"Yes. They'd like to meet with Starr tomorrow."

"Makes sense. The case was turned over to their office, and they're preparing to take it to a grand jury."

"What does that mean?" I ask.

"A jury will decide if charges should be brought against Officer Cruise."

"And Starr will have to testify to the grand jury," Daddy says.

Ms. Ofrah nods. "It's a bit different from a normal trial. There won't be a judge or a defense attorney present, and the DA will ask Starr questions."

"But what if I can't answer them all?"

"What do you mean?" Ms. Ofrah says.

"I – the gun in the car stuff. On the news they said there may have been a gun in the car, like that changes everything. I honestly don't know if there was."

Ms. Ofrah opens a folder that's on her desk, takes a piece of paper out, and pushes it toward me. It's a photograph of Khalil's black hairbrush, the one he used in the car.

"That's the so-called gun," Ms. Ofrah explains. "Officer

Cruise claims he saw it in the car door, and he assumed Khalil was reaching for it. The handle was thick enough, black enough, for him to assume it was a gun."

"And Khalil was black enough," Daddy adds.

A hairbrush.

Khalil died over a fucking hairbrush.

Ms. Ofrah slips the photograph back in the folder. "It'll be interesting to see how his father addresses it in his interview tonight."

Hold up. "Interview?" I ask.

Momma shifts a little in her chair. "Um … the officer's father has a television interview that's airing tonight."

I glance from her to Daddy. "And nobody told me?"

"'Cause it ain't worth talking about, baby," Daddy says.

I look at Ms. Ofrah. "So his dad can give his son's side to the whole world, and I can't give mine and Khalil's? He's gonna have everybody thinking One-Fifteen's the victim."

"Not necessarily," Ms. Ofrah says. "Sometimes these kinds of things backfire. And at the end of the day, the court of public opinion has no say in this. The grand jury does. If they see enough evidence, which they should, Officer Cruise will be charged and tried."

"If," I repeat.

A wave of awkward silence rolls in. One-Fifteen's father is his voice, but I'm Khalil's. The only way people will know his side of the story is if I speak out.

I look out the drive-through window at the car wash next door. Water cascades from a hose, making rainbows

215

against the sunlight like it did six years ago, right before bullets took Natasha.

I turn to Ms. Ofrah. "When I was ten, I saw my other best friend get murdered in a drive-by."

Funny how *murdered* comes out easily now.

"Oh." Ms. Ofrah sinks back. "I didn't— I'm so sorry, Starr."

I stare at my fingers and fumble with them. Tears well in my eyes. "I've tried to forget it, but I remember everything. The shots, the look on Natasha's face. They never caught the person who did it. I guess it didn't matter enough. But it did matter. *She* mattered." I look at Ms. Ofrah, but I can barely see her for all the tears. "And I want everyone to know that Khalil mattered too."

Ms. Ofrah blinks. A lot. "Absolutely. I—" She clears her throat. "I would like to represent you, Starr. Pro bono, in fact."

Momma nods, and she's teary-eyed too.

"I'll do whatever I can to make sure you're heard, Starr. Because just like Khalil and Natasha mattered, you matter and your voice matters. I can start by trying to get you a television interview." She looks at my parents. "If you're okay with that."

"As long as they don't reveal her identity, yeah," Daddy says.

"That shouldn't be a problem," she says. "We will absolutely make sure her privacy is protected."

A quiet buzzing comes from Daddy's way. He takes out

his phone and answers. The person on the other end shouts something, but I can't make it out. "Ay, calm down, Vante. Say that again?" The response makes Daddy stand up. "I'm coming. You call nine-one-one?"

"What's wrong?" Momma says.

He motions for us to follow him. "Stay with him, a'ight? We on the way."

CHAPTER 13

Mr. Lewis's left eye is swollen shut and blood drips onto his shirt from a slash on his cheek, but he refuses to go to the hospital.

Daddy's office has become an examining room, and Momma tends to Mr. Lewis with Daddy's help. I lean against the doorway and watch. DeVante stands even farther back in the store.

"It took five of 'em to take me down," Mr. Lewis says. "Five of 'em! Against one li'l ol' man. Ain't that something?"

"It's really something that you're alive," I say. Snitches get stitches doesn't apply to King Lords. More like snitches get graves.

Momma tilts Mr. Lewis's head to look at the cut on his cheek. "She's right. You're real lucky, Mr. Lewis. Don't even need stitches."

"King himself gave me that one," he says. "He ain't come in till them other ones got me down. Ol' punk ass, looking like a black Michelin Man."

I snort.

"This ain't funny," Daddy says. "I told you they was gon' come after you."

"And I told you I ain't scared! If this the worst they could do, they ain't did nothing!"

"Nah, this ain't the worst," says Daddy. "They could've killed you!"

"I ain't the one they want dead!" He stretches his fat finger my way, but he looks beyond me at DeVante. "That's the one you need to worry 'bout! I made him hide before they came in, but King said he know you helping that boy, and he gon' kill him if he find him."

DeVante backs away, his eyes wide.

I swear, in like two seconds Daddy grabs DeVante by his neck and slams him against the freezer. "What the hell you do?"

DeVante kicks and squirms and tries to pull Daddy's hands from his neck.

"Daddy, stop!"

"Shut up!" His glare never leaves DeVante. "I brought you in my house, and you ain't been honest 'bout why you hiding? King wouldn't want you dead unless you did something, so what you do?"

"Mav-rick!" Momma breaks his name down real good. "Let him go. He can't explain anything with you choking him."

Daddy releases, and DeVante bends over, gasping for air. "Don't be putting your hands on me!" he says.

"Or what?" Daddy taunts. "Start talking."

"Man, look, it ain't a big deal. King tripping."

Is he for real? "What did you do?" I ask.

DeVante slides onto the floor and tries to catch his breath. He blinks real fast for several seconds. His face scrunches up. Suddenly he's bawling like a baby.

I don't know anything else to do, so I sit in front of him. When Khalil would cry like that because his momma was messed up, I'd lift his head.

I lift DeVante's. "It's okay," I say.

That always worked with Khalil. It works with DeVante too. He stops crying as hard and says, "I stole 'bout five Gs from King."

"Dammit!" Daddy groans. "What the hell, man?"

"I had to get my family outta here! I was gonna handle the dudes that killed Dalvin, and shit, all that would do was make some GDs come after me. I was a dead man walking, straight up. I didn't want my momma and my sisters caught up in that. So I got them some bus tickets and got them outta town."

"That's why we can't get your momma on the phone," Momma realizes.

Tears fall around his lips. "She didn't want me coming anyway. Said I'd get them killed. Put me out the house before they left." He looks at Daddy. "Big Mav, I'm sorry. I should've told you the other day. I did change my mind 'bout killing them dudes though, but now King wants me dead. Please don't take me to him. I'll do anything. Please?"

"He bet' not!" Mr. Lewis limps out Daddy's office. "You help that boy, Maverick!"

Daddy stares at the ceiling like he could cuss God out.

"Daddy," I plead.

"A'ight! C'mon, Vante."

"Big Mav," he whimpers, "I'm sorry, please—"

"I'm not taking you to King, but we gotta get you outta here. Now."

Forty minutes later, Momma and I pull up behind Daddy and DeVante in Uncle Carlos's driveway.

I'm surprised Daddy knows how to get here. He never comes out here with us. Ne-ver. Holidays, birthdays, none of that. I guess he doesn't wanna deal with Nana and her mouth.

Momma and I get out her car as Daddy and DeVante get out the truck.

"This is where you're bringing him?" Momma says. "My brother's house?"

"Yeah," Daddy says, like it's no big deal.

Uncle Carlos comes from the garage, wiping oil off his hands with one of Aunt Pam's good towels. He shouldn't be home. It's the middle of a workday, and he never takes sick days. He stops wiping his hands, but the knuckles on one of them are still dark.

DeVante squints against the sunlight and looks around like we brought him to another planet. "Damn, Big Mav. Where we at?"

"Where are we?" Uncle Carlos corrects, and offers his hand. "Carlos. You must be DeVante."

221

DeVante stares at his hand. No manners at all. "How you know my name?"

Uncle Carlos awkwardly lets his hand fall to his side. "Maverick told me about you. We've discussed getting you out here."

"Oh!" Momma says with a hollow laugh. "Maverick's discussed getting him out here." She narrows her eyes at Daddy. "I'm surprised you even knew how to get out here, Maverick."

Daddy's nostrils flare. "We'll talk later."

"C'mon," Uncle Carlos says. "I'll show you your room."

DeVante stares at the house, his eyes all big. "What you do to get a house like this?"

"Dang, you're nosy," I say.

Uncle Carlos chuckles. "It's okay, Starr. My wife's a surgeon, and I'm a detective."

DeVante stops dead. He turns on Daddy. "What the fuck, man? You brought me to a cop?"

"Watch your mouth," Daddy says. "And I brought you to somebody who actually wanna help you."

"A cop though? If the homies find out, they gon' think I'm snitching."

"They're not your homies if you gotta hide from them," I say. "Plus Uncle Carlos wouldn't ask you to snitch."

"She's right," says Uncle Carlos. "Maverick's really serious about getting you out of Garden Heights."

Momma scoffs. Loudly.

"When he told us the situation, we wanted to help,"

Uncle Carlos goes on. "And it sounds like you need our help."

DeVante sighs. "Man, this ain't cool."

"Look, I'm on leave," says Uncle Carlos. "You don't have to worry about me getting information out of you."

"Leave?" I say. That explains the sweats in the middle of the day. "Why'd they put you on leave?"

He glances from me to Momma, and she probably doesn't know I see her shake her head real quick. "Don't worry about it, baby girl," he says, hooking his arm around me. "I needed a vacation."

It's so, so obvious. They put him on leave because of me.

Nana meets us at the front door. Knowing her, she's been watching through the window since we got here. She has one arm folded and takes a drag of her cigarette with the other. She blows the smoke toward the ceiling while staring at DeVante. "Who he supposed to be?"

"DeVante," Uncle Carlos says. "He's staying with us."

"What you mean he's staying with us?"

"Just what I said. He got in a little trouble in Garden Heights and needs to stay here."

She scoffs, and I know where Momma gets it from. "A li'l trouble, huh? Tell the truth, boy." She lowers her voice and asks with suspicious, squinted eyes, "Did you kill somebody?"

"Momma!" my momma says.

"What? I better ask before y'all have me sleeping in the house with a murderer, waking up dead!"

What in the... "You can't wake up dead," I say.

"Li'l girl, you know what I mean!" She moves from the doorway. "I'll be waking up in Jesus's face, trying to figure out what happened!"

"Like you going to heaven," Daddy mumbles.

Uncle Carlos gives DeVante a tour. His room is about as big as me and Seven's rooms put together. It doesn't seem right that he only has a little backpack to put in it, and when we go to the kitchen Uncle Carlos makes him hand that over.

"There are a few rules for living here," Uncle Carlos says. "One, follow the rules. Two" – he pulls the Glock from DeVante's backpack – "no weapons and no drugs."

"I know you ain't bring that in my house, Vante," Daddy says.

"King probably got money on my head. You damn right I got a piece."

"Rule three." Uncle Carlos speaks over him. "No cursing. I have an eight-year-old and a three-year-old. They don't need to hear that."

'Cause they hear it from Nana enough. Ava's new favorite word is "Goddammit!"

"Rule four," Uncle Carlos says, "go to school."

"Man," DeVante groans. "I already told Big Mav I can't go back to Garden High."

"We know," Daddy says. "Once we get in touch with your momma, we'll get you enrolled in an online program. Lisa's momma is a retired teacher. She can tutor you through it so you can finish the year out."

"Like hell I can!" Nana says. I don't know where she is, but I'm not surprised she's listening.

"Momma, stop being nosy!" Uncle Carlos says.

"Stop volunteering me for shit!"

"Stop cursing," he says.

"Tell me what to do again and see what happens."

Uncle Carlos's face and neck go red.

The doorbell rings.

"Carlos, get the door," Nana says from wherever she's hiding.

He purses his lips and leaves to answer. As he comes back I can hear him talking to somebody. Then somebody laughs, and I know that laugh 'cause it makes me laugh.

"Look who I found," Uncle Carlos says.

Chris is behind him in his white Williamson polo and khaki shorts. He has on the red-and-black Jordan Twelves that MJ wore when he had the flu during the '97 finals. Shoot, that makes Chris finer for some reason. Or I have a Jordan fetish.

"Hi." He smiles without showing teeth.

"Hi." I smile too.

I forget that Daddy is here and that I potentially have a big-ass problem on my hands. That only lasts about ten seconds though because Daddy asks, "Who you?"

Chris extends his hand to Daddy. "Christopher, sir. Nice to meet you."

Daddy gives him a twice-over. "You know my daughter or something?"

225

"Yeah." Chris stretches it kinda long and looks at me. "We both go to Williamson?"

I nod. Good answer.

Daddy folds his arms. "Well, do you or don't you? You sound a li'l unsure 'bout that."

Momma gives Chris a quick hug. All the while Daddy mean-mugs the hell outta him. "How are you doing, sweetie?" she asks.

"I'm fine. I didn't mean to interrupt anything. I saw your car, and Starr wasn't at school today, so I wanted to check on her."

"It's fine," says Momma. "Tell your mom and dad I said hello. How are they?"

"Hold up," Daddy says. "Y'all act like this dude been around a minute." Daddy turns to me. "Why ain't I never heard 'bout him?"

It's gonna take a hell of a lotta boldness to put myself out there for Khalil. Like "I once told my militant black daddy about my white boyfriend" kinda boldness. If I can't stand up to my dad about Chris, how can I stand up for Khalil?

Daddy always tells me to never bite my tongue for anyone. That includes him.

So I say it. "He's my boyfriend."

"Boyfriend?" Daddy repeats.

"Yeah, her boyfriend!" Nana pipes up again from wherever she is. "Hey, Chris baby."

Chris glances around, all confused. "Uh, hey, Ms. Montgomery."

Nana was the first to find out about Chris, thanks to her master snooping skills. She told me, "Go 'head, get your swirl on, baby," then proceeded to tell me about all of her swirling adventures, which I didn't need to know.

"The hell, Starr?" Daddy says. "You dating a white boy?"

"Maverick!" Momma snaps.

"Calm down, Maverick," Uncle Carlos says. "He's a good kid, and he treats her well. That's all that matters, isn't it?"

"You knew?" Daddy says. He looks at me, and I don't know if that's anger or hurt in his eyes. "*He* knew, and I didn't?"

This happens when you have two dads. One of them's bound to get hurt, and you're bound to feel like shit because of it.

"Let's go outside," Momma says tightly. "Now."

Daddy glares at Chris and follows Momma to the patio. The doors have thick glass, but I still hear her go off on him.

"C'mon, DeVante," Uncle Carlos says. "Gonna show you the basement and the laundry room."

DeVante sizes Chris up. "Boyfriend," he says with a slight laugh, and looks at me. "I should've known *you'd* have a white boy."

He leaves with Uncle Carlos. What the hell that's supposed to mean?

"Sorry," I tell Chris. "My dad shouldn't have gone off like that."

227

"It could've been worse. He could've killed me."

True. I motion him to sit at the counter while I get us some drinks.

"Who was that guy with your uncle?" he asks.

Aunt Pam ain't got one soda up in here. Juice, water, and sparkling water. I bet Nana has a stash of Sprite and Coke in her room though. "DeVante," I say, grabbing two apple juice boxes. "He got caught up in some King Lord stuff, and Daddy brought him to live with Uncle Carlos."

"Why was he looking at me like that?"

"Get over it, Maverick. He's white!" Momma shouts on the patio. "White, white, white!"

Chris blushes. And blushes, and blushes, and blushes.

I hand him a juice box. "*That's* why DeVante was looking at you that way. You're white."

"Okay?" he asks more than says. "Is this one of those black things I won't understand?"

"Okay, babe, real talk? If you were somebody else I'd side-eye the shit out of you for calling it that."

"Calling it what? A black thing?"

"Yeah."

"But isn't that what it is?"

"Not really," I say. "It's not like this kinda stuff is exclusive to black people, you know? The reasoning may be different, but that's about it. Your parents don't have a problem with us dating?"

"I wouldn't call it a problem," Chris says, "but we did talk about it."

228

"So it's not just a black thing then, huh?"

"Point made."

We sit at the counter, and I listen to his play-by-play of school today. Nobody walked out because the police were there, waiting for any drama.

"Hailey and Maya asked about you," he says. "I told them you were sick."

"They could've texted me and asked themselves."

"I think they feel guilty about yesterday. Especially Hailey. White guilt." He winks.

I crack up. My white boyfriend talking about white guilt.

Momma yells, "And I love how you insist on getting somebody else's child out of Garden Heights, but you want ours to stay in that hellhole!"

"You want them in the suburbs with all this fake shit?" Daddy says.

"If this is fake, baby, I'll take it over real any day. I'm sick of this! The kids go to school out here, I take them to church out here, their friends are out here. We can afford to move. But you wanna stay in that mess!"

"'Cause at least in Garden Heights people ain't gonna treat them like shit."

"They already do! And wait until King can't find DeVante. Who do you think he's gonna look at? Us!"

"I told you I'll handle that," Daddy says. "We ain't moving. It ain't even up for discussion."

"Oh, really?"

"Really."

229

Chris gives me a bit of a smile. "This is awkward."

My cheeks are hot, and I'm glad I'm too brown for it to show. "Yeah. Awkward."

He takes my hand and taps his fingertips against my fingertips, one at a time. He laces his fingers through mine, and we let our arms swing together in the space between us.

Daddy comes in and slams the door behind him. He zeroes straight in on our joined hands. Chris doesn't let go. Point for my boyfriend.

"We'll talk later, Starr." Daddy marches out.

"If this were a rom-com," Chris says, "you'd be Zoe Saldana and I'd be Ashton Kutcher."

"Huh?"

He sips his juice. "This old movie, *Guess Who*. I caught it when I had the flu a few weeks ago. Zoe Saldana dated Ashton Kutcher. Her dad didn't like that she was seeing a white guy. That's us."

"Except this isn't funny," I say.

"It can be."

"Nah. What's funny though is that you watched a rom-com."

"Hey!" he cries. "It was hilarious. More of a comedy than a rom-com. Bernie Mac was her dad. That guy was hilarious, one of the Kings of Comedy. I don't think it can be called a rom-com simply because he was in it."

"Okay, you get points for knowing Bernie Mac and that he was a King of Comedy—"

"*Everyone* should know that."

"True, but you don't get a pass. It was still a rom-com. I won't tell anyone though."

I lean over to kiss his cheek, but he moves his head, giving me no choice but to kiss him on the mouth. Soon we're making out, right there in my uncle's kitchen.

"Hem-hem!" Somebody clears their throat. Chris and I separate so fast.

I thought embarrassment was having my boyfriend hear my parents argue. Nope. Embarrassment is having my mom walk in on me and Chris making out. Again.

"Don't y'all think y'all should let each other breathe?" she says.

Chris blushes down to his Adam's apple. "I should go."

He leaves with a quick good-bye to Momma.

She raises her eyebrows at me. "Are you taking your birth control pills?"

"Mommy!"

"Answer my question. Are you?"

"Yeeees," I groan, putting my face on the countertop.

"When was your last cycle?"

Oh. My. Lord. I lift my head and flash the fakest of fake smiles. "We're fine. Promise."

"Y'all got some nerve. Your daddy was barely out the driveway, and y'all slobbering all over each other. You know how Maverick is."

"Are we staying out here tonight?"

The question catches her off guard. "Why would you think that?"

231

"Because you and Daddy—"

"Had a disagreement, that's all."

"A disagreement the whole neighborhood heard." Plus one the other night.

"Starr, we're okay. Don't worry about it. Your father's being … your father."

Outside, somebody honks his car horn a bunch of times.

Momma rolls her eyes. "Speaking of your father, I guess Mr. I'm-Gonna-Slam-Doors needs me to move my car so he can leave." She shakes her head and heads toward the front.

I throw Chris's juice away and search the cabinets. Aunt Pam may be picky when it comes to drinks, but she always buys good snacks, and my stomach is talking. I get some graham crackers and slather peanut butter on them. So good.

DeVante comes in the kitchen. "Can't believe you dating a white boy." He sits next to me and steals a graham cracker sandwich. "A wigga at that."

"Excuse you?" I say with a mouth full of peanut butter. "He is not a wigga."

"Please! Dude wearing J's. White boys wear Converse and Vans, not no J's unless they trying to be black."

Really? "My bad. I didn't know shoes determined somebody's race."

He can't say anything to that. Like I thought. "What you see in him anyway? For real? All them dudes in Garden Heights who would get with you in a second, and you looking at Justin Bieber?"

232

I point in his face. "Don't call him that. And what dudes? Nobody in Garden Heights is checking for me. Hardly anybody knows my name. Hell, even you called me Big Mav's daughter who work in the store."

"'Cause you don't come around," he says. "I ain't never seen you at a party, nothing."

Without thinking, I say, "You mean parties where people get shot at?" And as soon as it leaves my mouth, I feel like shit. "Oh my God, I'm sorry. I shouldn't have said that."

He stares at the countertop. "It's cool. Don't worry about it."

We quietly nibble on graham crackers.

"Um…" I say. The silence is brutal. "Uncle Carlos and Aunt Pam are cool. I think you'll like it here."

He bites another graham cracker.

"They can be corny sometimes, but they're sweet. They'll look out for you. Knowing Aunt Pam, she'll treat you like Ava and Daniel. Uncle Carlos will probably be tougher. If you follow the rules, you'll be okay."

"Khalil talked 'bout you sometimes," DeVante says.

"Huh?"

"You said nobody knows you, but Khalil talked 'bout you. I ain't know you was Big Mav's daughter who – I ain't know that was you," he says. "But he talked 'bout his friend Starr. He said you were the coolest girl he knew."

Some peanut butter gets stuck in my throat, but it's not the only reason I swallow. "How did you know – oh. Yeah. Both of y'all were King Lords."

I swear to God whenever I think about Khalil falling into that life, it's like watching him die all over again. Yeah, Khalil matters and not the stuff he did, but I can't lie and say it doesn't bother me or it's not disappointing. He knew better.

DeVante says, "Khalil wasn't a King Lord, Starr."

"But at the funeral, King put the bandana on him——"

"To save face," DeVante says. "He tried to get Khalil to join, but Khalil said nah. Then a cop killed him, so you know, all the homies riding for him now. King not 'bout to admit that Khalil turned him down. So he got folks thinking that Khalil repped King Lords."

"Wait," I say. "How do you know he turned King down?"

"Khalil told me in the park one day. We was posted up."

"So y'all sold drugs together?"

"Yeah. For King."

"Oh."

"He didn't wanna sell drugs, Starr," DeVante says. "Nobody really wanna do that shit. Khalil ain't have much of a choice though."

"Yeah, he did," I say thickly.

"No, he didn't. Look, his momma stole some shit from King. King wanted her dead. Khalil found out and started selling to pay the debt."

"What?"

"Yeah. That's the only reason he started doing that shit. Trying to save her."

234

I can't believe it.

Then again, I can. That was classic Khalil. No matter what his momma did, he was still her knight and he was still gonna protect her.

This is worse than denying him. I thought the worst of him. Like everybody else.

"Don't be mad at him," DeVante says, and it's funny because I can hear Khalil asking me not to be mad too.

"I'm not—" I sigh. "Okay, I was a little mad. I just hate how he's being called a thug and shit when people don't know the whole story. You said it, he wasn't a gangbanger, and if everybody knew why he sold drugs, then—"

"They wouldn't think he was a thug like me?"

Oh, damn. "I didn't mean…"

"It's cool," he says. "I get it. I guess I am a thug, I don't know. I did what I had to do. King Lords was the closest thing me and Dalvin had to a family."

"But your momma," I say, "and your sisters—"

"They couldn't look out for us like King Lords do," he says. "Me and Dalvin looked out for them. With King Lords, we had a whole bunch of folks who had our backs, no matter what. They bought us clothes and shit our momma couldn't afford and always made sure we ate." He looks at the counter. "It was just cool to have somebody take care of us for a change, instead of the other way around."

"Oh." A shitty response, I know.

"Like I said, nobody likes selling drugs," he says. "I hated that shit. For real. But I hated seeing my momma and my sisters go hungry, you know?"

"I don't know." I've never had to know. My parents made sure of that.

"You got it good then," he says. "I'm sorry they talking 'bout Khalil like that though. He really was a good dude. Hopefully one day they can find out the truth."

"Yeah," I say quietly.

DeVante. Khalil. Neither one of them thought they had much of a choice. If I were them, I'm not sure I'd make a much better one.

Guess that makes me a thug too.

"I'm going for a walk," I say, getting up. My head's all over the place. "You can have the rest of the graham crackers and peanut butter."

I leave. I don't know where I'm going. I don't know much of anything anymore.

CHAPTER 14

I end up at Maya's house. Truth be told, that's the farthest I can go in Uncle Carlos's neighborhood before the houses start looking the same.

It's that weird time between day and night when the sky looks like it's on fire and mosquitoes are on the hunt; all of the lights at the Yang house are already on, which is a lot of lights. Their house is big enough for me and my family to live with them and have a little wiggle room. There's a blue Infiniti Coupe with a dented bumper in the circular drive-way. Hailey can't drive for shit.

No lie, it stings a little knowing they hang out without me. That's what happens when you live so far away from your friends. I can't get mad about it. Jealous maybe. Not mad.

That protest shit though? Now that makes me mad. Mad enough to ring the doorbell. Besides, I told Maya the three of us could talk, so fine, we'll talk.

Mrs. Yang answers, her Bluetooth headset around her neck.

"Starr!" She beams and hugs me. "So good to see you. How is everyone?"

"Good," I say. She announces my arrival to Maya and lets me in. The aroma of Mrs. Yang's seafood lasagna greets me in the foyer.

"I hope it's not a bad time," I say.

"Not at all, sweetie. Maya's upstairs. Hailey too. You're more than welcome to join us for dinner... No, George, I wasn't talking to you," she says into her headset, then mouths at me, *"My assistant,"* and rolls her eyes a little.

I smile and take off my Nike Dunks. In the Yang house, shoe removal is part Chinese tradition, part Mrs. Yang likes people to be comfy.

Maya races down the stairs, wearing an oversized T-shirt and basketball shorts that almost hang to her ankles. "Starr!"

She reaches the bottom, and there's this awkward moment where her arms are out like she wants to hug me, but she starts lowering them. I hug her anyway. It's been a while since I got a good Maya hug. Her hair smells like citrus, and she hugs all tight and motherly.

Maya leads me to her bedroom. White Christmas lights hang from the ceiling. There's a shelf for video games, *Adventure Time* memorabilia all around, and Hailey in a beanbag chair, concentrating on the basketball players she's controlling on Maya's flat-screen.

"Look who's here, Hails," Maya says.

Hailey glances up at me. "Hey."

"Hey."

It's Awkward Central in here.

I step over an empty Sprite can and a bag of Doritos and sit in the other beanbag chair. Maya closes her door. An old-school poster of Michael Jordan, in his famous Jumpman pose, is on the back.

Maya belly flops onto her bed and grabs a controller off the floor. "You wanna join in, Starr?"

"Yeah, sure."

She hands me a third controller, and we start a new game – the three of us against a computer-controlled team. It's a lot like when we play in real life, a combination of rhythm, chemistry, and skill, but the awkwardness in the room is so thick it's hard to ignore.

They keep glancing at me. I keep my eyes on the screen. The animated crowd cheers as Hailey's player makes a three-pointer. "Nice shot," I say.

"Okay, cut the crap." Hailey grabs the TV remote and flicks the game off, turning to a detective show instead. "Why are you mad at us?"

"Why did you protest?" Since she wants to cut the crap, may as well get right to it.

"Because," she says, like that's reason enough. "I don't see what the big deal is, Starr. You said you didn't know him."

"Why does that make a difference?"

"Isn't a protest a good thing?"

"Not if you're only doing it to cut class."

"So you want us to apologize for it even though every-body else did it too?" Hailey asks.

239

"Just because everyone else did it doesn't mean it's okay."

Shit. I sound like my mother.

"Guys, stop!" Maya says. "Hailey, if Starr wants us to apologize, fine, we can apologize. Starr, I'm sorry for protesting. It was stupid to use a tragedy just to get out of class."

We look at Hailey. She sits back and folds her arms. "I'm not apologizing when I didn't do anything wrong. If anything, she should apologize for accusing me of being racist last week."

"Wow," I say. One thing that irks the hell out of me about Hailey? The way she can turn an argument around and make herself the victim. She's a master at this shit. I used to fall for it, but now?

"I'm not apologizing for what I felt," I say. "I don't care what your intention was, Hailey. That fried chicken comment felt racist to me."

"Fine," she says. "Just like I felt it was fine to protest. Since I won't apologize for what I felt, and you won't apologize for what you felt, I guess we'll just watch TV."

"Fine," I say.

Maya grunts like it's taking everything in her not to choke us. "You know what? If you two want to be this stubborn, fine."

Maya flicks through channels. Hailey does that BS move where you look at someone out the corner of your eye, but you don't want them to know that you care enough to look, so you avert your eyes. At this point it's whatever. I thought I came to talk, but yeah, I really want an apology.

I look at TV. A singing competition, a reality show, One-Fifteen, a celebrity dance – wait.

"Back up, back up," I tell Maya.

She flicks through the channels, and when he appears again, I say, "Right there!"

I've pictured his face so much. Actually seeing it again is different. My memory is pretty spot-on – a thin, jagged scar above his lip, bursts of freckles that cover his face and neck.

My stomach churns and my skin crawls, and I wanna get away from One-Fifteen. My instinct doesn't care that it's a photograph being shown on TV. A silver cross pendant hangs from his neck, like he's saying Jesus endorses what he did. We must believe in a different Jesus.

What looks like an older version of him appears on the screen, but this man doesn't have the scar on his lip, and there are more wrinkles on his neck than freckles. He has white hair, although there's still some streaks of brown in it.

"My son was afraid for his life," he says. "He only wanted to get home to his wife and kids."

Pictures flash on the screen. One-Fifteen smiles with his arms draped around a blurred-out woman. He's on a fishing trip with two small, blurred-out children. They show him with a smiley golden retriever, with his pastor and some fellow deacons who are all blurred out, and then in his police uniform.

"Officer Brian Cruise Jr. has been on the force for sixteen years," the voice-over says, and more pics of him as a cop are shown. He's been a cop for as long as Khalil was alive, and I wonder if in some sick twist of fate Khalil was only born for this man to kill.

"A majority of those years have been spent serving in Garden Heights," the voice-over continues, "a neighborhood notorious for gangs and drug dealers."

I tense as footage of my neighborhood, my home, is shown. It's like they picked the worst parts – the drug addicts roaming the streets, the broken-down Cedar Grove projects, gangbangers flashing signs, bodies on the sidewalks with white sheets over them. What about Mrs. Rooks and her cakes? Or Mr. Lewis and his haircuts? Mr. Reuben? The clinic? My family?

Me?

I feel Hailey's and Maya's eyes on me. I can't look at them.

"My son loved working in the neighborhood," One-Fifteen's father claims. "He always wanted to make a difference in the lives there."

Funny. Slave masters thought they were making a difference in black people's lives too. Saving them from their "wild African ways." Same shit, different century. I wish people like them would stop thinking that people like me need saving.

One-Fifteen Sr. talks about his son's life before the shooting. How he was a good kid who never got into trouble, always wanted to help others. A lot like Khalil. But then he talks about the stuff One-Fifteen did that Khalil will never get to do, like go to college, get married, have a family.

The interviewer asks about that night.

"Apparently, Brian pulled the kid over 'cause he had a broken taillight and was speeding."

Khalil wasn't speeding.

"He told me, 'Pop, soon as I pulled him over, I had a bad feeling,'" says One-Fifteen Sr.

"Why is that?" the interviewer asks.

"He said the kid and his friend immediately started cursing him out—"

We never cursed.

"And they kept glancing at each other, like they were up to something. Brian says that's when he got scared, 'cause they could've taken him down if they teamed up."

I couldn't have taken anyone down. I was too afraid. He makes us sound like we're superhumans. We're kids.

"No matter how afraid he is, my son's still gonna do his job," he says. "And that's all he set out to do that night."

"There have been reports that Khalil Harris was unarmed when the incident took place," the interviewer says. "Has your son told you why he made the decision to shoot?"

"Brian says he had his back to the kid, and he heard the kid say, 'I'm gon' show your ass today.'"

No, no, no. Khalil asked if I was okay.

"Brian turned around and saw something in the car door. He thought it was a gun—"

It was a hairbrush.

His lips quiver. My body shakes. He covers his mouth to

243

hold back a sob. I cover mine to keep from puking.

"Brian's a good boy," he says, in tears. "He only wanted to get home to his family, and people are making him out to be a monster."

That's all Khalil and I wanted, and you're making *us* out to be monsters.

I can't breathe, like I'm drowning in the tears I refuse to shed. I won't give One-Fifteen or his father the satisfaction of crying. Tonight, they shot me too, more than once, and killed a part of me. Unfortunately for them, it's the part that felt any hesitation about speaking out.

"How has your son's life changed since this happened?" the interviewer asks.

"All of our lives have been hell, honestly," his father claims. "Brian's a people person, but now he's afraid to go out in public, even for something as simple as getting a gallon of milk. There have been threats on his life, our family's lives. His wife had to quit her job. He's even been attacked by fellow officers."

"Physically or verbally?" the interviewer asks.

"Both," he says.

It hits me. Uncle Carlos's bruised knuckles.

"This is awful," Hailey says. "That poor family."

She's looking at One-Fifteen Sr. with sympathy that belongs to Brenda and Ms. Rosalie.

I blink several times. "What?"

"His son lost everything because he was trying to do his job and protect himself. His life matters too, you know?"

I cannot right now. I can't. I stand up or otherwise I will say or do something really stupid. Like punch her.

"I need to … yeah." I say all that I can and start for the door, but Maya grabs the tail of my cardigan.

"Whoa, whoa. You guys haven't worked this out yet," she says.

"Maya," I say, as calmly as possible. "Please let me go. I cannot talk to her. Did you not hear what she said?"

"Are you serious right now?" Hailey asks. "What's wrong with saying his life matters too?"

"His life always matters more!" My voice is gruff, and my throat is tight. "That's the problem!"

"Starr! Starr!" Maya says, trying to catch my eye. I look at her. "What's going on? You're Harry in *Order of the Phoenix* angry lately."

"Thank you!" Hailey says. "She's been in bitch mode for weeks but wants to blame me."

"Excuse you?"

There's a knock on the door. "Girls, is everything okay?" Mrs. Yang asks.

"We're fine, Mom. Video game stuff." Maya looks at me and lowers her voice. "Please, sit down. Please?"

I sit on her bed. Commercials replace One-Fifteen Sr. on the TV and fill in the gap of silence we've created.

I blurt out, "Why did you unfollow my Tumblr?"

Hailey turns toward me. "What?"

"You unfollowed my Tumblr. Why?"

She glances at Maya – quickly, but I notice – and goes,

"I don't know what you're talking about."

"Cut the bullshit, Hailey. You unfollowed me. Months ago. Why?"

She doesn't say anything.

I swallow. "Is it because of the Emmett Till picture?"

"Oh my God," she says, standing up. "Here we go again. I am not gonna stay here and let you accuse me of something, Starr—"

"You don't text me anymore," I say. "You freaked out about that picture."

"Do you hear her?" Hailey says to Maya. "Once again, calling me racist."

"I'm not calling you anything. I'm asking a question and giving you examples."

"You're insinuating!"

"I never even mentioned race."

Silence comes between us.

Hailey shakes her head. Her lips are thin. "Unbelievable." She grabs her jacket off Maya's bed and starts for the door. She stops, and her back is to me. "You wanna really know why I unfollowed you, Starr? Because I don't know who the hell you are anymore."

She slams the door on her way out.

The news program returns on the television. They show footage of protests all over the country, not just in Garden Heights. Hopefully none of them used Khalil's death to skip class or work.

Out of nowhere, Maya says, "That's not why."

She's staring at her closed door, her shoulders a bit stiff.

"Huh?" I say.

"She's lying," Maya says. "That's not why she unfollowed you. She said she didn't wanna see that shit on her dashboard."

I figured. "That Emmett Till picture, right?"

"No. All the 'black stuff,' she called it. The petitions. The Black Panther pictures. That post on those four little girls who were killed in that church. The stuff about that Marcus Garvey guy. The one about those Black Panthers who were shot by the government."

"Fred Hampton and Bobby Hutton," I say.

"Yeah. Them."

Wow. She's been paying attention. "Why didn't you tell me?"

She stares at her plush Finn on the floor. "I hoped she'd change her mind before you found out. I should've known better though. It's not like that's the first fucked-up thing she's said."

"What are you talking about?"

Maya swallows hard. "Do you remember that time she asked if my family ate a cat for Thanksgiving?"

"What? When?"

Her eyes are glossy. "Freshman year. First period. Mrs. Edwards's biology class. We'd just gotten back from Thanksgiving break. Class hadn't started yet, and we were talking about what we did for Thanksgiving. I told you guys my grandparents visited, and it was their first time

247

celebrating Thanksgiving. Hailey asked if we ate a cat. Because we're Chinese."

Ho–ly shit. I'm wracking my brain right now. Freshman year is so close to middle school; there's a huge possibility I said or did something extremely stupid. I'm afraid to know, but I ask, "What did I say?"

"Nothing. You had this look on your face like you couldn't believe she said that. She claimed it was a joke and laughed. I laughed, and then you laughed." Maya blinks. A lot. "I only laughed because I thought I was supposed to. I felt like shit the rest of the week."

"Oh."

"Yeah."

I feel like shit right now. I can't believe I let Hailey say that. Or has she always joked like that? Did I always laugh because I thought I had to?

That's the problem. We let people say stuff, and they say it so much that it becomes okay to them and normal for us. What's the point of having a voice if you're gonna be silent in those moments you shouldn't be?

"Maya?" I say.

"Yeah?"

"We can't let her get away with saying stuff like that again, okay?"

She cracks a smile. "A minority alliance?"

"Hell, yeah," I say, and we laugh.

"All right. Deal."

★ ★ ★

A game of NBA 2K15 later (I whooped Maya's butt), I'm walking back to Uncle Carlos's house with a foil-wrapped plate of seafood lasagna. Mrs. Yang never lets me leave empty-handed, and I never turn down food.

Iron streetlamps line the sidewalks, and I see Uncle Carlos from a few houses down, sitting on his front steps in the dark. He's chugging back something, and as I get closer, I can see the Heineken.

I put my plate on the steps and sit beside him.

"You better not have been at your li'l boyfriend's house," he says.

Lord. Chris is always "li'l" to him, and they're almost the same height. "No. I was at Maya's." I stretch my legs forward and yawn. It's been a long-ass day. "I can't believe you're drinking," I say through my yawn.

"I'm not drinking. It's one beer."

"Is that what Nana said?"

He cuts me a look. "Starr."

"Uncle Carlos," I say as firmly.

We battle it out, hard stare versus hard stare.

He sets the beer down. Here's the thing – Nana's an alcoholic. She's not as bad as she used to be, but all it takes is one hard drink and she's the "other" Nana. I've heard stories of her drunken rages from back in the day. She'd blame Momma and Uncle Carlos that their daddy went back to his wife and other kids. She'd lock them out the house, cuss at them, all kinds of stuff.

So, no. One beer isn't one beer to Uncle Carlos, who's

249

always been anti-alcohol.

"Sorry," he says. "It's one of those nights."

"You saw the interview, didn't you?" I ask.

"Yeah. I was hoping you didn't."

"I did. Did my mom see—"

"Oh yeah, she saw it. So did Pam. And your grandma. I've never been in a room with so many pissed-off women in my life." He looks at me. "How are you dealing with it?"

I shrug. Yeah, I'm pissed, but honestly? "I expected his dad to make him the victim."

"I did too." He rests his cheek in his palm, his elbow propped on his knee. It's not too dark on the steps. I see the bruising on his hand fine.

"So…," I say, patting my knees. "On leave, huh?"

He looks at me like he's trying to figure out what I'm getting at. "Yeah?"

Silence.

"Did you fight him, Uncle Carlos?"

He straightens up. "No, I had a discussion with him."

"You mean your fist talked to his eye. Did he say something about me?"

"He pointed his gun at you. That was more than enough."

His voice has a foreign edge to it. It's totally inappropriate, but I laugh. I have to hold my side I laugh so hard.

"What's so funny?" he cries.

"Uncle Carlos, you punched somebody!"

"Hey, I'm from Garden Heights. I know how to fight. I can get down."

250

I'm hollering right now.

"It's not funny!" he says. "I shouldn't have lost my cool like that. It was unprofessional. Now I've set a bad example for you."

"Yeah, you have, Muhammad Ali."

I'm still laughing. Now he's laughing.

"Hush," he says.

Our laughter dies down, and it's real quiet out here. Nothing to do but look at the sky and all the stars. There's so many of them tonight. It's possible that I don't notice them at home because of all the other stuff. Sometimes it's hard to believe Garden Heights and Riverton Hills share the same sky.

"You remember what I used to tell you?" Uncle Carlos says.

I scoot closer to him. "That I'm not named after the stars, but the stars are named after me. You were really trying to give me a big head, huh?"

He chuckles. "No. I wanted you to know how special you are."

"Special or not, you shouldn't have risked your job for me. You love your job."

"But I love you more. You're one reason I even became a cop, baby girl. Because I love you and all those folks in the neighborhood."

"I know. That's why I don't want you to risk it. We need the ones like you."

"The ones like me." He gives a hollow laugh. "You

251

know, I got pissed listening to that man talk about you and Khalil like that, but it made me consider the comments I made about Khalil that night in your parents' kitchen."

"What comments?"

"I know you were eavesdropping, Starr. Don't act brand-new."

I smirk. Uncle Carlos said "brand-new." "You mean when you called Khalil a drug dealer?"

He nods. "Even if he was, I knew that boy. Watched him grow up with you. He was more than any bad decision he made," he says. "I hate that I let myself fall into that mind-set of trying to rationalize his death. And at the end of the day, you don't kill someone for opening a car door. If you do, you shouldn't be a cop."

I tear up. It's good to hear my parents and Ms. Ofrah say that or see all the protestors shout about it. From my uncle the cop though? It's a relief, even if it makes everything hurt a little more.

"I told Brian that," he says, looking at his knuckles. "After I clocked him. Told the chief too. Actually, I think I screamed it loud enough for everybody in the precinct to hear. It doesn't take away from what I did though. I dropped the ball on Khalil."

"No, you didn't—"

"Yes, I did," he says. "I knew him, knew his family's situation. After he stopped coming around with you, he was out of sight and out of mind to me, and there's no excuse for that."

252

There's no excuse for me either. "I think all of us feel like that," I mutter. "That's one reason Daddy's determined to help DeVante."

"Yeah," he says. "Me too."

I look at all the stars again. Daddy says he named me Starr because I was his light in the darkness. I need some light in my own darkness right about now.

"I wouldn't have killed Khalil, by the way," Uncle Carlos says. "I don't know a lot of stuff, but I do know that."

My eyes sting, and my throat tightens. I've turned into such a damn crybaby. I snuggle closer to Uncle Carlos and hope it says everything I can't.

CHAPTER 15

It takes an untouched stack of pancakes for Momma to say, "All right, Munch. What's up?"

We have a table to ourselves in IHOP. It's early morning, and the restaurant's almost empty except for us and these big-bellied, bearded truckers stuffing their faces in a booth. Thanks to them, country music plays on the jukebox.

I poke my fork at my pancakes. "Not real hungry."

Somewhat a lie, somewhat the truth. I'm having a serious emotional hangover. There's that interview. Uncle Carlos. Hailey. Khalil. DeVante. My parents.

Momma, Sekani, and I spent the night at Uncle Carlos's house, and I know it was more because Momma's mad at Daddy than it was about the riots. In fact, the news said last night was the first semi-peaceful night in the Garden. Just protests, no riots. Cops were still throwing tear gas though.

Anyway, if I bring up my parents' fight, Momma's gonna tell me, "Stay outta grown folks' business." You'd think since it's partially my fault they fought, it *is* my business, but nope.

"I don't know who's supposed to believe that *you're* not hungry," Momma says. "You've always been greedy."

I roll my eyes and yawn. She got me up too early and said we were going to IHOP, just the two of us like we used to do before Sekani came along and ruined everything. He has an extra uniform at Uncle Carlos's and can go to school with Daniel. I only had some sweats and a Drake T-shirt – not DA office appropriate. I gotta go home and change.

"Thanks for bringing me here," I say. With my awful mood, I owe her that.

"Anytime, baby. We haven't hung out in a while. Somebody decided I wasn't cool anymore. I thought I was still cool, so whatever." She sips from her steaming mug of coffee. "Are you scared to talk to the DA?"

"Not really." Although I do notice the clock is only three and a half hours away from our nine-thirty meeting.

"Is it that BS of an interview? That bastard."

Here we go again. "Momma—"

"Got his damn daddy going on TV, telling lies," she says. "And who's supposed to believe a grown man was that scared of two *children*?"

People on the internet are saying the same thing. Black Twitter's been going in on Officer Cruise's dad, claiming his name should be Tom Cruise with that performance he put on. Tumblr too. I'm sure there are people who believe him – Hailey did – but Ms. Ofrah was right: it backfired. Folks who never met me or Khalil are calling BS.

So while the interview bothers me, it doesn't bother me *that* much.

"It's not really the interview," I say. "It's other stuff too."

"Like?"

"Khalil," I say. "DeVante told me some stuff about him, and I feel guilty."

"Stuff like what?" she says.

"Why he sold drugs. He was trying to help Ms. Brenda pay a debt to King."

Momma's eyes widen. "What?"

"Yeah. And he wasn't a King Lord. Khalil turned King down, and King's been lying to save face."

Momma shakes her head. "Why am I not surprised? King would do some mess like that."

I stare at my pancakes. "I should've known better. Should've known *Khalil* better."

"You had no way of knowing, baby," she says.

"That's the thing. If I would've been there for him, I—"

"Couldn't have stopped him. Khalil was almost as stubborn as you. I know you cared about him a lot, even as more than a friend, but you can't blame yourself for this."

I look up at her. "What you mean 'cared about him as more than a friend'?"

"Don't play dumb, Starr. Y'all liked each other for a long time."

"You think he liked me too?"

"Lord!" Momma rolls her eyes. "Between the two of us, I'm the old one—"

"You just called yourself old."

"*Older* one," she corrects, and shoots me a quick stank-eye, "and I saw it. How in the world did you miss it?"

"I dunno. He always talked about other girls, not me. It's weird though. I thought I was over my crush, but sometimes I don't know."

Momma traces the rim of her mug. "Munch," she says, and it's followed by a sigh. "Baby, look. You're grieving, okay? That can amplify your emotions and make you feel things you haven't felt in a long time. Even if you do have feelings for Khalil, there's nothing wrong with that."

"Even though I'm with Chris?"

"Yes. You're sixteen. You're allowed to have feelings for more than one person."

"So you're saying I can be a ho?"

"Girl!" She points at me. "Don't make me kick you under this table. I'm saying don't beat yourself up about it. Grieve Khalil all you want. Miss him, allow yourself to miss what could've been, let your feelings get out of whack. But like I told you, don't stop living. All right?"

"All right."

"Good. So that's two things," she says. "What else is up?"

What isn't up? My head is tight like my brain is overloaded. I'm guessing emotional hangovers feel a lot like actual hangovers.

"Hailey," I say.

She slurps her coffee. Loudly. "What that li'l girl do now?"

Here she goes with this. "Momma, you've never liked her."

"No, I've never liked how you've followed her like you can't think for yourself. Difference."

"I haven't—"

"Don't lie! Remember that drum set you begged me to buy. Why did you want it, Starr?"

"Hailey wanted to start a band, but I liked the idea too."

"Hold up, though. Didn't you tell me you wanted to play guitar in this 'band,' but Hailey said you should play drums?"

"Yeah, but—"

"Them li'l Jonas boys," she says. "Which one did you really like?"

"Joe."

"But who said you should be with the curly-headed one instead?"

"Hailey, but Nick was still fine as all get-out, and this is middle school stuff—"

"Uh-uh! Last year you begged me to let you color your hair purple. Why, Starr?"

"I wanted—"

"No. *Why*, Starr?" she says. "The real why."

Damn. There's a pattern here. "Because Hailey wanted me, her, and Maya to have matching hair."

"E-xact-damn-ly. Baby, I love you, but you have a history of putting your wants aside and doing whatever that li'l girl wants. Excuse me if I don't like her."

258

With all my receipts put out there like that, I say, "I can see why."

"Good. Realizing is the first step. So what she do now?"

"We had an argument yesterday," I say. "Really though, things have been weird for a while. She stopped texting me and unfollowed my Tumblr."

Momma reaches her fork onto my plate and breaks off a piece of pancake. "What is Tumblr anyway? Is it like Facebook?"

"No, and you're forbidden to get one. No parents allowed. You guys already took over Facebook."

"You haven't responded to my friend request yet."

"I know."

"I need Candy Crush lives."

"That's why I'll never respond."

She gives me "the look." I don't care. There are some things I absolutely refuse to do.

"So she unfollowed your Tumblr thingy," Momma says, proving why she can never have one. "Is that all?"

"No. She said and did some stupid stuff too." I rub my eyes. Like I said, it's too early. "I'm starting to wonder why we're friends."

"Well, Munch" – she gets another freaking piece of my pancakes – "you have to decide if the relationship is worth salvaging. Make a list of the good stuff, then make a list of the bad stuff. If one outweighs the other, then you know what you gotta do. Trust me, that method hasn't failed me yet."

"Is that what you did with Daddy after Iesha got pregnant?" I ask. "'Cause I'll be honest, I would've kicked him to the curb. No offense."

"It's all right. A lot of people called me a fool for going back to your daddy. Shoot, they may still call me a fool behind my back. Your nana would have a stroke if she knew this, but she's the real reason I stayed with your daddy."

"I thought Nana hated Daddy?" I think Nana still hates Daddy.

Sadness creeps into Momma's eyes, but she gives me a small smile. "When I was growing up, your grandmother would do and say hurtful things when she was drunk, and apologize the next morning. At an early age I learned that people make mistakes, and you have to decide if their mistakes are bigger than your love for them."

She takes a deep breath. "Seven's not a mistake, I love him to death, but Maverick made a mistake in his actions. However, all of his good and the love we share outweighs that one mistake."

"Even with crazy Iesha in our lives?" I ask.

Momma chuckles. "Even with crazy, messy, annoying Iesha. It's a little different, yeah, but if the good outweighs the bad, keep Hailey in your life, baby."

That might be the problem. A lot of the good stuff is from the past. The Jonas Brothers, *High School Musical*, our shared grief. Our friendship is based on memories. What do we have now?

"What if the good doesn't outweigh the bad?" I ask.

"Then let her go," Momma says. "And if you keep her in your life and she keeps doing the bad, let her go. Because I promise you, had your daddy pulled some mess like that again, I'd be married to Idris Elba and saying, 'Maverick who?'"

I bust out laughing.

"Now eat," she says, and hands me her fork. "Before I have no choice but to eat these pancakes for you."

I'm so used to seeing smoke in Garden Heights, it's weird when we go back and there isn't any. It's dreary because of a late-night storm, but we can ride with the windows down. Even though the riots stopped, we pass as many tanks as we pass lowriders.

But at home smoke greets us at the front door.

"Maverick!" Momma hollers, and we hurry toward the kitchen.

Daddy pours water on a skillet at the sink, and the skillet responds with a loud sizzle and a white cloud. Whatever he burned, he burned it bad.

"Hallelujah!" Seven throws his hands up at the table. "Somebody who can actually cook."

"Shut up," Daddy says.

Momma takes the skillet and examines the unidentifiable remains. "What was this? Eggs?"

"Glad to see you know how to come home," he says. He walks right by me without a glance or a good morning. He's still pissed about Chris?

Momma gets a fork and stabs at the charred food stuck

261

to the skillet. "You want some breakfast, Seven baby?"

He watches her and goes, "Um, nah. By the way, the skillet didn't do anything, Ma."

"You're right," she says, but she keeps stabbing. "Seriously, I can fix you something. Eggs. Bacon." She looks toward the hall and shouts, "The *pork* kind! Pig! Swine! All'a that!"

So much for the good outweighing the bad. Seven and I look at each other. We hate when they fight because we always get stuck in the middle of their wars. Our appetites are the greatest casualty. If Momma's mad and not cooking, we have to eat Daddy's struggle meals, like spaghetti with ketchup and hot dogs in it.

"I'll grab something at school." Seven kisses her cheek. "Thanks though." He gives me a fist bump on his way out, the Seven way of wishing me good luck.

Daddy returns wearing a backwards cap. He grabs his keys and a banana.

"We have to be at the DA's office at nine thirty," Momma says. "Are you coming?"

"Oh, Carlos can't do it? Since he the one y'all let in on secrets and stuff."

"You know what, Maverick—"

"I'll be there," he says, and leaves.

Momma stabs the skillet some more.

The DA personally escorts us to a conference room. Her name is Karen Monroe, and she's a middle-aged white lady who claims she understands what I'm going through.

Ms. Ofrah is already in the conference room along with some people who work at the DA's office. Ms. Monroe gives a long speech about how much she wants justice for Khalil and apologizes that it's taken this long for us to meet.

"Twelve days, to be exact," Daddy points out. "Too long, if you ask me."

Ms. Monroe looks a bit uncomfortable at that.

She explains the grand jury proceedings. Then she asks about that night. I pretty much tell her what I told the cops, except she doesn't ask any stupid questions about Khalil. But when I get to the part when I describe the number of shots, how they hit Khalil in his back, the look on his face—

My stomach bubbles, bile pools in my mouth, and I gag. Momma jumps up and grabs a garbage bin. She puts it in front of me quick enough to catch the vomit that spews from my mouth.

And I cry and puke. Cry and puke. It's all I can do.

The DA gets me a soda and says, "That'll be all today, sweetie. Thank you."

Daddy helps me to Momma's car, and people in the halls gawk. I bet they know I'm the witness from my teary, snotty face, and are probably giving me a new name – Poor Thing. As in, "Oh, that poor thing." That makes it worse.

I get in the car away from their pity and rest my head against the window, feeling like shit.

Momma parks in front of the store, and Daddy pulls up behind us. He gets out his truck and comes to Momma's side of the car. She rolls her window down.

"I'm going to the school," she tells him. "They need to know what's going on. Can she stay with you?"

"Yeah, that's fine. She can rest in the office."

Another thing puking and crying gets you – people talk about you like you're not there and make plans for you. Poor Thing apparently can't hear.

"You sure?" Momma asks him. "Or do I need to take her to Carlos?"

Daddy sighs. "Lisa—"

"Maverick, I don't give a flying monkey's ass what your problem is, just be there for your daughter. Please?"

Daddy moves to my side of the car and opens the door. "Come here, baby."

I climb out, blubbering like a little kid who skinned her knee. Daddy pulls me into his chest, rubbing my back and kissing my hair. Momma drives off.

"I'm sorry, baby," he says.

The crying, the puking don't mean anything anymore. My daddy's got me.

We go in the store. Daddy turns on the lights but keeps the closed sign in the window. He goes to his office for a second, then comes back to me and holds my chin.

"Open your mouth," he says. I open it, and his face scrunches up. "*Ill*. We gotta get you a whole bottle of mouthwash. 'Bout to raise the dead with that breath."

I laugh with tears in my eyes. Like I said, Daddy's talented that way.

He wipes my face with his hands, which are rough as sandpaper, but I'm used to them. He frames my face. I smile. "There go my baby," he says. "You'll be a'ight."

I feel normal enough to say, "Now I'm your baby? You haven't been acting like it."

"Don't start!" He goes down the medicine aisle. "Sounding like your momma."

"I'm just saying. You've been extra salty today."

He returns with a bottle of Listerine. "Here. Before you kill my produce with your breath."

"Like you killed those eggs this morning?"

"Ay, those were blackened eggs. Y'all don't know 'bout that."

"*Nobody* knows 'bout that."

A couple of rinses in the restroom transform my mouth from a swamp of puke residue to normal. Daddy waits on the wooden bench at the front of the store. Our older customers who can't walk much usually sit there as Daddy, Seven, or I get their groceries for them.

Daddy pats the spot next to him.

I sit. "You're gonna open back up soon?"

"In a li'l bit. What you see in that white boy?"

Damn. I wasn't expecting him to go right into it. "Besides the fact he's adorable—" I say, and Daddy makes a gagging sound, "he's smart, funny, and he cares about me. A lot."

"You got a problem with black boys?"

"No. I've had black boyfriends." Three of them. One

in fourth grade, although that doesn't really count, and two in middle school, which don't count either 'cause nobody knows shit about a relationship in middle school. Or about anything really.

"What?" he says. "I ain't know 'bout them."

"Because I knew you'd act crazy. Put a hit on them or something."

"You know, that ain't a bad idea."

"Daddy!" I smack his arm as he cracks up.

"Did Carlos know 'bout them?" he asks.

"No. He would've ran background checks on them or arrested them. Not cool."

"So why you tell him 'bout the white boy?"

"I didn't tell him," I say. "He found out. Chris lives down the street from him, so it was harder to hide. And let's be real here, Daddy. I've heard the stuff you've said about interracial couples. I didn't want you talking about me and Chris like that."

"Chris," he mocks. "What kinda plain-ass name is that?"

He's so petty. "Since you wanna ask me questions, do you have a problem with white people?"

"Not really."

"Not really?"

"Ay, I'm being honest. My thing is, girls usually date boys who are like their daddies, and I ain't gon' lie, when I saw that white – Chris," he corrects, and I smile. "I got worried. Thought I turned you against black men or didn't

266

set a good example of a black man. I couldn't handle that."

I rest my head on his shoulder. "Nah, Daddy. You haven't set a good example of what a black man should be. You've set a good example of what a *man* should be. Duh!"

"Duh," he mocks, and kisses the top of my head. "My baby."

A gray BMW comes to a sudden stop in front of the store.

Daddy nudges me off the bench. "C'mon."

He pulls me to his office and shoves me in. I catch a glimpse of King getting out the BMW before Daddy closes the door in my face.

Hands shaking, I crack open the door.

Daddy stands guard in the entrance of the store. His hand drifts to his waist. His piece.

Three other King Lords hop out the BMW, but Daddy calls out, "Nah. If you wanna talk, we do this alone."

King nods at his boys. They wait beside the car.

Daddy steps aside, and King lumbers in. I'm ashamed to admit it, but I don't know if Daddy stands a chance against King. Daddy isn't skinny or short, but compared to King, who's pure muscle at six feet, he looks tiny. It's damn near blasphemous to think like that though.

"Where he at?" King asks.

"Where who at?"

"You know who. Vante."

"How I'm supposed to know?" Daddy says.

"He was working here, wasn't he?"

"For a day or two, yeah. I ain't seen him today."

King paces and points his cigar at Daddy. Sweat glistens on the rolls of fat on the back of his head. "You lying."

"Why I gotta lie, King?"

"All the shit I did for you," King says, "and this how you repay me? Where he at, Big Mav?"

"I don't know."

"Where he at?" King yells.

"I said I don't know! He asked me for a couple hundred dollars the other day. I told him he had to work for it. So he did. I had some mercy and paid it all up front like a dumbass. He was supposed to come in today and didn't. End of story."

"Why he need money from you when he stole five Gs from me?"

"Hell if I know," Daddy says.

"If I find out you lying—"

"You ain't gotta worry 'bout that. Got too many problems of my own."

"Oh, yeah. I know 'bout your problems," King says, a laugh bubbling from him. "I heard Starr-Starr the witness they been talking 'bout on the news. Hope she know to keep her mouth shut when she supposed to."

"What the hell is that supposed to mean?"

"These cases always interesting," King says. "They dig for information. Shit, they try to find out more 'bout the person who died than the person who shot them. Make it seem like a good thing they got killed. They already saying Khalil sold drugs. That could mean problems for anybody

268

who may have been involved in his hustle. So people gotta be careful when they talking to the DA. Wouldn't want them to be in danger 'cause they ran their mouth."

"Nah," Daddy says. "The folks who were involved in the hustle need to be careful 'bout what they say or even think 'bout doing."

There are several agonizing seconds of Daddy and King staring each other down. Daddy's hand is at his waist like it's glued there.

King leaves, pushing the door hard enough to nearly break the hinges, the bell clanging wildly. He gets in his BMW. His minions follow, and he peels out, leaving the truth behind.

He's gonna mess me up if I rat on him.

Daddy sinks onto the old people's bench. His shoulders slump, and he takes a deep breath.

We close early and pick up dinner from Reuben's.

During the short drive home, I notice every car behind us, especially if it's gray.

"I won't let him do anything to you," Daddy says.

I know. But still.

Momma's beating the hell out of some steaks when we get home. First the skillet and now red meat. Nothing in the kitchen is safe.

Daddy holds up the bags for her to see. "I got dinner, baby."

It doesn't stop her from beating the steaks.

We all sit around the kitchen table, but it's the quietest dinner in Carter family history. My parents aren't talking. Seven's not talking. I'm definitely not talking. Or eating. Between the disaster at the DA's office and King, my ribs and baked beans look disgusting. Sekani can't sit still, like he's itching to give every detail of his day. I guess he can tell nobody's in the mood. Brickz chomps and slobbers over some ribs in his corner.

Afterward, Momma collects our plates and silverware. "All right, guys, finish your homework. And don't worry, Starr. Your teachers gave me yours."

Why would I worry about that? "Thanks."

She starts to pick up Daddy's plate, but he touches her arm. "Nah. I got it."

He takes all of the plates from her, dumps them in the sink, and turns the water on.

"Maverick, you don't have to do that."

He squirts way too much dishwashing liquid in the sink. He always does. "It's cool. What time you gotta be at the clinic in the morning?"

"I'll be off again tomorrow. I have a job interview."

Daddy turns around. "Another one?"

Another one?

"Yeah. Markham Memorial again."

"That's where Aunt Pam works," I say.

"Yeah. Her dad is on the board and recommended me. It's the Pediatrics Nursing Manager. This is my second interview for it actually. They want some of the

270

higher-ups to interview me this time."

"Baby, that's amazing," Daddy says. "That means you're close to getting it, huh?"

"Hopefully," she says. "Pam thinks it's as good as mine."

"Why didn't you guys tell us?" Seven asks.

"'Cause it's none of y'all business," Daddy says.

"And we didn't want to get your hopes up," Momma adds. "It's a competitive position."

"How much does it pay?" Seven's rude self asks.

"More than what I make at the clinic. Six figures."

"Six?" Seven and I say.

"Momma's gonna be a millionaire!" Sekani shouts.

I swear he doesn't know anything. "Six figures is the hundred thousands, Sekani," I say.

"Oh. It's still a lot."

"What time is your interview?" Daddy asks.

"Eleven."

"Okay, good." He turns around and wipes a plate. "We can look at some houses before you go to it."

Momma's hand goes across her chest, and she steps back. "What?"

He looks at me, then at her. "I'm getting us outta Garden Heights, baby. You got my word."

The idea is as crazy as a four-point shot. Living somewhere other than Garden Heights? Yeah, right. I'd never believe it if it wasn't Daddy saying it. Daddy never says something unless he means it. King's threat must've really got to him.

He scrubs the skillet that Momma stabbed this morning.

She takes it from him, sets it down, and grabs his hand. "Don't worry about that."

"I told you it's cool. I can get the dishes."

"Forget the dishes."

And she pulls him to their bedroom and closes the door.

Suddenly, their TV blares real loud, and Jodeci sings over it from the stereo. If that woman ends up with a fetus in her uterus, I will be completely done. *Done*.

"Ill, man," Seven says, knowing the deal too. "They're too old for that."

"Too old for what?" Sekani asks.

"Nothing," Seven and I say together.

"You think Daddy meant that though?" I ask Seven. "We're moving?"

He twists one of his dreads at the root. I don't think he realizes he's doing it. "Sounds like y'all are. Especially if Ma gets this job."

"*Y'all?*" I say. "You're not staying in Garden Heights."

"I mean, I'll visit, but I can't leave my momma and my sisters, Starr. You know that."

"Your momma put you out," Sekani says "Where else you gonna go, stupid?"

"Who you calling stupid?" Seven sticks his hand under his armpit, then rubs it in Sekani's face. The one time he did it to me I was nine. He got a busted lip, and I got a whooping.

"You're not gonna be at your momma's house anyway,"

272

I say. "You're going away to college, hallelujah, thank Black Jesus."

Seven raises his brows. "You want an armpit hand too? And I'm going to Central Community so I can stay at my momma's house and watch out for my sisters."

That stings. A little. I'm his sister too, not just them. *"House,"* I repeat. "You never call it home."

"Yeah, I do," he says.

"No, you don't."

"Yeah."

"Shut the hell up." I end that argument.

"Ooh!" Sekani holds his hand out. "Gimme my dollar!"

"Hell no," I say. "That shit doesn't work with me."

"Three dollars!"

"Okay, fine. I'll give you a three-dollar bill."

"I've never seen a three-dollar bill," he says.

"Exactly. And you'll never see my three dollars."

PART 2

FIVE WEEKS
AFTER IT

CHAPTER 16

Ms. Ofrah arranged for me to do an interview with one of the national news programs today – exactly a week before I testify before the grand jury next Monday.

It's around six o'clock when the limo that the news program sent arrives. My family's coming with me. I doubt my brothers will be interviewed, but Seven wants to support me. Sekani claims he does too, but really he's hoping he'll get "discovered" somehow with all those cameras around.

My parents told him about everything. As much as he gets on my nerves, it was sweet when he gave me a hand-made card that said "Sorry." Until I opened it. There was a drawing of me crying over Khalil, and I had devil horns. Sekani said he wanted it to be "real." Little asshole.

We all head out to the limo. Some neighbors watch curiously from their porches and yards. Momma made all of us, including Daddy, dress up like we're going to Christ Temple – not quite Easter formal but not "diverse church" casual. She says we're not gonna have the news people thinking we're "hood rats."

So as we're walking to the car, she's all, "When we get there, don't touch anything and only speak when somebody speaks to you. It's 'yes, ma'am' and 'yes, sir,' or 'no, ma'am' and 'no, sir.' Do I make myself clear?"

"Yes, ma'am," the three of us say.

"All right now, Starr," one of our neighbors calls out. I get that just about every day in the neighborhood now. Word's spreading around the Garden that I'm the witness. "All right now" is more than a greeting. It's a simple way people let me know they got my back.

The best part though? It's never "All right now, Big Mav's daughter who works in the store." It's always Starr.

We leave in the limo. I drum my fingers on my knee as I watch the neighborhood pass by. I've talked to detectives and the DA, and next week I'll talk to the grand jury. I've talked about that night so much I can repeat it back in my sleep. But the whole world will see this.

My phone vibrates in my blazer pocket. A couple of texts from Chris.

My mom wants to know what color your prom dress is.

Something about the tailor needs to know ASAP.

Oh, shit. The Junior-Senior Prom is Saturday. I haven't bought a dress. With all this Khalil stuff, I'm not sure I wanna go. Momma said I need to get my mind off things. I said no. She gave me "the look."

So I'm going to the damn prom. This dictatorship she's on? Not cool. I text Chris back.

Uh … light blue?

He responds:

You don't have a dress yet?

I've got plenty of time, I write back. **Just been busy.**

It's true. Ms. Ofrah prepared me for this interview every day after school. Some days we finished early, and I helped out around Just Us for Justice. Answered phones, passed out flyers, anything they needed me to do. Sometimes I listened in on their staff meetings as they discussed police reform ideas and the importance of telling the community to protest not riot.

I asked Dr. Davis if Just Us could have a roundtable discussion at Williamson like they do at Garden High. He said he didn't see the need.

Chris replies to my prom text:

Okay, if you say so

Btw Vante says sup.

About to kill him on Madden

He needs to stop calling me Bieber tho

After all that "white boy trying to be black" shit DeVante said about Chris, lately he's at Chris's house more than I am. Chris invited him over to play Madden, and all of a sudden they're "bros." According to DeVante, Chris's massive video game collection makes up for his whiteness.

I told DeVante he's a video game thot. He told me to shut up. We're cool like that though.

We arrive at a fancy hotel downtown. A white guy in a hoodie waits under the awning leading up to the door. He has a clipboard under his arm and a Starbucks cup in his hand.

Still, he somehow manages to open the limo door and shake our hands when we get out. "John, the producer. It's a pleasure to meet you." He shakes my hand a second time. "And let me guess, you're Starr."

"Yes, sir."

"Thank you so much for having the bravery to do this."

There's that word again. Bravery. Brave peoples' legs don't shake. Brave people don't feel like puking. Brave people sure don't have to remind themselves how to breathe if they think about that night too hard. If bravery is a medical condition, everybody's misdiagnosed me.

John leads us through all of these twists and turns, and I'm so glad I'm wearing flats. He can't stop talking about how important the interview is and how much they wanna get the truth out there. He's not exactly adding to my "bravery."

He takes us to the hotel courtyard, where some camera operators and other show people are setting up. In the middle of the chaos, the interviewer, Diane Carey, is getting her makeup done.

It's weird seeing her in the flesh and not as a bunch of pixels on TV. When I was younger, every single time I spent the night at Nana's house she made me sleep in one of her long-ass nightgowns, say my bedtime prayers for at least five minutes, and watch Diane Carey's news report so I could be "knowledgeable of the world."

"Hi!" Mrs. Carey's face lights up when she sees us. She comes over, and I gotta give the makeup lady props 'cause she follows her and keeps working like a pro. Mrs. Carey shakes our hands. "Diane. So nice to meet you all. And you must be Starr," she says to me. "Don't be nervous. This will simply be a conversation between the two of us."

The whole time she talks, some guy snaps photos of us. Yeah, this will be a normal conversation.

"Starr, we were thinking we could get shots of you and Diane walking and talking around the courtyard," John says. "Then we'll go up to the suite and do the conversations between you and Diane; you, Diane, and Ms. Ofrah; and finally you and your parents. After that, we'll be all set."

One of the production people mics me up as John gives me a rundown of this walk and talk thing. "It's only a transitional shot," he says. "Simple stuff."

Simple my ass. The first time, I practically power-walk. The second time, I walk like I'm in a funeral processional and can't answer Mrs. Carey's questions. I never realized walking and talking required so much coordination.

Once we get that right, we take an elevator to the top floor. John leads us to a huge suite – seriously, it looks like a penthouse – overlooking downtown. About a dozen people are setting up cameras and lighting. Ms. Ofrah's there in one of her Khalil shirts and a skirt. John says they're ready for me.

I sit in the loveseat across from Mrs. Carey. I've never been able to cross my legs, for whatever reason, so that's out the question. They check my mic, and Mrs. Carey tells me to relax. Soon, the cameras are rolling.

"Millions of people around the world have heard the name Khalil Harris," she says, "and they've developed their own ideas of who he was. Who was he to you?"

More than he may have ever realized. "One of my best friends," I say. "We knew each other since we were babies. If he were here, he'd point out that he was five months, two weeks, and three days older than me." We both chuckle at that. "But that's who Khalil is — was."

Damn. It hurts to correct myself.

"He was a jokester. Even when things were hard, he'd somehow find some light in it. And he…" My voice cracks.

I know it's corny, but I think he's here. His nosy ass would show up to make sure I say the right things. Probably calling me his number one fan or some annoying title that only Khalil can think of.

I miss that boy.

"He had a big heart," I say. "I know that some people call him a thug, but if you knew him, you'd know that wasn't the case at all. I'm not saying he was an angel or anything, but he wasn't a bad person. He was a…" I shrug. "He was a kid."

She nods. "He was a kid."

"He was a kid."

"What do you think about people who focus on the not-so-good aspect of him?" she asks. "The fact that he may have sold drugs?"

Ms. Ofrah once said that this is how I fight, with my voice.

So I fight.

"I hate it," I say. "If people knew why he sold drugs, they wouldn't talk about him that way."

Mrs. Carey sits up a little. "Why did he sell them?"

I glance at Ms. Ofrah, and she shakes her head. During all our prep meetings, she advised me not to go into details about Khalil selling drugs. She said the public doesn't have to know about that.

But then I look at the camera, suddenly aware that millions of people will watch this in a few days. King may be one of them. Although his threat is loud in my head, it's not nearly as loud as what Kenya said that day in the store.

Khalil would defend me. I should defend him.

So I gear up to throw a punch.

"Khalil's mom is a drug addict," I tell Mrs. Carey. "Anybody who knew him knew how much that bothered him and how much he hated drugs. He only sold them to help her out of a situation with the biggest drug dealer and gang leader in the neighborhood."

Ms. Ofrah noticeably sighs. My parents have wide eyes.

It's dry snitching, but it's snitching. Anybody who knows anything about Garden Heights will know exactly who I'm talking about. Hell, if they watch Mr. Lewis's interview they can figure it out.

But hey, since King wants to go around the neighborhood lying and saying Khalil repped his set, I can let the world know Khalil was forced to sell drugs for him. "His mom's life was in danger," I say. "That's the only reason he'd ever do something like that. And he wasn't a gang member—"

"He wasn't?"

"No, ma'am. He never wanted to fall into that type of life. But I guess—" I think about DeVante for some reason. "I don't understand how everyone can make it seem like it's okay he got killed if he was a drug dealer and a gangbanger."

A hook straight to the jaw.

"The media?" she asks.

"Yes, ma'am. It seems like they always talk about what he may have said, what he may have done, what he may not have done. I didn't know a dead person could be charged in his own murder, you know?"

The moment I say it, I know it's my jab to the mouth.

Mrs. Carey asks for my account of that night. I can't go into a lot of details – Ms. Ofrah told me not to – but I tell her we did everything One-Fifteen asked and never once cussed at him like his father claims. I tell her how afraid I was, how Khalil was so concerned about me that he opened the door and asked if I was okay.

"So he didn't make a threat on Officer Cruise's life?" she questions.

"No, ma'am. His exact words were, 'Starr, are you okay?' That was the last thing he said, and—"

I'm ugly crying, describing the moment when the shots rang out and Khalil looked at me for the last time; how I held him in the street and saw his eyes gloss over. I tell her One-Fifteen pointed his gun at me.

284

"He pointed his gun at you?" she asks.

"Yes, ma'am. He kept it on me until the other officers arrived."

Behind the cameras, Momma puts her hand over her mouth. Fury sparks in Daddy's eyes. Ms. Ofrah looks stunned.

It's another jab.

See, I only told Uncle Carlos that part.

Mrs. Carey gives me Kleenex and a moment to get myself together. "Has this situation made you fearful of cops?" she eventually asks.

"I don't know," I say truthfully. "My uncle's a cop. I know not all cops are bad. And they risk their lives, you know? I'm always scared for my uncle. But I'm tired of them assuming. Especially when it comes to black people."

"You wish that more cops wouldn't make assumptions about black people?" she clarifies.

"Right. This all happened because *he*" – I can't say his name – "assumed that we were up to no good. Because we're black and because of where we live. We were just two kids, minding our business, you know? His assumption killed Khalil. It could've killed me."

A kick straight to the ribs.

"If Officer Cruise were sitting here," Mrs. Carey says, "what would you say to him?"

I blink several times. My mouth waters, but I swallow. No way I'm gonna let myself cry or throw up from thinking about that man.

If he were sitting here, I don't have enough Black Jesus in me to tell him I forgive him. Instead I'd probably punch him. Straight up.

But Ms. Ofrah says this interview is the way I fight. When you fight, you put yourself out there, not caring who you hurt or if you'll get hurt.

So I throw one more blow, right at One-Fifteen.

"I'd ask him if he wished he shot me too."

CHAPTER 17

My interview aired yesterday on Diane Carey's *Friday Night News Special*. This morning, John the producer called and said it's one of the most-watched interviews in the network's history.

A millionaire, who wishes to remain anonymous, offered to pay my college tuition. John said the offer was made right after the interview aired. I think it's Oprah, but that's just me because I've always imagined she's my fairy godmother and one day she'll come to my house saying, "You get a car!"

The network's already got a bunch of emails in support of me. I haven't seen any of them, but I received the best message in a text from Kenya.

Bout time you spoke out.

Don't let this fame go to your head tho.

The interview trended online. When I looked this morning, people were still talking about it. Black Twitter and Tumblr have my back. Some assholes want me dead.

King's not too happy either. Kenya told me he's heated that I dry snitched.

The Saturday news programs discussed the interview too, dissecting my words like I'm the president or something. This one network is outraged by my "disregard for cops." I'm not sure how they got that out the interview. It's not like I was on some NWA "Fuck the Police" type shit. I simply said I'd ask the man if he wished he shot me too.

I don't care. I'm not apologizing for how I feel. People can say what they want.

But it's Saturday, and I'm sitting in a Rolls-Royce on my way to prom with a boyfriend who isn't saying much of anything to me. Chris is more interested in his phone.

"You look nice," I tell him. Which he does. His black tux with a light-blue vest and tie match the strapless tea-length gown I have on. His black leather Chuck Taylors are also a good match to my silver sequined ones. The dictator, a.k.a. my mom, bought my outfit. She has pretty good taste.

Chris says, "Thanks. You too," but it's so robotic, like he's saying what he's supposed to and not what he wants to. And how does he know what I look like? He's barely looked at me since he picked me up from Uncle Carlos's house.

I have no clue what's wrong with him. Things have been fine between us, as far as I know. Now, out of nowhere, he's all moody and silent. I would ask the driver to take me back to Uncle Carlos's, but I look too cute to go home.

The driveway at the country club is lit with blue lights, and golden balloon arches hang over it. We're in the only Rolls-Royce among a sea of limos, so of course people look when we pull up to the entrance.

The driver opens the door for us. Mr. Silent climbs out first and actually helps me out. Our classmates whoop and cheer and whistle. Chris wraps his arm around my waist, and we smile for pictures like everything's all good. Chris takes my hand and wordlessly escorts me inside.

Loud music greets us. Chandeliers and flashing party lights light up the ballroom. Some committee decided the theme should be Midnight in Paris, so there's a huge Eiffel Tower made out of Christmas lights. Looks like just about every junior and senior at Williamson is on the dance floor.

Let me say it. A Garden Heights party and a Williamson party are two very different things. At Big D's party, people Nae-Naed, Hit the Quan, twerked and stuff. At prom, I honestly don't know what the hell some of them are doing. Lots of jumping and fist pumping and attempts at twerking. It's not bad. Just different. Way different.

It's weird though – I'm not as hesitant to dance here as I was at Big D's party. Like I said, at Williamson I'm cool by default because I'm black. I can go out there and do a silly dance move I made up, and everyone will think it's the new thing. White people assume all black people are experts on trends and shit. There's no way in hell I'd try that at a Garden Heights party though. You make a fool of yourself one time, and that's it. Everybody in the neighborhood will know and nobody will forget.

In Garden Heights, I learn how to be dope by watching. At Williamson, I put my learned dopeness on display. I'm not even *that* dope, but these white kids think I am and that goes a long way in high school politics.

I start to ask Chris if he wants to dance, but he lets my hand go and heads toward some of his boys.

Why did I come to prom again?

"Starr!" somebody calls. I look around a couple of times and finally spot Maya waving at me from a table.

"Girl-lee!" she says when I get there. "You look good! I know Chris went crazy when he saw you."

No. He nearly *drove* me crazy. "Thanks," I say, and give her a once-over. She's wearing a pink knee-length strapless dress. A pair of sparkly silver stilettos gives her about five more inches of height. I applaud her for making it this far in them. I hate heels. "But if anybody's looking good tonight, it's you. You clean up nice, Shorty."

"Don't call me that. Especially since She Who Must Not Be Named gave me that nickname."

Damn. She Voldemorted Hailey. "Maya, you don't have to take sides, you know."

"She's the one not speaking to us, remember?"

Hailey's been on some silent treatment shit since the incident at Maya's house. I mean damn, I call you out on something, so I'm wrong and deserve the cold shoulder? Nah, she's not guilt-tripping me like that. And when Maya admitted to Hailey that she told me why Hailey unfollowed my Tumblr, Hailey stopped speaking to Maya, claiming she won't talk to either of us until we apologize. She's not used to both of us turning on her like this.

Whatever. She and Chris can form a club for all I care.

Call it the Silent Treatment League of Young, Rich Brats.

I'm in my feelings just a tad. I hate that Maya got pulled into it though. "Maya, I'm sorry—"

"No need," she says. "Don't know if I told you, but I brought up the cat thing to her. After I told her about Tumblr."

"Really?"

"Yeah. And she told me to get over it." Maya shakes her head. "I'm still mad at myself for letting her say it in the first place."

"Yeah. I'm mad at myself too."

We get quiet.

Maya nudges my side. "Hey. We minorities have to stick together, remember?"

I chuckle. "Okay, okay. Where's Ryan?"

"Getting some snacks. He looks good tonight, if I say so myself. Where's your guy?"

"Don't know," I say. And don't care at the moment.

The beautiful thing about best friends? They can tell when you don't wanna talk, and they don't push it. Maya hooks her arm through mine. "C'mon. I did not get dressed up to stand around."

We head for the dance floor and jump and fist-pump along with the rest of them. Maya takes those heels off and barefoots it. Jess, Britt, and some of the other girls from the team join us, and we make our own little dancing circle. We lose our minds when my cousin-through-marriage, Beyoncé, comes on. (I swear I'm related to Jay-Z somehow. Same last name – we have to be.)

We sing loudly with Cousin Bey until we almost go hoarse, and Maya and I are really into it. I may not have Khalil, Natasha, or even Hailey, but I have Maya. She's enough.

After six songs, we head back to our table, our arms draped around each other. I carry one of Maya's shoes, and the other one dangles from her wrist by the strap.

"Did you see Mr. Warren do the robot?" Maya asks between laughs.

"Did I? I didn't know he had it in him."

Maya stops. She looks around without looking at anything at all. "Don't look, but look to the left," she mutters.

"The hell? Which one is it?"

"Look to the left," she says through her teeth. "But quickly."

Hailey and Luke are arm in arm in the entrance, posing for pictures, and I can't even throw shade – with her gold-and-white dress and his white tux, they're cute. I mean, just 'cause we've got beef doesn't mean I can't compliment her, you know? I'm even happy she's with Luke. It took long enough.

Hailey and Luke walk in our direction but brush right past us, her shoulder a couple of inches away from mine. She flashes us stank-eye. This chick. I probably shoot one back. Sometimes I give stank-eyes and don't realize I'm giving them.

"Yeah, that's right," Maya says to Hailey's back. "You better keep walking."

Lord. Maya can go from zero to one hundred a little too quick. "Let's get something to drink," I say, pulling her with me. "Before you hurt yourself."

We get some punch and join Ryan at our table. He's stuffing his face with finger sandwiches and meatballs, crumbs falling onto his tux. "Where y'all been?" he asks.

"Dancing," Maya says. She steals one of his shrimp. "You didn't eat all day, did you?"

"Nope. I was about to starve to death." He nods at me. "What's up, Black Girlfriend?"

We joke around about that whole "only two black kids in the class are supposed to date" thing. "What's up, Black Boyfriend?" I say, and I steal a shrimp too.

What do you know, Chris remembers he came with somebody and walks over to our table. He says hey to Maya and Ryan, then asks me, "You wanna take pictures or something?"

His tone is all robotic again. On a scale of one to ten on the "I'm done" meter, I'm at about fifty. "No thanks," I tell him. "I'm not taking pictures with somebody who doesn't wanna be here with me."

He sighs. "Why do you have to have an attitude?"

"Me? You're the one giving me the cold shoulder."

"Dammit, Starr! Do you wanna take a fucking picture or not?"

The "done" meter blows up. Ka-boom. Blown to pieces. "Hell no. Go take one and shove it up your ass."

I march off, ignoring Maya's calls for me to come back.

293

Chris follows me. He tries to grab my arm, but I snatch away and keep walking. It's dark outside, but I easily find the Rolls-Royce parked along the driveway. The chauffeur isn't around, or otherwise I would ask him to take me home. I hop in the back and lock the doors.

Chris knocks on the window. "Starr, c'mon." He puts his hands against the window like they're binoculars and he's trying to look through the tint. "Can we talk?"

"Oh, now you wanna talk to me?"

"You're the one who wouldn't talk to me!" He bows his head, pressing his forehead against the glass. "Why didn't you tell me you were the witness they've been talking about?"

He asks it softly, but it's hard as a sucker punch in the gut.

He knows.

I unlock the door and scoot over. Chris climbs in next to me.

"How did you find out?" I ask.

"The interview. Watched it with my parents."

"They didn't show my face though."

"I knew your voice, Starr. And then they showed the back of you as you walked with that interview lady, and I've watched you walk away enough to know what you look like from the back, and … I sound like a pervert, don't I?"

"So you knew me by my ass?"

"I … yeah." His face goes red. "But that wasn't all. Everything made sense, like how upset you got about the protest and about Khalil. Not that that wasn't stuff to get upset about, 'cause it was, but it—" He sighs. "I'm sinking here, Starr. I just knew it was you. And it was, wasn't it?"

I nod.

"Babe, you should've told me. Why would you keep something like that from me?"

I tilt my head. "Wow. I saw someone get murdered, and you're acting like a brat 'cause I didn't tell you?"

"I didn't mean it like that."

"But you think about that for a second," I say. "Tonight you could hardly say two words to me because I didn't tell you about one of the worst experiences of my life. You ever seen somebody die?"

"No."

"I've seen it twice."

"And I didn't know that!" he says. "I'm your boyfriend, and I didn't know any of that." He looks at me, the same hurt in his eyes like there was when I snatched my hands away weeks ago. "There's this whole part of your life that you've kept from me, Starr. We've been together over a year now, and you've never mentioned Khalil, who you claim was your best friend, or this other person you saw die. You didn't trust me enough to tell me."

My breath catches. "It's – it's not like that."

"Really?" he says. "Then what is it like? What are we? Just *Fresh Prince* and fooling around?"

"No." My lips tremble, and my voice is small. "I … I can't share that part of me here, Chris."

295

"Why not?"

"Because," I croak. "People use it against me. Either I'm poor Starr who saw her friend get killed in a drive-by, or Starr the charity case who lives in the ghetto. That's how the teachers act."

"Okay, I get not telling people around school," he says. "But I'm not them. I would never use that against you. You once told me I'm the only person you could be yourself around at Williamson, but the truth is you *still* didn't trust me."

I'm one second away from ugly crying. "You're right," I say. "I didn't trust you. I didn't want you to just see me as the girl from the ghetto."

"You didn't even give me the chance to prove you wrong. I wanna be there for you. You gotta let me in."

God. Being two different people is so exhausting. I've taught myself to speak with two different voices and only say certain things around certain people. I've mastered it. As much as I say I don't have to choose which Starr I am with Chris, maybe without realizing it, I have to an extent. Part of me feels like I can't exist around people like him.

I am not gonna cry, I am not gonna cry, I am not gonna cry.

"Please?" he says.

That does it. Everything starts spilling out.

"I was ten. When my other friend died," I say, staring at the French tips on my nails. "She was ten too."

"What was her name?" he asks.

"Natasha. It was a drive-by. It's one of the reasons my parents put me and my brothers in Williamson. It was the closest they could get to protecting us a little more. They bust their butts for us to go to that school."

Chris doesn't say anything. I don't need him to.

I take a shaky breath and look around. "You don't know how crazy it is that I'm even sitting in this car," I say. "A Rolls freaking Royce. I used to live in the projects in a one-bedroom apartment. I shared the room with my brothers, and my parents slept on a fold-out couch."

The details of life back then are suddenly fresh. "The apartment smelled like cigarettes all the damn time," I say. "Daddy smoked. Our neighbors above us and next to us smoked. I had so many asthma attacks, it ain't funny. We only kept canned goods in the cabinets 'cause of the rats and roaches. Summers were always too hot, and winters too cold. We had to wear coats inside and outside.

"Sometimes Daddy sold food stamps to buy clothes for us," I say. "He couldn't get a job for the longest time, 'cause he's an ex-con. When he got hired at the grocery store, he took us to Taco Bell, and we ordered whatever we wanted. I thought it was the greatest thing in the world. Almost better than the day we moved out the projects."

Chris cracks a small smile. "Taco Bell is pretty awesome."

"Yeah." I look at my hands again. "He let Khalil come with us to Taco Bell. We were struggling, but Khalil was like our charity case. Everybody knew his momma was a crackhead."

I feel the tears coming. Fuck, I'm sick of this. "We were real close back then. He was my first kiss, first crush. Before

297

he died, we weren't as close anymore. I mean, I hadn't seen him in months and…" I'm ugly crying. "And it's killing me because he was going through so much shit, and I wasn't there for him anymore."

Chris thumbs my tears away. "You can't blame yourself."

"But I do," I say. "I could've stopped him from selling drugs. Then people wouldn't be calling him a thug. And I'm sorry I didn't tell you; I wanted to, but everybody who knows I was in the car acts like I'm made out of glass. You treated me normal. You *were* my normal."

I'm an absolute mess right now. Chris takes my hand and pulls me onto his lap so I'm straddling him. I bury my face in his shoulder and cry like a big-ass baby. His tux is wet, my makeup is ruined. Awful.

"I'm sorry," he says, rubbing my back. "I was an ass tonight."

"You were. But you're my ass."

"I've been watching *myself* walk away?"

I look at him and seriously punch his arm. He laughs and the sound of it makes me laugh. "You know what I mean! You're my normal. And that's all that matters."

"All that matters." He smiles.

I hold his cheek and let my lips reintroduce themselves to his. Chris's are soft and perfect. They taste like fruit punch too.

Chris pulls back with a gentle tug to my bottom lip. He presses his forehead against mine and looks at me. "I love you."

The "I" has appeared. My response is easy. "I love you too."

Two loud knocks against the window startle us. Seven presses his face against the glass. "Y'all bet' not be doing nothing!"

The best way to get turned all the way off? Have your brother show up.

"Seven, leave them alone," Layla whines behind him. "We were about to dance, remember?"

"That can wait. I gotta make sure he's not getting some from my sister."

"You won't get any if you don't stop acting so ridiculous!" she says.

"I don't care. Starr, get out this car. I ain't playing!"

Chris laughs into my bare shoulder. "Did your dad tell him to keep an eye on you?"

Knowing Daddy... "Probably so."

He kisses my shoulder and his lips linger there a few seconds. "Are we good now?"

I peck him back on the lips. "We're good."

"Good. Let's go dance."

We get out the car, and Seven yells about us sneaking off and threatens to tell Daddy. Layla pulls him back inside as he says, "And if she push out a little Chris in nine months, we gon' have a problem, partna!"

Ridiculous. Re-damn-diculous.

The music is still bumping inside. I try not to laugh as Chris really does turn the Nae-Nae into a No-No. Maya and Ryan join us on the dance floor, and they give me these "What the hell?" looks at Chris's moves. I shrug and go with it.

Toward the end of a song, Chris leans down to my ear and says, "I'll be right back."

He disappears into the crowd. I don't think anything of it until about a minute later when his voice comes over the speakers, and he's next to the DJ in the booth.

"Hey, everybody," he says. "My girl and I had a fight earlier."

Oh, Lord. He's telling all of our business. I look at my Chucks and shield my face.

"And I wanted to do this song, our song, to show you how much I love you and care about you, Fresh Princess."

A bunch of girls go, "Awww!" His boys whoop and cheer. I'm thinking, please don't let him sing. Please. But there's this familiar *boomp … boomp, boomp, boomp.*

"Now this is a story all about how my life got flipped turned upside down," Chris raps. "And I'd like to take a minute, just sit right there, I'll tell you how I became the prince of a town called Bel-Air."

I smile way too hard. *Our* song. I rap along with him, and mostly everyone joins in. Even the teachers. At the end, I cheer louder than anybody.

Chris comes back down, and we laugh and hug and kiss. Then we dance and take silly selfies, flooding dashboards and timelines around the world. When prom is over, we let Maya, Ryan, Jess, and some of our other friends ride with us to IHOP. Everybody has somebody on their lap. At IHOP, we eat way too many pancakes and dance to songs on the jukebox. I don't think about Khalil or Natasha.

It's one of the best nights of my life.

CHAPTER 18

On Sunday, my parents take me and my brothers on a trip.

It seems like a normal visit to Uncle Carlos's house until we pass his neighborhood. A little over five minutes later, a brick sign surrounded by colorful shrubs welcomes us to Brook Falls.

Single-story brick houses line freshly paved streets. Black kids, white kids, and everything in between play on the sidewalks and in yards. Open garage doors show all of the junk inside, and bikes and scooters lay abandoned in yards. Nobody's worried about their stuff getting stolen in the middle of the day.

It reminds me of Uncle Carlos's neighborhood yet it's different. For one, there's no gate around it, so they're not keeping anyone out or in, but obviously people feel safe. The houses are smaller, more homey looking. And straight up? There are more people who look like us compared to Uncle Carlos's neighborhood.

Daddy pulls into the driveway of a brown-brick house at the end of a cul-de-sac. Bushes and small trees decorate the yard, and a cobblestone walkway leads up to the front door.

"C'mon, y'all," Daddy says.

We hop out, stretching and yawning. Those forty-five-minute drives aren't a joke. A chubby black man waves at us from the driveway next door. We wave back and follow my parents up the walkway. Through the glass of the front door, the house appears empty.

"Whose house is this?" Seven asks.

Daddy unlocks the door. "Hopefully ours."

When we go inside, we're standing in the living room. There's a strong stench of paint and polished hardwood floors. Two halls, one on each side, lead away from the living room. The kitchen is right off from the living room with white cabinets, granite countertops, and stainless-steel appliances.

"We wanted you guys to see it," Momma says. "Look around."

I can't lie, I'm afraid to move. "This is *our* house?"

"Like I said, we hope so," Daddy replies. "We're waiting for the mortgage to be approved."

"Can we afford it?" Seven asks.

Momma raises an eyebrow. "Yes, we can."

"But like down payments and stuff—"

"Seven!" I hiss. He's always in somebody's business.

"We got everything taken care of," Daddy says. "We'll rent the house in the Garden out, so that's gon' help with the monthly payments. Plus…" He looks at Momma with this sly grin that's kinda adorable, I gotta admit.

"I got the nurse manager job at Markham," she says, smiling. "I start in two weeks."

"For real?" I say, and Seven goes, "Whoa," while Sekani shouts, "Momma's rich!"

"Boy, ain't nobody rich," Daddy says. "Calm down."

"But this helps," says Momma. "A lot."

"Daddy, you're okay with us living out here with the fake people?" Sekani asks.

"Where you get that from, Sekani?" Momma says.

"Well, that's what he always says. That people out here are fake, and that Garden Heights is real."

"Yeah, he does say that," says Seven.

I nod. "All. The. Time."

Momma folds her arms. "Care to explain, Maverick?"

"I don't say it *that* much—"

"Yeah, you do," the rest of us say.

"A'ight, I say it a lot. I may not have been one hundred percent right on all of this—"

Momma coughs, but there's a "Ha" hidden in it.

Daddy glares at her. "But I realize being real ain't got anything to do with where you live. The realest thing I can do is protect my family, and that means leaving Garden Heights."

"What else?" Momma questions, like he's being grilled in front of the class.

"And that living in the suburbs don't make you any less black than living in the hood."

"Thank you," she says with a satisfied smile.

"Now are y'all gon' look around or what?" Daddy asks.

Seven hesitates to move, and since he's hesitant, Sekani is too. But shoot, I want first dibs on a room. "Where are the bedrooms?"

Momma points to the hall on the left. I guess Seven and Sekani realize why I asked. The three of us exchange looks.

We rush for the hall. Sekani gets there first, and it's not my best moment, but I sling his scrawny butt back.

"Mommy, she threw me!" he whines.

I beat Seven to the first room. It's bigger than my current room but not as big as I want. Seven reaches the second one, looks around, and I guess he doesn't like it. That leaves the third room as the biggest one, and it's at the end of the hall.

Seven and I race for it, and it's like Harry Potter versus Cedric Diggory trying to get to the Goblet of Fire. I grab Seven's shirt, stretching it until I have a good enough grip to pull him back and get ahead of him. I beat him to the room and open the door.

And it's smaller than the first one.

"I call dibs!" Sekani shouts. He shimmies in the doorway of the first room, the biggest of the three.

Seven and I rock, paper, scissor it for the second-biggest room. Seven always goes with rock or paper, so I easily win.

Daddy leaves to get lunch, and Momma shows us the rest of the house. My brothers and I have to share a bathroom again. Sekani's finally learned aim etiquette and the art of flushing, so it's fine, I guess. The master suite is on the other hallway. There's a laundry room, an unfinished basement, and a two-car garage. Momma says we'll get a basketball hoop on wheels. We can keep it in the garage, roll it in front of the house, and play in the cul-de-sac sometimes. A wooden fence surrounds the backyard, and there's plenty of space for Daddy's garden and Brickz.

"Brickz can come out here, right?" I ask.

"Of course. We aren't gonna leave him."

Daddy brings burgers and fries, and we eat on the kitchen floor. It's super quiet out here. Dogs bark sometimes, but wall-rattling music and gunshots? Not happening.

"So, we're gonna close in the next few weeks or so," Momma says, "but since it's the end of the school year, we'll wait until you guys are out for summer to move."

"'Cause moving ain't no joke," Daddy adds.

"Hopefully, we can get settled in before you go off to college, Seven," Momma says. "Plus it gives you a chance to make your room yours, so you can have it for holidays and the summer."

Sekani slurps his milk shake and says with a mouth full of froth, "Seven said he's not going to college."

Daddy says, "What?"

Seven glares at Sekani. "I didn't say I wasn't going to college. I said I wasn't going *away* to college. I'm going to Central Community so I can be around for Kenya and Lyric."

"Oh, hell no," Daddy says.

"You can't be serious," says Momma.

306

Central Community is the junior college on the edge of Garden Heights. Some people call it Garden Heights High 2.0 'cause so many people from Garden High go there and take the same drama and bullshit with them.

"They have engineering classes," Seven argues.

"But they don't have the same opportunities as those schools you applied to," Momma says. "Do you realize what you're passing up? Scholarships, internships—"

"The chance for me to finally have a Seven-free life," I add, and slurp my milk shake.

"Who asked you?" Seven says.

"Yo' momma."

Low blow, I know, but that response comes naturally. Seven flicks a fry at me. I block it and come this close to flipping him off, but Momma says, "You bet' not!" and I lower my finger.

"Look, you not responsible for your sisters," Daddy says, "but I'm responsible for you. And I ain't letting you pass up opportunities so you can do what two grown-ass people supposed to do."

"A dollar, Daddy," Sekani points out.

"I love that you look out for Kenya and Lyric," Daddy tells Seven, "but there's only so much you can do. You can choose whatever college you want, and you'll be successful. But you choose because that's where you wanna be. Not because you trying to do somebody else's job. You hear me?"

"Yeah," Seven says.

Daddy hooks his arm around Seven's neck and pulls him

307

closer. Daddy kisses his temple. "I love you. And I always got your back."

After lunch we gather in the living room, join hands, and bow our heads.

"Black Jesus, thank you for this blessing," Daddy says. "Even when we weren't so crazy about the idea of moving—"

Momma clears her throat.

"Okay, when *I* wasn't so crazy about the idea of moving," Daddy corrects, "you worked things out. Thank you for Lisa's new job. Please help her and continue to be with her when she does extra shifts at the clinic. Help Sekani with his end-of-the-year tests. And thank you, Lord, for helping Seven do something I didn't, get a high school diploma. Guide him as he chooses a college and let him know you're protecting Kenya and Lyric.

"Now, Lord, tomorrow is a big day for my baby girl as she goes before this grand jury. Please give her peace and courage. As much as I wanna ask you to work this case out a certain way, I know you already got a plan. I ask for some mercy, God. That's all. Mercy for Garden Heights, for Khalil's family, for Starr. Help all of us through this. In your precious name—"

"Wait," Momma says.

I peek out with one eye. Daddy does too. Momma never, *ever* interrupts prayer.

"Uh, baby," says Daddy, "I was finishing up."

"I have something to add. Lord, bless my mom, and thank you that she went into her retirement fund and gave

308

us the money for the down payment. Help us turn the basement into a suite so she can stay here sometimes."

"No, Lord," Daddy says.

"Yes, Lord," says Momma.

"No, Lord."

"Yes."

"No, amen!"

We get home in time to catch a playoffs game.

Basketball season equals war in our house. I'm a LeBron fan through and through. Miami, Cleveland, it doesn't matter. I ride with him. Daddy hasn't jumped off the Lakers ship yet, but he likes LeBron. Seven's all about the Spurs. Momma's an "anybody but LeBron" hater, and Sekani is a "whoever is winning" fan.

It's Cleveland versus Chicago tonight. The battle lines are drawn – me and Daddy versus Seven and Momma. Seven jumps on that "anybody but LeBron" bandwagon of hateration too.

I change into my LeBron jersey. Every time I don't wear it, his team loses. Seriously, I'm not even lying. I can't wash it either. Momma washed my last jersey right before Finals, and Miami lost to the Spurs. I think she did it on purpose.

I take my lucky spot in the den in front of the sectional. Seven comes in and steps over me, putting his big bare foot near my face. I smack it away. "Get your crusty foot outta my face."

309

"We'll see who's joking later. Ready for a butt whooping?"

"You mean am I ready to give one? Yep!"

Momma peeks around the doorway. "Munch, you want some ice cream?"

I gape at her. She *knows* I don't eat dairy products during games. Dairy gives me gas, and gas is bad luck.

She grins. "How about a sundae? Sprinkles, strawberry syrup, whipped cream."

I cover my ears. "La-la-la-la-la, go away, LeBron hater. La-la-la-la-la."

Like I said, basketball season equals war, and my family has the dirtiest tactics.

Momma returns with a big bowl, shoveling ice cream into her mouth. She sits on the sectional and lowers her bowl into my face. "You sure you don't want some, Munch? It's your favorite too. Cake batter. So good!"

Be strong, I tell myself, but damn, that ice cream looks good. Strawberry syrup glistens on it and a big dollop of whipped cream sits pretty on top. I close my eyes. "I want a championship more."

"Well, you aren't getting that, so you may as well enjoy some ice cream."

"Ha!" Seven goes.

"What's all this smack up in here?" Daddy asks.

He takes the recliner on the sectional, his lucky spot. Sekani scurries in and sits behind me, propping his bare feet on my shoulders. I don't mind. They haven't matured and funkified yet.

"I was offering Munch some of my sundae," Momma says. "You want some, baby?"

"Heck, nah. You know I don't eat dairy during games." See? It's serious.

"You and Seven may as well get ready for this butt whooping Cleveland 'bout to give y'all," says Daddy. "I mean, it ain't gon' be a Kobe butt whooping, but it's gon' be a good one."

"Amen!" I say. Except the Kobe part.

"Boy, bye," Momma tells him. "You're always picking sorry teams. First the Lakers—"

"Ay, a three-peat ain't a sorry team, baby. And I don't always pick sorry teams." He grins. "I picked your team, didn't I?"

Momma rolls her eyes, but she's grinning too, and I hate to admit it but they're kinda cute right now. "Yeah," she says, "that's the only time you picked right."

"Uh-huh," Daddy says. "See, your momma played for Saint Mary's basketball team, and they had a game against Garden High, my school."

"And we whooped their butts too," Momma says, licking ice cream off her spoon. "Them li'l girls ain't have anything on us. I'm just saying."

"Anyway, I'm there to watch some of the homeboys play after the girls' game," Daddy says, looking at Momma. This is so adorable, I can't stand it. "I got there early and saw the finest girl ever, and she was playing her ass off on the court."

311

"Tell them what you did," says Momma, although we know.

"Ay, I was trying to—"

"Nah, nah, tell them what you did," she says.

"I tried to get your attention."

"Uh-uh!" Momma says, getting up. She hands me her bowl and stands in front of the TV. "You were like this on the sideline," she says, and she kinda leans to the side, holding her crotch and licking her lips. We crack up. I can so see Daddy doing that too.

"During the middle of a game!" she says. "Standing there looking like a pervert, just watching me."

"But you noticed me," Daddy says. "Right?"

"'Cause you looked like a fool! Then, during halftime, I'm on the bench, and he's behind me, talking about" – she deepens her voice – "'Ay! Ay, shorty. What's your name? You know you looking good out there. Can I get your number?'"

"Dang, Pops, you didn't have any game," Seven says.

"I had game!" Daddy argues.

"Did you get her number that night though?" Seven says.

"I mean, I was working on it—"

"Did you get her number?" I repeat Seven's question.

"Nah," he admits, and we're hollering laughing. "Man, whatever. Hate all y'all want. I eventually did something right."

"Yeah," Momma admits, running her fingers through my hair. "You did."

* * *

By the second quarter of Cleveland versus Chicago, we're yelling and shouting at the TV. When LeBron steals the ball, I jump up, and bam! He dunks it.

"In yo' face!" I yell at Momma and Seven. "In yo' face!"

Daddy gives me a high five and claps. "That's what I'm talking 'bout!"

Momma and Seven roll their eyes.

I sit in my "game time" position – knees pulled in, right arm draped over my head and holding my left ear, and my left thumb in my mouth. Don't hate. It works. Cleveland's offense and defense is on point. "Let's go, Cavs!"

Glass shatters. Then, *pop, pop, pop, pop.* Gunshots.

"Get down!" Daddy yells.

I'm already down. Sekani comes down next to me, then Momma on top of us, and she wraps her arms around us. Daddy's feet thud toward the front of the house and the hinges on the front door squeak as it swings open. Tires screech off.

"Mothaf—" Gunshots cut Daddy off.

My heart stops. For a split second, I visit a world without my dad, and it doesn't seem like much of a world at all.

But his footsteps rush back in. "Y'all a'ight?"

The weight on top of me lifts. Momma says she's okay, and Sekani says he is too. Seven echoes them.

Daddy's holding his Glock. "I shot at them fools," he says between heavy breaths. "I think I hit a tire. Ain't never seen that car before."

313

"Did they shoot in the house?" Momma asks.

"Yeah, a couple shots through the front window," he says. "They threw something too. Landed in the living room."

I head for the front.

"Starr! Get back here!" Momma calls.

I'm too curious and too hardheaded. Glass shards glisten all over Momma's good sofa. A brick sits in the middle of the floor.

Momma calls Uncle Carlos. He gets to our house in half an hour.

Daddy hasn't stopped pacing the den, and he hasn't put his Glock down. Seven takes Sekani to bed. Momma has her arm around me on the sectional and won't let go.

Some of our neighbors checked in, like Mrs. Pearl and Ms. Jones. Mr. Charles from next door rushed over, holding his own piece. None of them saw who did it.

Doesn't matter who did it. It was clearly a message for me.

I have this sick feeling like I got when I ate ice cream and played in hot weather too long when I was younger. Ms. Rosalie said the heat "boiled" my stomach and that something cool would settle it. Nothing cool can settle this.

"Did you call the police?" Uncle Carlos asks.

"Hell nah!" says Daddy. "How I know it wasn't them?"

"Maverick, you still should've called," Uncle Carlos says. "This needs to be recorded, and they can send someone to guard the house."

"Oh, I got somebody to guard the house. Don't worry about that. It definitely ain't gon' be no crooked pig who may have been behind this."

"King Lords could've done this!" says Uncle Carlos. "Didn't you say King made a veiled threat against Starr because of her interview?"

"I'm not going tomorrow," I say, but I have a better chance of being heard at a Drake concert.

"It ain't no damn coincidence that somebody's trying to scare us the night before she testifies to the grand jury," Daddy says. "That's some shit your buddies would do."

"You'd be surprised at how many of us want justice in this case," says Uncle Carlos. "But of course, classic Maverick. Every cop is automatically a bad cop."

"I'm not going tomorrow," I repeat.

"I ain't say every cop is a bad cop, but I ain't gon' stand here like a fool, thinking that some of them don't do dirty shit. Hell, they made me lay face-down on the sidewalk. And for what? 'Cause they could!"

"It could've been either one of them," Momma says. "Trying to figure out who did it will get us nowhere. The main thing is making sure Starr is safe tomorrow—"

"I said I'm not going!" I shout.

They finally hear me. My stomach holds a roiling boil. "Yeah, it could've been King Lords, but what if it was the cops?" I look at Daddy and remember that moment weeks ago in front of the store. "I thought they were gonna kill you," I croak. "Because of me."

315

He kneels in front of me and sits the Glock beside my feet. He lifts my chin. "Point one of the Ten-Point Program. Say it."

My brothers and I learned to recite the Black Panthers' Ten-Point Program the same way other kids learn the Pledge of Allegiance.

"'We want freedom,'" I say. "'We want the power to determine the destiny of our black and oppressed communities.'"

"Say it again."

"'We want freedom. We want the power to determine the destiny of our black and oppressed communities.'"

"Point seven."

"'We want an immediate end to police brutality,'" I say, "'and the murder of black people, other people of color, and oppressed people.'"

"Again."

"'We want an immediate end to police brutality and the murder of black people, other people of color, and oppressed people.'"

"And what did Brother Malcolm say is our objective?"

Seven and I could recite Malcolm X quotes by the time we were thirteen. Sekani hasn't gotten there yet.

"'Complete freedom, justice, and equality,'" I say, "'by any means necessary.'"

"Again."

"'Complete freedom, justice, and equality, by any means necessary.'"

"So why you gon' be quiet?" Daddy asks.

Because the Ten-Point Program didn't work for the Panthers. Huey Newton died a crackhead, and the government crushed the Panthers one by one. *By any means necessary* didn't keep Brother Malcolm from dying, possibly at the hands of his own people. Intentions always look better on paper than in reality. The reality is, I may not make it to the courthouse in the morning.

Two loud knocks at the front door startle us.

Daddy straightens up, grabs his Glock, and leaves to answer. He says what's up to somebody, and there's a sound like palms slapping. Then a male voice says, "You know we got you, Big Mav."

Daddy returns with some tall, wide-shouldered guys dressed in gray and black. It's a lighter gray than what King and his folks wear. It takes a hood-trained eye to notice it and understand. This is a different set of King Lords.

"This is Goon." Daddy points to the shortest one, in front with the ponytails. "Him and his boys gon' provide security for us tonight and tomorrow."

Uncle Carlos folds his arms and gives the King Lords a hard look. "You asked King Lords to guard the house when King Lords may have put us in this position?"

"They don't mess with King," Daddy says. "They Cedar Grove King Lords."

Shit, they may as well be GDs then. Sets make all the difference in gangbanging, not colors. The Cedar Grove King Lords have been beefing with King's set, the West Side King Lords, for a while now.

"You need us to fall back, Big Mav?" Goon asks.

"Nah, don't worry about him," Daddy says. "Y'all do what y'all came to do."

"Nothing but a thang," Goon says, and gives Daddy dap. Him and his boys head back outside.

"Are you serious right now?" Uncle Carlos yells. "You really think gangbangers can provide adequate security?"

"They strapped, ain't they?" Daddy says.

"Ridiculous!" Uncle Carlos looks at Momma. "Look, I'll go with you to the courthouse tomorrow as long as they aren't coming too."

"Punk ass," Daddy says. "Can't even protect your niece 'cause you scared of what it'll look like to your fellow cops if you're working with gangbangers."

"Oh, you wanna go there, Maverick?" Uncle Carlos says.

"Carlos, calm down."

"No, Lisa. I wanna make sure I got this right. Does he mean the same niece I took care of while he was locked up? Huh? The one I took to her first day of school because he took a charge for his so-called boy? The one I held when she cried for her daddy?"

He's loud, and Momma stands in front of him to keep him from Daddy.

"You can call me as many names as you want, Maverick, but don't you ever say I don't care about my niece and nephews! Yeah, that's right, nephews! Seven too. When you were locked up—"

318

"Carlos," Momma says.

"No, he needs to hear this. When you were locked up, I helped Lisa every time your sorry-ass baby momma dropped Seven off on her for weeks at a time. Me! I bought clothes, food, provided shelter. My Uncle Tom ass! Hell no, I don't wanna work with criminals, but don't you ever insinuate I don't care about any of those kids!"

Daddy's mouth makes a line. He's silent.

Uncle Carlos snatches his keys off the coffee table, gives my forehead two pecks, and leaves. The front door slams shut.

CHAPTER 19

The smell of hickory bacon and the sound of way too many voices wake me up.

I blink to soothe my eyes from the assault my neon-blue walls are giving them. It takes me a few minutes lying here to remember it's grand jury day.

Time to see if I'll fail Khalil or not.

I put my feet in my slippers and head toward the unfamiliar voices. Seven and Sekani are at school by now, plus their voices aren't that deep. I should be worried about some unknown dudes seeing me in my pajamas, but that's the beauty of sleeping in tanks and basketball shorts. They won't see much.

The kitchen's standing-room-only. Guys in black slacks, white shirts, and ties are at the table or standing against the wall, shoveling food in their mouths. They have tattoos on their faces and hands. A couple of them give me quick nods and mumble "S'up" through mouths full of food.

The Cedar Grove King Lords. Damn, they clean up nicely.

Momma and Aunt Pam work the stove as skillets full of

bacon and eggs sizzle, blue flames dancing beneath them. Nana pours juice and coffee and runs her mouth.

Momma barely looks over her shoulder and says, "Morning, Munch. Your plate's in the microwave. Come get these biscuits out for me, please."

She and Aunt Pam move to the ends of the stove, stirring the eggs and turning the bacon. I grab a towel and open the oven. The aroma of buttery biscuits and a heat wave hit me head-on. I pick the pan up with the towel, and that thing is still too hot to hold for long.

"Over here, li'l momma," Goon says at the table.

I'm glad to put it down. Not even two minutes after I set it on the table, every last biscuit is gone. Goddamn. I grab my paper towel–covered plate from the microwave before the King Lords inhale it too.

"Starr, get those other plates for your dad and your uncle," Aunt Pam says. "Take them outside, please."

Uncle Carlos is here? I tell Aunt Pam, "Yes, ma'am," stack their plates on top of mine, grab the hot sauce and some forks, and leave as Nana starts one of her "back in my theater days" stories.

Outside, the sunlight's so bright it makes the paint on my walls seem dim. I squint and look around for Daddy or Uncle Carlos. The hatch on Daddy's Tahoe is up, and they're sitting on the back of it.

My slippers scuff against the concrete, sounding like brooms sweeping the floor. Daddy looks around the truck. "There go my baby."

I hand him and Uncle Carlos a plate and get a kiss to the cheek from Daddy in return. "You sleep okay?" he asks.

"Kinda."

Uncle Carlos moves his pistol from the space between them and pats the empty spot. "Keep us company for a bit."

I hop up next to them. We unwrap the plates that have enough biscuits, bacon, and eggs for a few people.

"I think this one's yours, Maverick," Uncle Carlos says. "It's got turkey bacon."

"Thanks, man," Daddy says, and they exchange plates.

I shake hot sauce on my eggs and pass Daddy the bottle. Uncle Carlos holds his hand out for it too.

Daddy smirks and passes it down. "I would've thought you were too refined for some hot sauce on your eggs."

"You do realize this is the house I grew up in, right?" He covers his eggs completely in hot sauce, sets the bottle down, and licks his fingers for the sauce that got on them. "Don't tell Pam I ate all of this though. She's always on me about watching my sodium."

"I won't tell if you won't tell," Daddy says. They bump fists to seal the deal.

I woke up on another planet or in an alternate reality. Something. "Y'all cool all of a sudden?"

"We talked," Daddy says. "It's all good."

"Yep," says Uncle Carlos. "Some things are more important than others."

I want details, but I won't get them. If they're good though, I'm good. And honestly? It's about damn time.

"Since you and Aunt Pam are here, where's DeVante?" I ask Uncle Carlos.

"At home for once and not playing video games with your li'l boyfriend."

"Why does Chris always have to be 'li'l' to you?" I ask. "He's not little."

"You better be talking about his height," says Daddy.

"Amen," Uncle Carlos adds, and they fist-bump again.

So they've found common complaining ground – Chris. Figures.

Our street is quiet for the most part this morning. It usually is. The drama always comes from people who don't live here. Two houses down, Mrs. Lynn and Ms. Carol talk in Mrs. Lynn's yard. Probably gossiping. Can't tell either one of them anything if you don't want it spread around Garden Heights like a cold. Mrs. Pearl works in her flower bed across the street with a little help from Fo'ty Ounce. Everybody calls him that 'cause he always asks for money to buy a "Fo'ty ounce from the licka sto' real quick." His rusty shopping cart with all of his belongings is in Mrs. Pearl's driveway, a big bag of mulch on the bottom of it. Apparently he has a green thumb. He laughs at something Mrs. Pearl says, and people two streets over probably hear that guffaw of his.

"Can't believe that fool's alive," Uncle Carlos says. "Would've thought he drank himself to death by now."

"Who? Fo'ty Ounce?" I ask.

"Yeah! He was around when I was a kid."

"Nah, he ain't going nowhere," says Daddy. "He claims the liquor keeps him alive."

"Does Mrs. Rooks live around the corner?" Uncle Carlos asks.

"Yep," I say. "And she still makes the best red velvet cakes you ever had in your life."

"Wow. I told Pam I have yet to taste a red velvet cake as good as Mrs. Rooks's. What about um…" He snaps his fingers. "The man who fixed cars. Lived at the corner."

"Mr. Washington," says Daddy. "Still kicking it and still does better work than any automotive shop around. Got his son helping him too."

"Li'l John?" Uncle Carlos asks. "The one that played basketball but got on that stuff?"

"Yep," says Daddy. "He been clean for a minute now."

"Man." Uncle Carlos pushes his red eggs around his plate. "I almost miss living here sometimes."

I watch Fo'ty Ounce help Mrs. Pearl. People around here don't have much, but they help each other out as best they can. It's this strange, dysfunctional-as-hell family, but it's still a family. More than I realized until recently.

"Starr!" Nana calls from the front door. People two streets over probably hear her like they heard Fo'ty Ounce. "Your momma said hurry up. You gotta get ready. Hey, Pearl!"

Mrs. Pearl shields her eyes and looks our way. "Hey, Adele! Haven't seen you in a while. You all right?"

"Hanging in there, girl. You got that flowerbed looking

324

good! I'm coming by later to get some of that Birds of Paradise."

"All right."

"You not gon' say hey to me, Adele?" Fo'ty Ounce asks. When he talks, it jumbled together like one long word.

"Hell nah, you old fool," Nana says. The door slams behind her.

Daddy, Uncle Carlos, and I crack up.

The Cedar Grove King Lords trail us in two cars, and Uncle Carlos drives me and my parents. One of his off-duty buddies occupies the passenger's seat. Nana and Aunt Pam trail us too.

All these people though, and none of them can go in the grand jury room with me.

It takes fifteen minutes to get to downtown from Garden Heights. There's always construction work going on for some new building. Garden Heights has dope boys on corners, but downtown people in business suits wait for crossing lights to change. I wonder if they ever hear the gunshots and shit in my neighborhood.

We turn onto the street where the courthouse is, and I have one of those weird déjà-vu moments. I'm three, and Uncle Carlos drives Momma, Seven, and me to the courthouse. Momma cries the entire drive, and I wish Daddy were here because he can always get her to stop crying. Seven and I hold Momma's hands as we walk into a courtroom. Some cops bring Daddy out in an orange jumpsuit.

He can't hug us because he's handcuffed. I tell him I like his jumpsuit; orange is one of my favorite colors. But he looks at me real seriously, and says, "Don't you ever wear this, you hear me?"

All I remember after that is the judge saying something, Momma sobbing, and Daddy telling us he loves us as the cops haul him off. For three years I hated the courthouse because it took Daddy from us.

I'm not thrilled to see it now. News vans and trucks are across the street from the courthouse, and police barricades separate them from everybody else. I now know why people call it a "media circus." It seriously looks like the circus is setting up in town.

Two traffic lanes separate the courthouse from the media frenzy, but I swear they're a world away. Hundreds of people quietly kneel on the courthouse lawn. Men and women in clerical collars stand at the front of the crowd, their heads bowed.

To avoid the clowns and their cameras, Uncle Carlos turns onto the street alongside the courthouse. We go in through the back door. Goon and another King Lord join us. They flank me and don't hesitate to let security check them for weapons.

Another security guard leads us through the courthouse. The farther we go, the fewer people we pass in the halls. Ms. Ofrah waits beside a door with a brass plate that says Grand Jury Room.

She hugs me and asks, "Ready?"

For once I am. "Yes, ma'am."

"I'll be out here the whole time," she says. "If you need to ask me something, you have that right." She looks at my entourage. "I'm sorry, but only Starr's parents are allowed to watch in the TV room."

Uncle Carlos and Aunt Pam hug me. Nana pats my shoulder as she shakes her head. Goon and his boy give me quick nods and leave with them.

Momma's eyes brim with tears. She pulls me into a tight hug, and it's at that moment, of all the moments, that I realize I've gotten an inch or two taller than she is. She plants kisses all over my face and hugs me again. "I'm proud of you, baby. You are so brave."

That word. I hate it. "No, I'm not."

"Yeah, you are." She pulls back and pushes a strand of hair away from my face. I can't explain the look in her eyes, but it knows me better than I know myself. It wraps me up and warms me from the inside out. "Brave doesn't mean you're not scared, Starr," she says. "It means you go on even though you're scared. And you're doing that."

She leans up slightly on her tiptoes and kisses my forehead as if that makes it true. For me it kinda does.

Daddy wraps his arms around both of us. "You got this, baby girl."

The door to the grand jury room creaks open, and the DA, Ms. Monroe, looks out. "We're ready if you are."

I walk into the grand jury room alone, but somehow my parents are with me.

The room has wood-paneled walls and no windows. About twenty or so men and women occupy a U-shaped table. Some of them are black, some of them aren't. Their eyes follow us as Ms. Monroe leads me to a table in front of them with a mic on it.

One of Ms. Monroe's colleagues swears me in, and I promise on the Bible to tell the truth. I silently promise it to Khalil too.

Ms. Monroe says from the back of the room, "Could you please introduce yourself to the grand jurors?"

I scoot closer to the mic and clear my throat. "My name—" My small voice sounds like a five-year-old's. I sit up straight and try again. "My name is Starr Carter. I'm sixteen years old."

"The mic is only recording you, not projecting your voice," Ms. Monroe says. "As we have our conversation, we need you to speak loud enough for everyone to hear, okay?"

"Yes—" My lips brush the mic. Too close. I move back and try again. "Yes, ma'am."

"Good. You came here on your own free will, is that correct?"

"Yes, ma'am."

"You have an attorney, Ms. April Ofrah, correct?" she says.

"Yes, ma'am."

"You understand you have the right to consult with her, correct?"

"Yes, ma'am."

"You understand you're not the focus of any criminal charges, correct?"

Bullshit. Khalil and I have been on trial since he died. "Yes, ma'am."

"Today, we want to hear in your own words what happened to Khalil Harris, okay?"

I look at the jurors, unable to read their faces and tell if they really want to hear my words. Hopefully they do. "Yes, ma'am."

"Now, since we have that understanding, let's talk about Khalil. You were friends with him, right?"

I nod, but Ms. Monroe says, "Please give a verbal response."

I lean toward the mic and say, "Yes, ma'am."

Shit. I forgot the jurors can't hear me on it and it's only for recording. It doesn't make any sense that I'm so nervous.

"How long did you know Khalil?"

The same story, all over again. I become a robot who repeats how I knew Khalil since I was three, how we grew up together, the kind of person he was.

When I finish, Ms. Monroe says, "Okay. We're going to discuss the night of the shooting in detail. Are you okay with that?"

The un-brave part of me, which feels like most of me, shouts no. It wants to crawl up in a corner and act as if none of this ever happened. But all those people outside are praying for me. My parents are watching me. Khalil needs me.

I straighten up and allow the tiny brave part of me to speak. "Yes, ma'am."

PART 3

EIGHT WEEKS
AFTER IT

CHAPTER 20

Three hours. That's how long I was in the grand jury room. Ms. Monroe asked me all kinds of questions. What angle was Khalil at when he was shot? Where did he pull his license and registration from? How did Officer Cruise remove him from the car? Did Officer Cruise seem angry? What did he say?

She wanted every single detail. I gave her as much as I could.

It's been over two weeks since I talked to the grand jury, and now we're waiting for their decision, which is similar to waiting for a meteor to hit. You know it's coming, you're just not exactly sure when and where it'll hit, and there ain't shit you can do in the meantime but keep living.

So we're living.

The sun is out today, but the rain fell in sheets as soon as we pulled into the parking lot of Williamson. When it rains like that while the sun's out, Nana says the devil is beating his wife. Plus, it's Friday the thirteenth, a.k.a. the devil's day, according to Nana. She's probably holed up in the house like it's doomsday.

Seven and I dash from the car into the school. The atrium's busy as usual with people talking to their little cliques or playing around. The school year's almost over, so everybody's goof-off levels are at their highest, and white-kid goofing off is a category of its own. I'm sorry, but it is. Yesterday a sophomore rode down the stairs in the janitor's garbage can. His dumb ass got suspension and a concussion. Stupid.

I wiggle my toes. The one day I wear Chucks it decides to rain. They're miraculously dry.

"You're good?" Seven asks, and I doubt it's about the rain. He's been way more protective lately, ever since we got word that King's still pissed I dry snitched. I heard Uncle Carlos tell Daddy it gave the cops another reason to watch King closely.

Unless King threw the brick, he hasn't done anything. *Yet.* So Seven's always on guard, even all the way out here at Williamson.

"Yeah," I tell him. "I'm good."

"All right."

He gives me dap and goes off to his locker.

I head for mine. Hailey and Maya are talking at Maya's locker nearby. Actually, Maya's doing most of the talking. Hailey's got her arms folded and rolls her eyes a lot. She sees me down the hall and gets this smug expression.

"Perfect," she says when I get closer. "The liar is here."

"Excuse me?" It's way too early for this bullshit.

"Why don't you tell Maya how you flat-out lied to us?"

334

"What?"

Hailey hands me two pictures. One is Khalil's thug-shot, as Daddy calls it. One of the pictures they've shown on the news. Hailey printed it off the internet. Khalil wears a smirk, gripping a handful of money and throwing up a sideways peace sign.

The other picture, he's twelve. I know because I'm twelve in it too. It's my birthday party at this laser tag place downtown. Khalil's on one side of me, shoveling strawberry cake into his mouth, and Hailey's on my other side, grinning for the camera along with me.

"I thought he looked familiar," Hailey says as smugly as she looks. "He *is* the Khalil you knew. Isn't he?"

I stare at the two Khalils. The pictures only show so much. For some people, the thugshot makes him look just like that – a thug. But I see somebody who was happy to finally have some money in his hand, damn where it came from. And the birthday picture? I remember how Khalil ate so much cake and pizza he got sick. His grandma hadn't gotten paid yet, and food was limited in their house.

I knew the whole Khalil. That's who I've been speaking up for. I shouldn't deny any part of him. Not even at Williamson.

I hand the pictures back to Hailey. "Yeah, I knew him. So what?"

"Don't you think you owe us an explanation?" she says. "You owe me an apology too."

"Um, what?"

"You've basically picked fights with me because you were upset about what happened to him," she says. "You even accused me of being racist."

"But you have said and done some racist stuff. So…" Maya shrugs. "Whether Starr lied or not doesn't make it okay."

Minority alliance activated.

"So, since I unfollowed her Tumblr because I didn't wanna see any more pictures of that mutilated kid on my dashboard—"

"His name was Emmett Till," says Maya.

"Whatever. So because I didn't want to see that disgusting shit, I'm racist?"

"No," Maya says. "What you said about it was racist. And your Thanksgiving joke was definitely racist."

"Oh my God, you're still upset about that?" Hailey says. "That was so long ago!"

"Doesn't make it okay," I say. "And you can't even apologize for it."

"I'm not apologizing because it was only a joke!" she shouts. "It doesn't make me a racist. I'm not letting you guys guilt trip me like this. What's next? You want me to apologize because my ancestors were slave masters or something stupid?"

"Bitch—" I take a deep breath. Way too many people are watching. I cannot go angry black girl on her. "Your joke was hurtful," I say, as calmly as I can. "If you give a damn about Maya, you'd apologize and at least try to see why it hurt her."

"It's not my fault she can't get over a *joke* from freaking *freshman* year! Just like it's not my fault you can't get over what happened to Khalil."

"So I'm supposed to 'get over' the fact he was murdered?"

"Yes, get over it! He was probably gonna end up dead anyway."

"Are you serious?" Maya says.

"He was a drug dealer and a gangbanger," Hailey says. "Somebody was gonna kill him eventually."

"Get over it?" I repeat.

She folds her arms and does this little neck movement. "Um, yeah? Isn't that what I said? The cop probably did everyone a favor. One less drug dealer on the—"

I move Maya out the way and slam my fist against the side of Hailey's face. It hurts, but damn it feels good.

Hailey holds her cheek, her eyes wide and her mouth open for several seconds.

"Bitch!" she shrieks. She goes straight for my hair like girls usually do, but my ponytail is real. She's not pulling it out.

I hit at Hailey with my fists, and she slaps and claws me upside my head. I push her off, and she hits the floor. Her skirt goes up, and her pink drawers are out for everybody to see. Laughter erupts around us. Some people have their phones out.

I'm no longer Williamson Starr or even Garden Heights Starr. I'm pissed.

I kick and hit at Hailey, cuss words flying out my mouth.

People gather around us, chanting "Fight! Fight!" and one fool even shouts, "World Star!"

Shit. I'm gonna end up on that ratchet site.

Somebody yanks my arm, and I turn, face-to-face with Remy, Hailey's older brother.

"You crazy bi—"

Before he can finish "bitch," a blur of dreadlocks charges at us and pushes Remy back.

"Get your hands off my sister!" Seven says.

And then they're fighting. Seven throws blows like nobody's business, knocking Remy upside his head with several good hooks and jabs. Daddy used to take both of us to the boxing gym after school.

Two security guards run over. Dr. Davis, the headmaster, marches toward us.

An hour later, I'm in Momma's car. Seven trails us in his Mustang.

All four of us have been sentenced to three days' suspension, despite Williamson's zero-tolerance policy. Hailey and Remy's dad, a Williamson board member, thought it was outrageous. He said Seven and I should be expelled because we "started it," and that Seven shouldn't be allowed to graduate. Dr. Davis told him, "Given the circumstances" – and he looked straight at me – "suspension will suffice."

He knows I was with Khalil.

"This is exactly what *They* expect you to do," Momma

says. "Two kids from Garden Heights, acting like you ain't got any sense!"

They with a capital *T*. There's Them and then there's Us. Sometimes They look like Us and don't realize They are Us.

"But she was running her mouth, saying Khalil deserved—"

"I don't care if she said she shot him herself. People are gonna say a whole lot, Starr. It doesn't mean you hit somebody. You gotta walk away sometimes."

"You mean walk away and get shot like Khalil did?"

She sighs. "Baby, I understand—"

"No you don't!" I say. "*Nobody* understands! *I* saw the bullets rip through him. *I* sat there in the street as he took his last breath. *I've* had to listen to people try to make it seem like it's okay he was murdered. As if he deserved it. But he didn't deserve to die, and I didn't do anything to deserve seeing that shit!"

WebMD calls it a stage of grief – anger. But I doubt I'll ever get to the other stages. This one slices me into millions of pieces. Every time I'm whole and back to normal, something happens to tear me apart, and I'm forced to start all over again.

The rain lets up. The devil stops beating his wife, but I beat the dashboard, punching it over and over, numb to the pain of it. I wanna be numb to the pain of all of this.

"Let it out, Munch." My mom rubs my back. "Let it out."

I pull my polo over my mouth and scream until there aren't any screams left in me. If there are any, I don't have the energy to get them out. I cry for Khalil, for Natasha, even for Hailey, 'cause damn if I didn't just lose her for good too.

When we turn on our street, I'm snot-nosed and wet-eyed. Finally numb.

A gray pickup and a green Chrysler 300 are parked behind Daddy's truck in the driveway. Momma and Seven have to park in front of the house.

"What is this man up to?" Momma says. She looks over at me. "You feel better?"

I nod. What other choice do I have?

She leans over and kisses my temple. "We'll get through this. I promise."

We get out. I'm one hundred percent sure the cars in the driveway belong to King Lords and Garden Disciples. In Garden Heights you can't drive a car that's gray or green unless you claim a set. I expect yelling and cussing when I get inside, but all I hear is Daddy saying, "It don't make no sense, man. For real, it don't."

It's standing-room-only in the kitchen. We can't even get in 'cause some guys are in the doorway. Half of them have green somewhere in their outfits. Garden Disciples. The others have light gray on somewhere. Cedar Grove King Lords. Mr. Reuben's nephew, Tim, sits beside Daddy at the table. I've never noticed that cursive GD tattoo on his arm.

"We don't know when the grand jury gon' make their

decision," Daddy says. "But if they decide not to indict, y'all gotta tell these li'l dudes not to burn this neighborhood down."

"What you expect them to do then?" says a GD at the table. "Folks tired of the bullshit, Mav."

"Straight up," says the King Lord Goon, who's at the table too. His long plaits have ponytail holders on them like I used to wear way back in the day. "Nothing we can do 'bout it."

"That's bullshit," says Tim. "We can do something."

"We can all agree the riots got outta hand, right?" says Daddy.

He gets a bunch of "yeahs" and "rights."

"Then we can make sure it doesn't go down like that again. Talk to these kids. Get in their heads. Yeah, they mad. We all mad, but burning down our neighborhood ain't gon' fix it."

"Our?" says the GD at the table. "Nigga, you said you moving."

"To the *suburbs*," Goon mocks. "You getting a minivan too, Mav?"

They all laugh at that.

Daddy doesn't though. "I'm moving, so what? I'll still have a store here, and I'll still give a damn what happens here. Who is it gon' benefit if the whole neighborhood burns down? Damn sure won't benefit none of us."

"We gotta be more organized next time," says Tim. "For one, make sure our brothers and sisters know they can't destroy black-owned businesses. That messes it up for all of us."

"For real," says Daddy. "And I know, me and Tim out the game, so we can't speak on some things, but all these territory wars gotta be put aside somehow. This is bigger than some street shit. And honestly all the street shit got these cops thinking they can do whatever they want."

"Yeah, I feel you on that," says Goon.

"Y'all gotta come together somehow, man," Daddy says. "For the sake of the Garden. The last thing they'd ever expect is some unity around here. A'ight?"

Daddy slaps palms with Goon and the Garden Disciple. Then Goon and the Garden Disciple slap palms with each other.

"Wow," Seven says.

It's huge that these two gangs are in the same room together, and for my daddy to be the one behind it? Crazy.

He notices us in the doorway. "What y'all doing here?"

Momma inches into the kitchen, looking around. "The kids got suspended."

"Suspended?" Daddy says. "For what?"

Seven passes him his phone.

"It's online already?" I say.

"Yeah, somebody tagged me in it."

Daddy taps the screen, and I hear Hailey running her mouth about Khalil, then a loud smack.

Some of the gang members watch over Daddy's shoulder. "Damn, li'l momma," one says, "you got hands."

"You crazy bi— ," Remy says on the phone. A bunch of smacks and oohs follow.

"Look at my boy!" Daddy says. "Look at him!"

"I ain't know your li'l nerdy ass had it in you," a King Lord teases.

Momma clears her throat. Daddy stops the video.

"A'ight, y'all," he says, serious all of a sudden. "I gotta handle some family business. We'll meet back up tomorrow."

Tim and all the gang members clear out, and cars crank up outside. Still no gunshots or arguing. They could've broken out into a gangsta rendition of "Kumbaya" and I wouldn't be any more shocked than I am.

"How did you get all of them in here and keep the house in one piece?" Momma asks.

"I got it like that."

Momma kisses him on the lips. "You certainly do. My man, the activist."

"Uh-huh." He kisses her back. "Your man."

Seven clears his throat. "We're standing right here."

"Ay, y'all can't complain," Daddy says. "If you wouldn't have been fighting, you wouldn't have to see that." He reaches over and pinches my cheek a little. "You a'ight?"

The dampness hasn't left my eyes yet, and I'm not exactly smiling. I mutter, "Yeah."

Daddy pulls me onto his lap. He cradles me and switches between kissing my cheek and pinching it, going over and over in a real deep voice, "What's wrong with you? Huh? What's wrong with you?"

And I'm giggling before I can stop myself.

Daddy gives me a sloppy, wet kiss to my cheek and lets me up. "I knew I'd get you laughing. Now what happened?"

"You saw the video. Hailey ran her mouth, so I popped her. Simple as that."

"That's your child, Maverick," Momma says. "Gotta hit somebody because she didn't like what they said."

"Mine? Uh-uh, baby. That's all you." He looks at Seven. "Why were you fighting?"

"Dude came at my sister," Seven says. "I wasn't gonna let him."

As much as Seven talks about protecting Kenya and Lyric, it's nice that he has my back too.

Daddy replays the video, starting with Hailey saying, "He was probably gonna end up dead anyway."

"Wow," Momma says. "That li'l girl has a lot of nerve."

"Spoiled ass don't know a damn thing and running her mouth," says Daddy.

"So, what's our punishment?" Seven asks.

"Go do your homework," Momma says.

"That's it?" I say.

"You'll also have to help your dad at the store while you're suspended." She drapes her arms over Daddy from behind. "Sound okay, baby?"

He kisses her arm. "Sounds good to me."

If you can't translate Parentish, this is what they really said:

Momma: I don't condone what you did, and I'm not

saying it's okay, but I probably would've done it too. What about you, baby?

Daddy: Hell yeah, I would've.

I love them for that.

PART 4

TEN WEEKS
AFTER IT

CHAPTER 21

Still no decision from the grand jury, so we're still living.

It's Saturday, and my family is at Uncle Carlos's house for a Memorial Day weekend barbecue, which is also serving as Seven's birthday/graduation party. He turns eighteen tomorrow, and he officially became a high school graduate yesterday. I've never seen Daddy cry like he did when Dr. Davis handed Seven that diploma.

The backyard smells like barbecue, and it's warm enough that Seven's friends swim in the pool. Sekani and Daniel run around in their trunks and push unsuspecting people in. They get Jess. She laughs about it and threatens to get them later. They try it once with me and Kenya and never again. All it takes is some swift kicks to their asses.

But DeVante comes up behind us and pushes me in. Kenya shrieks as I go under, getting my freshly done cornrows soaked and my J's too. I have on board shorts and a tankini, but they're new and cute, meaning they're supposed to be looked at, not swam in.

I break the surface of the water and gulp in air.

"Starr, you okay?" Kenya calls. She's run about five feet away from the pool.

"You not gon' help me get out?" I say.

"Girl, nah. And mess up my outfit? You seem all right."

Sekani and Daniel whoop and cheer for DeVante like he's the greatest thing since Spider-Man. Bastards. I climb out that pool so fast.

"Uh-oh," DeVante says, and the three of them take off in separate directions. Kenya goes after DeVante. I run after Sekani because dammit, blood is supposed to be thicker than pool water.

"Momma!" he squeals.

I catch him by his trunks and pull them way up, almost to his neck, until he has the worst wedgie ever. He gives a high-pitched scream. I let go, and he falls on the grass, his trunks so far up his butt it looks like he's wearing a thong. That's what he gets.

Kenya brings DeVante to me, holding his arms behind him like he's under arrest. "Apologize," she says.

"No!" Kenya yanks on his arms. "Okay, okay, I'm sorry!"

She lets go. "Better be."

DeVante rubs his arm with a smirk. "Violent ass."

"Punk ass," she snips back.

He flicks his tongue at her, and she goes, "Boy, bye!"

This is flirting for them, believe it or not. I almost forget DeVante's hiding from her daddy. They act like they've forgotten too.

DeVante gets me a towel. I snatch it and dry my face as I head to the poolside loungers with Kenya. DeVante sits beside her on one.

Ava skips over with her baby doll and a comb, and I naturally expect her to shove them into my hands. She hands them to DeVante instead.

"Here!" she tells him, and skips off.

And he starts combing the doll's hair! Kenya and I stare at him for the longest.

"What?" he says.

We bust out laughing.

"She got you trained!" I say.

"Man." He groans. "She cute, okay? I can't tell her no." He braids the doll's hair, and his long thin fingers move so quickly, they look like they'll get tangled. "My li'l sisters did me like this all the time."

His tone dips when he mentions them. "You heard from them or your momma?" I ask.

"Yeah, about a week ago. They at my cousin's house. She live in like the middle of nowhere. Mom's been a mess 'cause she didn't know if I was okay. She apologized for leaving me and for being mad. She want me to come stay with them."

Kenya frowns. "You leaving?"

"I don't know. Mr. Carlos and Mrs. Pam said I can stay with them for my senior year. My momma said she'd be okay with that, if it means I stay outta trouble." He examines his handiwork. The doll has a perfect French braid.

"I gotta think about it. I kinda like it out here."

Salt-N-Pepa's "Push It" blasts from the speakers. That's one song Daddy shouldn't play. The only thing worse would be that old song "Back That Thang Up." Momma loses her damn mind when it comes on. Really, just say, "Cash Money Records, takin' over for the '99 and the 2000," and she suddenly becomes ratchet as hell.

She and Aunt Pam both go, "Heeey!" to Salt-N-Pepa and do all these old dance moves. I like nineties shows and movies, but I do not wanna see my mom and auntie reenact that decade in dance. Seven and his friends circle around them and cheer them on.

Seven's the loudest. "Go, Ma! Go, Aunt Pam!"

Daddy jumps in the middle of the circle behind Momma. He puts both hands behind his head and moves his hips in a circle.

Seven pushes Daddy away from Momma, going, "Nooo! Stooop!" Daddy gets around him, and dances behind Momma.

"Uh-uh," Kenya laughs. "That's *too* much."

DeVante watches them with a smile. "You were right about your aunt and uncle, Starr. They ain't too bad. Your grandma kinda cool too."

"Who? I know you don't mean Nana."

"Yeah, her. She found out I play spades. The other day, she took me to a game after she finished tutoring me. She called it extra-credit work. We been cool ever since."

Figures.

Chris and Maya walk through the gate, and my stomach gets all jittery. I should be used to my two worlds colliding, but I never know which Starr I should be. I can use some slang, but not too much slang, some attitude, but not too much attitude, so I'm not a "sassy black girl." I have to watch what I say and how I say it, but I can't sound "white."

Shit is exhausting.

Chris and his new "bro" DeVante slap palms, then Chris kisses my cheek. Maya and I do our handshake. DeVante nods at her. They met a few weeks ago.

Maya sits beside me on the lounger. Chris squeezes his big butt between us, pushing both of us aside a little.

Maya flashes him a stink eye. "Seriously, Chris?"

"Hey, she's my girlfriend. I get to sit next to her."

"Um, no? Besties before testes."

Kenya and I snicker, and DeVante goes, "Damn."

The jitters ease up a bit.

"So you're Chris?" Kenya says. She's seen pictures on my Instagram.

"Yep. And you're Kenya?" He's seen pictures on my Instagram too.

"The one and only." Kenya eyes me and mouths, *He is fine!* Like I didn't know that already.

Kenya and Maya look at each other. Their paths last crossed almost a year ago at my Sweet Sixteen, if you can consider that path-crossing. Hailey and Maya were at one table, Kenya and Khalil at another table with Seven. They never talked.

"Maya, right?" Kenya says.

Maya nods. "The one and only."

Kenya's lips curl up. "Your kicks are cute."

"Thanks," Maya says, checking them out for herself. Nike Air Max 95s. "They're supposed to be running shoes. I never run in them."

"I don't run in mine neither," Kenya says. "My brother's the only person I know who actually runs in them."

Maya laughs.

Okay. This is good so far. Nothing to worry about.

Until Kenya goes, "So where blondie at?"

Chris snorts. Maya's eyes widen.

"Kenya, that ain't – that's not her name," I say.

"You knew who I was talking about though, didn't you?"

"Yep!" Maya says. "She's probably somewhere licking her wounds after Starr kicked her ass."

"What?" Kenya shouts. "Starr, you ain't tell me about that!"

"It was, like, two weeks ago," I say. "Wasn't worth talking 'bout. I only hit her."

"*Only* hit her?" Maya says. "You Mayweathered her."

Chris and DeVante laugh.

"Wait, wait," Kenya says. "What happened?"

So I tell her about it, without really thinking about what I say or how I sound. I just talk. Maya adds to the story, making it sound worse than it was, and Kenya eats it up. We tell her how Seven gave Remy a couple of hits, which

354

has Kenya beaming, talking about, "My brother don't play."
Like he's only *her* brother, but whatever. Maya even tells her
about the Thanksgiving cat thing.

"I told Starr we minorities gotta stick together," Maya
says.

"So true," says Kenya. "White people been sticking
together forever."

"Well…" Chris blushes. "This is awkward."

"You'll get over it, boo," I say.

Maya and Kenya crack up.

My two worlds just collided. Surprisingly, everything's
all right.

The song changes to "Wobble." Momma runs over and
pulls me up. "C'mon, Munch."

I can't dig my feet in the grass fast enough. "Mommy,
no!"

"Hush, girl. C'mon. Y'all too!" she hollers back to my
friends.

Everybody lines up on the grassy area that's become the
makeshift dance floor. Momma pulls me to the front row.
"Show 'em how it's done, baby," she says. "Show 'em how
it's done!"

I stay still on purpose. Dictator or not, she's *not* gonna
make me dance. Kenya and Maya egg her on in egging me
on. Never thought they'd team up against me.

Shoot, before I know it, I'm wobbling. I have duck lips
too, so you know I'm feeling it.

I talk Chris through the steps, and he keeps up. I love

him for trying. Nana joins in, doing a shoulder shimmy that's not the Wobble, but I doubt she cares.

The "Cupid Shuffle" comes on, and my family leads everybody else on the front row. Sometimes we forget which way is right and which is left, and we laugh way too hard at ourselves. Embarrassing dancing and dysfunction aside, my family's not so bad.

After all that wobbling and shuffling, my stomach begs for some food. I leave everybody else doing the "Bikers Shuffle," which is a whole new level of shuffling, and most of our party guests are lost as hell.

Aluminum serving trays crowd the kitchen counter. I stack a plate with some ribs, wings, and corn on the cob. I scoop a nice amount of baked beans on there somehow. No potato salad. That's the devil's food. All that mayonnaise. I don't care if Momma made it, I'm not touching that mess.

I refuse to eat outside, too many bugs that could get on my food. I plop down at the dining room table, and I'm about to go in on my plate.

But the damn phone rings.

Everybody else is outside, leaving me to answer. I shove a chicken wing in my mouth. "Hello?" I chomp in the other person's ear. Rude? Definitely. Am I starving? Hell yeah.

"Hi, this is the front security gate. Iesha Robinson is asking to visit your residence."

I stop chewing. Iesha was MIA at Seven's graduation, which she was invited to, so why did she show up to the party she wasn't invited to? How did she even find out about

356

it? Seven didn't tell her, and Kenya swore she wouldn't. She lied and told her momma and daddy she was hanging with some other friends today.

I take the phone outside to Daddy because, shit, I don't know what to do. I go out at a good time too. He's trying – and failing – to Nae-Nae. I have to call him a second time for him to stop that atrocity and come over.

He grins. "You ain't know your daddy had it in him, did you?"

"I still don't. Here." I hand him the phone. "That's neighborhood security. Iesha's at the security gate."

His grin disappears. He plugs one ear and puts the phone to the other. "Hello?"

The security guard talks for a moment. Daddy motions Seven to the patio. "Hold on." He covers the receiver. "Your momma at the gate. She wanna see you."

Seven's eyebrows knit together. "How did she know we're here?"

"Your grandma's with her. Didn't you invite her?"

"Yeah, but not Iesha."

"Look, man, if you want her to come back for a li'l bit, it's cool," Daddy says. "I'll make DeVante go inside so she won't see him. What you wanna do?"

"Pops, can you tell her—"

"Nah, man. That's your momma. You handle that."

Seven bites his lip for a moment. He sighs through his nose. "All right."

★ ★ ★

Iesha pulls up out front. I follow Seven, Kenya, and my parents to the driveway. Seven always has my back. I figure he needs me to have his too.

Seven tells Kenya to stay back with us and goes toward Iesha's pink BMW.

Lyric jumps out the car. "Sevvie!" She runs to him, the ball-shaped ponytail holders on her hair bouncing. I hated wearing those things. All it takes is one hitting you between your eyes and you're done. Lyric launches into Seven's arms, and he swings her around.

I can't lie, I always get a little jealous when I see Seven with his other sisters. It doesn't make sense, I know. But they share a momma, and it makes things different between them. It's like they have a stronger bond or something.

But there's no way in hell I'd trade Momma for Iesha. Nope.

Seven keeps Lyric on his hip and hugs his grandma with one arm.

Iesha gets out. A bob haircut has replaced her down-to-the-ass Indian import. She doesn't even try to tug her hot-pink dress down that obviously rode up her thighs during the drive. Or maybe it didn't ride up and that's where it always was.

Nope. Wouldn't trade Momma for anything.

"So you gon' have a party and not invite me, Seven?" Iesha asks. "A *birthday* party at that? I'm the one who gave birth to your ass!"

Seven glances around. At least one of Uncle Carlos's

neighbors is looking. "Not now."

"Oh, hell yes now. I had to find out from my momma because my own son couldn't be bothered to invite me." She sets her sharp glare on Kenya. "And this li'l fast thang lied to me about it! I oughta whoop your ass."

Kenya flinches like Iesha already hit her. "Momma—"

"Don't blame Kenya," says Seven, setting Lyric down. "I asked her not to tell you, Iesha."

"Iesha?" she echoes, all in his face. "Who the hell you think you talking to like that?"

What happens next is like when you shake a soda can real hard. From the outside, you can't tell anything is going on. But then you open it, and it explodes.

"This is why I didn't invite you!" Seven shouts. "This! Right now! You don't know how to act!"

"Oh, so you ashamed of me, Seven?"

"You're fucking right I'm ashamed of you!"

"Whoa!" Daddy says. Stepping between them, he puts his hand on Seven's chest. "Seven, calm down."

"Nah, Pops! Let me tell her how I didn't invite her because I didn't wanna explain to my friends that my step-mom isn't my mom like they think. Or how I never once corrected anybody at Williamson who made the assumption. Hell, it wasn't like she ever came to any of my stuff, so why bother? You couldn't even show up to my graduation yesterday!"

"Seven," Kenya pleads. "Stop."

"No, Kenya!" he says, his sights square on their momma.

359

"I'll tell her how I didn't think she gave a damn about my birthday, 'cause guess what? She never has! 'You didn't invite me, you didn't invite me,'" he mocks. "Hell no, I didn't. And why the fuck should I?"

Iesha blinks several times and says in a voice like broken glass, "After all I've done for you."

"All you've done for me? What? Putting me out the house? Choosing a man over me every single chance you got? Remember when I tried to stop King from whooping your ass, Iesha? Who did you get mad at?"

"Seven," Daddy says.

"Me! You got mad at me! Said I made him leave. That's what you call 'doing' for me? That woman right there" – he stretches his arm toward Momma – "did everything you were supposed to and then some. How dare you stand there and take credit for it. All I ever did was love you." His voice cracks. "That's it. And you couldn't even give that back to me."

The music has stopped, and heads peek over the back-yard fence.

Layla approaches him. She hooks her arm through his. He allows her to take him inside. Iesha turns on her heels and starts for her car.

"Iesha, wait," Daddy says.

"Nothing to wait for." She throws her door open. "You happy, Maverick? You and that trick you married finally turned my son against me. Can't wait till King fuck y'all up for letting that girl snitch on him on TV."

My stomach clenches.

"Tell him try it if he wants and see what happens!" says Daddy.

It's one thing to hear gossip that somebody plans to "fuck you up," but it's a whole different thing to hear it from somebody who would actually know.

But I can't worry about King right now. I have to go to my brother.

Kenya's at my side. We find him on the bottom of the staircase. He sobs like a baby. Layla rests her head on his shoulder.

Seeing him cry like that … I wanna cry. "Seven?"

He looks up with red, puffy eyes that I've never seen on my brother before.

Momma comes in. Layla gets up, and Momma takes her spot on the steps.

"Come here, baby," she says, and they somehow hug.

Daddy touches my shoulder and Kenya's. "Go outside, y'all."

Kenya's face is scrunched up like she's gonna cry. I grab her arm and take her to the kitchen. She sits at the counter and buries her face in her hands. I climb onto the stool and don't say anything. Sometimes it's not necessary.

After a few minutes, she says, "I'm sorry my daddy's mad at you."

This is the most awkward situation ever – my friend's dad possibly wants to kill me. "Not your fault," I mumble.

"I understand why my brother didn't invite my momma,

361

but…" Her voice cracks. "She going through a lot, Starr. With him." Kenya wipes her face on her arm. "I wish she'd leave him."

"Maybe she afraid to?" I say. "Look at me. I was afraid to speak out for Khalil, and you went off on me about it."

"I didn't go off."

"Yeah, you did."

"Trust me, no, I didn't. You'll know when I go off on you."

"Anyway! I know it's not the same, but…" Good Lord, I never thought I'd say this. "I think I understand Iesha. It's hard to stand up for yourself sometimes. She may need that push too."

"So you want me to go off on her? I can't believe you think I went off on you. Sensitive ass."

My mouth flies open. "You know what? I'm gonna let that slide. Nah, I ain't say you need to go off on her, that would be stupid. Just…" I sigh. "I don't know."

"I don't either."

We go silent.

Kenya wipes her face again. "I'm good." She gets up. "I'm good."

"You sure?"

"Yes! Stop asking me that. C'mon, let's go back out there and stop them from talking about my brother, 'cause you know they're talking."

She heads for the door, but I say, "*Our* brother."

Kenya turns around. "What?"

362

"*Our* brother. He's mine too."

I didn't say it in a mean way or even with an attitude, I swear. She doesn't respond. Not even an "okay." Not that I expected her to suddenly go, "Of course, he's *our* brother, I'm extremely sorry for acting like he wasn't yours too." I hoped for something though.

Kenya goes outside.

Seven and Iesha unknowingly hit the pause button on the party. The music's off, and Seven's friends stand around, talking in hushed tones.

Chris and Maya walk up to me. "Is Seven okay?" Maya asks.

"Who turned the music off?" I ask. Chris shrugs.

I pick up Daddy's iPod from the patio table, our DJ for the afternoon that's hooked up to the sound system. Scrolling through the playlist, I find this Kendrick Lamar song Seven played for me one day, right after Khalil died. Kendrick raps about how everything will be all right. Seven said it's for both of us.

I hit play and hope he hears it. It's for Kenya too.

Midway through the song, Seven and Layla come back out. His eyes are puffy and pink but dry. He smiles at me a little and gives a quick nod. I return it.

Momma leads Daddy outside. They're both wearing cone-shaped birthday hats, and Daddy carries a huge sheet cake with candles lit on top of it.

"Happy birthday to ya!" they sing, and Momma does

363

this not-as-embarrassing shoulder bounce. "Happy birthday to ya! Happy birth-day!"

Seven smiles from ear to ear. I turn the music down.

Daddy sets the cake on the patio table, and everybody crowds around it and Seven. Our family, Kenya, DeVante, and Layla – basically, all the black people – sing the Stevie Wonder version of "Happy Birthday." Maya seems to know it. A lot of Seven's friends look lost. Chris does too. These cultural differences are crazy sometimes.

Nana takes the song way too far and hits notes that don't need to be hit. Momma tells her, "The candles are about to go out, Momma!"

She's so damn dramatic.

Seven leans down to blow the candles out, but Daddy says, "Wait! Man, you know you don't blow no candles out till I say something."

"Aww, Pops!"

"He can't tell you what to do, Seven," Sekani chirps. "You're grown now!"

Daddy shoots Sekani an up-and-down look. "Boy—" He turns to Seven. "I'm proud of you, man. Like I told you, I never got a diploma. A lot of young brothers don't get theirs. And where we come from, a lot of them don't make it to eighteen. Some do make it, but they're messed up by the time they get there. Not you though. You're going places, no doubt. I always knew that.

"See, I believe in giving my kids names that mean something. Sekani, that means merriment and joy."

I snort. Sekani side-eyes me.

"I named your sister Starr because she was my light in the darkness. Seven, that's a holy number. The number of perfection. I ain't saying you're perfect, nobody is, but you're the perfect gift God gave me. I love you, man. Happy birthday and congratulations."

Daddy affectionately clasps Seven's neck. Seven grins wider. "Love you too, Pops."

The cake is one of Mrs. Rooks's red velvets. Everybody goes on and on about how good it is. Uncle Carlos pigs out on at least three slices. There's more dancing, laughing. All in all, it's a good day.

Good days don't last forever though.

PART 5

THE DECISION –
THIRTEEN WEEKS
AFTER IT

CHAPTER 22

In our new neighborhood I can simply tell my parents "I'm going for a walk" and leave.

We just got off the phone with Ms. Ofrah, who said the grand jury will announce their decision in a few hours. She claims only the grand jurors know the decision, but I've got a sinking feeling I know it. It's always the decision.

I stick my hands in the pockets of my sleeveless hoodie. Some kids race past on bikes and scooters. Nearly knock me over. Doubt they're worried about the grand jury's decision. They aren't hurrying inside like the kids back home are probably doing.

Home.

We started moving into our new house this past weekend. Five days later, this place doesn't feel like home yet. It could be all the unpacked boxes or the street names I don't know. And it's almost too quiet. No Fo'ty Ounce and his creaky cart or Mrs. Pearl hollering a greeting from across the street.

I need normal.

I text Chris. Less than ten minutes later, he picks me up in his dad's Benz.

The Bryants live in the only house on their street that has a separate house attached to it for a butler. Mr. Bryant owns eight cars, mostly antiques, and a garage to store them all.

Chris parks in one of the two empty spots.

"Your parents gone?" I ask.

"Yep. Date night at the country club."

Most of Chris's house looks too fancy to live in. Statues, oil paintings, chandeliers. A museum more than a home. Chris's suite on the third floor is more normal looking. There's a leather couch in his room, right in front of the flat-screen TV and video game systems. His floor is painted to look like a half basketball court, and he can play on an actual hoop on his wall.

His California King–size bed has been made, a rare sight. I never knew there was anything larger than a king-size bed before I met him. I pull my Timbs off and grab the remote from his nightstand. As I throw myself onto his bed, I flick the TV on.

Chris steps out his Chucks and sits at his desk, where a drum pad, a keyboard, and turntables are hooked up to a Mac. "Check this out," he says, and plays a beat.

I prop myself up on my elbows and nod along. It's got an old-school feel to it, like something Dre and Snoop would've used back in the day. "Nice."

"Thanks. I think I need to take some of that bass out

though." He turns around and gets to work.

I pick at a loose thread on his comforter. "Do you think they're gonna charge him?"

"Do you?"

"No."

Chris spins his chair back around. My eyes are watery, and I lie on my side. He climbs in next to me so we're facing each other.

Chris presses his forehead against mine. "I'm sorry."

"You didn't do anything."

"But I feel like I should apologize on behalf of white people everywhere."

"You don't have to."

"But I want to."

Lying in his California King–size bed in his suite in his gigantic house, I realize the truth. I mean, it's been there all along, but in this moment lights flash around it. "We shouldn't be together," I say.

"Why not?"

"My old house in Garden Heights could fit in your house."

"So?"

"My dad was a gangbanger."

"My dad gambles."

"I grew up in the projects."

"I grew up with a roof over my head too."

I sigh and start to turn my back to him.

He holds my shoulder so I won't. "Don't let this stuff get in your head again, Starr."

"You ever notice how people look at us?"

"What people?"

"People," I say. "It takes them a second to realize we're a couple."

"Who gives a fuck?"

"Me."

"Why?"

"Because you should be with Hailey."

He recoils. "Why the hell would I do that?"

"Not Hailey. But you know. Blond. Rich. White."

"I prefer: Beautiful. Amazing. Starr."

He doesn't get it, but I don't wanna talk about it anymore. I wanna get so caught up in him that the grand jury's decision isn't even a thing. I kiss his lips, which always have and always will be perfect. He kisses me back, and soon we're making out like it's the only thing we know how to do.

It's not enough. My hands travel below his chest, and he's bulging in more than his arms. I start unzipping his jeans.

He grabs my hand. "Whoa. What are you doing?"

"What do you think?"

His eyes search mine. "Starr, I want to, I do—"

"I know you do. And it's the perfect opportunity." I trail kisses along his neck, getting each of those perfectly placed freckles. "Nobody's here but us."

"But we can't," he says, voice strained. "Not like this."

"Why not?" I slip my hand in his pants, heading for the bulge.

"Because you're not in a good place."

I stop.

He looks at me, and I look at him. My vision blurs. Chris wraps his arms around me and pulls me closer. I bury my face in his shirt. He smells like a perfect combination of Lever soap and Old Spice. The thump of his heart is better than any beat he's ever made. My normal, in the flesh.

Chris rests his chin on top of my head. "Starr…"

He lets me cry as much as I need to.

My phone vibrates against my thigh, waking me up. It's almost pitch-black in Chris's room – the red sky shines a bit of light through his windows. He sleeps soundly and holds me like that's how he always sleeps.

My phone buzzes again. I untangle myself out of Chris's arms and crawl to the foot of the bed. I fish my phone from my pocket. Seven's face lights up my screen.

I try not to sound too groggy. "Hello?"

"Where the hell are you?" Seven barks.

"Has the decision been announced?"

"No. Answer my question."

"Chris's house."

Seven sucks his teeth. "I don't even wanna know. Is DeVante over there?"

"No. Why?"

"Uncle Carlos said he walked out a while ago. Nobody's seen him since."

My stomach clenches. "What?"

"Yeah. If you weren't fooling around with your boyfriend, you'd know that."

"You're really making me feel guilty right now?"

He sighs. "I know you're going through a lot, but damn, Starr. You can't disappear on us like that. Ma's looking for you. She's worried sick. And Pops had to go protect the store, in case … you know."

I crawl back to Chris and shake his shoulder. "Come get us," I tell Seven. "We'll help you look for DeVante."

I send Momma a text to let her know where I am, where I'm going, and that I'm okay. I don't have the guts to call her. And have her go off on me? Nah, no thanks.

Seven is talking on his phone when he pulls into the driveway. By the look on his face, somebody's gotta be dead.

I throw open the passenger door. "What's wrong?"

"Kenya, calm down," he says. "What happened?" Seven listens and looks more horrified by the second. Then he suddenly says, "I'm on my way," and tosses the phone on the backseat. "It's DeVante."

"Whoa, wait." I'm holding the door, and he's revving up his engine. "What happened?"

"I don't know. Chris, take Starr home—"

"And let you go to Garden Heights by yourself?" But shoot, actions are louder. I climb in the passenger seat.

"I'm coming too," Chris says. I let my seat forward, and he climbs in the back.

Luckily, or unluckily, Seven doesn't have time to argue. We pull off.

Seven cuts the forty-five-minute drive to Garden Heights to thirty. The entire drive I plead with God to let DeVante be okay.

The sun's gone by the time we get off the freeway. I fight the urge to tell Seven to turn around. This is Chris's first time in my neighborhood.

But I have to trust him. He wants me to let him in, and this is the most "in" he could get.

At the Cedar Grove Projects there's graffiti on the walls and broken-down cars in the courtyard. Under the Black Jesus mural at the clinic, grass grows up through the cracks in the sidewalk. Trash litters every curb we pass. Two junkies argue loudly on a corner. There's lots of hoopties, cars that should've been in the junkyard a long time ago. The houses are old, small.

Whatever Chris thinks doesn't come out his mouth.

Seven parks in front of Iesha's house. The paint is peeling, and the windows have sheets in them instead of blinds and curtains. Iesha's pink BMW and King's gray one make an L shape on the yard. The grass is completely gone from years of them parking there. Gray cars fitted with rims sit in the driveway and along the street.

Seven turns his ignition off. "Kenya said they're all in the backyard. I should be good. Y'all stay here."

Judging by those cars, for one Seven there's about fifty

King Lords. I don't care if King is pissed at me, I'm not letting my brother go in there alone. "I'm coming with you."

"No."

"I said I'm coming."

"Starr, I don't have time for—"

I fold my arms. "Try and make me stay."

He can't, and he won't.

Seven sighs. "Fine. Chris, stay here."

"Hell no! I'm not staying out here by myself."

We all get out. Music echoes from the backyard along with random shouts and laughter. A pair of gray high-tops dangle by their laces from the utility line in front of the house, telling everybody who can decipher the code that drugs are sold here.

Seven takes the steps two at a time and throws the front door open. "Kenya!"

Compared to the outside, the inside is five-star-hotel nice. They have a damn chandelier in the living room and brand-new leather furniture. A flat-screen TV takes up a whole wall, and tropical fish swim around in a tank on another wall. The definition of "hood rich."

"Kenya!" Seven repeats, going down the hall.

From the front door I see the back door. A whole lot of King Lords dance with women in the backyard. King's in the middle in a high-backed chair, his throne, puffing on a cigar. Iesha sits on the arm of the chair, holding a cup and moving her shoulders to the music. Thanks to the dark screen on the door, I can see outside but chances are they can't see inside.

Kenya peeks into the hall from one of the bedrooms. "In here."

DeVante lies on the floor in the fetal position at the foot of a king-size bed. The plush white carpet is stained with his blood as it trickles from his nose and mouth. There's a towel beside him, but he's not doing anything with it. One of his eyes has a fresh bruise around it. He groans, clutching his side.

Seven looks at Chris. "Help me get him up."

Chris has paled. "Maybe we should call—"

"Chris, man, c'mon!"

Chris inches over, and the two of them sit DeVante up against the bed. His nose is swollen and bruised, and his upper lip has a nasty cut.

Chris passes him the towel. "Dude, what happened?"

"I walked into King's fist. Man, what you think happened? They jumped me."

"I couldn't stop them," Kenya says, all stuffed-up sounding like she's been crying. "I'm so sorry, DeVante."

"This shit ain't your fault, Kenya," DeVante says. "Are you a'ight?"

She sniffs and wipes her nose on her arm. "I'm okay. He only pushed me."

Seven's eyes flash. "Who pushed you?"

"She tried to stop them from beating my ass," DeVante says. "King got mad and pushed her out the—"

Seven marches to the door. I catch his arm and dig my feet into the carpet to keep him from moving, but he ends up pulling me with him. Kenya grabs his other arm. In this moment, he's *our* brother, not just mine or hers.

"Seven, no," I say. He tries to pull away, but my grip and Kenya's grip are steel. "You go out there and you're dead."

His jaw is hard, his shoulders are tense. His narrowed eyes are set on the doorway.

"Let. Me. Go," he says.

"Seven, I'm okay. I promise," Kenya says. "But Starr's right. We gotta get Vante outta here before they kill him. They just waiting for the sun to set."

"He put his hands on you," Seven snarls. "I said I wouldn't let that happen again."

"We know," I say. "But please don't go back there."

I hate stopping him because I promise, I want somebody to whoop King's ass. It can't be Seven. No way in hell. I can't lose him too. I'd never be normal again.

He snatches away from us, and the sting that would usually come with that gesture is missing. I understand his frustration like it's mine.

The back door squeaks and slams closed.

Shit.

We freeze. Feet thump against the floor, drawing nearer. Iesha appears in the doorway.

Nobody speaks.

She stares at us, sipping from a red plastic cup. Her lip is

378

curled up slightly, and she takes her sweet time to speak, like she's getting a kick out of our fear.

Chomping on some ice, she looks at Chris and says, "Who this li'l white boy y'all done brought up in my house?"

Iesha smirks and eyes me. "I bet he yours, ain't he? That's what happens when you go to them white folks' schools." She leans against the doorframe. Her gold bracelets jingle as she lifts her cup to her lips again. "I would've paid to see Maverick's face the day you brought this one home. Shit, I'm surprised Seven got a black girl."

At his name Seven snaps out his trance. "Can you help us?"

"Help you?" she echoes with a laugh. "What? With DeVante? What I look like helping him?"

"Momma—"

"Now I'm Momma?" she says. "What happened to that 'Iesha' shit from the other week? Huh, Seven? See, baby, you don't know how the game work. Let Momma explain something to you, okay? When DeVante stole from King, he earned an ass whooping. He got one. Anybody who helps him is asking for it too, and they better be able to handle it." She looks at me. "That goes for dry snitches too."

All it takes is her hollering for King...

Her eyes flick toward the back door. The music and laughter rise in the air. "I tell y'all what," she says, and turns to us. "Y'all better get DeVante's sorry ass out my bedroom. Bleeding on my carpet and shit. And got the nerve to use one of my damn towels? Matter of fact, get him and that snitch out my house."

Seven says, "What?"

"You deaf too?" she says. "I said get them out my house. And take your sisters."

"What I gotta take them for?" Seven says.

"Because I said so! Take them to your grandma's or something, I don't care. Get them out my face. I'm trying to get my party on, shit." When none of us moves, she says, "Go!"

"I'll get Lyric," Kenya says, and leaves.

Chris and Seven each take one of DeVante's hands and pull him up. DeVante winces and cusses the whole way. Once on his feet, he bends over, holding his side, but slowly straightens up and takes steadying breaths. He nods. "I'm good. Just sore."

"Hurry up," Iesha says. "Damn. I'm tired of looking at y'all."

Seven's glare says what he doesn't.

DeVante insists he can walk, but Seven and Chris lend their shoulders for support anyway. Kenya's already at the front door with Lyric on her hip. I hold the door open for all of them and look toward the backyard.

Shit. King's rising off his throne.

Iesha goes out the back door, and she's in his face before he can fully stand up. She grabs his shoulders and guides him back down, whispering in his ear. He smiles widely and leans back into his chair. She turns around so her back

380

is to him, the view he really wants, and starts dancing. He smacks her ass. She looks my way.

I doubt she can see me, but I don't think I'm one of the people she's trying to see anyway. They've gone to the car.

Suddenly I get it.

"Starr, c'mon," Seven calls.

I jump off the porch. Seven holds his seat forward for me and Chris to climb in the back with his sisters. Once we're in, he drives off.

"We gotta get you to the hospital, Vante," he says.

DeVante presses the towel against his nose and looks at the blood staining it. "I'll be a'ight," he says, like that quick observation tells him what a doctor can't. "We lucky Iesha helped us, man. For real."

Seven snorts. "She wasn't helping us. Somebody could be bleeding to death, and she would be more worried about her carpet and getting her party on."

My brother is smart. So smart that he's dumb. He's been hurt by his momma so much that when she does something right he's blind to it. "Seven, she did help us," I say. "Think about it. Why did she tell you to take your sisters too?"

"'Cause she didn't wanna be bothered. As always."

"No. She knows King will go off when he sees DeVante's gone," I say. "If Kenya's not there, Lyric's not there, who do you think he's gon' take it out on?"

He says nothing.

Then, "Shit."

The car makes an abrupt stop, lurching us forward then

sideways as Seven makes a wide U-turn. He hits the gas, and houses blur past us.

"Seven, no!" Kenya says. "We can't go back!"

"I'm supposed to protect her!"

"No, you're not!" I say. "She's supposed to protect you, and she's trying to do that now."

The car slows down. It comes to a complete stop a few houses away from Iesha's.

"If he—" Seven swallows. "If she – he'll kill her."

"He won't," Kenya says. "She's lasted this long. Let her do this, Seven."

A Tupac song on the radio makes up for our silence. He raps about how we gotta start making changes. Khalil was right. 'Pac's still relevant.

"All right," Seven says, and he makes another U-turn. "All right."

The song fades off. "This is the hottest station in the nation, Hot 105," the DJ says. "If you're just tuning in, the grand jury has decided not to indict Officer Brian Cruise Jr. in the death of Khalil Harris. Our thoughts and prayers are with the Harris family. Stay safe out there, y'all."

CHAPTER 23

It's a quiet ride to Seven's grandma's house.

I told the truth. I did everything I was supposed to do, and it wasn't fucking good enough. Khalil's death wasn't horrible enough to be considered a crime.

But damn, what about his life? He was once a walking, talking human being. He had family. He had friends. He had dreams. None of it fucking mattered. He was just a thug who deserved to die.

Car horns honk around us. Drivers shout the decision to the rest of the neighborhood. Some kids around my age stand on top of a car as they shout, "Justice for Khalil!"

Seven maneuvers around it all and parks in his grandma's driveway. He's silent and unmoving at first. Suddenly he punches the steering wheel. "Fuck!"

DeVante shakes his head. "This some bullshit."

"Fuck!" Seven croaks. He covers his eyes and rocks back and forth. "Fuck, fuck, fuck!"

I wanna cry too. Just can't.

"I don't understand," Chris says. "He killed Khalil.

He should go to prison."

"They never do," Kenya mutters.

Seven hastily wipes his face. "Fuck this. Starr, whatever you wanna do, I'm down. You wanna burn some shit up, we'll burn some shit up. Give the word."

"Dude, are you crazy?" Chris says.

Seven turns around. "*You* don't get it, so shut up. Starr, what you wanna do?"

Anything. *Everything.* Scream. Cry. Puke. Hit somebody. Burn something. Throw something.

They gave me the hate, and now I wanna fuck everybody, even if I'm not sure how.

"I wanna do something," I say. "Protest, riot, I don't care—"

"*Riot?*" Chris echoes.

"Hell yeah!" DeVante gives me dap. "That's what I'm talking 'bout!"

"Starr, think about this," Chris says. "That won't solve anything."

"And neither did talking!" I snap. "I did everything right, and it didn't make a fucking difference. I've gotten death threats, cops harassed my family, somebody shot into my house, all kinds of shit. And for what? Justice Khalil won't get? They don't give a fuck about us, so fine. I no longer give a fuck."

"But—"

"Chris, I don't need you to agree," I say, my throat tight. "Just try to understand how I feel. Please?"

384

He closes and opens his mouth a couple of times. No response.

Seven gets out and holds his seat forward. "C'mon, Lyric. Kenya, you staying here or you coming with us?"

"Staying," Kenya says, her eyes wet from earlier. "In case Momma shows up."

Seven nods heavily. "Good idea. She'll need somebody."

Lyric climbs off Kenya's lap and runs up the walkway. Kenya hesitates. She looks back at me. "I'm sorry, Starr," she says. "This ain't right."

She follows Lyric to the front door, and their grandma lets them inside.

Seven returns to the driver's seat. "Chris, you want me to take you home?"

"I'm staying." Chris nods, as if he's settling with himself. "Yeah, I'm staying."

"You sure you up for this?" DeVante asks. "It's gon' get wild out here."

"I'm sure." He eyes me. "I want everyone to know that decision is bullshit."

He puts his hand on the seat with his palm facing up. I put my hand on his.

Seven cranks up the car and backs out the driveway. "Somebody check Twitter, find out where everything's going down."

"I got you." DeVante holds up his phone. "Folks headed to Magnolia. That's where a lot of shit happened last—" He winces and grabs his side.

"Are *you* up for this, Vante?" Chris asks.

DeVante straightens up. "Yeah. I got beat worse than this when I got initiated."

"How'd they get you anyway?" I ask.

"Yeah. Uncle Carlos said you walked off," says Seven. "That's a long-ass walk."

"Man," DeVante groans in that DeVante way. "I wanted to visit Dalvin, a'ight? I took the bus to the cemetery. I hate that he by himself in the Garden. I didn't want him to be lonely, if that make sense."

I try not to think about Khalil being alone in Garden Heights, now that Ms. Rosalie and Cameron are going to New York with Ms. Tammy and I'm leaving too. "It makes sense."

DeVante presses the towel against his nose and lip. The bleeding's slacked up. "Before I could catch the bus back, King's boys snatched me up. I thought I'd be dead by now. For real."

"Well, I'm glad you're not," Chris says. "Gives me more time to beat you in Madden."

DeVante smirks. "You a crazy-ass white boy if you think that's gon' happen."

Cars are up and down Magnolia like it's a Saturday morning and the dope boys are showing off. Music blasts, horns blare, people hang out car windows, stand on the hoods. The sidewalks are packed. It's hazy out, and flames lick the sky in the distance.

I tell Seven to park at Just Us for Justice. The windows are boarded up and "Black owned" is spray-painted across them. Ms. Ofrah said they would be leading protests around the city if the grand jury didn't indict.

We head down the sidewalk, just walking with no particular place to go. It's more crowded than I realized. About half the neighborhood is out here. I throw my hoodie over my hair and keep my head down. No matter what that grand jury decided, I'm still "Starr who was with Khalil," and I don't wanna be seen tonight. Just heard.

A couple of folks glance at Chris with that "what the hell is this white boy doing out here" look. He stuffs his hands in his pockets.

"Guess I'm noticeable, huh?" he says.

"You're sure you wanna be out here?" I ask.

"This is kinda how it is for you and Seven at Williamson, right?"

"A lot like that," Seven says.

"Then I can deal."

The crowds are too thick. We climb on top of a bus stop bench to get a better view of everything going on. King Lords in gray bandanas and Garden Disciples in green bandanas stand on a police car in the middle of the street, chanting, "Justice for Khalil!" People gathered around the car record the scene with their phones and throw rocks at the windows.

"Fuck that cop, bruh," a guy says, gripping a baseball bat. "Killed him over nothing!"

He slams the bat into the driver's side window, shattering the glass.

It's on.

The King Lords and GDs stomp out the front window. Then somebody yells, "Flip that mothafucka!"

The gangbangers jump off. People line up on one side of the car. I stare at the lights on the top, remembering the ones that flashed behind me and Khalil, and watch them disappear as they flip the car onto its back.

Someone shouts, "Watch out!"

A Molotov cocktail sails toward the car. Then – *whoompf!* It bursts into flames.

The crowd cheers.

People say misery loves company, but I think it's like that with anger too. I'm not the only one pissed – everyone around me is. They didn't have to be sitting in the passenger's seat when it happened. My anger is theirs, and theirs is mine.

A car stereo loudly plays a record-scratching sound, then Ice Cube says, *"Fuck the police, coming straight from the underground. A young nigga got it bad 'cause I'm brown."*

You'd think it was a concert the way people react, rapping along and jumping to the beat. DeVante and Seven yell out the lyrics. Chris nods along and mumbles the words. He goes silent every time Cube says "nigga." As he should.

When that hook hits, a collective "Fuck the police" thunders off Magnolia Avenue, probably loud enough to reach the heavens.

I yell it out too. Part of me is like, "What about Uncle Carlos the cop?" But this isn't about him or his coworkers who do their jobs right. This is about One-Fifteen, those detectives with their bullshit questions, and those cops who made Daddy lie on the ground. Fuck them.

Glass shatters. I stop rapping.

A block away, people throw rocks and garbage cans at the windows of the McDonald's and the drugstore next to it.

One time I had a really bad asthma attack that put me in the emergency room. My parents and I didn't leave the hospital until like three in the morning, and we were starving by then. Momma and I grabbed hamburgers at that McDonald's and ate while Daddy got my prescription from the pharmacy.

The glass doors at the drugstore shatter completely. People rush in and eventually come back out with arms full of stuff.

"Stop!" I yell, and others say the same, but looters continue to run in. A glow of orange bursts inside, and all those people rush out.

"Holy shit," Chris says.

In no time the building is in flames.

"Hell yeah!" says DeVante. "Burn that bitch down!"

I remember the look on Daddy's face the day Mr. Wyatt handed him the keys to the grocery store; Mr. Reuben and all those pictures on his walls, showing years and years of a legacy he's built; Ms. Yvette walking into her shop every morning, yawning; even pain-in-the-ass Mr. Lewis with his top-of-the-line haircuts.

Glass shatters at the pawnshop on the next block. Then at the beauty supply store near it.

Flames pour out both, and people cheer. A new battle cry starts up:

The roof, the roof, the roof is on fire! We don't need no water, let that mothafucka burn!

I'm just as pissed as anybody, but this … this isn't it. Not for me.

DeVante's right there with them, yelling out the new chant. I backhand his arm.

"What?" he says.

Chris nudges my side. "Guys…"

A few blocks away, a line of cops in riot gear march down the street, followed closely by two tanks with bright lights.

"This is not a peaceful assembly," an officer on a loud-speaker says. "Disperse now, or you will be subject to arrest."

The original battle cry starts up again: "Fuck the police! Fuck the police!"

People hurl rocks and glass bottles at the cops.

"Yo," Seven says.

"Stop throwing objects at law enforcement," the officer says. "Exit the streets immediately or you will be subject to arrest."

The rocks and bottles continue to fly.

Seven hops off the bench. "C'mon," he says, as Chris and I climb off too. "We need to get outta here."

"Fuck the police! Fuck the police!" DeVante continues to shout.

"Vante, man, c'mon!" says Seven.

"I ain't scared of them! Fuck the police!"

There's a loud pop. An object sails into the air, lands in the middle of the street, and explodes in a ball of fire.

"Oh shit!" DeVante says.

He hops off the bench, and we run. It's damn near a stampede on the sidewalk. Cars speed away in the street. It sounds like the Fourth of July behind us; pop after pop after pop.

Smoke fills the air. More glass shatters. The pops get closer, and the smoke thickens.

Flames eat away at the cash advance place. Just Us for Justice is fine though. So is the car wash on the other side of it, "black owned" spray-painted on one of its walls.

We hop into Seven's Mustang. He speeds out the back entrance of the old Taco Bell parking lot, hitting the next street over.

"The hell just happened?" he says.

Chris slumps in his seat. "I don't know. I don't want it to happen again though."

"Niggas tired of taking shit," DeVante says, between heavy breaths. "Like Starr said, they don't give a fuck about us, so we don't give a fuck. Burn this bitch down."

"But they don't live here!" Seven says. "They don't give a *damn* what happens to this neighborhood."

"What we supposed to do then?" DeVante snaps. "All

that 'Kumbaya' peaceful shit clearly don't work. They don't listen till we tear something up."

"Those businesses though," I say.

"What about them?" DeVante asks. "My momma used to work at that McDonald's, and they barely paid her. That pawnshop ripped us off a hell of a lot of times. Nah, I don't give a fuck about neither one of them bitches."

I get it. Daddy almost lost his wedding ring to that pawnshop once. He actually threatened to burn it down. Kinda ironic it's burning now.

But if the looters decide to ignore the "black owned" tags, they could end up hitting our store. "We need to go help Daddy."

"What?" Seven says.

"We need to go help Daddy protect the store! In case looters show up."

Seven wipes his face. "Shit, you're probably right."

"Ain't nobody gon' touch Big Mav," says DeVante.

"You don't know that," I say. "People are pissed, DeVante. They're not thinking shit out. They're doing shit."

DeVante eventually nods. "A'ight, fine. Let's go help Big Mav."

"Think he'll be okay with me helping out?" Chris asks. "He didn't seem to like me last time."

"Seem to?" DeVante repeats. "He straight up mean-mugged your ass. I was there. I remember."

Seven snickers. I smack DeVante and tell him, "Shush."

"What? It's true. He was mad as hell that Chris is white.

But ay? You spit that NWA shit like you did back there, maybe he'll think you're a'ight."

"What? Surprised a white boy knows NWA?" Chris teases.

"Man, you ain't white. You light-skinned."

"Agreed!" I say.

"Wait, wait," Seven says over our laughter, "we gotta test him to see if he really is black. Chris, you eat green bean casserole?"

"Hell no. That shit's disgusting."

The rest of us lose it, saying, "He's black! He's black!"

"Wait, one more," I say. "Macaroni and cheese. Full meal or a side dish?"

"Uh…" Chris's eyes dart around at us.

DeVante mimics the *Jeopardy!* music.

"How to earn a black card for three hundred, Alex," Seven says in an announcer's voice.

Chris finally answers, "Full meal."

"Aww!" the rest of us groan.

"Whomp-whomp-whomp!" DeVante adds.

"Guys, it is! Think about it. You get protein, calcium—"

"Protein is meat," DeVante says. "Not no damn cheese. I wish somebody would give me some macaroni, calling it a meal."

"It's like the easiest, quickest meal ever though," Chris says. "One box, and you're—"

"And that's the problem," I say. "Real macaroni and cheese doesn't come from a box, babe. It eventually comes

393

from an oven with a crust bubbling on top."

"Amen." Seven holds his fist to me, and I bump it.

"Ohhh," Chris says. "You mean the kind with bread-crumbs?"

"What?" DeVante yells, and Seven goes, "Breadcrumbs?"

"Nah," I say. "I mean there's like a crust of cheese on top. We gotta get you to a soul food restaurant, babe."

"This fool said breadcrumbs." DeVante sounds seriously offended. "Breadcrumbs."

The car stops. Up ahead a Road Closed sign blocks the street with a cop car in front of it.

"Damn," Seven says, backing up and turning around. "Gotta find another way to the store."

"They probably got a lot of roadblocks around the neighborhood tonight," I tell him.

"Fucking breadcrumbs." DeVante still can't get over it. "I swear, I don't understand white people. Breadcrumbs on macaroni, kissing dogs on the mouth—"

"Treating their dogs like they're their kids," I add.

"Yeah!" says DeVante. "Purposely doing shit that could kill them, like bungee jumping."

"Calling Target 'Tar-jay,' like that makes it fancier," says Seven.

"Fuck," Chris mutters. "That's what my mom calls it."

Seven and I bust out laughing.

"Saying dumb shit to their parents," DeVante continues. "Splitting up in situations when they clearly need to stick together."

394

Chris goes, "Huh?"

"Babe, c'mon," I say. "White people always wanna split up, and when they do something bad happens."

"That's only in horror movies though," he says.

"Nah! Shit like that is always on the news," says DeVante. "They go on a hiking trip, split up, and a bear kills somebody."

"Car breaks down, they split up to find help, and a serial killer murders somebody," Seven adds.

"Like, have y'all ever heard that there's power in numbers?" DeVante asks. "For real though."

"Okay, fine," Chris says. "Since you guys want to go there with white people, can I ask a question about black people?"

Cue the record scratching. No lie, all three of us turn and look at him, including Seven. The car veers off to the side of the road, scraping against the curb. Seven cusses and gets it back on the street.

"I mean, it's only fair," Chris mumbles.

"Guys, he's right," I say. "He should be able to ask."

"Fine," says Seven. "Go ahead, Chris."

"Okay. Why do some black people give their kids odd names? I mean, look at you guys' names. They're not normal."

"My name normal," DeVante says, all puffed-up sounding. "I don't know what you talking about."

"Man, you named after a dude from Jodeci," Seven says.

"And you named after a number! What's your middle name? Eight?"

"Anyway, Chris," Seven says, "DeVante's got a point. What makes his name or our names any less normal than yours? Who or what defines 'normal' to you? If my pops were here, he'd say you've fallen into the trap of the white standard."

Color creeps into Chris's neck and face. "I didn't mean — okay, maybe 'normal' isn't the right word."

"Nope," I say.

"I guess uncommon is the word instead?" he asks. "You guys have *uncommon* names."

"I know 'bout three other DeVantes in the neighborhood though," says DeVante.

"Right. It's about perspective," says Seven. "Plus, most of the names white people think are unusual actually have meanings in various African languages."

"And let's be real, some white people give their kids 'uncommon' names too," I say. "That's not limited to black people. Just 'cause it doesn't have a De- or a La- on the front doesn't make it okay."

Chris nods. "True enough."

"Why you have to use 'De-' as an example though?" DeVante asks.

We stop again. Another roadblock.

"Shit," Seven hisses. "I gotta go the long way. Through the east side."

"East side?" DeVante says. "That's GD territory!"

"And that's where most of the riots happened last time," I remind them.

Chris shakes his head. "Nope. Can't go there then."

"Nobody's thinking about gangbanging tonight," Seven says. "And as long as I stay away from the major streets, we'll be all right."

Gunshots go off close by – a little too close by – and all of us jump. Chris actually yelps.

Seven swallows. "Yeah. We'll be all right."

CHAPTER 24

Because Seven said we'd be all right, everything goes wrong.

Most of the routes through the east side are blocked off by police, and it takes Seven forever to find one that isn't. About halfway to the store the car grunts and slows down.

"C'mon," Seven says. He rubs the dashboard and pumps the gas. "C'mon, baby."

His baby basically says "fuck it" and stops.

"Shit!" Seven rests his head on the steering wheel. "We're out of gas."

"You're kidding, right?" Chris says.

"I wish, man. It was low when we left your house, but I thought I could wait a while before I got gas. I know my car."

"You obviously don't know shit," I say.

We're next to some duplex houses. I don't know what street this is. I'm not familiar with the east side like that. Sirens go off nearby, and it's as hazy and smoky as the rest of the neighborhood.

"There's a gas station not too far from here," Seven says.

"Chris, can you help me push it?"

"As in, get out the protection of this car and push it?" Chris asks.

"Yeah, that. It'll be all right." Seven hops out.

"That's what you said before," Chris mumbles, but he climbs out.

DeVante says, "I can push too."

"Nah, man. You need to rest up," says Seven. "Just sit back. Starr, get behind the wheel."

This is the first time he's ever let anyone else drive his "baby." He tells me to put the car in neutral and guide it with the steering wheel. He pushes next to me. Chris pushes on the passenger side. He constantly glances over his shoulder.

The sirens get louder, and the smoke thickens. Seven and Chris cough and cover their noses with their shirts. A pickup truck full of mattresses and people speeds by.

We reach a slight hill, and Seven and Chris jog to keep up with the car.

"Slow down, slow down!" Seven yells. I pump the brakes. The car stops at the bottom of the hill.

Seven coughs into his shirt. "Hold on. I need a minute."

I put the car in park. Chris bends over, trying to catch his breath. "This smoke is killing me," he says.

Seven straightens up and slowly blows air out his mouth. "Shit. We'll get to the gas station faster if we leave the car. The two of us can't push it all the way."

The hell? I'm sitting right here. "I can push."

"I know that, Starr. Even if you did, we'll still be faster

without it. Damn, I don't wanna leave it here though."

"How about we split up?" Chris says. "Two of us stay here, two of us go get some gas — and this is that white-people shit you guys were talking about, isn't it?"

"Yes," the rest of us say.

"Told you," says DeVante.

Seven folds his hands and rests them on top of his dreads. "Fuck, fuck, fuck. We gotta leave it."

I get Seven's keys, and he grabs a gas can from the trunk. He caresses the car and whispers something to it. I think he says he loves it and promises to come back. Lord.

The four of us start down the sidewalk and pull our shirts over our mouths and noses. DeVante limps but swears he's all right.

A voice in the distance says something, I can't make it out, and there's a thunderous response like from a crowd.

Chris and I walk behind the other two. His hand falls to his side, and he brushes up against me, his sly way of trying to hold my hand. I let him.

"So this is where you used to live?" he says.

I forgot this is his first time in Garden Heights. "Yeah. Well, not this side of the neighborhood. I'm from the west side."

"West siiiiiide!" Seven says, as DeVante throws up a W. "The best siiiiiide!"

"On my momma!" DeVante adds.

I roll my eyes. People go too far with that "what side of the neighborhood you from" mess. "You saw that big apartment complex we passed? Those are the projects we lived in when I was younger."

Chris nods. "That place where we parked – was that the Taco Bell your dad took you and Seven to?"

"Yeah. They opened a new one closer to the freeway a few years ago."

"Maybe we can go there together one day," he says.

"Bruh," DeVante butts in. "Please tell me you ain't considering taking your girl to Taco Bell for a date. *Taco Bell?*"

Seven hollers laughing.

"Excuse me, was anybody talking to y'all?" I ask.

"Ay, you my friend, I'm trying to help you out," says DeVante. "Your boy ain't got no game."

"I have game!" Chris says. "I'm letting my girl know I'm happy to go with her anywhere, no matter what neighborhood it's in. As long as she's there, I'm good."

He smiles at me without showing his teeth. I do too.

"Psh! It's still Taco Bell," says DeVante. "By the end of the night it'll be Taco Hell with them bubble guts."

The voice is a bit louder now. Not clear yet. A man and a woman run by on the sidewalk, pushing two shopping carts with flat-screen TVs in them.

"They wilding out here," DeVante says with a chuckle, but grabs his side.

"King kicked you, didn't he?" Seven says. "With those big-ass Timbs on, right?"

DeVante whistles a breath out. He nods.

"Yeah, he did that to my momma once. Broke most of her ribs."

A Rottweiler on a leash in a fenced-in yard barks and struggles to come after us. I stomp my foot at it. It squeals and jumps back.

"She's all right," Seven says, though it seems like he's trying to convince himself. "Yeah. She's fine."

A block away, people stand around in a four-way intersection, watching something on one of the other streets.

"You need to exit the street," a voice announces from a loudspeaker. "You are unlawfully blocking traffic."

"A hairbrush is not a gun! A hairbrush is not a gun!" a voice chants from another loudspeaker. It's echoed back by a crowd.

We get to the intersection. A red, green, and yellow school bus is parked on the street to our right. It says Just Us for Justice on the side. A large crowd is gathered in the street to our left. They point black hairbrushes into the air.

The protestors are on Carnation. Where it happened.

I haven't been back here since that night. Knowing this is where Khalil... I stare too hard, the crowd disappears, and I see him lying in the street. The whole thing plays out before my eyes like a horror movie on repeat. He looks at me for the last time and—

"A hairbrush is not a gun!"

The voice snaps me from my daze.

Ahead of the crowd a lady with twists stands on top of a police car, holding a bullhorn. She turns toward us, her fist raised for black power. Khalil smiles on the front of her T-shirt.

"Ain't that your attorney, Starr?" Seven asks.

"Yeah." Now I knew Ms. Ofrah was about that radical life, but when you think "attorney" you don't really think "person standing on a police car with a bullhorn," you know?

"Disperse immediately," the officer repeats. I can't see him for the crowd.

Ms. Ofrah leads the chant again. "A hairbrush is not a gun! A hairbrush is not a gun!"

It's contagious and echoes all around us. Seven, DeVante, and Chris join in.

"A hairbrush is not a gun," I mutter.

Khalil drops it into the side of the door.

"A hairbrush is not a gun."

He opens the door to ask if I'm okay.

Then pow-pow—

"A hairbrush is not a gun!" I scream loud as I can, fist high in the air, tears in my eyes.

"I'm going to invite Sister Freeman to come up and give a word about the injustice that took place tonight," Ms. Ofrah says.

She hands the bullhorn to a lady who's also in a Khalil shirt, and she hops off the patrol car. The crowd lets her through, and Ms. Ofrah heads toward another coworker who's standing near the bus at the intersection. She spots me and does a double-take.

"Starr?" she says, making her way over. "What are you doing out here?"

"We... I... When they announced the decision, I wanted to do something. So we came to the neighborhood."

She eyes beat-up DeVante. "Oh my God, did you get caught in the riots?"

DeVante touches his face. "Damn, I look that bad?"

"That's not why he looks like that," I tell her. "But we did get caught in the riots on Magnolia. It got crazy over there. Looters took over."

Ms. Ofrah purses her lips. "Yeah. We heard."

"Just Us for Justice was fine when we left," Seven says.

"Even if it's not, it's okay," says Ms. Ofrah. "You can destroy wood and brick, but you can't destroy a movement. Starr, does your mother know you're out here?"

"Yeah." Don't even sound convincing to myself.

"Really?"

"Okay, no. Please don't tell her."

"I have to," she says. "As your attorney I have to do what's in your best interest. Your mom knowing you're out here is in your best interest."

No, it's not, 'cause she'll kill me. "But you're *my* attorney. Not hers. Can't this be a client confidentiality thing?"

"Starr—"

"Please? During the other protests, I watched. And talked. So now I wanna do something."

"Who said talking isn't doing something?" she says.

404

"It's more productive than silence. Remember what I told you about your voice?"

"You said it's my biggest weapon."

"And I mean that." She stares at me a second, then sighs out her nose. "You want to fight the system tonight?"

I nod.

"C'mon then."

Ms. Ofrah takes my hand and leads me through the crowd.

"Fire me," she says.

"Huh?"

"Tell me you no longer want me to represent you."

"I no longer want you to represent me?" I ask.

"Good. As of now I'm not your attorney. So if your parents find out about this, I didn't do it as your attorney but as an activist. You saw that bus near the intersection?"

"Yeah."

"If the officers react, run straight to it. Got it?"

"But what—"

She takes me to the patrol car and motions at her colleague. The lady climbs off and hands Ms. Ofrah the bullhorn. Ms. Ofrah passes it over to me.

"Use your weapon," she says.

Another one of her coworkers lifts me and sets me on top of the cop car.

About ten feet away there's a shrine for Khalil in the middle of the street; lit candles, teddy bears, framed pictures, and balloons. It separates the protestors from a cluster

405

of officers in riot gear. It's not nearly as many cops as it was on Magnolia, but still … they're cops.

I turn toward the crowd. They watch me expectantly.

The bullhorn is as heavy as a gun. Ironic since Ms. Ofrah said to use my weapon. I have the hardest time lifting it. Shit, I have no idea what to say. I put it near my mouth and press the button.

"My—" It makes a loud, earsplitting noise.

"Don't be scared!" somebody in the crowd yells. "Speak!"

"You need to exit the street immediately," the cop says.

You know what? Fuck it.

"My name is Starr. I'm the one who saw what happened to Khalil," I say into the bullhorn. "And it wasn't right."

I get a bunch of "yeahs" and "amens" from the crowd.

"We weren't doing anything wrong. Not only did Officer Cruise assume we were up to no good, he assumed we were criminals. Well, Officer Cruise is the criminal."

The crowd cheers and claps. Ms. Ofrah says, "Speak!"

That amps me up.

I turn to the cops. "I'm sick of this! Just like y'all think all of us are bad because of some people, we think the same about y'all. Until you give us a reason to think otherwise, we'll keep protesting."

More cheers, and I can't lie, it eggs me on. Forget trigger happy – speaker happy is more my thing.

"Everybody wants to talk about how Khalil died," I say. "But this isn't about how Khalil died. It's about the fact that he lived. His life mattered. Khalil lived!" I look at the cops again. "You hear me? Khalil lived!"

"You have until the count of three to disperse," the officer on the loudspeaker says.

"Khalil lived!" we chant.

"One."

"Khalil lived!"

"Two."

"Khalil lived!"

"Three."

"Khalil lived!"

The can of tear gas sails toward us from the cops. It lands beside the patrol car.

I jump off and pick up the can. Smoke whizzes out the end of it. Any second it'll combust.

I scream at the top of my lungs, hoping Khalil hears me, and chuck it back at the cops. It explodes and consumes them in a cloud of tear gas.

All hell breaks loose.

The cops stampede over Khalil's shrine, and the crowd runs. Someone grabs my arm. Ms. Ofrah.

"Go to the bus!" she says.

I get about halfway there when Chris and Seven catch me.

"C'mon!" Seven says, and they pull me with them.

I try to tell them about the bus, but explosions go off and thick white smoke engulfs us. My nose and throat burn as if I swallowed fire. My eyes feel like flames lick them.

Something whizzes overhead, then an explosion goes off in front of us. More smoke.

"DeVante!" Chris croaks, looking around. "DeVante!"

We find him leaning against a flickering streetlight. He coughs and heaves. Seven lets me go and grabs him by the arm.

"Shit, man! My eyes! I can't breathe."

We run. Chris grips my hand as tight as I grip his. There are screams and loud pops in every direction. Can't see a thing for the smoke, not even the Just Us bus.

"I can't run. My side!" DeVante says. "Shit!"

"C'mon, man," Seven says, pulling him. "Keep going!"

Bright lights barrel down the street through the smoke. A gray pickup truck on oversized wheels. It stops beside us, the window rolls down, and my heart stops, waiting for the gun to come pointing out, courtesy of a King Lord.

But Goon, the Cedar Grove King Lord with the ponytails, looks at us from the driver's seat, a gray bandana over his nose and mouth. "Get in the back!" he says.

Two guys and a girl around our age, wearing white bandanas on their faces, help us into the back of the truck. It's an open invitation and other people climb in, like this white man in a shirt and tie and a Latino holding a camera on his shoulder. The white man looks oddly familiar. Goon drives off.

DeVante lies in the bed of the truck. He holds his eyes and rolls in agony. "Shit, man! Shit!"

"Bri, get him some milk," Goon says through the back window.

Milk?

"We're out, Unc," says the girl in the bandana.

"Fuck!" Goon hisses. "Hold on, Vante."

Tears and snot drip down my face. My eyes are damn near numb from burning.

The truck slows down. "Get li'l homie," Goon says.

The two guys in the bandanas grab some kid on the street by his arms and lift him into the truck. The kid looks around thirteen. His shirt is covered in soot, and he coughs and heaves.

I get into a coughing fit. Snorting is like hacking up hot coals. The man in the shirt and tie hands me his dampened handkerchief.

"It'll help some," he says. "Put it against your nose and breathe through it."

It gives me a small amount of clean air. I pass it to Chris, he uses it, passes it to Seven beside him. Seven uses it and passes it to someone else.

"As you can see, Jim," the man says, looking at the camera, "there are a lot of youth out here protesting tonight, black and white."

"I'm the token, huh?" Chris mutters to me before coughing. I'd laugh if it didn't hurt.

"And you have people like this gentlemen, going around the neighborhood, helping out where they can," the white man says. "Driver, what's your name?"

The Latino turns the camera toward Goon.

"Nunya," Goon says.

"Thank you, Nunya, for giving us a ride."

Woooow. I realize why he looks familiar though. He's a national news anchor, Brian somebody.

"This young lady here made a powerful statement earlier," he says, and the camera points toward me. "Are you really the witness?"

I nod. No point hiding anymore.

"We caught what you said back there. Anything else you'd like to add for our viewers?"

"Yeah. None of this makes sense."

I start coughing again. He leaves me alone.

When my eyes aren't closed I see what my neighborhood has become. More tanks, more cops in riot gear, more smoke. Businesses ransacked. Streetlights are out, and fires keep everything from being in complete darkness. People run out of the Walmart and carry armfuls of items, looking like ants rushing from an anthill. The untouched businesses have boarded-up windows and graffiti that says "black owned."

We eventually turn onto Marigold Avenue, and even with the fire in my lungs I take a deep breath. Our store is in one piece. The windows are boarded up with that same "black owned" tag on them, like it's lamb's blood protecting the store from the plague of death. The street is pretty still. Top Shelf Spirits and Wine is the only business with broken windows. It doesn't have a "black owned" tag either.

Goon stops in front of our store. He jumps out, comes to the back of the truck, and helps everyone out. "Starr, Sev, y'all got a key?"

I pat my pockets for Seven's keys and toss them to Goon. He tries each key until one unlocks the door. "In here, y'all," he says.

Everyone including the cameraman and reporter go in the store. Goon and one of the guys in the bandana get DeVante and carry him inside. No sign of Daddy.

I crawl onto the floor and fall on my stomach, blinking fast. My eyes burn and fill with tears.

Goon sets DeVante on the old people's bench before running toward the refrigerator.

He rushes back with a gallon of milk and pours it onto DeVante's face. The milk momentarily turns him white. DeVante coughs and sputters. Goon pours more.

"Stop!" DeVante says. "You 'bout to drown me!"

"I bet your eyes ain't hurting no more though," Goon replies.

I half-crawl, half-run to the refrigerators and get a gallon for myself. I pour it on my face. The relief comes in seconds.

People pour milk onto their faces while the cameraman records it all. An older lady drinks from a gallon. Milk pools on the floor, and a college-aged guy lies face-down in it and gasps for air.

When people get the relief they need, they leave. Goon grabs a bunch of cartons of milk and asks, "Ay, can we take this in case somebody needs it on the street?"

Seven nods and sips from a carton.

"Thanks, li'l homie. If I see your pops again I'll tell him y'all here."

411

"You saw our—" I cough and sip some milk, dousing the flames in my lungs. "You saw our dad?"

"Yeah, a li'l while ago. He was looking for y'all."

Oh, shit.

"Sir," the reporter says to Goon, "can we ride along? We'd like to see more of the neighborhood."

"Ain't no thang, homie. Hop in the back." He turns to the camera and twists his fingers so they resemble a K and an L. "Cedar Grove Kings, baby! Crowns up! Addi-o!" He gives the King Lord call. Leave it to Goon to throw gang signs on live TV.

They leave us alone in the store. Seven, Chris and I are in the pool of milk with our knees up to our chests. DeVante's arms and legs dangle off the old people's bench. He chugs back some milk.

Seven takes his phone from his pocket. "Damn. My phone's dead. Starr, you got yours?"

"Yeah." I have way too many voice mails and way too many texts, most of them from Momma.

I play the voice mails first. They start out safe enough with Momma saying, *"Starr baby, call me as soon as you get this, okay?"*

But they soon become, *"Starr Amara, I know you're getting these messages. Call me. I'm not playing."*

They progress to, *"See, you've taken this too far. Carlos and I are heading out the door right now, and you better pray to God we don't find you!"*

And on the last message, left a few minutes ago, Momma

412

says, *"Oh, so you can't return my calls, but you can lead protests, huh? Momma told me she saw you on live TV, giving speeches and throwing tear gas at cops! I swear I'm gon' snatch your life if you don't call me!"*

"We in deep shit, man," DeVante says. "Deep shit."

Seven glances at his watch. "Damn. We've been gone about four hours."

"Deep shit," DeVante repeats.

"Maybe the four of us can get a place in Mexico?" says Chris.

I shake my head. "Not far enough for our mom."

Seven picks at his face. The milk has dried and formed a crust. "All right, we need to call them. And if we call from the office phone, Ma will see it on the caller ID and know we're not lying when we say we're here. That'll help, right?"

"We're at least three hours too late for any help," I say.

Seven stands and gives me and Chris a hand up. He helps DeVante off the bench. "C'mon. Make sure y'all sound remorseful, all right?"

We head for Daddy's office.

The front door creaks. Something thuds onto the floor.

I turn around. A glass bottle with flaming cloth—

Whoomf! The store is suddenly lit bright orange. A heat wave hits like the sun dropped in. Flames lick the ceiling and block the door.

CHAPTER 25

An entire aisle is already engulfed.

"The back door," Seven says, choked up. "The back door!"

Chris and DeVante follow us down the narrow hall near Daddy's office. It leads to the restroom and the back door where deliveries are unloaded. Smoke's already filling the hall.

Seven pushes the door. It doesn't budge. He and Chris ram their shoulders against it, but it's bulletproof, shoulder-proof, everything-proof. The burglar bars won't let us out anyway.

"Starr, my keys," Seven croaks.

I shake my head. I gave them to Goon, and the last time I saw them he left them in the front door.

DeVante coughs. It's getting harder to breathe with all the smoke. "Man, we can't die up in here. I don't wanna die."

"Shut up!" Chris says. "We're not gonna die."

I cough into the crook of my arm. "Daddy may have a

spare," I say, and my voice is thin. "In his office."

We rush back down the hall, but the office door is locked too.

"Fuck!" Seven screams.

Mr. Lewis limps into the middle of the street. He grips a baseball bat in each hand. He glances around, like he's trying to figure out where the smoke is coming from. With the boards on the windows, he can't see the inferno in the store unless he looks through the front door.

"Mr. Lewis!" I scream as loud as I can.

The guys join in. The smoke strangles our voices. The flames dance feet away, but I swear it's like I'm standing in them.

Mr. Lewis limps toward the store, squinting his eyes. They widen as he looks in through the door, straight at us on the other side of the flames. "Oh Lord!"

He limps into the street faster than I've ever seen him move. "Help! These kids stuck up in here! Help!"

There's a loud crackling to our right. The fire takes out another shelf.

Mr. Reuben's nephew, Tim, runs over and opens the front door, but the flames are too much.

"Go to the back door!" he calls to us.

Tim almost beats us getting there. He yanks hard on the door, and the glass rattles. The way he's pulling, the door will come off eventually. We don't have eventually time though.

Tires screech outside.

Moments later, Daddy runs up to the back door.

"Watch out," he tells Tim, moving him out the way.

Daddy fumbles for his keys and sticks several in the lock while muttering, "Please, God. Please."

I can barely see Seven, Chris, or DeVante for all the smoke, and they're coughing and wheezing next to me.

A click. The knob turns. The door flies open. We rush out. Fresh air fills my lungs.

Daddy pulls me and Seven through the alley, around the corner, and across the street to Reuben's. Tim gets DeVante and Chris. They make us sit on the sidewalk.

Tires screech again, and Momma goes, "Oh my God!"

She runs over, Uncle Carlos on her heels. She holds my shoulders and helps me lie on the sidewalk.

"Breathe, baby," she says. "Breathe."

But I have to see. I sit up.

Daddy attempts to run into the store for God knows what. The flames swat him back. Tim rushes a bucket of water from his uncle's restaurant. He runs into our store and douses it on the flames, but he's forced to jump back too.

People trickle onto the street, and more buckets of sloshing water are hauled into the store. Ms. Yvette carries one from her beauty shop. Tim tosses it onto the fire. Flames eat away at the roof, and smoke billows from the windows of the barbershop next door.

"My shop!" Mr. Lewis cries. Mr. Reuben stops him from running toward it. "My shop!"

Daddy stands in the middle of the street, breathing hard,

looking helpless. A crowd has gathered, and people watch with their hands pressed to their mouths.

Bass rattles nearby. Daddy slowly turns his head.

The gray BMW is parked in the intersection near the liquor store. King leans up against it. Some other King Lords stand alongside him and sit on the hood of the car. They laugh and point.

King stares straight at Daddy and takes out his cigarette lighter. He sparks a flame.

Iesha said King was gonna fuck *us* up because I dry snitched. That meant my whole family.

This is it.

"You son of a bitch!" Daddy marches toward King, and King's boys advance toward Daddy. Uncle Carlos stops him. The King Lords reach for their pieces and tell Daddy to bring it. King laughs like it's a comedy show.

"You think this shit funny?" Daddy yells. "Punk ass, always hiding behind your boys!"

King stops laughing.

"Yeah, I said it! I ain't scared of you! You ain't shit to be scared of! Trying to burn up some kids, you fucking coward!"

"Oh uh-uh!" Momma starts for King, and Uncle Carlos has to work overtime to hold her back too.

"He burned Maverick's store down!" Mr. Lewis announces to everybody, in case we didn't hear. "King burned Maverick's store down!"

It bubbles around the crowd, and narrowed eyes set on King.

Of course, that's when the cops and the fire truck decide to show up. Of course. Because that's how it works in Garden Heights.

Uncle Carlos convinces my parents to back away. King lifts his cigar to his lips, eyes gleaming. I wanna get one of Mr. Lewis's baseball bats and knock him upside his head.

The firefighters get to work. The cops order the crowd to back up. King and his boys are really amused now. Shit, it's like the cops are helping them out.

"You need to be getting them!" Mr. Lewis says. "They the ones who started the fire!"

"That old man don't know what he talking about," King says. "All this smoke done got to him."

Mr. Lewis starts to charge at King, and an officer has to hold him back. "I ain't crazy! You did start it! Everybody know it!"

King's face twitches. "You better watch yourself, lying on folks."

Daddy glances back at me, and there's this expression on his face that I've never seen before. He turns around to the cop who's holding Mr. Lewis and says, "He ain't lying. King did start it, Officer."

Ho–ly shit.

Daddy snitched.

"It's my store," he says. "I know he started the fire."

"Did you see him do it?" the cop asks.

No. That's the problem. We know King did it, but if nobody saw it…

"I saw him," Mr. Reuben says. "He did it."

"I saw him too," Tim says.

"So did I," Ms. Yvette adds.

And shit, now the crowd is echoing the same thing, pointing at King and his boys. I mean, everybody's snitching. The rules no fucking longer apply.

King reaches for his car door, but some of the officers draw their guns and order him and his boys to the ground.

An ambulance arrives. Momma tells them about our smoke inhalation. I snitch and tell them about DeVante, although his black eye makes it obvious he needs help. They let the four of us sit on the curb, and they put oxygen masks on us. I thought I wasn't that bad anymore, but I forgot how nice clean air is. I've been breathing in smoke since I got to Garden Heights.

They look at DeVante's side. It's purple-looking, and they tell him he'll need to go in for X-rays. He doesn't wanna go in the ambulance, and Momma assures the paramedics that she'll take him in herself.

I rest my head on Chris's shoulder as we hold hands, oxygen masks on both of us. I'm not gonna lie and say tonight was better because he was here – frankly this has been one fucked-up night, nothing could make it better – but it doesn't hurt that we went through it together.

My parents come our way. Daddy's lips thin, and he mumbles something to Momma. She elbows him and says, "Be nice."

She sits between Chris and Seven. Daddy hovers over

me and Chris at first, as if he's expecting us to make room for him.

"Maverick," Momma says.

"A'ight, a'ight." He sits on the other side of me.

We watch the firefighters put out the flames. No point though. They're only saving a shell of the store.

Daddy sighs, rubbing his bald head. "Damn, man."

My heart aches. We're losing a family member, for real. I've spent most of my life in that store. I move my head off Chris and rest it on Daddy's shoulder. He puts his arm around me and kisses my hair. I don't miss that smug look that crosses his face. Petty.

"Wait a minute." He pulls away. "Where the hell y'all been?"

"That's what I wanna know," Momma says. "Acting like you can't answer my texts or calls!"

Really? Seven and I almost died in a fire, and they're mad 'cause we didn't call them? I lift my mask and say, "Long night."

"Oh, I'm sure it was," Momma says. "We got ourselves a li'l radical, Maverick. All on the news, throwing tear gas at the cops."

"After they threw it at us," I point out.

"Whaaat?" Daddy says, but in that impressed way. Momma cuts him a side-eye, and he says in a more stern tone, "I mean, what? What you do that for?"

"I was mad." I fold my arms onto my knees and stare at my Timbs through the gap. "That decision wasn't right."

Daddy puts his arm around me again and rests his head against mine. A Daddy-snuggle. "Nah," he says. "It wasn't."

"Hey," Momma beckons me to look at her. "The decision may not have been right, but it's not your fault. Remember what I said? Sometimes things will go wrong—"

"But the key is to keep doing right." My eyes drift to my Timbs again. "Khalil still deserved better than that."

"Yeah." Her voice thickens. "He did."

Daddy looks past me at my boyfriend. "So... Plain-Ass Chris."

Seven snorts. DeVante snickers. Momma goes, "Maverick!" as I say, "Daddy!"

"At least it's not white boy," Chris says.

"Exactly," Daddy says. "It's a step up. You gotta earn my tolerance in increments if you gon' date my daughter."

"Lord." Momma rolls her eyes. "Chris, baby, you've been out *here* all night?"

The way she says it, I can't help but laugh. She's basically asking him, "You do realize you're in the hood, right?"

"Yes, ma'am," Chris says. "All night."

Daddy grunts. "Maybe you do got some balls then."

My mouth drops, and Momma says, "Maverick Carter!" Seven and DeVante crack up.

But Chris? Chris says, "Yes, sir, I'd like to think I do."

"Daaaaamn," says Seven. He reaches to give Chris dap, but Daddy cuts him a hard eye and he pulls his hand back.

"A'ight, Plain-Ass Chris," Daddy says. "Boxing gym, next Saturday, you and me."

421

Chris lifts his oxygen mask so fast. "I'm sorry, I shouldn't have said—"

"Calm down, I'm not gon' fight you," Daddy says. "We gon' train. Get to know each other. You been seeing my daughter for a minute now. I gotta know you, and you can learn a lot about a man at a boxing gym."

"Oh…" Chris's shoulders relax. "Okay." He puts the oxygen mask back on.

Daddy grins. It's a little too mischievous for my liking. He's gonna kill my poor boyfriend.

The cops load King and his boys into patrol cars, and the crowd claps and cheers. Finally, something to celebrate tonight.

Uncle Carlos strolls over. He's got on a wifebeater and shorts, which is so not Uncle Carlos, yet something about him still looks detectivey. He's been in cop mode since his colleagues arrived.

Uncle Carlos gives this old-man grunt as he lowers himself onto the sidewalk next to DeVante. He grabs the back of DeVante's neck the same way Daddy grabs Seven's. Man hugs, I call them.

"I'm glad you're safe, kid," he says. "Even if you do look like a truck ran over you twice."

"You not mad I left without telling y'all?"

"Of course I'm mad. I'm actually pissed. But I'm happier that you're safe. Now, my mom and Pam, that's a whole different story. I can't save you from their wrath."

"Are you putting me out?"

"No. You're grounded, probably for the rest of your life, but that's only because we love you."

DeVante cracks a smile.

Uncle Carlos pats his knees. "Sooo … thanks to all these witnesses, we should get King for arson."

"Oh, for real?" Daddy says.

"Yep. It's a start, but not really enough. He'll be out by the end of the week."

And back to the same ol' shit. With targets this time.

"If y'all knew where King's stash was," DeVante says, "would that help?"

Uncle Carlos says, "Probably, yeah."

"If somebody agreed to rat on him, would that help?"

Uncle Carlos turns completely toward him. "Are you saying you want to turn witness?"

"I mean…" DeVante pauses. "Will it help Kenya, her momma, and her sister?"

"If King went to jail?" says Seven. "Yeah. A lot."

"It'll help the whole neighborhood, honestly," Daddy says.

"And I'll be protected?" DeVante asks Uncle Carlos.

"Absolutely. I promise."

"And Uncle Carlos always keeps his promises," I say.

DeVante nods for a moment. "Then I guess I will turn witness."

Ho-ly shit again. "You're sure about that?" I ask.

"Yeah. After seeing you face those cops the way you did, I don't know, man. That did something to me," he says.

"And that lady said our voices are weapons. I should use mine, right?"

"So you're willing to become a snitch," Chris says.

"On King," Seven adds.

DeVante shrugs. "I already need the stitches. Might as well snitch."

CHAPTER 26

It's around eleven the next morning, and I'm still in bed. After the longest night ever I had to seriously get reacquainted with my pillow.

My mom flicks on the lights in my new room – good Lord, it's too many lights in here. "Starr, your partner in crime is on the phone," she says.

"Who?" I mumble.

"Your protest partner in crime. Momma told me she saw her hand you that bullhorn on TV. Putting you in danger like that."

"But she didn't mean to put me in—"

"Oh, I've dealt with her already, don't worry. Here. She wants to apologize to you."

Ms. Ofrah does apologize for putting me in a bad situation and for the way things turned out with Khalil, but she says she's proud of me.

She also says she thinks I have a future in activism.

Momma leaves with the phone, and I turn onto my side. Tupac stares back at me from a poster, a smirk on his face.

The Thug Life tattoo on his stomach looks bolder than the rest of the photo. It was the first thing I put in my new room. Kinda like bringing Khalil with me.

He said Thug Life stood for "The Hate U Give Little Infants Fucks Everybody." We did all that stuff last night because we were pissed, and it fucked all of us. Now we have to somehow un-fuck everybody.

I sit up and grab my phone off my nightstand. There are texts from Maya, who saw me on the news and thinks I'm dope personified, and texts from Chris. His parents grounded him, but he says it was so worth it. It really was.

There's another text. From Hailey, of all people. Two simple words:

I'm sorry.

Not what I expected; not that I expected to get *anything* from her; not that I even wanna deal with her. This is the first time she's spoken to me since our fight. I'm not complaining. She's been nonexistent to me too. I respond anyway.

Sorry for what?

I'm not being petty. Petty would be saying, "New number, who dis?" There's a damn near endless list of things she could be apologizing for.

About the decision, she says.

And that you're upset with me.

Haven't been myself lately.

Just want everything to be how it used to be.

The sympathy for the case is nice, but she's sorry I'm

upset? That's not the same as apologizing for her actions or the garbage she said. She's sorry I reacted the way I did.

Oddly enough, I needed to know that.

You see, it's like my mom said – if the good outweighs the bad, I should keep Hailey as a friend. There's a shit ton of bad now, an *overload* of bad. I hate to admit that a teeny-tiny part of me hoped Hailey would see how wrong she was, but she hasn't. She may not ever see that.

And you know what? That's fine. Okay, maybe not *fine,* because it makes her a shitty-ass person, but I don't have to wait around for her to change. I can let go. I reply:

Things will never be the way they used to be.

I hit send, wait for the text to go through, and delete the conversation. I delete Hailey's number from my phone too.

I stretch and yawn as I creep down the hall. The layout of our new house is way different than our old one, but I think I can get used to it.

Daddy clips some roses at the kitchen counter. Next to him Sekani inhales a sandwich, and Brickz stands on his hind legs with his paws on Sekani's lap. He watches the sandwich the same way he watches a squirrel.

Momma flips switches on the wall. One causes a grinding noise in the sink, and another turns the lights off and on.

"Too many switches," she mumbles, and notices me. "Oh look, Maverick. It's our li'l revolutionary."

Brickz scuttles over to me and jumps up my legs, tongue wagging.

"Morning," I tell him, and scratch behind his ears.

427

He gets down and returns to Sekani and the sandwich.

"Do me a favor, Starr," Seven says, searching through a box that has "Kitchen Stuff" written on it in my handwriting. "Next time, be more specific about what type of kitchen stuff is in the box. I've gone through three, trying to find plates."

I climb onto a stool at the counter. "Lazy butt, isn't that what paper towels are for?"

Seven narrows his eyes. "Hey, Pops, guess where I picked Starr up from yester—"

"The plates are in the bottom of that box," I say.

"Thought so."

My middle finger wants to extend so bad.

Daddy says, "You bet' not have been at that boy's house, I know that."

I force a smile. "No. Of course not."

I'm gonna kill Seven.

Daddy sucks his teeth. "Uh-huh." He goes back to work on his roses. An entire bush lies on the counter. The roses are dry, and some of the petals have fallen off. Daddy sets the bush in a clay pot and pours dirt over the roots.

"Will they be all right?" I ask.

"Yeah. A li'l damaged, but alive. I'm gon' try something different with them. Putting them in new soil can be like hitting a reset button."

"Starr," Sekani says, mouth full of wet bread and meat. Nasty. "You're in the newspaper."

"Stop talking with your mouth full, boy!" Momma scolds.

428

Daddy nods toward the newspaper on the counter. "Yeah. Check it out, Li'l Black Panther."

I'm on the front page. The photographer caught me mid-throw. The can of tear gas smokes in my hand. The headline reads "The Witness Fights Back."

Momma rests her chin on my shoulder. "They've discussed you on every news show this morning. Your nana calls every five minutes, telling us a new channel to watch." She kisses my cheek. "I know you better not scare me like that again."

"I won't. What are they saying on the news?"

"They calling you brave," Daddy says. "But you know, that one network gotta complain, saying you put them cops in danger."

"I didn't have a problem with those cops. I had a problem with that tear gas can, and they threw it first."

"I know, baby. Don't even stress it. That whole network can kiss my—"

"Dollar, Daddy." Sekani grins up at him.

"Roses. They can kiss my roses." He smudges dirt on Sekani's nose. "You ain't getting another dollar outta me."

"He knows," Seven says, glaring at Sekani. Sekani gets guilty puppy-dog eyes that could give Brickz some competition.

Momma moves her chin off my shoulder. "Okay. What's that about?"

"Nothing. I told Sekani we gotta be careful with money now."

429

"He said we might have to go back to Garden Heights too!" Sekani rats. "Do we?"

"No, of course not," Momma says. "Guys, we'll make this work."

"Exactly," Daddy says. "If I have to sell oranges on the side of the street like the Nation brothers, we'll make it."

"Is it okay to leave though?" I ask. "I mean, the neighborhood is messed up. What are people gonna think about us leaving instead of helping fix it?"

Never, ever thought I'd say something like that, but last night has me thinking about all of this so differently, about me differently. About Garden Heights differently.

"We still can help fix it," Daddy says.

"Right. I'm gonna do extra shifts at the clinic," Momma says.

"And I'm gon' figure something out to do about the store till I get it renovated," says Daddy. "We ain't gotta live there to change things, baby. We just gotta give a damn. A'ight?"

"All right."

Momma kisses my cheek and runs a hand over my hair. "Look at you. Community minded all of a sudden. Maverick, what time did the claims agent say he was coming?"

Daddy closes his eyes and pinches the space between them. "In a couple of hours. I don't even wanna see it."

"It's okay, Daddy," Sekani says, with a mouth full of sandwich. "You don't have to go by yourself. We'll go with you."

So we do. Two police cars block off the entrance to

430

Garden Heights. Daddy shows them his ID and explains why we need to go in. I'm able to breathe during the whole exchange, and they let us through.

Damn, I see why they aren't letting people in though. Smoke has taken up a permanent residence, and glass and all kinds of trash litter the streets. We pass so many blackened frames of what used to be businesses.

The store is the hardest to see. The burned roof folds into itself like the slightest wind will knock it over. The bricks and burglar bars protect charred rubble.

Mr. Lewis sweeps the sidewalk in front of his shop. It's not as bad off as the store, but a broom and a dustpan won't make it better.

Daddy parks in front of the store, and we get out. Momma rubs and squeezes Daddy's shoulder.

"Starr," Sekani whispers, and looks back at me. "The store—"

His eyes have tears in them, and then mine do too. I drape my arms over his shoulders and hug him to me. "I know, man."

A loud creaking sound approaches and somebody whistles a tune. Fo'ty Ounce pushes his shopping cart down the sidewalk. As hot as it is, he's wearing his camouflage coat.

He comes to an abrupt stop in front of the store, like he just noticed it.

"Goddamn, Maverick," he says in that fast, Fo'ty Ounce way where it all sounds like one word. "What the hell happened?"

431

"Man, where were you last night?" Daddy says. "My store got burned up."

"I went on the other side of the freeway. Couldn't stay here. Oh nooo, I knew these fools would go crazy. You got insurance? I hope you do. I got insurance."

"What for?" I ask, because seriously?

"My life!" he says, like it's obvious. "You gon' rebuild, Maverick?"

"I don't know, man. I gotta think about it."

"You have to 'cause now we won't have no store. Everybody else gon' leave and never come back."

"I'll think about it."

"Okay. If you need anything, let me know." And he pushes his cart down the sidewalk but comes to an abrupt stop again. "The liquor store gone too? Oh nooo!"

I snicker. Only Fo'ty Ounce.

Mr. Lewis limps over with his broom. "That fool got a point. Folks will need a store around here. Everybody else gon' leave."

"I know," Daddy says. "It's just – it's a lot, Mr. Lewis."

"I know it is. But you can handle it. I told Clarence what happened," he says of Mr. Wyatt, his friend who used to own the store. "He thinks you oughta stick around. And we were talking, and I think it's about time for me to do like him. Sit on a beach, watch some pretty women."

"You're closing the shop?" Seven asks.

"Who's gonna cut my hair?" Sekani adds.

Mr. Lewis looks down at him. "Not my problem. Since

432

you gon' be the only store around here, Maverick, you'll need more space when you rebuild. I wanna give you the shop."

"What?" Momma sputters.

"Whoa, now, wait a minute, Mr. Lewis," Daddy says.

"Wait nothing. I got insurance, and I'm gonna get more than enough from that. Ain't nothing I can do with a burned-up shop. You can build a nice store, give folks something to be proud to shop in. All I ask is that you put up some pictures of Dr. King alongside your Newey Whoever-He-Was."

Daddy chuckles. "Huey Newton."

"Yeah. Him. I know y'all moving, and I'm glad, but the neighborhood still needs more men like you. Even if you just running a store."

The insurance man arrives a little later, and Daddy gives him a tour of what's left. Momma gets some gloves and garbage bags from the truck, passes them to me and my brothers, and tells us to get to work. It's kinda hard with people driving by and honking their horns. They yell out stuff like "Keep y'all heads up" or "We got your back!"

Some of them come and help out, like Mrs. Rooks and Tim. Mr. Reuben brings us ice-cold bottles of water, 'cause this sun ain't no joke. I sit on the curb, sweating, tired, and one hundred percent ready to be done. We aren't anywhere near finished.

A shadow casts over me, and somebody says, "Hey."

I shield my eyes as I look up. Kenya's wearing an over-sized T-shirt and some basketball shorts. They look like Seven's.

"Hey."

She sits next to me and pulls her knees up to her chest. "I saw you on TV," she says. "I told you to speak out, but damn, Starr. You took it kinda far."

"It got people talking though, didn't it?"

"Yeah. Sorry about the store. I heard my daddy did it."

"He did." No point in denying it, shoot. "How's your momma?"

Kenya pulls her knees closer. "He beat her. She ended up in the hospital. They kept her overnight. She got a concussion and a whole bunch of other stuff, but she'll be okay. We saw her a li'l while ago. The cops came, and we had to leave."

"Really?"

"Yeah. They raided our house earlier and wanted to ask her some questions. Me and Lyric gotta stay with Grandma right now."

DeVante struck already. "You okay with that?"

"I'm relieved, actually. Messed up, huh?"

"Nah, not really."

She scratches one of her cornrows, which somehow makes all of them move in the same back-and-forth motion. "I'm sorry for calling Seven my brother and not our brother."

"Oh." I kinda forgot about that. It seems minor after everything that's happened. "It's all right."

"I guess I called him my brother 'cause … it made it feel like he really was my brother, you know?"

"Um, he is your brother, Kenya. I honestly get jealous of how much he wants to be with you and Lyric."

"Because he thinks he has to be," she says. "He wants to be with y'all. I mean, I get why. He and Daddy don't get along. But I wish he wanted to be my brother sometimes and didn't feel like he had to be. He ashamed of us. 'Cause of our momma and my daddy."

"No, he's not."

"Yeah, he is. You ashamed of me too."

"I've never said that."

"You didn't have to, Starr," she says. "You never invited me to hang out with you and them girls. They were never at your house when I was. Like you ain't want them to know I was your friend too. You were ashamed of me, Khalil, even the Garden, and you know it."

I go quiet. If I face the truth, as ugly as it is, she's right. I was ashamed of Garden Heights and everything in it. It seems stupid now though. I can't change where I come from or what I've been through, so why should I be ashamed of what makes me, me? That's like being ashamed of myself.

Nah. Fuck that.

"Maybe I was ashamed," I admit. "But I'm not anymore. And Seven's not ashamed of you, your momma, or Lyric. He loves y'all, Kenya. So like I said, *our* brother. Not just mine. Trust, I'm more than happy to share if it means getting him off my back."

"He can be a pain in the ass, can't he?"

"Girl, yes."

We laugh together. As much as I've lost, I've gained some good stuff too. Like Kenya.

"Yeah, all right," she says. "I guess we can share him."

"Chop-chop, Starr," Momma calls, clapping her hands as if that'll make me move faster. Still on her dictatorship, I swear. "We've got work to do. Kenya, I got a bag and some gloves with your name on them if you wanna help out."

Kenya turns to me like, *seriously*?

"I can share her too," I say. "Matter of fact, please take her."

We laugh and stand up. Kenya glances around at the rubble. More neighbors have joined in on cleaning up, and they form a line that moves trash out the store and into the trash cans on the curb.

"So what y'all gon' do now?" Kenya asks. "With the store, I mean."

A car honks at us, and the driver yells out to let us know he has our back. The answer comes easily.

"We'll rebuild."

Once upon a time there was a hazel-eyed boy with dimples. I called him Khalil. The world called him a thug.

He lived, but not nearly long enough, and for the rest of my life I'll remember how he died.

Fairy tale? No. But I'm not giving up on a better ending.

It would be easy to quit if it was just about me, Khalil, that night, and that cop. It's about way more than that though. It's about Seven. Sekani. Kenya. DeVante.

It's also about Oscar.

Aiyana.

Trayvon.

Rekia.

Michael.

Eric.

Tamir.

John.

Ezell.

Sandra.

Freddie.

Alton.

Philando.

It's even about that little boy in 1955 who nobody recognized at first – Emmett.

The messed-up part? There are so many more.

Yet I think it'll change one day. How? I don't know. When? I definitely don't know. Why? Because there will always be someone ready to fight. Maybe it's my turn.

Others are fighting too, even in the Garden, where sometimes it feels like there's not a lot worth fighting for. People are realizing and shouting and marching and demanding. They're not forgetting. I think that's the most important part.

Khalil, I'll never forget.

I'll never give up.
I'll never be quiet.
I promise.

AUTHOR'S NOTE

I remember the first time I saw Emmett Louis Till.

I couldn't have been more than eight years old. I came across his photo in a Jet magazine that marked the anniversary of his death. At the time I was convinced he wasn't real, or at least that he wasn't a person. What was supposed to be his face was mutilated beyond recognition. He looked more like a prop from a movie to me; a monster from some over-the-top horror flick.

But he was a person, a boy, and his story was a cautionary tale, even for a black girl in Mississippi who was born more than three decades after he died. "Know your worth," my mom would say, "but also know that not everyone values you as much as I do."

Still, Emmett wasn't real to me. There was no way I'd ever have to worry about anything like that happening to me or to someone I knew. Things had changed, even in Mississippi, which is unfortunately more known for its racism than anything else. Nobody ever told me to sit on the back of the bus or made me drink from a "Colored" fountain. I never saw a KKK member. I had never been called nigger. Emmett and the stories of his time were history. The present had its own problems.

I grew up in a neighborhood that's notorious for all the wrong reasons: drug dealers, shootings, crime, insert other "ghetto" stereotypes here. I wasn't worried about the KKK wandering onto my street; I was more worried about the gunshots I heard at night. Yet, while those things were daily threats, they were slightly outweighed by the good – the things you wouldn't see unless you lived there. My neighbors were family. The neighborhood drug dealer was a superhero who gave kids money for snacks and beat up pedophiles who tried to snatch little girls off the street. The cops could be superheroes too, but I was taught at a young age to be "mindful" around them. So were my friends. We'd all heard stories, and though they didn't come with mutilated photos, they were realer than Emmett.

But just like Emmett, I remember the first time I saw the video of Oscar Grant.

I was a transfer student in my first year at the fine arts college I'd later graduate from. It was in a nicer part of town than where I lived, but only ten minutes away from it, and it was very, very white. A majority of the time I was the only black student in my creative writing classes. I did everything I could so no one would label me as the "black girl from the hood." I would leave home, blasting Tupac, but by the time I arrived to pick up a friend, I was listening to the Jonas Brothers. I kept quiet whenever race came up in discussions, despite the glances I'd get because as the "token black girl," I was expected to speak.

But Oscar did something to me. Suddenly, Emmett

wasn't history. Emmett was still reality.

The video was shocking for multiple reasons, one being that someone actually caught it on tape. This was undeniable evidence that had never been provided for the stories I'd heard. Yet my classmates, who had never heard such tales, had their own opinions about it.

"He should've just done what they said."

"He was resisting."

"I heard he was an ex-con and a drug dealer."

"He had it coming. Why are people so mad?"

"They were just doing their job."

I hate to admit it, but I still remained silent.

I was hurt, no doubt. And angry. Frustrated. Straight-up pissed. I knew plenty of Oscars. I grew up with them and I was friends with them. This was like being told that they deserved to die.

As the unrest took place in Oakland, I wondered how my community would react if that happened to one of our Oscars. I also wondered if my classmates would make the same comments if I became an Oscar. I wasn't an ex-con or a drug dealer, but I was from a neighborhood they were afraid to visit. They once jokingly said it was full of criminals, not knowing that's where I lived until months later.

From all of those questions and emotions, *The Hate U Give* was born.

I've always told stories. When I can't find a way to say the words out loud, I create characters who do it for me. *The Hate U Give* started as a short story my senior year. It was cathartic at the time, and I thought I was done telling Starr and Khalil's story because I foolishly hoped Oscar wouldn't happen again.

But then there was Trayvon. Michael. Eric. Tamir. There were more conversations just like the ones I heard at school but on a wider scale. Politicians and officials echoed my classmates, which led to more anger and disappointment for me, my peers, and the kids in my neighborhood who saw themselves in those gentlemen. In the midst of it, three words suddenly created a variety of reactions whenever uttered: Black Lives Matter.

I did the only thing I knew how to do: I expressed my feelings through story, in hopes that I would give a voice to every kid who feels the same way I do. As we witness injustice, prejudice, and racism rear their ugly heads again in this political climate both in the US and abroad, I think it's even more important to let young people know that they aren't alone in their frustration, fear, anger, and sadness. We must also provide glimmers of light in the midst of the darkness. I hope that I've done that.

But my ultimate hope is that every single person who reads *The Hate U Give* walks away from it understanding those feelings and sharing them in some way. And then, maybe then, Emmett Louis Till can truly become history.

ACKNOWLEDGEMENTS

There's a chance that this will sound like a rapper's award acceptance speech, so in true rapper fashion I first have to thank my Lord and Savior, Jesus Christ. I'm not worthy of all that you have done for me. Thank you for all of the people you placed in my life that made this book possible:

Brooks Sherman, superhero agent extraordinaire, friend, and the ultimate "Gangster in a V-Neck Sweater." From day one you've been my biggest cheerleader, a psychologist every now-and-then, and have gone gangster on my behalf when necessary. You are the Dopest, with a capital D. Starr is lucky to have you in her corner, and I'm even luckier.

Molly Ker Hawn, my UK agent extraordinaire – Cookie Lyon wishes she were you. If I could, I'd give you all the caramel cake in the world and a million thank yous.

The phenomenal team at the Bent Agency, including Jenny Bent, Victoria Cappello, Charlee Hoffman, John Bowers.

A HUGE thank you to everyone at Walker Books for your hard work and enthusiasm. You've made this girl from "across the pond" feel truly special. I couldn't have asked for a better UK team. Special thanks to Annalie Grainger, Gill Evans, Frances Taffinder and Maria Soler Canton. You are superheroes!

Donna Bray, when people look up "bad-ass," your picture should appear next to the definition. It should also appear next to "genius" and "brilliant." This book is so much stronger because of you. I'm humbled to have an editor who not only believes in Starr and her story as much as you do, but an editor who also believes in me. Thank you for "getting" it.

Christy Garner, thank you for often being light in darkness and for always seeing good in my stories (and me) even when they're (and I'm) a mess. Your friendship is a gift.

Team Double Stuff: Becky Albertalli, Stefani Sloma, and Nic Stone. You ladies may have questionable taste in Oreos, but there's no question that I love you. It's an honor to call you my friends.

My B-Team siblings with shout-outs to Sarah Cannon, Golden Oreo Partner-in-Crime Adam Silvera, Lianne Oelke, Heidi Schulz, Jessica Cluess, Brad McLelland, Rita Meade, and Mercy Brown.

The entire We Need Diverse Books crew. Ellen Oh, you are a gem to kid's lit and a gem in my life. Extra special thanks to the Walter Dean Myers Grant committee. I'm forever grateful.

Tupac Shakur, I never met you, but your wisdom and your words inspire me daily. Whether you're in "Thugz Mansion" or hiding out in Cuba somewhere, I hope this story does your message justice.

Joe Maxwell, thank you for your guidance and your love. Many, many, MANY blessings to you.

My phenomenal CP's, beta readers, and homies: Michelle Hulse, Chris Owens, Lana Wood Johnson, Linda Jackson, Dede Nesbitt, Katherine Webber, S.C., Ki-Wing Merlin, Melyssa Mercado, Bronwyn Deaver, Jeni Chappelle, Marty Mayberry (aka one of the first people to ever read the query for this book), Jeff Zentner (Hov!), all my Tweeps, and everyone at Sub It Club, Absolute Write, and Kidlit AOC. My apologies if I didn't name you. I love you all.

My Wakanda ladies: Camryn Garrett, L.L. McKinney, and Adrianne Russell. You are black girl magic personified.

June Hardwick, thank you for your insight, expertise, and for being you. You inspire me more than you know.

The Team Coffeehouse Queens: Brenda Drake, Nikki Roberti, and Kimberly Chase. You were some of the first people outside of friends and family who loved my words. I owe you so much. Brenda, thank you in particular for being such a pillar for the writing community.

My #WordSmiths crew, you rock!

To Mom, Ma, Momma, and my biggest champion, Julia Thomas: You are the ultimate light in the darkness; a true "Starr." I'm blessed that you're my mom and hope to be half the woman you are. When Dr. Maya Angelou described a "Phenomenal Woman," she described you. Thank you for loving me as I am.

And to every kid in Georgetown and in all "the Gardens" of the world: your voices matter, your dreams matter, your lives matter. Be roses that grow in concrete.

Photo © Anissa Hidouk

ANGIE THOMAS was born, raised and still resides in Jackson, Mississippi. She is a former teen rapper whose greatest accomplishment was having an article about her in *Right On!* magazine. She has a BFA in Creative Writing and is a winner of the inaugural Walter Dean Myers Grant 2015, awarded by We Need Diverse Books. *The Hate U Give* is her first novel. Follow her online at www.angiethomas.com or on Twitter: @angiecthomas.

🐦 #TheHateUGive

@WalkerBooksUK